AGE

OF

ARROGANCE

TIMOTHY WOLFF

Partnered with Willow Wraith Press.
Visit our website at **Willowwraithpress.com**.

ISBN: 979-8-9907730-0-4 (Paperback)
ISBN: 979-8-9867655-9-4 (Hardcover)
ISBN: 979-8-9867655-8-7 (eBook)
ISBN: 979-8-9907730-1-1 (Audiobook)

Any references to historical events, real people, or real places are used fictitiously. Names, characters, and places are products of the author's imagination.

Front cover image by Alejandro Colucci
Edited by Jonathan Oliver
World map by Chaim Holtjer
Title page image by Coe Landsell
Book design by Lorna Reid
First printing edition 2024.

MAP

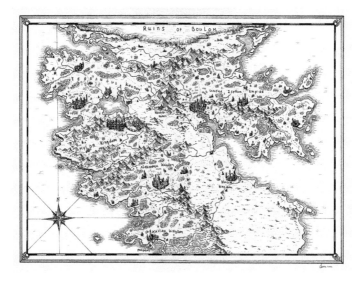

TEARS OF THE MAELSTROM RECAP

After seven months unconscious, Zeen finally wakes in Terrangus with Serenna by his side. He learns of Emperor Francis, Empress Mary (who is expecting a child), and new entities known as Vanguards: those who have surrendered their freewill to serve the God of Wisdom/ Arrogance. Their reunion is short-lived as the Goddess of Fear unleashes a Harbinger after David accidently tortures the Time God. With Francis and Mary unable to join the Guardians, Serenna reluctantly recruits Vanguard Five (Robert Cavare) and Dumiah Bloom: the zephum mechanist. Warlord Sardonyx forces his son Tempest to join the Guardians as a one-time combatant.

The Guardians succeed in slaying the Harbinger at great cost. Pyith is slain and Tempest has a permanently wounded leg. The Goddess of Valor reveals herself to Serenna as the ascended Everleigh and they train back in Mylor, while Zeen attempts to help Tempest avoid the wrath of Sardonyx. David is enraged by Fear's actions and vows to create a realm without gods.

David does not create a realm without gods. He defeats Francis, but is easily beaten by Arrogance, who imprisons him in the Terrangus dungeons, where he reunites with Nyfe. After spending time with Tempest, Zeen learns the God of Death is speaking to the zephum. Riots in Terrangus grow worse as the number of

Vanguards increase. Vanguard Five uses the chaos to escort David out of Terrangus and back into Mylor. David and Serenna's reunion is cut short as Valor openly attacks Fear. While Valor is defeated, Serenna takes the opportunity to grab the Herald of Valor's scythe off the ground. David knocks the scythe out of her hands before Serenna can slay Fear.

Zeen is banished from Vaynex after a skirmish to protect Tempest. He returns to Mylor, then does adult things with Serenna. Their fun reminds David of his lost Melissa, so he drinks himself silly until Valor demands his service as the next engager. He agrees, accepts some armor from Senator Charles, then trains in the gardens. Serenna accepts a meeting with Alanammus Archon Faelen Gabriel. He proposes assassinating Francis to limit Arrogance's influence at the upcoming wedding.

The riots grow worse in Terrangus. Nyfe is made into Vanguard Omega, then after Francis and Mary are nearly killed in Terrangus, Francis uses the Herald of Arrogance staff to burn his own subjects, saving their lives but creating an atmosphere of terror.

Tempest and Sardonyx are betrayed in a Vaynex uprising. Zeen ends up slaying Warmaker Dubnok, father to Eltune, before being sent back to Mylor with Bloom. Tempest finally accepts the God of Death's offer to become a Harbinger. He lays waste to all the warmakers, then eventually, his own father.

With the Guardian team still reeling, Arrogance and Valor convince Serenna to accept Vanguards Omega (Nyfe) and Five into the Guardian team, with Davd as their Engager. The team portals to Vaynex. Eltune begs their aid in restoring order, but Serenna denies him. Tempest is eventually defeated, then finds himself in the Great Plains in the Sky with his father, the newly-ascended God of Tradition. There is no resurrection, but a final farewell.

Back in Mylor, David goes sober and reminisces with Bloom over the mountains in the outskirts. Serenna introduces Valor to Landon, since Guardian Everleigh was always his favorite. Everleigh reveals Landon is her son and they have a teary reunion.

Mary gives birth to her son, Calvin. Francis is in awe at the child in his arms, and vows to pay any price to give him Serenity. If he must cross the line between damaged and broken, he will gladly do so.

CHAPTER 1

BURDEN OF PERFECTION

itting on the Terrangus throne, Emperor Francis Haide sighed as he leaned his head into his left hand. Ever since the birth of his son Calvin eight months ago, the throne felt…invisible. It was odd and, a bit ironic, considering how often Nyfe had used the phrase "Invisible Guardian" to torment him during simpler times.

But these days, the only phrase Nyfe—now Vanguard Omega—could speak was, "Yes, Emperor." In a perfect world, it was all anyone would say.

The crowd of senators, soldiers, and people with enough gold to visit the castle but not enough gold for Francis to remember their names all flooded the throne room halls, mesmerized by Empress Mary and their child. General Marcus had vetted them all of course. Can't risk any of the rioters putting the royal family in danger. The mere thought drew sweat from Francis's brow, so he grasped the Herald of Arrogance with both hands and took a deep breath. *Would they dare? Calvin should never have to pay the debts of his father, but cowards always target the helpless. If anyone dares, for their sake, they better die in the attempt.*

People gave oohs and ahhs, laughed, applauded, enthralled as the baby did… baby things. *Did Mother treat me this way? Parading me around like a dog?* It was all so undignified. Francis had assumed this nonsense would end after a few weeks, months at worst, but here they were, entertaining the easily entertained, treating the future emperor like an actor in amateur theater.

"Are you unwell, Emperor?" asked General Marcus from the left side of the throne.

Francis tightened the grip on his staff. "Well? No, General, I am not well. Too much risk. Too many people. Too much *everything*. They could strike at any moment. We should be solidifying our defenses before the wedding, not inviting potential assassins to my very throne!" *Perhaps Wisdom was correct and I need a new general. Unfortunately, I think Marcus is the best of the worst. If only this kingdom had a better selection.*

Marcus chuckled, which seemed an inappropriate response. "You have a father's mind. Try to relax, Emperor. With all these Vanguards, Terrangus Castle is the safest place in the realm. I guess, well, this is what perfection looks like."

It was the god's turn to chuckle from behind the throne. "Oh, my dear General," Wisdom said, remaining invisible. "Look around. Expand your imagination. Would you consider *this* to be perfect?"

Marcus looked around, but it was unlikely he had the capacity to expand anything thought-wise. "I sure hope not."

"If you hold even the *slightest* thread of doubt, then rest assured, perfection has not yet prevailed. But the time shall soon arrive. Sooner than my original hypothesis, I dare say. *Oh*, is that a chill in the air? Cold winds on a temperate spring morning always spell danger to the complacent. You may have a job to do, General. An important job indeed."

A chill? I don't feel anything. Oh well. It seemed Wisdom always enjoyed playing with words. Maybe he could explain in greater detail after the room cleared—

"Francis!" Mary's voice rang from the center of the hall, snapping him to attention in a way only she knew how. "Stop slouching up there and come down. Your subjects yearn to see you! Leave your staff by the throne."

He couldn't recall exactly when she had stopped referring to them as their "people" but it was a welcome change, nonetheless. But leave his staff? Truly? He rose, keeping the staff in-hand, pretending he hadn't heard that last line. Lying without words is a weapon all leaders should master if they crave stability. "Coming, my beloved."

The oohs and ahhs dissipated as Emperor Francis Haide, Architect of Paradise, Herald of Serenity, approached with his staff sheathed behind his back. Was their silence meant to be a slight? Of course. They loved *Mary*. They loved *Calvin*. The cornucopia of snails infesting his throne room loved Francis's family, but no one loved the man who provided for them. *Is this the burden of perfection? Have I fallen too far to ever reclaim their love?*

"Francis? Hello?" Oh, Mary's voice again. Her tone shifted to annoyance, suggesting she had said his name more than once. Best to respond before she shifted to the tone that would often come next.

"Forgive me, there is much on my mind." *Not that any of these people would know what that's like. I need more words. A compliment?* "You look simply ravishing, my future empress. And you too, little Calvin. Um, not ravishing but handsome. You know what I mean." Damn them all for snickering.

Mary gestured to the crowd to stop their noise, then said, "Say hello to Daddy!" as she coerced Calvin into waving.

Calvin laughed, waving at Francis, but staring at Mary. Every child has a favorite parent, and it seemed most children choose the mother. The boy had such a large heart inside his tiny frame. Perhaps the mind would follow in time.

Francis surrendered his dignity and waved back, holding back a sigh as the onlookers said, "Aww" and clutched their hearts like they had witnessed the most precious act in the realm. Who were these people? Why were they here? Marcus was usually competent, but had he really vetted *everyone*?

"There is someone you should meet," Mary said. Despite the cacophony of people, her voice was always as clear as the skies of Serenity. "This is Sabastian, master of the Blacksmiths' Guild. He has a little son of his own named Francis."

And that is interesting…why? "A pleasure to meet you,

7

Blacksmith." Surely, none of them expected him to address the child. By Francis's educated guess, the child was at least three, which made his name a convenience rather than a planned honor.

The blacksmith bowed, then nudged his son forward, who said, "Mr. Emperor, if I work hard and tend to my duties, will I become wise and strong like you?"

Ugh. Children stop being cute the moment they can speak. *You are the son of a blacksmith. When you have a child, you will be the father of a blacksmith. That's where the dream begins and where it ends. I envy you, in a way. Such a life never has to consider the price of paradise, never has to weigh how much a person can be damaged before they are considered broken. When Serenity graces our realm, you will scantily tell the difference.*

Oh, I'm taking too long to respond. "My boy, keep your wits about you, and the glory of Serenity itself will be the limit of what you can accomplish."

The crowd cheered, enamored as their emperor lied to them. After all these years, it would seem lying was a simple task. You conjure what people wish to hear, then yell it out loud. Let them cheer. If Francis was forced to be an actor, he may as well be the lead role—

"*Get down!*"

Hmm? Was that Marcus? Get down from what—

Until that moment, Francis had never been stabbed. A "sharp pain" seemed an ironic description, but a sharp pain indeed coursed through his upper-shoulder. He clutched the wound, immediately finding blood, too much blood. The room went silent. That was unlikely, considering everyone rushing around making a mess of things.

Marcus tackled his assailant to the ground…a senator? He looked somewhat familiar. What an ungrateful cur. Out of all the people who could have grievances with Francis, the nobles have done just fine under his rule.

Sound returned as Francis collapsed into the arms of Mary. It was startling enough to break the light-headedness. "Mary, I told you. It's not safe. It's never safe. Nothing is safe. Enemies… everywhere. All around. They yearn so badly to be unhappy. They cling to it like some sort of…some sort of…" Out of all the sounds that barraged him, Calvin's cries wounded him the most. A son should never see their father's fragility until they are perceptive of their own.

"Hush," Mary said, cupping his face. "Save your energy. I've seen my share of stab wounds. None of your organs are in danger. In fact…they couldn't have done a better job avoiding a fatal blow if they tried. Just keep your eyes open and stay awake. Look at me!"

Actually, sleep was a great idea. He rested his eyes, using Mary's soft hand as a pillow…

"*Look at me!*"

They met eyes for a brief moment, and all pain subsided in the face of Mary's terror. It was nice that someone cared. Mother never did. Certainly not any of the Guardians.

Their intimate moment was dashed as the Vanguards arrived, analyzed Francis, and told Mary to tend to Calvin. They addressed the injury like it was a mathematical equation, not being gentle as they pressed the wound to stop the bleeding, then cleaned the blood and pressed it together with bandages. A comforting warmth came from their wands; Francis would have fallen asleep if not for the floating deity above him.

"Unacceptable. Simply unacceptable," Arrogance yelled from above. "This results from putting safety in the arms of imperfection. What say you, General?"

Marcus was obviously flustered; sweat poured down his face as he drew his sword to the senator's neck. "I cannot excuse my failure, but allow me the task of sending this traitor to the void."

"You will do no such thing," Arrogance said, drifting towards him. "Interrogate this wretched husk. I want to know everything. And I mean everything."

Marcus pressed his blade against the senator's neck harder. "That's absurd!"

"No, my dear General, there is only one thing I classify as absurd, and such moments exemplify my rationale. Vanguards, escort our two prisoners down below. I have tolerated imperfection for far too long. At least enjoy the irony of it. By committing your grandest failure, you have secured the pinnacle of your destiny."

"I would sooner die," Marcus said with a grimace. "Francis...I was always loyal to your family. I commanded good men to their deaths to protect you and yours. Don't...don't do this to me. Banish me if you must, but don't take away who I am. *Please.*"

Francis groaned as he leaned up. "Think of it as addition, not subtraction. We are taking nothing away other than your weakness. When all is said and done, you will be my finest Vanguard. Considering the alternative is to hang, your lack of gratitude is a disappointment. To join Serenity's Vanguard is the zenith of esteem."

Marcus threw his sword to the ground, his eyes filled with tears. "Every tyrant eventually runs out of people to hang. I spit on your esteem. If there was any truth to it, *you* would be a Vanguard. *Mary* would be a Vanguard. Your *son* would be a Vanguard."

Never. "My family is already perfect. They don't allow murderers to roam free in the throne room. I will pardon your insults as a moment of passion, and allow you to usher in the paradise of Serenity by my side. Vanguards, take him away."

Francis expected some sort of objection from Mary, but she was several feet away, tending to the distraught baby Calvin. By the way he flailed and screamed, one would think he was the one who had been stabbed. Oh well, such was life. Mary obviously loved them both...but Francis was well aware who held priority.

CHAPTER 2

A WAR OF LIES

erenna Morgan leaned against the balcony of her gardens with Zeen by her side, gazing out towards the mountains on the outskirts. Her lilies had grown nicely since the dawn of spring—a beautiful distraction from the fact she *still* hadn't told Zeen about Archon Gabriel's proposal to assassinate Francis. Fortunately, withholding information and lying are not the same thing.

"It's funny," said Zeen, squinting his eyes towards the view. "I always feel a bit distant out here. It's like we're drifting above the mountains from inside those clouds. I suppose that's a good thing, right? Like a sort of peace? Maybe this is what Serenity is like."

Serenna sighed. "We make our own Serenity. It's what Francis and Arrogance never understood. Happiness built on the pain of others is the most vile illusion. They have long surrendered the excuse of ignorance."

Zeen gave her a light kiss on the cheek. "My dear, you're too tense. If the wedding is such a concern, perhaps we should cancel? You haven't been eating much lately."

Since when does he pay attention to that? Does he suspect anything? "After all the delays from rioting, they are fools to continue this ceremony. It's not safe. Not for them. Not for us." Ironically, Serenna yearned for an opportunity to lose the burden of choice. If they canceled the wedding or at least delayed it further, next week wouldn't be a realm-changing event.

"I agree! So does Valor. I probably shouldn't say this, but she wants me to dissuade you from going. Honestly, it's humbling that she believes I can alter your judgment. But if the 'Pact Breaker' must go, I will be at your side."

Serenna smiled at him. It was…nice to be in a relationship. The glamor and lust had subsided and, to her relief, love didn't diminish but changed from a burning flame to a cozy warmth. The familiarity and comfort of family. "She asked you? That doesn't seem like the protocol of Valor—"

"Do not speak on my behalf, Crystal Girl," Valor said from behind. "We must choose an alternate path to reason when the mind yields to the heart. As of now, it may all be for naught. The puppet emperor of Arrogance was wounded last night in an assassination attempt."

Serenna froze, her grip tightening on the railing. Assassination? It would make no sense for Archon Gabriel to play his hand so early. Maybe the rioters? Her information on Terrangus these days was shaky at best, but the Vanguards were said to have crushed most of them. What of the zephum? Warlord Dubnok held no love for Francis and his god, but assassination was too dishonorable for zephum preference. *If he's already dead, my hands are clean. Forgive me for wishing such a fate…*

"That's terrible. Is he okay?" asked Zeen, gazing up at Valor with wide eyes. "What about little Calvin? Surely, they wouldn't dare. Please tell me they wouldn't dare…"

Oh gods, baby Calvin. I hope he didn't catch a glimpse of the violence. Could I truly leave a child with no father? What about Mary? Ending a life is never a singular task. The ripples of pain echo, creating monsters where heroes once stood.

"Based on the wound, the would-be assassin was either a novice or an absolute professional at incompetence. I refuse to believe the Wielder of Lies would allow such an attack under his watch."

"Welcome news," said Zeen after a deep breath. "It was probably one of the rioters. I don't see any of the other kingdoms risking involvement."

Valor glared at him, then at Serenna with pure disdain. "If we challenge Arrogance to a war of lies, we shall not prevail. Guardian Zeen, I wish to speak to the Crystal Girl alone."

Great...

"Do you want me to leave?" asked Zeen.

"That won't be necessary," Valor said, creating a platinum-tinted portal by her side. "I suggest you train for the days ahead. Serenna. *Get in.*"

As much as she despised the term "Crystal Girl," there were very few things more unsettling than hearing the goddess use her real name.

*

Serenna stepped into the dream of Mylor, her eyes drifting to the crescent moon far off in the distance. It had been several months since she had been here, but each arrival always felt like the first time. The lilies swayed with the breeze, illuminating a pale glory that never seemed to exist in the real world...

Archon Gabriel sat on a chair near the balcony, sipping a steaming beverage with a smile. "Welcome, Serenna. Please, have a seat." He gestured to the open spot beside him as Valor stood by the balcony.

"Archon or not, you wield no power in Valor's realm. What are you doing here?"

"At ease, Guardian," Valor said. "Put your grievances aside until the true threat is abolished."

"Wise words," Gabriel said with a grin. "You would do well to absorb her guidance. It's not often we find ourselves with a deity who doesn't suffer from divine madness."

"*Silence!*" Valor yelled, which shook the entire gardens and mountains. The aura at the end of her scythe radiated pure platinum energy. "Limit your childish urges while within my domain. *Both* of you."

"Yes, Goddess," they both said, nearly in unison. It was worth the scolding to see Gabriel tilt his head down in fear. For all his smugness, there was no doubt who held the power in here.

Valor let the lingering silence amplify their shame then said, "I am forced to believe this…*assassination* is nothing more than a ploy by Arrogance. So far, the two of you have proven unprepared, inefficient, uncooperative, and deceptive. Heed my words: neither of you will attend the wedding. Am I clear?"

"We must go!" Gabriel said, letting an interesting amount of desperation seep into his voice. "I have no qualms about canceling our original arrangement but, regardless, my presence is mandatory. Other people's weddings are always an archon's burden."

Valor scoffed. "Ignorance, it would seem, is the true archon's burden. Go if you must. You are an expendable pawn in a war that rages beyond your comprehension."

"You sound like him," Gabriel said with a smirk. "One of the unintended consequences of war is watching our reflection morph into our enemy. I still advise that we kill the puppet. Whether divine or mortal, chaos waits for no one. Watch a Haide fall, watch a kingdom rise."

"But how?" asked Serenna. "After last night, Arrogance will have every contingency accounted for. Perhaps Valor is correct, and we should reconvene for a better opportunity." *I don't want this. Puppet or not, I could never murder Francis. Deep down, he is still a fellow Guardian. And, somehow, a father…*

Gabriel tapped the head of the cane anxiously. "There won't *be* a better opportunity. Don't you understand? We lose ground in this war each day they convert more Vanguards. Inaction is a slow, grinding defeat."

It took every ounce of restraint not to grab him by the throat. "You *dare* speak of inaction to me? You left Mylor to rot. Heed my words, Archon: Inaction is not slow nor grinding to those losing their homes. It is agony. It is pure agony."

"I learn from my mistakes, Guardian. You should try it one day. I believe our time here is concluded. Do the right thing—"

"*Enough*," said Valor. "Neither of you have any understanding of risk and reward. If you indeed must attend, Francis cannot be the only target. Arrogance must die. No matter the cost, no matter how dire it may seem, Arrogance must be slain. It is simply not worth the risk otherwise."

Gabriel sighed. "Everleigh…Valor…is that even possible?"

"For me, anything is possible," Valor said, glaring at him. "Consider your role unchanged. Focus your efforts on Francis. It will allow me an opportunity to slay the true enemy. It will likely cost my life in the process, but sacrifice is the protocol of Valor."

After a long pause, Gabriel said, "Very well. If we're going through with this madness, I need the evening to ensure contingencies. I was a sore loser as a child. Would knock the board over instead of admitting defeat. Never made many friends…but I *never* lost." He left through the portal Valor had crafted for him.

Serenna took a deep breath. What an absurd turn of events that the Pact Breaker was demanding inaction. "Am I a fool?" she asked Valor.

"He taps his cane to alleviate his fear. The cost of a silver tongue is often paid for by neglecting the rest of the body."

That doesn't answer my question at all. "Perhaps it's foolish of me to abandon the only opportunity for a joint-kingdom cooperative."

Valor let out a faint snicker, which was more terrifying than it had any right to be. "He is no use to you. When the darkness rises, Guardians stand alone. I will speak openly: I doubt your resolve in slaying the puppet emperor. Are you capable of accomplishing said task?"

Yes. Maybe. I don't know. "I could, and I shall. Hesitation is not the protocol to Valor."

Serenna expected a grin, nod, some sort of approval, but the goddess never appeared more somber as she gazed into the crescent moon. "Though it wounds my heart, I believe you." Valor paused, then turned towards Serenna. "You are worthy, Guardian. Perhaps you always were. I offer you two gifts: the first is my artifact, the Valor of Mylor."

It was impossible to tell how long her pause was before Serenna finally took the scythe from her arms. As her hands fully gripped the wooden shaft, it took every ounce of restraint to avoid erupting into her platinum form. It would take time to control such power. Such wrath. "There are no words for my gratitude. I must ask, what is the second gift?"

"My condolences."

CHAPTER 3

THE PATH OF A TYRANT

I t had been nine days since David's last drink.

He materialized in the Vaynex Guardian portal, squinting his eyes as the shape of several zephum guards gained clarity in his view. Aside from the mage, there were eight warriors total, all covered tail-to-snout in heavy chainmail armor. Since the uprising, Warlord Eltune Dubnok had kept a small force by the portal at all times. Whether through paranoia or efficiency, the zephum had handled the aftermath of Tempest and done what they had always done best.

Survive.

The God of Tradition had demanded they tolerate David's presence, but tolerance is a state far closer to hatred than love. "Well met," David said, shifting his shoulders as the burden of his own armor pressed against him. "Tradition has granted me an audience with Warlord Eltune Dubnok. I know the way but, if you prefer to lead, I will follow."

He received grunts in response. Fair enough, any greeting that wasn't a sword in his throat was a welcome gesture. Zeen would have been the better choice for such a task, but slaying Dubnok's father during the uprising had closed that door and opened it for David, the new ambassador of Mylor…

The longer he lived, the stranger the realm had become.

The guards moved towards the citadel halls. While they never mentioned with words to accompany them, it seemed wise to follow their lead. Despite how much the realm had changed, the citadel halls appeared nearly the same as decades past. Torches illuminated the throne and stone council seats, along with the paintings of zephum heroes scattered all over the ceiling and walls. To his shame, he still didn't recognize any of them. Pyith deserved the honor and, dammit, so did Tempest. David would not *dare* voice such an opinion out loud, but every monster deserves a chance at redemption. Maybe he was spending too much time with Zeen.

David entered the center space surrounded by empty citadel chairs. There was no council, only Warlord Eltune, Guardian Bloom, and the enormous figure of a statue he recognized all too well.

Sardonyx Claw. The God of Tradition.

David kneeled in front of Warlord Eltune, nearly grinning from the memory of how he had used to kneel for Grayson. The grin died as he remembered that on most of those occasions, he had Melissa by his side. Those who claim history is doomed to repeat itself have probably never observed how a broken past lingers upon the future.

"You're late, Ambassador," Eltune said, leaning back onto his throne. The wide-eyed gentle zephum from David's memory had long since faded, replaced by a young kid trying to become what the realm expected of him. "If you weren't a Guardian, I would have you sleeping in the sand for your insult. Do humans believe their time is more precious than our own? *Answer me.*"

Ah, so Dubnok had chosen the path of a tyrant. An efficient path, but one that often finds the void sooner than most. *All this bravado. He's compensating for his fear. Interesting. Do I lean on that, or yield to his authority?* David rose, glared into his eyes, and said, "Never threaten a weary man with rest, Warlord. Since time is a scarce commodity, I will get straight to the point. There was an unsuccessful attempt on Emperor Francis's life last evening in his throne room. In the name of mutual cooperation, my superiors encourage you not to attend the upcoming wedding." It would never feel normal referring to Serenna as his superior and, yet, there was a comfort to it. Superior, leader: the fancier the title, the harsher the burdens.

"Oh shit," Bloom said. "Assassination? Good thing they didn't finish the job. I didn't waste all that gold on my new red silk dress for nothing. Leave it to humans to master the art of murder just to fuck it up when the realm needs it most—"

"Silence!" Dubnok yelled, slamming his hand on the throne. The long pause suggested he was unaware of such news. Strange that Sardonyx didn't feel the need to update them. "I am fortunate enough never to have set foot in Terrangus. Father claimed it was a human-infested hovel. Why does this change anything? I have no qualms with the Arrogant One's puppet. Let the humans drown in their pride. We can win this war without ever grasping our swords."

Ah, so the zephum position is weaker than anticipated. I'm not surprised. They never reopened trade with Terrangus. It's a miracle the clans haven't split up again.

Bloom snickered. "Wake up, Boss. The humans were obviously looking to kill him themselves. Since someone fucked up the job, someone else has to do it. I'll take a fat guess and say it's the woman who hangs out with a crazy goddess."

"Well?" asked Dubnok, with a hint of discomfort. "Is that true, Ambassador? Did someone 'fuck up the job,' as my Guardian states bluntly?"

Valor advised not to discuss assassination in an open space but that door is already wide open. "All in perspective, Warlord. Our enemy deals in lies. It would be foolish to assume the Arrogant One would allow such an attack on his emperor."

"All humans deal in lies. Dishonor has always been a crutch for your soft skulls." Eltune rose from his throne and spit on the ground. "Why have you not brought Zeen? Did you truly believe you could enter my domain, ignore my demands, and be allowed safe exit? Sardonyx never repeated himself as warlord, a tradition I intend to continue."

David put his hand on the hilt of his blade. May as well meet an empty threat with one of his own. "For as long as I live, you will never harm the boy. I will not speak ill of your father, but most warriors dig their own graves."

To his surprise—and relief—Eltune simply grinned at the gesture. "Indeed they do. From my understanding, you nearly dug your own. There is honor in your blood, Guardian. You hold a reputation among my people as Fear's *whore*, but I accept there is more to your tale. Are you attending the wedding?"

"Not by choice. I never cared for other people's weddings. Part of me expects it will be my final day in the realm."

"Expect, or hope?" asked Eltune. "I see why you were chosen as Mylor's ambassador. Blades cannot threaten an enemy who yearns for them. I eagerly await this wedding. There is nothing more honorable than to watch a ceremony of life end in death. You hold my blessing to move about the citadel, but enter the sands at your own risk. Whatever you remember of my home, I assure you those memories are long gone. Reality has failed, yet Vaynex is eternal." Eltune left towards his chambers, eerily similar to the way Sardonyx had done after his audiences.

Bloom walked up and hugged David, nearly crushing his back with her monstrous embrace. Pyith would have been proud. "Ah, Boss, it's good to see someone with some real nuts again. Gods, I almost wish Tempest was still alive. Eltune is the ugliest zephum I've ever laid with, and believe me, that's a low bar. How are your mountains doing?"

He wasn't sure why Bloom felt the need to offer that information, but he smiled anyway. "It is good to see you again, Bloom. I'm rather disappointed you never came to visit."

"I mean, you're good in my book, but the rest of the humans aren't worth shit." She snickered for a moment before yielding to silence. "Listen, if I left for even a single day, this entire kingdom would fall apart. It's held together by blood and swords."

"Blood and swords hold a lot more together than Vaynex, my friend. But on a serious matter, can you convince him to miss the wedding?"

"I can barely convince him to bathe. Every day I look at him pisses me off all the more. He's just a confused kid trying to act like Sardonyx, but everyone goes along with the charade because there's no alternative. We had it good for a while. A long time, really. I think everyone knows we won't survive another succession. It's not like Terrangus where you can throw any bearded human on the throne and restore order. Listen, Boss, if we lose Eltune, this shithole will become whatever's worse than a shithole."

Another Boulom. There is no title worse than Fallen Kingdom. The end of an entire civilization. The catalyst for Arrogance, Fear, Strength… the catalyst of everything. "Do you have any suggestions?"

She rubbed her snout, gazing at the God of Tradition statue as if it had the answers. "That's a bad omen if you're asking me. Offer him Zeen. That way, everyone wins. Eltune can save face and miss the wedding, and you guys can go fucking die in Terrangus without bringing the rest of us down with you."

"You know I can't do that."

"And you know I can't change his mind. Sounds like we're both fucked. Care for some ale?"

Ah, zephum ale. It had been exactly nine days since David's last drink. Total victory would likely never occur, but he had found small victories over the vice. "Too early. Besides, I never drink on the job."

"You may as well. Not like you could do much worse as ambassador. Alright, listen. I've wanted to show you this for a while. You're never gonna believe it."

David grinned, but kept his distance. Knowing Bloom, that sentence could mean anything.

Bloom stepped back and grabbed a fire-detonator off her belt. She threw it in the air and, as it began to come back down, she did a slight twitch of her neck. The detonator erupted dangerously close to the paintings of zephum heroes on the ceiling, sending fragments of fire and steel crashing down to the ground.

David didn't mean to flinch at the explosion but he hadn't heard that sound in months. It was like being slapped by the past. In better days, he would watch Melissa practice detonating for hours. Maybe he would take Bloom on that drink offer after all.

"So? What do you think? Am I the best mechanist in the realm?"

"Perhaps, but I remain unimpressed. Let me know when you can detonate without that weird neck twitch."

"Ah, fuck you. I bet Melissa did the same thing but your eyes were always looking lower—"

"*GUARDIANS!*" a booming voice yelled from behind. If the detonator was startling, the statue morphing into the form of Sardonyx nearly sent David to his knees. "Tradition requires your services. Heed my command!"

"Well met, Sardonyx," David said. He had to actively stop himself from including the title Warlord. "What…do you ask of us?"

"This is a demand, not a request! The Time Lord requires the removal of a mage dabbling in the dishonorable craft. Both of you must travel to Nuum at once. Fear will provide instructions from there."

David grit his teeth. The timing was terribly inconvenient, but arguing with an immortal Sardonyx seemed…unwise. "Must we go now? I dare not allow Serenna and Zeen to attend the wedding without me."

Tradition let out a sigh that echoed throughout the citadel halls. "Learn to let go, my friend. They are in the hands of Valor, and they are in worthy hands indeed. Do you accept me as your warlord, human?"

"Forever." The word came out naturally. "Bloom, we must leave at once. Make a last effort to persuade Eltune, then portal us to Nuum."

"Not happening, Boss." Bloom glared at Sardonyx. "My place is with Eltune. Vaynex lives or dies with that stupid fuck."

David held back a grin. To defy Sardonyx was the sort of insanity only someone like Bloom would attempt—

"Fair point, Guardian," Tradition said with a nod, then turned to David. "Old friend, I must request you fulfill this task on your own. It is not a glorious task, but it is the sort that keeps the realm intact. I have learned…much in my time as a god. Too much, perhaps. No warlord finds any defeat acceptable, but to lose this would be to lose everything."

Gods forgive him, but he welcomed the news. A shame that he needed violence to find purpose, but to be reunited with Fear…so be it. "Noelami and I will deal with the time mage."

"Indeed you shall! It will be *GLORIOUS!*"

Glorious, indeed…

CHAPTER 4

YOU'RE NOT OFF TO SLAY ARROGANCE, ARE YOU?

een's smile quickly faded as Serenna tumbled out of the portal with Valor's scythe in her hands. He knew very little about scythes, but based on the pure rage emanating off Serenna, that was likely for the best. Bright platinum rays glittered at the edge of the blade; he wanted to look away but couldn't. It was like that time in Mylor, when she had temporarily changed into a Harbinger. Those days were best left in the past, remembered by all but discussed by none.

"My love?" he said, though there was no way she heard him through her energy. *Do I approach her? It's Serenna. The answer is yes. The answer is always yes.*

Unfortunately, this time, the answer was no. Zeen approached, then got launched into a flowerbed by an eruption of platinum energy. While they cushioned his fall, there would be hell to pay later for *again* crushing her lilies.

"I can't...STOP IT!" she yelled, falling to her knees. Serenna shielded herself in a crystal that remained visible, shattered the shield, then made a new one and let it fade out of view. She gasped for air, her hands trembling at the base of the scythe. "Too much... I...I believe everything is okay now."

It didn't seem okay now, but Zeen forced himself up and eased over. Serenna was always drawn to forbidden powers without much regard for the cost. Not that she ever asked, but it never seemed worth it. "Ah, so Valor finally gave you the artifact. Dare I ask what you were discussing in there?" It was most likely a Harbinger, but hmm, Valor didn't relinquish her weapon when Tempest had threatened the realm, why would she do it now? Maybe it was something to do with Francis and Wisdom...

"I owe you the truth, and an apology. But today, I can only offer you one."

Well, that was ominous. "Am I allowed a choice? I always prefer the truth. Whatever it may be."

"Do you trust me, Zeen?"

Surely trust and doubt weren't absolutes. He trusted Serenna with his heart and his life, but still, her judgment tended to be a bit rash. The trembling woman wielding a glowing scythe while a trickle of blood ran down her left eye inspired more fear than confidence. *Hmm, let's take a wild guess and see how she reacts. I'll pick something completely absurd and work my way down.* "Of course I do, but I'm worried. You're not off to slay Arrogance, are you?"

Serenna twitched and glanced away. Damn, really? How long had she been planning this? No wonder she had been so nervous over the wedding.

"My dear, is that wise? I mean, Arrogance defeated David at his full power. I'm not saying you aren't powerful or anything, but, I mean...what if you can't win? I cannot lose you after everything." *If it's at the wedding, I'll be dead too.*

After lots of shifting around, her eyes went back to his. "Have you no faith in me? Have I ever let you down?"

"It's bad enough we live under the constant threat of Harbingers, now we have to storm into a god's domain and face him under his own rules? Serenna, I believe in you, I really do, but victory is never guaranteed. If I've learned anything from war, it's that the easiest way to stay alive is to avoid battle unless absolutely necessary—"

"He threatened my father," Serenna said, exchanging her apologetic glance for a classic glare. "We can ignore his tyranny until the Vanguards arrive at our doorstep, or we can bring the battle to him *now*."

I don't think we're gonna win this one. "You know I'm always with you but we should still discuss this with the others. Does David know? What about Valor?"

She paused, which probably meant yes to both. Was Zeen that blind? "I prefer not to speak of this in the open. Arrogance has eyes and ears everywhere. All around us."

"This is no way to live. Haven't we spent enough time being afraid?"

"*Exactly.* Zeen, I know my ambiguity is frustrating. All I can do right now is ask you to trust me. If we can win, it will usher in the dawn of a new age. No price is too high for such a thing."

"Most prices never seem too high until it's time to pay them. That being said, I will do my part." He stepped back, drew his sword, and entered his battle stance. "I'm curious to see if I can still deflect your crystals now that you wield an artifact. Shall we train?" Zeen forced a smile. He could barely keep up with the Wings of Mylor: to face an artifact of the gods would be laughable undertaking.

"We shall." Serenna gave a faint smile before a grimace took over. She seemed intent on hiding the pain brought on by the staff, which could only mean she was in agony. A crystal spike materialized in front of her, shimmering with a platinum wrath that burned his eyes.

Zeen clutched his sword and fixed his stance. Could he really deflect such a powerful spike? It didn't seem likely, but as it soared forward, that choice was no longer his own. He flailed his sword up, bracing himself for either a sharp pain in his wrist or a *very* swift death if Serenna's aim was off.

Instead, the spike froze about a foot or two away from Zeen's sword. Sweat poured down his face despite the freezing aura emanating from the crystal. "Halt," said Valor, with her arm stretched forward. She clenched her hand then the spike shattered into countless mirror-like fragments. "While I admire your eagerness, you are ill-prepared to train in such a manner just yet. You lack control, Crystal Girl. Had I not interfered, you would be in need of a new paramour."

Whew. Thank you, Goddess, Zeen thought, but didn't want to mention Serenna's lack of control. The simple truth was that spike would've been the last that he had ever seen before going to the void. "But *why?*" asked Serenna, huffing on her knees. "My aim is absolute. I am no simple amateur."

Valor scoffed. "The clear sign of any amateur is how adamantly they deny the rank in the face of failure. Now, rise and make another attempt. Stop focusing on the form and trust the spike to fulfill its purpose. Every crystal you bring into this realm, whether spike or shield, is an extension of yourself. Treat it as such, and control will be as natural as breathing. You are capable of breathing, are you not?"

The goddess grinned, but Zeen didn't find the joke very funny. Apparently, neither did Serenna, as she rushed up and formed three smaller spikes. She launched them one-by-one but…they were slow. And weak. Zeen didn't just deflect the spikes, he shattered them with three focused swipes. *Should I hold back? I don't want her to feel bad…*

"One more attempt," Valor said, shaking her head. "Fail me again, and the opportunity to wield my scythe shall vanish forever. Training the unworthy is not the protocol of Valor."

Okay, no matter what, I'll make this one look good. I know how badly she wants that artifact.

Serenna parted the hair from her eyes in that aggressive way she did whenever she was angry, then clutched her scythe and radiated with a bright platinum aura. A new spike materialized, thicker than the first one, with a more vibrant shimmer. It seemed rather chilly outside all of a sudden. Before Zeen could examine the spike further, she launched it forward.

Fortunately, Serenna aimed it far enough away to avoid hitting him, because by the time Zeen swung up, the spike had already flown past him and out towards the mountains. If this were anything resembling a true battle, he would be dead. "Wow. Is that from the scythe? I've never seen a crystal spike, or any spell for that matter, move so quickly."

"Indeed," she said with a smile, watching the crystal as it crashed into a mountain. "I wouldn't risk our future if I didn't believe victory was within our grasp. The last time I wielded this staff, I nearly ended the Goddess of Fear. I saw it, Zeen. I brought fear to the eyes of Fear."

To be fair, the crystal spike was impressive. It was one of the most impressive things he had ever seen. But Arrogance had defeated David. Quite handily, based on David's own account of the battle. "Valor," Zeen said, with a faint sigh. "Forgive me for asking, but can we really win?"

"It remains to be seen. Lean on the others. Lean on each other. I attempted the task alone in my mortal days. I was doomed to fail before I ever stepped foot in Terrangus. Mortals will always outnumber the divine. It is the one and only advantage of your kind."

That's not very encouraging. "Are you certain about this, my dear?"

"*Yes*, I am certain, and I tire of you questioning my judgment. This is why I kept our mission a secret. That and if you were made aware, the entire realm would know by nightfall."

He snickered. "That is likely the truth. I'm with you, but please be honest with me. We're lovers now. Lovers should never keep secrets."

"Fair enough, my love. No secrets." She gave him a light kiss on the cheek, which alleviated *most* of his worries, but something about this seemed off. It reminded him of the days when General Nyfe would lie about the enemy's true numbers to keep morale high, and Nyfe was about the last thing he wanted to think about. *She isn't telling me everything. If the lie is so terrible, what could possibly be the truth?*

CHAPTER 5

NUMBERS AND LIES

ary Walker kissed baby Calvin and laid him in the crib beside her bed. He always looked so adorable when he slept, which, unfortunately, was not often. As he lay there, all she wanted to do was hold him to her chest and hug him until the sun went down, giving him all the little comforts a baby needs to keep smiling. It was terrifying how much she loved him. Francis was her future husband, but this little boy, this tiny lump of love, filled her with a fury that was near- maddening.

Anyone or anything that put her child at risk would be annihilated.

"Will you watch him, Ruby?" she asked, already knowing the answer. Having her sister reside in the castle was one of the small blessings that came with the rank of Empress. Ruby was the only person she trusted with Calvin other than Francis. Mother would've been helpful too, but she had refused to visit, which was expected, but still disappointing. She hadn't seen Mother in so long…

"Right away, Empress!" Ruby said, standing firm at attention. Damn, she was tiny. The two of them were about the same size as kids when they would brawl, but Ruby had stopped instigating fights as Mary continued to grow larger. Apparently, the key to sisterly peace was lean arms and broad shoulders.

Mary sighed, a terrible habit from spending all that time with Francis. "Don't call me that. It's weird coming from you."

"Weird? Oh please, you were always Mother's little Empress. It took the realm a bit more time to figure out what I always knew. Have to admit though, Francis was a surprise. Always guessed you would end up with some muscular ex-soldier with a drinking problem."

"Francis surprises me every day." *And not always for the best.* "Well, I have an errand that requires my attention. Don't...please don't let any of the Vanguards take him while I'm gone. Or Wisdom. Especially Wisdom."

"Sorry, but there isn't a damn thing I can do if Mr. *God* comes storming in. He's probably already in here now. As for the Vanguards, they seem harmless, to me at least. Maybe because they're bald?" Ruby brushed her red hair to the side with a chuckle. "Mary, it's going to be okay. We're lucky our would-be assassin ended up being a fool. Heard it was a senator. You know anything about him?"

"Ask me again after I return." They hugged, then Mary left towards the door. Despite her efforts, she couldn't resist glancing back at Ruby and Calvin. Her sister was trustworthy, but Ruby was right: if Arrogance had any plans for Calvin, no one could stop him. Perhaps they were still on the same side, but with Francis recovering in a private healing ward, nothing was certain.

Mary left her chambers, pushing by the Vanguards assigned to her door. It was unsettling that they didn't ask where she was going, but just another disadvantage of being guarded by murderers.

Her hopes for a quick trek to the dungeons were ruined by an unruly crowd, rushing her like hungry cats with cries and moans, barraging her with phrases like, "Is the emperor well? What of the assassin? What are you doing for our safety? What are you doing to calm the riots?" Mary stopped listening to any questions beginning with, "What are you doing to..." These people would have to wait. If Francis...*when* Francis recovered, he could go back to giving his subjects vague, unhelpful answers. *If the gods are cruel and he doesn't make it...am I the sole ruler until Calvin is of age? That's impossible. Right?*

She took a deep breath and resisted the urge to grab her shield. Those military instincts would always be the first ones to rise.

Probably because they had kept her alive all those years. "My fellow people of Terrangus," she yelled, an annoying phrase she had stolen from Francis, who had probably stolen it from someone else. "Our emperor is well, but needs time to rest. The wedding is still scheduled for the end of the week, and our general has reported several victories over the rioters. You have nothing to fear." Hopefully, at least one of those statements was true. Lying was a loathsome act, but it came in handy in scenarios like this. If she had learned anything from Francis, it was that using the right lie at the right time can get people to stop speaking to you.

The murmurs and whining continued but, fortunately, the Vanguards finally did their jobs and not-so-gently pushed the people back, giving Mary room to breathe and an opportunity to make her not-so-discreet exit. She slowed her pace as she traveled down the stairs. They were steeper than she remembered, and an ominous chill made her shiver. She hadn't been this far down since David had been captured after his battle against Arrogance last year. For most people, this was a one-way journey. Rot in a cell until you die or convert into a Vanguard. The farther she walked, the less it seemed likely the senator-assassin would have any helpful answers. For all she knew, Arrogance had already dealt with him.

It wasn't too late to turn back, but she kept going. Part of her wished a Vanguard would send her back upstairs so she could return as a failure and not a coward. Vanguard Five stood at the entrance, staring at her with dissociated eyes. He was one of the only Vanguards she recognized, but it was by appearance only. The man once known as Robert Cavare was a shell of his former self. Arrogance had tightened his hold on Five after his short stint as a Guardian. She had begged Francis to keep Robert alive, but looking at him now, perhaps that was more cruel than merciful.

"Good morning, Empress," Five said with a bow. Perhaps some part of her old friend still remained; none of the other Vanguards ever bowed or showed any reverence other than repeatedly calling her Empress. "As you may have guessed, we have been expecting you."

Of course. It was foolish to think I would've made it this far unless it was allowed. "I'm free to pass?"

"Not only free, but encouraged. What future wife wouldn't want to interrogate her betrothed's near-murderer?" Five gestured towards the dank cell at the end of the dungeon, the same chamber that had held Nyfe before he became a Vanguard. "The truth, Empress, is all yours."

At this point, I don't even want to know. She eased up to the cell, pushing the fear back down into her gut. Why was she afraid? It was just a senator. Some old bastard who had probably lost all his investments as the riots became worse. "*You,*" she said, clutching the cell bars. "Your name. Now." Anything that resembled fear vanished into rage at the sight of the broken old man lying there. *This* was the man that had nearly murdered her Francis? *This* was the man that had forced innocent baby Calvin to witness violence?

The man struggled to rise. His right eye was swollen shut and blood stained his beard. The Vanguards had not been kind. One of the few times she appreciated them. "My name? The empress bitch doesn't even know her own subjects—"

"Unless you want to feel a mother's wrath, you will give me a name. Now." Part of her wished he would decline. Violence was always a great release, and to unleash it upon one who had harmed her family would be all the more sweet.

"Garrett Oakes. Son of Braylen. There was a time when emperors and archons knew our name better than their own kin. Do you know how debt works, Empress? I wager not, being a common soldier draped in gold."

She gestured for Five to open the cell. To her pleasant surprise, the Vanguard obliged. Garrett was likely goading her into making a mistake, but this "common soldier" wasn't going to tolerate such insolence from anyone, let alone the man who had attacked her family. Mary rushed in the moment Five opened the door. Garrett swung in that wide, sloppy way non-combatants always did, and she caught the blow with ease.

What a pathetic attempt. With his right arm hooked, she

grabbed him by the belt and slammed him to the ground. She ignored his groans and pressed harder. Odd that he wasn't really struggling or resisting her in any way. *He...he wants me to kill him. Interesting.* She let up, keeping her grip tight without pushing his head into the gravely floor. "If you seek a quick death, tell me everything."

That drew a smile, which confirmed her suspicions. "Debt is the most powerful magic ever conceived by god or man. Wealth is but a string of numbers and lies, its value conjured by those who own it. I lost everything in under a year. When my own fortune vanished, I turned to those who owed me theirs. The veil was lifted. In the end, no one had anything to offer but broken promises."

Mary gave him a quick punch across the face, withholding enough force to keep him awake. "I did not come here for riddles. Why did you do it?"

His breathing slowed after he spit out blood. After what the Vanguards had done, the next blow would likely be his last. "Family. Every terrible thing I have ever done has been for my family. You're asking the wrong question. Not why did I do it, but why *didn't*—"

Mary flinched back as Five drove his staff into Garrett's neck. "Why?" she asked, rising and drawing her shield. "Did I command such a thing?"

"Pardon, Empress, but the command was given from God himself. When actors forget their role, their role comes to an abrupt end. Do not despair. The void was always the endpoint for that one."

His words: why didn't *I do it? I wasn't meant to hear that.* After an awkward pause, she lowered her shield. Five wasn't even looking at her, so there was no threat. "Robert, I'm sorry. Had I known, perhaps I wouldn't have interfered. If you ever prefer...*that*, give me the word and I shall free you."

Five finally looked away from the corpse and into Mary. Maybe it was her imagination, but she swore there was a deep sadness in his eyes. "There is no Robert. Only Five. At ease, Empress. I have never been happier."

CHAPTER 6

GODS HAVE NO FRIENDS

here is Noelami?

David took the seat at the far side of the tavern, away from all the cheerful people having the time of their lives. It had been ten days without a drink. While it felt like a victory, there was a sinking feeling that normal people didn't keep track of such things. Travel to Nuum had been a brutal endeavor with the Guardian portals closed off. It had taken hours to arrive last night through the heavily defended outskirts portal. The guards had refused to believe he was *that* David and, to be fair, he couldn't blame them. The ex-leader of the Guardians was surely not this broken old man in light clothes with a bizarre-looking sword sheathed by his side. They had changed their minds when David placed ten gold pieces in the leader's hand. That had settled the argument. No wordsmith alive could ever match the persuasion of gold.

If there was one advantage to the brutal Nuum sun, David's dark skin attracted less attention throughout the city. Or perhaps everyone knew him, but just didn't care. "Another water, please," he said to the barkeep, who obliged. David was parched, but not for water. Maybe if he kept drinking it, the *other* urges would fade. Ah, to have some Nuum wine. Miserable places always provide the best ways to avoid reality. The scent was maddening. Bars smell different when we're sober. Whatever our drink of choice is the aroma that lingers in the air. *Maybe I could just have one while I wait for Fear...*

No. Time mages weren't the sort of enemy to battle while inebriated. Besides, it felt good to know clarity again. To remember events that took place more than a day ago. To sleep peacefully—

"A tavern? Truly?" Noelami's voice. She sat next to him, dressed in a white tunic to guard against the sun. Despite her royal status, she looked completely at home within the rundown hovel. "You were wise to show restraint. What has Sardonyx told you so far?"

"The usual nothing. My presence here was urgent, and was to be *glorious*. It is endearing that becoming a god has not changed him."

She *almost laughed, which brought a smile to his face. "Endearing is one way to put it. It's…difficult to deal with him. He refers to me only as Fear. I suppose to him, that is all I am. All I can be. The only one still remaining from my time is Ermias. And of course, we're at odds. It's* far too late to turn back now. One of us is going to die."

What does any of this have to do with our time mage? David thought, but he was always hesitant to question Fear. She seemed off. Distracted. Conflicted? "I am not from your Boulom, but I dare claim the title of friend."

"Gods have no friends, only tools that fade with time. Yet, here we are. There are difficult days ahead, David. Do not mistake my actions as cruel. I always play the long game. And I always win."

Hmm, that was rather ominous. "For a tool, I have come to know you very well. Now, where is my time mage? I'm not feeling the urgency."

"Patience, Guardian. Take it from one who has existed for nearly four centuries. The value of time is infinite, but there is never an excuse to squander the joyful moments."

He leaned in close. "What aren't you telling me? Are you in danger? Has Arrogance targeted you?" After an awkward pause, nearly nose-to-nose, he backed away and sipped his water. Noelami was no fool; she almost certainly knew of the plot to attack her once-lover through Francis. If David had learned anything in his life, it was the power of a loss that cannot heal. To experience loss is one matter, but to experience the anticipation of such pain must be crippling.

"Your silence is daunting. When the time comes, will you protect him?"

"How *dare* you ask me that. I have always acted in the name of balance."

"You speak in the name of balance, but my existence is proof you sometimes wander from the path."

Noelami sighed. "There was a time...a *short* time, where you met your potential. I don't often make mistakes but, when I do, the results are catastrophic. Too much power brings out the worst in anyone. I can only imagine how it will affect Sardonyx after a century or two."

David always wondered why she had never offered a replacement to the Herald of Fear. His current blade was stronger than most, but his old wrath had been a power most mortals could only dream of. "It's the loss that alters us, not the power."

"I wonder if you recall a time when you told me the opposite. Regardless," she said, sounding annoyed. Did he press her too far? "We have a mission to accomplish. If we linger too long, Sardonyx will involve himself and ruin everything. It will be difficult. Your target is Montgomery Wraith."

"Monty? The senator's son?" He nearly shivered despite the heat. Nuum always had the worst of luck. At least it wasn't a Harbinger this time. "And how will I manage that? Simply walk into the palace and state my intentions?"

"In a sense, yes. Senator Wraith has already left for Terrangus to attend the Haide wedding. Monty has been plotting his scheme to control time for the past few months. I would have acted sooner but the opportunity never presented itself. There is no room for error when kingdom leaders are involved. Approach the palace and state your intentions as an ambassador of Mylor. They will know the rest."

David scoffed. "Great. Perhaps you are unaware of your reputation, but if I were a gambling man, I would wager my death before I even enter the palace."

"I am despised in this part of the realm, but more importantly,

I am feared. Have you learned nothing in our time together? Fear is the true guardian of our realm. Everything else is a means to an end. Now go. Your realm and my own are both at stake. I would not send you if there was even the slightest possibility of failure."

David rose and offered his hand. Fear would always speak a strong game, but friendship tends to corrode the chains of authority. "May we meet again," he said as she accepted his grasp.

To his deep surprise, nearly knocking him over, she pulled him in and hugged him. It was a desperate embrace, the one given to those we never expect to see again. "Whatever happens, do not doubt my intentions. And do not falter."

If she bothered to read his fear, she would know the former was already a lost cause.

CHAPTER 7

ILLUSION OF SAFETY

een rustled his fancy white jacket as he sat down at the desk next to his bed, pulling up his socks to make his feet more comfortable. Until recently, he had eagerly been awaiting the wedding of Francis and Mary. It had been a *long* time since his last celebration outside of Mylor. But, of course, Serenna and her buddy Valor had designed a plan to attack a deranged god in his own domain, surrounded by his own guards. Unfortunately, being a good influence was not often the protocol of Valor.

Serenna was probably correct about the looming danger to the other kingdoms, but was immediate action the most logical response? Zeen was always the last to know anything. And, if *he* knew, it was certain Wisdom—or was it Arrogance? To be honest, that whole thing was terribly confusing—already knew. Oh well. Zeen would continue the plan that had gotten him this far in life: shut up and take orders.

While he waited for Serenna, he pulled up his stack of papers for *Rinso Volume IV* and turned to the page where he had left off yesterday. Ugh, where to start? A few people had suggested it was easier to plot these things, but Zeen preferred to pull up a page and write whatever came to mind. Hmm, if they were going to battle Wisdom, Rinso should battle Death!

Rinso was walking forward, he wrote, *moving quickly as he walked towards the steel gates of Terrangus. Rinso blinked his eyes from the rain that came down from the skies. Rinso did not enjoy being wet.*

The rain was like blood — red blood — Coming down from the skies — a reminder of his battle against a harbinger — a Harbinger of DEATH!

He reread the passage. Perfect! Zeen wasn't entirely sure how those dash things worked, but it seemed imperative to use them at every opportunity.

His door creaked open. "Zeen?"

He caught his breath as Serenna entered. She was draped in a loosely fitted platinum dress that matched the tint of her hair, with shiny white gloves on both hands. Her hair was pulled back in a bun, revealing her entire face, which was a rare but wonderful sight. Perhaps it had been silly to assume she would've attended the wedding in her Guardian armor, but she did everything in her armor. Nearly everything.

"How do I look?" she asked. It was likely she already knew the answer was amazing, beautiful, or some variation of both, but Zeen would never turn down an opportunity to remind her.

"Darling, you are simply *dashing*," he said with a smile. "When did you get that dress? It must've been hidden behind all your armor."

"Father bought it for me last month. A failed negotiation tactic on his part, but I welcome the gift. Perhaps in better times, I could wear something like this every day. It's not the most comfortable of garments but I'll make do."

"How about for the next Harbinger, we all wear fancy clothes? Instead of a helmet, we can force David to sport a pointy hat." Like any bad comedian, he laughed at his own joke. If Serenna in noble clothes was a rare sight, David would be a flying unicorn.

Serenna's head tilted down, killing the already weak laughter. "Zeen…the plan hasn't changed. I need you to acknowledge that."

Of course not, but it didn't seem necessary to linger on the fear. "Are you certain? This has been the best year of my life. I mean, look at you! How am I supposed to do battle with you looking like *that*?"

She giggled, and the red tint of her blushing face brought him a not-so-gentle warmth. "Happiness is both inspiration and the end goal. Don't yield to complacency when dark clouds are on the horizon." She approached and fixed his collar. "I understand your hesitation. I would be lying if I claimed not to feel it myself. But the realm needs protection. The realm needs *us*. We could smile, turn our backs, and grow old together, but that lingering cloud would only expand until it was all that remained. I know you, Zeen. By now, I know you very, *very* well. At the end, despite our happiness, we would look to the clouds and weep, knowing we did nothing."

Whatever she had done to his shirt made it feel much tighter. "Well, alright. You know, be kind and love each other ended up a lot more complex than I initially thought. Crazy to think this could be our last day alive. Hey, how much time before we're expected?"

"More than enough." She took the hint as she pushed him down onto their bed. It had been a chore to get all those clothes on, but getting them off was much easier.

*

Zeen took a deep breath as he materialized in the Terrangus outskirts portal. Rain dripped down his head, doing its best to hide the sweat. Even after all those years, the damned portals still made him uneasy. To be fair, everything made him uneasy today, and that was even after the stress release from earlier.

"Hello," he said awkwardly to the ten or so Vanguards standing by the portal. Apparently, this portal was the only one still active in Terrangus from the outside. Mylor was the same way. From what he had been told, all the kingdoms have been on the defensive with the rise of Arrogance.

Serenna materialized a few moments later, which was convenient since none of the Vanguards had returned his welcome. The Herald of Valor said hello without words: the scythe glowed a pale white at the edge of the blade, which honestly looked pretty awesome as it meshed with the stormy Terrangus darkness.

"Guardian Serenna Morgan. And guest," one of the Vanguards said... Oh! It was Mr. Five. "I am your escort to the wedding. Our host thought it most fitting for a Guardian to accompany the Guardians. Thank you for allowing me the honor to guide you."

Guest? How rude, Zeen thought, but didn't complain out loud. He nearly jumped as Serenna took him by the arm. There was a slight tremble in her grip; she was clearly as nervous as Zeen, perhaps even more so. "It's good to see you, Robert. You look well." *All things considered...*

"Well doesn't begin to describe it," Five said with a smile. An empty smile, the kind Forsythe had used to make. "I feel... *immaculate.* On an unfortunate note, our host has requested all guests with magical aptitude relinquish their respective staffs." Five reached out his hand to Serenna. Did he seriously expect her to comply?

She tightened her grip on Zeen's arm. "Does this look like a staff to you?"

"I know exactly what that is. An instrument of destruction. I wager I would die screaming if I even laid hands upon the shaft. Odd, that you chose to bring such wrath to a joining of royal lovers. A less inclined individual may perceive such a notion as a threat."

"The last emperor made several attempts on my life, and the one before that threw me in a prison cell after I defended his kingdom. I keep my staff, or Zeen and I shall head back to Mylor. I imagine the emperor would be most displeased."

Please just send us back. This is an opportunity to have the wedding without any realm-shattering events. Surely he knows Serenna isn't wielding that scythe without intent.

Five had a dissociated gaze into the stormy clouds above. After a few awkward moments of nothing but rain tapping down, he said, "Very well. I have received confirmation from God that you and your guest are welcome with weapons intact. If such...*toys* fulfill your illusion of safety, who are we to stand in your way?"

We should get the hell out of here, Zeen thought but refused to say as Serenna gripped his arm. Not all fears are created equal. One of the less fortunate talents from war was gauging the probability of victory based on your opponent's confidence. There is nothing more thrilling than to chase a weakened unit, with those crazy poses where weapons are held high and everyone is yelling. Everything about this screamed retreat, but maybe it was all lies, bluffs, or even delusions.

His name *was* Arrogance, after all.

"Thank you for understanding. Let us proceed," Serenna said, then followed Five with Zeen on her arm. The sight of Vanguards everywhere made an already uncomfortable trip more so. It took him a few moments to realize many of them were women with shaved heads. This wasn't how Zeen remembered his home. Although it kind of was, which was the strangest feeling of all. Most of the shops and inns had already been rebuilt to their former glory, though he barely recognized anyone. They couldn't all be dead but, how many had become Vanguards? Other than Five and...the *other* one, they all appeared the same.

"Where is everyone?" asked Serenna, and that was a great question. For a wedding, the streets were mostly empty. Even the standard trading and yelling was unnaturally soft.

"Whatever do you mean?" said Five with a hint of sarcasm. He had probably been anticipating the question. "Just because you don't see them, doesn't mean they aren't there."

Retreat. Retreat. Retreat...

Serenna smirked. "I wouldn't be surprised to see a small turnout. Even by Terrangus standards, your emperor and *god* have a meager amount of allies. That is the problem with lies, Robert. If even a single person knows the truth, the lie is vulnerable."

Five immediately stopped and shot Serenna an odd-looking glare. It was so unnatural, like someone who had never seen a human before attempting to convey anger. "Do not overestimate our patience. Refer to me as Robert again at your own risk."

"We meant no disrespect," Zeen said before Serenna could respond. The look on her face made it clear "Robert, Robert, Robert" was about to happen. "With all the tension, it has been months since we interacted with your kind." *Hmm, I could have worded that better...*

"Indeed," said Five. "The realm is so desperate to be unhappy, they craft their shields and walls and huddle together, reveling in their ignorance. I used to be one of them. My fate is both a miracle and a curse. A miracle, because I have seen paradise. It is a real, tangible thing. A curse, because I must see it alone."

The anger left Serenna's face, but the slight squint of her eyes showed pity. It was a quiet journey as they entered the military ward gates. Strange to think Zeen had lived here most of his life. By now the Vanguard to soldier ratio was nearly one-to-one. Most of the normal people stared in awe of Serenna and her scythe, but the Vanguards couldn't be less interested. They walked around, issuing bland orders in bland voices. Interestingly enough, it seemed they were organizing for a major battle—

Nyfe walked out from the castle entrance, draped in his white armor that covered his entire face other than his glowing eyes. "I'll take it from here, Five. Oh, how I missed you two! Such wonderful, precious friends. Thank you for abandoning me in Vaynex. You clearly knew what joy awaited me back home. Thank you, from the bottom of my heart."

Too many memories rushed up at once. Zeen's long miserable years under General Nyfe, acting as a glorified murderer. His first Harbinger of Fear with David, Pyith, and Melissa. The day he had faced Nyfe and died... "Stay away," Zeen said, drawing his sword by instinct. If this was the end, he would take Nyfe down with him.

"It's fine," Serenna said, which was wrong. It wasn't fine. It wasn't fine at all. She leaned into Zeen's ear and whispered, "It's all tricks and lies. Do not allow him the opportunity to break your concentration. If anything goes amiss, you have my word: Nyfe will be the first one to die."

Right now, it looks like I'll be the first one to die, he thought, sheathing his sword. "Lead the way...from a distance."

"Whatever our special guest demands," Nyfe said, gesturing to them to follow him into the castle.

So they did, and Zeen expected the usual cacophony that had usually awaited him inside the castle doors—even more so with a wedding about to commence. But there was nothing. No yells, no loud banging, no soldiers marching around pretending to be useful. *There is no wedding. He's taking us to a private room for an execution.* Zeen nearly grabbed his sword but yielded to his instincts as a soldier. If anyone was going to act, Serenna would have to be first.

Such is the chain of command. "Where are you taking us?" Zeen finally asked. If he couldn't act, he may as well speak.

"You were always too tense," Nyfe said, pausing before the doors to the hallway before the throne room. "To be fair, it made you into a good soldier, nearly a great one. Good enough…to make me envy you for time. After that whole Harbinger thing, I thought I was wrong. Meaningless or not, my entire life was wasted, rotting in cells. It wasn't until God showed me the truth did I realize: a life without enlightenment is a fate more cruel than any prison crafted by man. Guardian Serenna. Guardian Zeen. It was a path of violence and woe, but it led me to Serenity. I am finally happy."

Serenna sighed. "Of course you are. Delusion is the cornerstone of happiness."

That brought a chuckle from Nyfe, who led them to the throne room doors. It was difficult to admit, but the man *did* seem happier. *What if we're wrong? Can we coexist with Vanguards?* The whole thing was far above Zeen's head. For whatever good Wisdom had done for the realm, he had threatened Serenna's father last year. Hmm…

The doors opened, revealing an empty throne room and a glowing portal. "What sorcery is this?" asked Serenna. Her grip tightened on Zeen's arm and, to be honest, it was starting to hurt.

"My dear Serenna," Wisdom's voice called out. The vibration rumbled within the room, bouncing off the walls over and over. "Be a good guest and step inside.

"Serenity awaits."

CHAPTER 8

A COMFORTING LIE

ow do I look?" asked Mary, shifting to watch the side of her wedding dress glimmer in her reflection. It fit nicely; apparently the stress of the past few months had done an impressive job in slimming her figure. It was both a relief and a disappointment. Okay, it was more disappointing than she would admit. Most of her muscles had faded since becoming Empress and mother. It's easy to name ourselves warrior, soldier, Engager, but our body is our true identity. And Mary's identity had forever shifted to Empress.

"I actually hate how beautiful you look," Ruby said, analyzing her like she was a horse up for auction. "You always had the better face, but now that you're slim, I got nothing."

"Oh, stop it. If nothing else, you're still Mother's favorite. That should count for something."

"That's only become true recently. Not to get political, but sending your Vanguard buddies out there to silence people who don't agree with the royal family isn't winning you any friends."

"Sometimes you win friends. Sometimes you lose enemies. Besides, why do I need them when I have you—"

"When you have *us*," a voice called out from the doorway. A voice Mary hadn't heard in nearly two years.

"Mother…you came," Mary said, resisting the urge to rush over and hug her. Gods, she was a tiny woman, but Mother would always wield an authority that would put any general to shame. "This means the realm to me. Thank you."

"You won't be thanking me in a moment. But first, where is my grandson?"

Oh no, she thought, pointing to the crib where baby Calvin was sleeping, then cringed as Mother rushed over and picked him up without permission. There were less than a handful of people in the entire realm who could do such a thing without meeting the noose.

"Scrawny little man. Are you feeding him? Or are you too obsessed with murdering your own people that you forget they require food? Hmm? Speak!"

Gods, she always did this. It was like Mary was thirteen again, getting scolded for running in front of Alanammus Tower. She had been so excited to see Archon Addison Haide in person. What a bizarre turn of events she was to marry her son. "I... I... Ruby, leave us *now.*"

"Sorry, sis. No way I'll miss—"

"*Get out!*" Mary yelled, which woke Calvin and immediately made him cry.

"Look at that, even my grandson knows a tyrant when he sees one. Is this how I raised you? Could you even imagine what your father would say if he could see you now?"

Just like that, all the rage dissipated. Mary stared into her mother and, for the first time in her life, felt nothing. "Father is dead. He died a meaningless death in a meaningless war. If we had better leadership, he would still be with us today. Perhaps he would've walked me down the aisle." The thought nearly brought tears to her eyes. Not because it was impossible, but because she had never even considered it. Life had changed too much in too short an amount of time.

"Meaningless? Oh, it's worse than I imagined. I don't even recognize you anymore. It's like a Harbinger wearing my daughter's skin. Here," she said, handing Mary back her son, "take him away from me. I will not become attached to a grandchild destined to become the next tyrant."

"Mom... Francis isn't a tyrant." Doubt made the words weaker than intended. It's rare that benevolent leaders find a blade in their chest. "Behind all the lies and slander is a good man trying to repair a shattered kingdom. I could introduce you to him."

"I would sooner drown," she said, then left.

Ruby leaned against the wall, staring out the window. She likely regretted not leaving the room earlier. "Sorry about that. I knew she was mad but didn't know it went so deep. I wouldn't have brought her here. Is there anything I can do?"

Mary sighed as Calvin continued to cry in her arms. So, everyone decided it was tyrants now and not just tyrant. It was far worse than she had ever thought. If Mary's own mother couldn't stand her presence, the regular people of Terrangus must despise her on a level rivaling the God of Death. The assassination attempt on Francis was just a taste of things to come. "Tonight...will you stay here with him? I have a very ominous feeling about the wedding and my instincts are usually right. You're the only one I trust. The only one that still loves me."

"Oh, Mary," Ruby said, giving her an embrace before taking Calvin. "Of course I'll watch over my tiny nephew, though it may be a challenge to spoil a future emperor. Mother is...has always been stubborn. I know you're doing your best. Keep your head up. These things always work out in the end. We always remember leaders for the good and not the bad. Otherwise, there wouldn't be a single beloved emperor in Terrangus history."

Things were truly dire if Ruby had to offer a comforting lie. Although that raised an interesting point: Terrangus had no real beloved emperors. Adrial Forsythe was said to be wise, but her son and heir Grayson had nearly destroyed the realm with his brash judgment. Could Francis be the exception? With Arrogance pulling the strings, it seemed impossible. "Aren't weddings supposed to be joyous events? We should just cancel."

"Hush, and wipe that tear. Have a few glasses of wine, enjoy the celebration, and try to be happy. I would wish you good luck with the marital affairs, but based on this little man in my arms, you already know what to expect. Let's go. I'll escort you to the portal."

Her chamber door swung open, nearly hitting Ruby in the face. "Mary!" Francis said, his eyes darting everywhere while he fidgeted all over. Ugh, the Herald of Arrogance was sheathed behind his back, but he looked...well, he looked great in his pristine white robes, bulky shoulder pads, and shimmering gold crown. Something in his boots definitely made him a few inches taller but she wouldn't mention that.

"Da?" Calvin said, reaching his tiny hands out to Francis. Ah, his first word, and a devastating blow to Mary. All children have a favorite parent and, like Mary, Calvin had chosen his father.

The utter dismay on Francis's face was silly enough to calm the wave of despair flowing through her. "Well look at that," Mary said, forcing her smile to push the other feelings down. Zeen would be proud. "His first word is Da. Congratulations are in order, my beloved."

"Ah, what a joyous day," Francis said. "And Mary, you look simply ravishing! If there was a Goddess of Beauty, you would be her muse! I take it your servant here is going to watch our son? Do you trust her?"

Mary smiled. "With my life. Francis, I would like you to meet my sister, Ruby." *I would like to introduce you to my mother too but that will never happen.*

"I see it!" Francis said, his eyes lighting up. "Look at that hair, the green eyes, the hooked shape of the nose...you are truly Mary's sister. It is a pleasure and honor to see you, my lady."

He's awfully confident today. He must...is he excited to finally marry me?

"The pleasure is all mine, Emperor. Now, you two run along and have your ceremony. I'll watch over the little one. With some nudging, I can get his second word to be 'Aunt.'"

"There's no rush," Francis said, losing his smile. "Are you certain you don't wish to...uh, discuss family history or some variation of the sort?"

Ah, he's stalling. "It's time, my beloved. We're about to be joined forever as one. We'll have all the time in the realm to discuss that stuff while we grow old and die."

Francis sighed, rubbing the spot where his wound was. "It seems unlikely I'm going to reach old age. There is a foreboding sense in the air. At first I thought it was just me being…me, but something is amiss."

"Then we'll deal with it together," Mary said, taking his arm. "It's time, Francis.

"Serenity awaits."

CHAPTER 9

AGE MUST BE A CRUEL POISON

t had been eleven days since David's last drink. He had slept better most of those nights, but it had been a long time since he struggled as he did last night. Something was terribly wrong, and it seemed everyone in the realm knew what it was other than him. David stood in front of the Nuum palace. With the heat smothering him, it was one of the most exquisite-looking, but least comfortable strongholds in the entire realm. Opulence is no match for a vengeful sun.

"Halt," the guard said, pointing his halberd forward as David approached. "Senator Wraith is on leave. The palace will not accept an audience with any outsiders until his return. Nuum is full. Return to your own kingdom at once."

Hmm. Noelami had said the palace was expecting him, but name-dropping Fear didn't seem like a rational plan. "What makes you think I'm an outsider?"

"A native wouldn't appear lost in their own home. Listen, I don't know who you are or where you're from, but consider it a blessing that I'm giving you a final warning. Nuum is full. Return to your kingdom at once."

David sighed, his hand drifting to his sword sheath. "My friend, that is not going to happen. Monty is expecting me and I can ill afford to waste valuable time. Now, either call your superior, or summon a healer." Hopefully, those words would get the job done.

Any violence against the guards—even if justified—would ruin the entire mission.

"Fucking foreigners," the lead guard said, stepping back into a battle stance and holding his halberd forward. Well, shit—

"Stop," the other one said, frozen as if he had seen Fear herself. Maybe he had. "Evan, wait. It's him."

"Truly?" Even asked, lowering his halberd. He approached and analyzed David with a confused look on his face. "You must be mistaken. This can't be Fear's chosen. Look at him!"

"*She* confirmed it. Let's go, there is no time to waste."

"Shit. Oh, shit. Alright, let's get moving."

David smiled as he pulled his hand back and stepped forward. Odd that he couldn't see Fear if they could. While it would've been nice if she had warned the guards ahead of time, at least no violence had occurred—

A *very* sharp pain manifested in the back of David's head. It only lasted a moment before the pain and all other senses faded entirely.

*

His eyes eased open. Gently at first, but the throbbing sensation in his skull was like a bucket of cold water thrown onto his face. "Where am I?" he asked out loud. Musty air, sandy grounds, wails in the distance and...bars. He patted where his sword should be, sighing at the obvious result.

"David Williams," a familiar voice called out from the other side of the bars. "Imagine my surprise to find that the man who saved my father's kingdom is now out to destroy it. You barely resemble my memories. Age must be a cruel poison."

"An interesting observation from one dabbling in time," David said, forcing himself up. "Why, Monty? Have you any idea what game you're playing?"

Monty licked his lips. Despite everything, it was nice to see the boy grown into a man. "A game where I win and Father loses. A game of retribution. I doubt you could understand."

David nearly laughed at the thought of Nuum betraying Fear

until he considered that meant a Harbinger would arrive. With the wedding taking place, such timing would be catastrophic. "I murdered an emperor, my once-closest friend, in cold blood. Take it from one who embraced vengeance and made it their entire identity. You begin the journey with nothing. You complete it with even less."

"Always so dramatic. Enjoy the next few hours of rest. Once the wedding begins, you are to be executed."

David grinned at the bluff. Perhaps the threat would've held more weight in his younger years, but convincing Nuum of all places to execute a Guardian would be madness. "Monty, stop this nonsense. There is nothing to be afraid of. You haven't crossed the point of no return. Release me, vow to stop dabbling in time magic, and no harm will come to anyone. Neither of us believes you would ever harm a Guardian, even the least useful one." He forced a smile, though he hated the reality of slaying Monty at the first opportunity. Unfortunately, time magic is *always* a one-way journey.

"Of course not, but you misunderstand. I must kill you today, so that I never have to kill you yesterday. A pity: that means this conversation will never have occurred. A lost opportunity to rub it in your face when the realm achieves Serenity."

"Serenity? Oh no. Oh…no."

"Oh, *yes*," he said, his eyes growing large as he grabbed the bars. "And how fortunate that I trusted him! It's all come to pass exactly as he foretold. The Guardians are at the wedding and Fear's assassin is locked away. The rest…is up to me. If I can cast the spell before a Harbinger arrives, we win. Oh, curse me if you must David, but consider how wonderful it all will be!"

David sighed and went back to leaning against the wall. His head still throbbed, but it didn't seem to matter anymore. "Monty, you fucking fool. I swear no matter what sins your father committed, none of them will ever come close to your own if you go through with this. It's not too late…"

"Farewell, David. Forgive me for not attending your execution, but I must ensure that it never occurs at all."

He watched Monty leave, not bothering to beg him to stay. *May Fear save us all.*

*

The opening of his prison cell made David immediately wake. Ah, it was the two guards from the palace gates. While he had no chance to fight them unarmed, he would leave the cell on his own terms. What amateurs: if David were ten years younger, *maybe* he could have...

"It's time, Guardian," one of them said. Was it Evan? With the helmet covering most of his face, he couldn't tell them apart.

"A welcome upgrade from 'fucking foreigner.'"

"She didn't tell us everything," the other one said. "Had we known, perhaps this could've gone differently. As it stands, we are in great danger."

By "she," David assumed they were referring to Fear. He flinched as Evan held out David's sword. "No tricks? I will warn you once. Betray me while I wield this blade and I will not hesitate to slay you both."

"No tricks. Take it and please follow us. Wraith forgive me, but we must slay Montgomery."

"We?" asked David, taking his blade.

"Indeed. Forgive our...transgressions from earlier. We had specific orders from the One True Empress to keep you apprehended until further orders. I will not guess her motives, but they seem to want you away from Terrangus. Not sure when Arrogance got involved, but it made a mess of everything. I think we've all been played."

Away from the wedding. By the gods... "The Guardians are in danger. I must leave here immediately."

"No!" Evan yelled, grabbing his hand. If David wasn't lost in thought, he would've retaliated. "Listen, we'll break our orders and escort you to the portal but only after Montgomery is slain. David, you're the wisest Guardian. You know what must be done."

Fuck, he thought, letting out a drawn-out sigh. "All too well. We must make haste. Time, unfortunately, is not on our side."

CHAPTER 10

PLATINUM SONATA

Francis wasn't cold but his hands wouldn't stop shaking. What an annoying habit to follow his already tense nerves. There was no doubt that Francis, Mary, and all their guests were somewhere in Serenity, but it wasn't the usual sky garden. To be clear, it *was* a sky garden, with the sunny skies, fluffy clouds, even the waterfall flowing by the wedding arch, but something about the tone didn't match the upbeat atmosphere that normally followed these events. The most probable reason was the replica of Boulom Cathedral that stood behind them. An odd if not thoughtless choice by Wisdom. The simple-minded folk who undeservingly found their way into Serenity would have no idea what significance the structure represented. The arrival of the first Harbinger. The cataclysm of everything leading to this moment.

By Wisdom's glory, it was difficult to admit, but the cathedral put even Alanammus Tower to shame, a reminder that the future had yet to transcend the past. The grand structure was a mix of ivory on the primary sections and azure near the top, with the magic-infused light posts glowing on all four corners of the rectangular shape. Above the doorway were enormous pillars holding up a stained-glass window engraved with Wisdom's sun mask. How interesting, the original inhabitants of Boulom wouldn't have known who Wisdom was, so perhaps it was a touch added by their host of the evening—

Mary grabbed his hand. Hopefully, she wouldn't mind how

sweaty it was. How did she manage to remain so calm and stoic? Are weddings just a normal event for most people? It was difficult to articulate his concerns. There was no doubt in his mind that Mary— the mother of their child—was the only woman he desired for the rest of his life. She was sheer and utter perfection, a crimson-haired angel bestowed upon the realm from the heavens above, the greatest argument that perhaps there was a Goddess of Beauty and she already walked among them. Maybe the crowd of people triggered his nerves? Having Warlord Eltune Dubnok and Guardian Bloom in attendance didn't help matters.

And Serenna. Oh, Serenna, Serenna.

Why was she sitting there with a scythe behind her back like a common brute? She managed to put even the zephum to shame, but at least she wore some real clothes and not that dingy armor. And why did Zeen have a sword as well? Hmm. To attack Francis in Terrangus was one thing, but here? In *Serenity*? He almost wished they would try, just for an opportunity to display the superiority of the Herald of Arrogance.

"It's okay," Mary said, giving his hand a light squeeze. "All this ceremony does is confirm the truth we both already know. I am yours, and you are mine. Forever."

"Forever," he said, clutching her hand as they began their walk down the grassy aisle. It was pleasant to have a strong wife. She probably didn't know or care how much effort he was putting into holding her hand. Hopefully, she didn't mind all the sweat either. It's a damnable feeling when we can't see it on our face but feel it drip down.

At least the music was perfect. Cellos, violins, and a bass floated in the air, waving side to side as they played their concerto in unison: Thaddeus Emmanuel's *Platinum Sonata* in A major, to be precise. Unlike the chaotic tone of the more popular but less beautiful *Mylor March* in B sharp, the tone was more...mature. While most guests cling to the dancing, wine, yelling—all the insufferable aspects of weddings—wiser men know that marriage is a calculated risk and should be celebrated with the proper subtlety.

Francis smiled as the concerto slowed to its second movement. The bass notes diminished to the background, a friendly rumble heard only by those who knew how to listen. The soft vibration was like a soothing glass of wine, a gentle reminder from art itself that no matter how stressful the realm could be, greater minds would always prevail.

The music came to a close, and Mary released his hand as they arrived at the head of the podium. If she held any doubt about her choice of a husband, there was none to be found on her face. May the gods bless her for being so wonderful to a man who never deserved it.

Several of the guests watching from behind gasped as Wisdom materialized at the podium. Thankfully, God had chosen the more welcoming form and not Arrogance. It was one of the few times the platinum smile on the sun mask outshone the black frown. Perhaps it was from the rays of sunlight or, hopefully, God was truly pleased.

"Welcome friends, guests, those who could be either but chose to be neither. Guardians, archons, warlords, all our favorite senators escorted by predators. Today is a joyous day. A celebration. A gathering to behold something so *precious*, so *dear* to both mortals and divine alike. A joining of royal lovers. Heralds of the new age of Serenity." Wisdom chuckled, his bulging eyes drifting around the mask. "That was your cue to applaud."

Light claps filled the air but it was obviously out of obedience rather than admiration. Out of all the things that baffled Francis, the realm's distrust for Lord Wisdom was atop the list. It was more tragic than anything else. Who fears opportunity more than fools? All of them: every single one of them would benefit from Wisdom's guidance, and yet they struggled against it with every essence of their being.

"What a journey it has been," Wisdom said, gesturing with his spectral hands, ignoring Bloom's exaggerated groan. "If only dear Addison Haide could see us now. Ah, to cast me out from Alanammus, just to have me officiate her son's wedding. The absurdity of freewill truly works in mysterious ways. Hopefully, not for much longer."

Wisdom cleared his throat as the wind stopped. If his pause was for cheers, none came. "I didn't know what to make of you two at first. What seemed like chaos in motion was love unyielding. So precious. So innocent. So…familiar. Like remnants of a dream estranged to those who sleep no longer. Like a yawn on the edge of oblivion. A shadow on the lightest corner of heaven. Time beyond time. Screams beyond whispers. An echo, upon echo, upon echo… When our time in this realm comes to an end, we are nothing more, nothing less, than all we did not do. Mary, Francis. You stand here upon the precipice of forever. From henceforth, you are of one body. One heart. One mind. You may now kiss your empress."

The words brought clarity where anxiety once stood. He turned to his future…*current* wife and waited for her to act first. They met eyes, but not lips. Was she second-guessing her future? The cruelest of tragedies always occur at the peak of joy. A heart must learn to smile before it can scream. Nothing. Neither of them were moving. Was it seconds or minutes? Impossible to tell—

She lunged forward and kissed him, wrapping her arms around him in a way that made it difficult to mimic the gesture. It was too loud to be afraid. The people finally cheered, despite how little they loved him. Maybe…they had changed their minds? Was Francis finally the beloved ruler he was always meant to be? "I love you," she whispered, easing her grip but holding his hand high in the air.

While the gesture seemed absurd, it made the people cheer, so he whispered back, "I love you too," and kept his hand high. Life had never been better, but as they walked back to Boulom Cathedral, the anxiety from earlier made itself known. To be honest, he didn't want to enter. His only experience within the structure had been watching Wisdom's mortal days before he became the Harbinger that destroyed Boulom. An odd location to celebrate a grand new future.

*

Francis sighed, sitting at his private table with Mary beside him. Feasting after a wedding always seemed an obscure tradition. The task had already been completed. *Why are you people still here? Run back to whichever rotten kingdom you hail from…*

Or just keep dancing and yelling inside a foreign structure. Of course they would choose that option. It was rather annoying how few people came to congratulate Francis. Mary had so many visitors one would think *she* was the true ruler of Terrangus. Perhaps that was the plan? Grant Mary the Haide name, then throw Francis into the garbage where he always belonged. *I wager one of them will attempt to slay me tonight. But who? Let them try. I could burn each and every one of them into ash before they ever knew my intentions.*

Francis pushed his wine glass away. What once numbed the senses brought nothing but rage and doubt, two completely different emotions that somehow worked in unison. Hmm. Maybe if he drank a bit more, it would expedite the evening's close. Drinking alone is said to be a loathsome act, but there is nothing more lonely than being surrounded by everyone but no one in particular.

"Draw your sword, human!" Warlord Eltune yelled, pointing his blade at Zeen in the middle of the now-empty dance area. Hopefully, such nonsense would mean the end of the party. It was a wonder the zephum managed to behave as adults for long as they did.

Mary rushed over to the scene, but Francis sat at his table, eyeing the Vanguards stationed throughout the Cathedral. It was rather odd that they didn't seem concerned about the potential realm-shattering event. What held their attention?

"My dear Francis," Arrogance whispered through his thoughts. *"Avert your eyes from the obvious distraction and ponder a thought. Who, oh who, isn't reacting to this display appropriately? Here's a hint: she stands with weapon in hand by the corner. But stay alert, for she does not stand alone. Show our unfortunate guests what occurs when pawns rise against God.*

"It's time, Francis. Kill them. Kill every single one of them."

Serenna held her scythe with both hands. How sad that it had to be her. She had chosen violence and now, in doing so, she had chosen to die.

CHAPTER II

DANDELIONS IN THE WIND

hile Serenna couldn't have asked for a better distraction than the drunken warlord threatening Zeen, the plan had failed long before it ever begun. She tightened the grip on her scythe as she met eyes with Francis. By Valor's grace, he knew her intentions. There would be no turning back now.

So be it.

Serenna erupted into her platinum form, carefully allowing her energy to mesh with the wrath of Valor's scythe. With the room filled with hostile forces, overstoring her power wouldn't be an issue. Vanguards rushed over from every direction while she shielded herself and formed a crystal spike. *You better uphold your end of the bargain, Archon,* she thought, hovering her spike to aim the perfect strike. To her enormous relief, several Alanammus gold cloaks drew their swords and engaged the Vanguards while Archon Gabriel protected them in crystal shields.

Eltune cocked his head at Zeen, then examined the room. "What is this… Ah, human treachery! What a glorious way to slay the Arrogant One! Strength without honor—is *chaos!*" He smiled before rushing into the fray with Bloom by his side. It was incredible how little coordination it took to have everyone turn against Francis. Hatred is never an ideal to strive for, but nothing unifies desperate people more quickly.

Serenna launched her spike forward. Francis's glare never changed; it was like he was frozen in time, wielding his Arrogance staff but not casting any spells. She swore the eye on the staff was staring directly at her, daring her to strike.

A Vanguard jumped in front of the spike, taking the edge through his chest and crashing downwards. He was clearly dead, but with the empty expression that was always present on their faces, it was difficult to notice any change.

"Yes, I am well aware," Francis said out loud, likely to Arrogance, who hadn't revealed himself yet. "I know. I know. I know." He clutched his staff and erupted into a yellow-tinted aura. Letting out a desperate wail, he thrust his arms forward, sending a blinding ray of light towards her.

Serenna groaned as she yielded energy to the scythe to quickly form a spike. Sometimes offense is the only practical defense, so she launched her spike at the blast to stop it from consuming her. Platinum and lighting collided in the middle of the hall, exploding, sending fragments of shattered crystals in every direction. Then a blast came from directly above her; Serenna dove behind one of the tables, crashing awkwardly into the chairs, then forced herself up to avoid becoming an easy target.

Francis must have lost sight of her in the chaos, for he blasted an adjacent table, incinerating both gold cloaks and his own Vanguards within the vicinity. What a sad fate to surrender one's freewill in the name of a higher power, only for said power to burn them without a moment's hesitation.

"Child, I am engaged against Arrogance within the shadows and cannot assist. Stop acting like an amateur and refresh your shield," Valor's voice whispered through her thoughts. The tone of her voice was surprisingly frantic. *"And fix your posture! Remember, while you are protected by shields, it takes only one rogue shard to eliminate the Puppet Emperor. Defense has always been your strongest attribute but offense is the only path to victory. By Noelami's mercy, may we both succeed."*

Fair enough. Serenna crafted several tiny spikes and hovered them in a spread-out formation. It would have been preferable to improve the form, but with soldiers clashing against Vanguards all around her, precision yielded to caution. She launched them simultaneously towards Francis's table.

His aura shifted to green as he fell backwards, casting a mountainous terrain that surrounded himself and Mary at the last second. The spikes thrust into the wall of earth but not through them, creating a bizarre cascade of shimmering light on soil in the middle of the cathedral.

More energy. MORE! Deep down, the ecstasy of destruction always lingered. Power tore from her chest, ripping through her insides to amplify the pale glow of the scythe. Let him hide behind his mountains. She turned her attention to the Vanguards who were overrunning the gold cloaks. Her hands shook, gripping the handle of her blade. The ratio of fallen allies to enemies was concerning, but at least she had plenty of targets to choose from. *Too much energy... Have to release... Something must die...*

You.

She picked a lone Vanguard at random and trapped him within a crystal prison. Hopefully, it was Nyfe, but the platinum rays dancing in front of her eyes made it impossible to tell. Ripping the prison in two was incredible, if only to stop the accumulating pain. It gave her a moment to breathe before the scythe would demand more. Sweat poured down her face or, more likely, blood. How anyone could battle with a scythe for a prolonged period of time was—

"Are you okay?" Zeen asked, grabbing her shoulder from behind.

She jumped. *I must be more careful. If it was anyone other than Zeen, that would've been the end.* "Don't sneak up on me! We must get through that wall of earth before we are overrun. If we can force Arrogance to reveal himself, I should be able to slay him and end this madness." An odd sensation filled her thoughts, like someone was trying to speak but couldn't be heard.

An eruption of orange came from within the earthy terrain, blasting rocks and soil in all directions. A glowing Francis stood within the inferno, his aura seething with fiery energy. "You thought to face me here?" he yelled, stepping forward.

A brave or delusional gold cloak rushed him, only to be incinerated by a burst of flame. It was the only time Serenna had ever seen a man slain by fire without screaming. He simply crumbled into ash.

"It is simply *outrageous* that my god is labeled arrogant, yet Valor is the one storming the heavens to end paradise. And why? What have I ever done to you? Are you so overcome with psychotic urges to always interfere, no matter the cost? You have taken Pact Breaker, a *slur*, and made it your entire identity. *No.* You don't get to win, Serenna. Not this time. Serenity is upon us. And it begins with your end."

Serenna took a deep breath, refreshing her crystal shield and stepping forward. For as long as she had known him, Francis always had the worst monologues. The open section of the hall was a disadvantage against flame, but time was running out.

Bloom must have been out of gadgets; every time Serenna glanced in her direction, the zephum was slashing with blades instead of detonators. Zeen and Eltune stood back-to-back, protecting each other's flank, slaying Vanguard after Vanguard. Father was... Where the hell was Father?

Enough. Everything depends on me. It always did.

Serenna cast a barrier directly around her and then a barrier to protect the barrier. She was covered in a fortress of shimmering platinum before she crafted a monstrous spike in the middle of the air. Her right leg gave out, but she was able to fall to one knee. It was a bit alarming that no pain followed. The only pain was from her insides; it felt like tiny daggers were poking her organs in some obscure torture. But as she stared at the prodigious crystal spike that could take down an entire castle, it was worth it. Pain is the temporary price for a permanent victory. The muffled voice continued to nag Serenna from the back of her mind.

Francis created his own elemental monstrosity, a seething ball of flame. Even through the platinum tint of her barrier, the vibrant orange from the inferno was blinding. It was as if the sun itself was about to crash into Serenity.

"*Sah...mustn't...decept...*"

"What do you *want?*" she yelled to the muffled voice.

The unintelligible whispers continued, but were drowned out by Arrogance chuckling above Francis. So, the god had finally revealed himself. Perhaps Valor had been defeated, but it was fitting for one named Arrogance to gloat while Serenna still held the power to end gods. One last fatal mistake.

She launched the spike directly at the sun mask of Arrogance while Francis launched his inferno towards her. There was little hope her shields and barriers would stop the flame, and that was okay. There had been some wonderful days with Zeen in the past few months. How cruel of the realm not to give them more, but when it comes to happiness, we can only take what is given—

"*I love you, Crystal Girl, and I forgive you. Fear not! For Mylor has never fallen. Her mountains are stained red from the blood of those who tried.*"

The illusion of the sun mask faded, revealing Arrogance holding Valor in place. Serenna's crystal spike tore through Valor's neck. The goddess fell from the air with a pained wail that echoed throughout the cathedral halls. So much blood seeped out from the wound; Serenna had never wondered if gods could bleed, but like most unasked questions, only an unfortunate truth waited in the shadows. The incoming inferno burned her eyes but all she could do was watch Arrogance laugh hysterically over the fallen goddess. Valor clutched at her throat, shaking on the ground. Her eyes closed as she rolled onto her back, then her body slowly dissipated into white specks, flowing out like dandelion seeds in the wind.

With the numbness, it took a moment to realize the scythe had vanished from her hands. Serenna held nothing: no scythe, no hope of victory, no chance of seeing tomorrow. She had killed her own goddess and punishment was enroute. Fire is a cruel end. After her failures, perhaps a cruel end was all she deserved...

The inferno erupted.

It felt like slow motion as her barriers collapsed one after the other. To the Herald of Valor's credit, the glass shattered, but did not melt. Her own crystal shield was all that remained as the flame soared. Tiny cracks followed by large ones chiseled at the fading sphere.

Flames blocked her view as she was launched backwards. The soreness and sharp pain from the scythe yielded to a burning sensation. Serenna screamed. She screamed until her throat tore, but no sound pierced the deep rumble of the flames. She crashed to the ground. The impact shattered her already weakened shield, leaving her in a broken daze, shivering. If any mercy in the realm remained, perhaps a Vanguard would put Serenna out of her misery.

Instead, Arrogance chuckled. The illusion was truly gone; the god above her radiated such raw energy, it was difficult to breathe.

"And so it seems failure is the protocol of Valor. Why so glum, Serenna? You have managed a feat no mortal has ever achieved: you have slain a god! The worst one, of course, but a goddess all the same. Now, how about we play a game?"

Arrogance clapped his spectral hands, and the entire world shook as sections of the cathedral changed into some bizarre-looking nighttime garden. A biting wind blew through the grass, as a crimson sun rose in the distance. A broken mind may have found it beautiful, but it was layered in so many lies, any description would fail to find truth. "The royal family and I will be quite the busy bees in the upcoming months. Serenna, this can go one of two ways. Most of these people are worthless," he said, gesturing to Warlord, Archon, and Father, "but the Guardians intrigue me. Become my Vanguard and I will spare them. Most of them. Some of them. Choose well, for either way, this is the final choice you'll ever have the burden of making."

It took a moment for it to sink in that Arrogance was speaking to her. Some unholy mesh of physical agony and self-loathing made her feel realms away. Only then did she realize all her remaining allies were on their knees with Vanguards behind them. "Just kill me," she forced out, gasping for air. "You already know my answer. My service has ended." It was freeing to say it. Gods, was this how David had felt all those years? *Oh David, forgive me for placing such a burden on you. I did my best. Gods above and below, please believe that I did my best.*

"Is that so? Wrong answer, my dear." Arrogance pointed to her father, then Nyfe dragged his blade across his throat. "I told you, Serenna. I told you I would kill your father all that time ago, and you didn't believe me. Do you believe me now? *Speak.* I want to hear the words. Do you believe me now?"

"*No!*" she screamed but it didn't matter. If there was an emptiness beyond feeling nothing, it strangled out what few tears remained. She could've looked away, but she didn't. *I did this. Everyone warned me. Every single person warned me.* Her father's lips moved but no words came out. Eventually he stopped moving. His suffering ended but hers was just beginning. "My answer hasn't changed. Just…get it over with." Zeen was probably next. For as cruel as their fate was, at least it would be over. Let the Harbingers take them. Let the Harbingers take them all.

Arrogance chuckled again, snapping his fingers towards Archon Gabriel. "I used to believe you were a clever one, Archon, but you went out of your way to prove me wrong. The only time great minds are at odds is when only one great mind exists."

"Do I get any final words?" asked Gabriel. "A chance to explain myself? I didn't do all this…just to lose out on paradise."

"For you, dear friend? Speak away, speak away. I would *love* to hear you explain your way out of this one. But speak wisely. You are but a moment from being the second archon I have sent to the void."

Archon Gabriel smiled. For as much as she hated the man, if anyone had a plan to get out of this travesty, it would be him. "Interesting choice of words," he said, rising slowly without his cane. Oh gods, that look. She already knew what it meant.

"I am nothing. I am forever. I am the end."

CHAPTER 12

A WISE AND FINAL CHOICE

een grabbed his sword and dove behind one of the broken tables as Gabriel ascended into the air on wings of void energy. The sight was somehow both horrifying and welcoming, but Zeen couldn't stop glancing at Senator Morgan. Serenna's father lay there, unmoving, blood still pouring from his neck. And Valor. Zeen had indirectly killed a god but he had never seen one die. No matter the result of tonight's battle, life would never be the same—

Serenity rumbled as a familiar laugh filled the skies. "I may not be welcome in your world, Ermias," Death yelled, "but take this as a reminder that you will never be safe from my wrath. Hide in your dreams. Hide in your illusions. Let your celebration of life end in a storm of death. A perfect testament to the inevitable. I am nothing. I am forever. I am the end."

Wisdom created a ball of swirling energies and threw it towards the sky. While the power seething from the blast made Zeen shiver, it apparently had no effect on Death, whose laughter only grew louder.

"*No!*" Wisdom yelled, turning back to the Harbinger. "Let none escape! Tonight shall not be in vain!"

What the hell was he talking about... Ah. Gabriel triggered the portal they had all arrived through hours ago. He covered Serenna in a void-tinted crystal sphere and launched her through. He then did the same to Bloom. Zeen wondered why Eltune wasn't next until he saw Vanguards standing over the warlord's corpse.

Forgive me, old friend, Zeen thought with a sigh. At least Eltune had died fighting by Zeen's side. Hopefully, his hatred towards Zeen had died before he did.

The portal closed, and with it, Zeen's chance of going back home. At least Serenna and Bloom had escaped. Between them and David, the realm was in good hands—

Zeen jumped to the side, barely avoiding Nyfe's slash. Battling his nemesis would be a welcome distraction before going to the void. *I'll finally take you down for good. Let this be my final service to the realm.* Zeen dodged another slash and swiped upwards, catching his wrist. Nyfe groaned in pain, but whatever mercy Zeen had felt during better days was long gone.

Both combatants flinched as the fully transformed Gabriel roared in the middle of the cathedral. The old man must've been powerful; his seething void energy resembled the day in Mylor when Serenna had tapped into Death's power. It was surreal to watch Francis and Mary battle the Harbinger in unison while still in their wedding outfits. Zeen had no idea where Mary had found a shield, but she looked reminiscent of her days in the Koulva mines, the way she blocked and pushed forward.

It was easy to dodge as Nyfe swung again. Was the man always so slow? Today was likely Zeen's final day, but there was a comfort in surpassing his former general.

Maybe not.

A quick swipe hit nothing but air, then Nyfe's dagger caught the side of Zeen's cheek. Zeen was too tense to feel pain, but it was impossible to ignore the blood flowing from the cut. By pure instinct Zeen swung again, crashing into his dagger. Zeen pressed forward to overpower him and nearly stumbled when Nyfe disengaged with a quick step back. Zeen swung up to block whatever the hell was coming next. Fortunately, he deflected. Unfortunately, he couldn't avoid the follow-up swipe at his arm. All the pain hit at once and Zeen nearly fell over from the shock.

Nyfe gave a faint smirk, though his eyes twitched as if the act brought him agony. He held his dagger in front of him and rushed forward.

This ends now.

Zeen threw his sword forward, hard enough to knock someone's head off, and sprinted at Nyfe, who awkwardly blocked the flying blade and fell to one leg. Zeen ignored the pain as he tackled Nyfe to the ground; he leaned in with his shoulder as he punched him in the face, over and over. This sort of strategy had never been encouraged during his time in the military. Mounting an enemy during battle was an invitation to get taken out by someone looking for an easy kill. Zeen rained down blow after blow until the throbbing pain in his fists surrendered to numbness. It took a moment to realize the silence wasn't in his head, but the madness had subsided. Dead Vanguards and gold cloaks were scattered around the room, with the fallen Gabriel sprawled out in front of the glowing Vanguard Five.

Wisdom did a slow clap with Mary and Francis by his side. Their once-beautiful garments were drenched in blood. "Mr. Zeen," he said with a chuckle. "Would you kindly stop thrashing my Vanguard? I lost quite a few of them today and would prefer to limit my losses."

Zeen forced himself up even though his legs didn't want to. "Do your worst. I beat him. After everything, I beat him. You can never take that away from me."

"Indeed you did," Wisdom said. After a pause, he made a gesture, which reopened the portal. "Vanguard Five, escort our dear emperor and his new wife back to the healing ward. I will rejoin you shortly."

Five nodded and took Mary by the arm, even though Francis was in worse shape. Zeen tried to smile at his old friend, but she actively avoided eye contact. Ah, well. That's how it goes sometimes.

"It was kind of you not to kill me in front of them," Zeen said. "Francis never liked me, but Mary still does." He took a deep breath, taking a final moment to observe the aftermath of madness throughout the room. "I'm ready. Go ahead."

Zeen closed his eyes, awaiting a moment of sharp pain before it all ended. At least Serenna had gotten away. If any of the Guardians had to die it may as well be him. It was cruel to keep Zeen waiting for as long as he did. *What are you waiting for?*

"How would you like to lead the Vanguards?" asked Wisdom, floating above Nyfe. "I thought this one would suffice. A rare mistake on my part."

Zeen laughed at the absurdity. "You know I won't do that."

"Do not *ever* presume to tell me what I know," Wisdom said. The tone of his voice was more…violent would be the only way to explain it. The smile faded entirely, and the eyes went from that tired stare to a bulging rage. "You misinterpret my intentions… Vanguard Ultra."

"Sorry, I don't think so. I already died once. It was an undeserved privilege to last for as long as I did. There is nothing more you can do to me."

An icy gust of wind blew through the air. "Oh? Nothing? I will kill Francis. I will kill Mary. I will kill David. When they're dead, I'll kill Serenna. When she's dead, I'll kill every last *miserable* zephum. When they're dead…I'll kill Calvin."

"You're lying," Zeen said, even though he didn't believe it. "You always lie."

Arrogance lifted a hand, which hovered Charles Morgan's body in the air. He then snapped his finger and the flying body slammed into Zeen, knocking him down. "When I destroyed Boulom, I destroyed the part of me willing to compromise. Those fables…the Rinso ones, I *despise* them. It takes a true ideal like heroism and dilutes it into childish nonsense. I am the hero, Zeen, because I will do anything, *anything* in order to usher in Serenity. Give me your answer. I do not ask twice."

"If I accept…I will never battle my friends. You must swear this to me—"

"This is *not* a negotiation. You will do whatever I say, whenever I say it. Accept now or Mary dies. I'll have her buried in her wedding dress."

Zeen sighed, fighting back tears. He had no doubt Arrogance would kill her. He had no doubt Arrogance would kill them all. *Please forgive me for this.*

"I accept."

"Ah. A wise and final choice. Welcome...Vanguard Ultra."

CHAPTER 13

THE LEGACY OF BOULOM, PART ONE

t had been eleven days since David's last drink, but he had a feeling that streak was coming to an end. He crashed through the door, with Evan and the other guard by his side. It was a relief to see the shock in Monty's eyes as he gripped his staff and fell over. It was *not* a relief to see two Vanguards erupt into a blue and yellow glow.

"By the gods," Evan said. "What are those? Why are they draped in the deceiver's garments?"

David rushed the blue one. Lightning would be a problem in close quarters, but nothing was more dangerous than ice. He swung his blade and clashed with the Vanguard's oak staff, knocking it from his hands and ending the blue glow. As David's sword pierced through his chest; he nearly admired how uninterested the Vanguard appeared to be that he was dying. If we could all be so lucky—

A bolt of lightning blasted Evan out of the room, immediately filling the small room with the stench of burning flesh. Since David didn't know the other man's name, he was promoted to New Evan. New Evan missed his Vanguard with a swing, then took an oak staff right to the helmet, knocking him to the ground with a groan.

The skirmish gave David enough time to rush forward and jab his blade into the Vanguard's neck. It was far from a clean blow; he had to rip the sword out and force it through twice before the blade finally pierced to the other side.

"*Why* won't it work?" Monty yelled, flipping through the pages in some book while his staff glowed white. "I followed every letter of every word! It cannot happen this way! Paradise must... Serenity must..."

"If it's any consolation, you are not the first to fall for his treachery. And I fear...you are far from the last. Farewell, Monty. May you find redemption in the void." David ignored his final cries as he stabbed him in the neck. What a sad waste of life. David had been there on his tenth name day, out of respect for Senator Wraith—*and* the additional benefit of getting paid twenty gold to attend. Fucking Arrogance had ruined everything. "Can you rise?" asked David, reaching out a hand to Evan.

After a groan, Evan took his hand and rose. "That...that was a Vanguard, wasn't it? I never saw one up close until now. The royal family claims they are eight feet tall and roar like a zephum. I don't understand—why did Monty do it? Time magic is forbidden! It is a miracle that Fear hasn't punished us with a Harbinger."

"All lies, nothing but lies on top of lies. Arrogance obviously gave him fake instructions to lure me away. Hmm. You said earlier that Fear was expecting me. I will not believe she fell for any deception. When I arrived, what was your purpose?" He would usually end such questions with a threat, but David's bloody sword would be more efficient than any hostile words.

Evan sighed. "Our orders were to contain you until the wedding was over. That changed when...the lizard god appeared. By the fallen empress, he rode a unicorn! A flying unicorn!"

Oh, Noelami. This wasn't the way to do it. "I must get to Terrangus immediately. Can you escort me to the outskirts portal before they find Monty's body? I'll never leave this kingdom alive if we don't make haste."

"Only if you take me with you."

"Now is not the time to be bold. Listen, there are very few scenarios where this trip to Terrangus is not a one-way journey. Think carefully about your decision. Do you have anyone special waiting for you?"

"A betrothed I have done nothing to deserve. Take me with you. Give her a reason to love me."

David studied the fool. Ah, to be so young. "So be it. If you won't take no for an answer, then lead the way."

Evan's eyes lit up as he smiled. "Follow me and act normal. No one should recognize you unless you draw attention to us."

He followed Evan through the halls, keeping his head down and sword sheathed. It was a depressing convenience to be unknown in a kingdom he had saved about seven times by now. Apparently, there was no need to remember heroes once the threat had been vanquished.

It only took a few minutes into their walk down the long, poorly designed palace stairs until screams came from Monty's room. "Shit," Evan said, glancing behind him. "We should walk faster. This place will be on lockdown any minute now."

"Keep steady and remain uninteresting. If we start rushing, the only place we will end up is a prison cell. Trust me, there are few places less comfortable."

*

Thank the gods that statement had turned out to be true. No one had bothered them as they casually left the palace. *Gods, I need a drink,* he thought, walking through the busy Nuum streets. Having Evan by his side certainly made the trip easier. Merchants selling their wares stared him down but kept their distance, likely wondering why a random old man was being escorted through the marketplace by a palace guard.

It took about an hour to reach the portal; being accompanied by Evan allowed them to skip the queue. Any feelings of thirst or hunger faded as David glanced at the rocky structure. *Something tells me I'll never come back here.* He sighed and turned to Evan. "What is her name?"

"What?"

"Don't be a fool. What is her name?"

After an awkward pause, Evan glared at him. A pitiful anger

filled his eyes. "Maria. Whatever you're planning, I need to come with you and give her a reason to be proud of me."

"Pride," David said with a laugh. "I was proud once. Now, all I can do is linger on and love a memory. Go home, and be grateful you found someone to travel your journey of life with. Don't leave her loving a memory. It is a wound that never heals."

Tears ran down Evan's cheek as he grabbed him. "I…fuck. I will never forget you, David."

"If I've learned anything, you will, and that's okay. You'll lean back in her arms, watch the sunset with your child, and never think of me again. Pride and happiness are two entirely different journeys." David walked up to the portal mage and said, "Terrangus."

"No time for jokes. I have a queue here."

"Terrangus."

She cocked her head. Maybe David's eyes told her whatever she needed to know, for she triggered the ebony glow without speaking a word.

David took a deep breath and entered.

*

He appeared in the Terrangus outskirts, surrounded by Vanguards who stared at him but otherwise had no reaction. Cold Terrangus rain poured down his bald ebony head. He missed his hair, particularly when it rained. He missed Melissa. He missed Tempest and Pyith. Noelami forgive him but he even missed Grayson. He missed…better days. It would be a fool's journey to enter the gates of Terrangus…

But when you're destined to lose, it's best to lose on your own terms.

The trade district would never change. Sure, the shops were different, the people were different, the things being sold were different, but it was just the same old kingdom trying on different masks. That's what Arrogance could never understand. Serenity already existed. Serenity is the realm around us, the evolution of our loves and memories, the way a house may alter its structure but the home never changes.

Vanguards infested the trade district and military ward, not engaging David but staring into him. He pitied all of them and paused before he passed by the noble district. Part of him was tempted to visit Melissa's home one last time, if only to say goodbye to the past—

"*STOP!*" Fear's voice rang through his thoughts. "*May the gods damn you for coming here. Have you lost your senses? I kept you away for your own protection. We can still salvage our realm. Don't make it all for nothing.*"

David laughed out loud right outside Terrangus Castle, uncaring if it brought any attention. "I tire of being the only one left. One way or the other, this ends now."

"*Serenna still remains. Rejoin her and rebuild the Guardians. Without them, it is only a matter of time before the entire realm becomes a smoldering ode to Boulom.*"

"Then take care of her. As long as we have Fear, the realm will always have a Guardian."

Vanguards opened the gates and he stepped through. It was eerily quiet, certainly not the atmosphere for a wedding of two of the most powerful people in the realm. Vanguards were stationed all through the castle halls, staring at David but otherwise unmoving. It would never feel normal to approach the throne doors knowing that Grayson would not be on the other side, and it didn't help that the doors were already opened. David stepped inside, then flinched as both doors slammed behind him.

"Welcome, David Williams," Arrogance said, hovering above the throne. A man who wasn't Francis was sitting on the throne in Vanguard armor with a glowing white sword behind his back. "Where do we draw the line between fashionably late and rude? And I don't recall offering you a plus one, so please ask Fear to leave us. It would be a shame to lose two goddesses in one evening, yes?"

"I am alone. I have been alone for a long time now. You offered me the role of Vanguard in this very room all those months ago. Release Zeen and I will take his place."

Arrogance chuckled. "Aside from in the mirror, you are the boldest man I have ever laid eyes upon. You see, worth is a dynamic concept, an ever-changing quantitative value that comes and goes with the tide. I hate to be the bearer of reality, Lord David, but you are *worthless*."

"We shall see," David said, drawing his blade and approaching. "This is the last time I'll ask nicely. Release Zeen. Release him now."

"Release me from what?" the man on the throne said... Zeen? By the gods, it was him. He rose from the throne and drew his sword: some glowing monstrosity that could not have been from their realm. "It's rude to stare, David. The blade is a gift from God. A sword from the very kingdom of Boulom. I've always favored naming weapons, so I declare this blade the Legacy of Boulom."

"Zeen...resist him. You must resist. Serenna has returned to Mylor. Join me and reunite with her."

At least that ended his smile. Zeen stared at his blade in confusion, then screamed and fell to one knee. When he rose, it was like staring into a stranger. No smile, no wide eyes, none of the things that made Zeen special. "It's all coming back now. We fought here, about two years ago. You struck me in the face. I think it's about time I return the favor."

There wasn't time to think as Zeen approached. Maybe David could incapacitate him, but, more likely, the only way to truly free Zeen would be to end him. It would be an unforgivable loss to force upon the realm, but the idea of Zeen becoming a tyrant's murderer was too much. *Forgive me, old friend.* David swung his blade at Zeen's head, hoping to end it in a single blow.

Zeen easily dodged, then countered with a wide swing. The odd-looking blade filled the air with a whistle as David forced his sword up to block.

He managed to do so, but by Fear's mercy, the blow was powerful. The block sent David staggering a few steps back. He took a deep breath and rushed at Zeen. If he couldn't win a sword duel, perhaps he could take it hand-to-hand combat. David had never excelled at such tactics, but the unknown is always superior to a losing strategy.

Zeen was too quick. He caught David, prevented his tackle,

then elbowed him in the face. "You really should have joined the winning side while you still had the chance. Best you can do now is die with honor. Never meant much to me but the zephum may respect it. Prepare yourself. The next strike won't be an elbow. What was that stupid phrase you used to say? 'Show me your violence'? I have seen the extent of your violence, and I'm left wanting."

David wiped the blood off his nose, only to find more flowing down. It was most likely broken, but that was the least of his problems. Fine, if this was the end, David would go down with a fight. "Forgive me, Zeen. If we reunite in the Great Plains in the Sky, your first drink is on me." He rushed in before Zeen could respond and swung.

Zeen parried, but looked more cautious. Maybe he sensed David's willingness to slay him. Zeen made three quick strikes, doing that usual low, low, high nonsense, which David easily dodged.

It was the best and—most likely—final opportunity. David stepped forward and swung, close enough that it should be impossible to dodge. Zeen groaned as he parried from an awkward angle. Vanguard or not, the blow must have damaged his wrist.

If Zeen wanted to see some violence, it was enroute in the form of a thrust. He flinched out of the way but didn't manage to avoid the entire strike. David's blade tore through his armor, grazing him on the side.

David pushed down the guilt and followed through with a vicious strike towards the head. His blade met Zeen's, and David put every remaining drop of his strength into pushing him back—

Zeen disengaged and slashed David in the leg. It wasn't a clean enough blow to disable him but it forced David to hobble, making it impossible to dodge the next blow. Zeen's blade made a clean cut through David's shoulder, knocking him to the ground and losing his sword.

David crawled towards the sword, then screamed as Zeen stepped on his hand. It was over. What a bizarre fate to hope that

Zeen of all people would give him a merciful death. What a cruel fate to know that wouldn't happen.

Zeen slammed his glowing blade on David's sword, shattering it—

"Halt," Arrogance said, floating above them. "Where is your sense of fairness? The man doesn't have a blade!"

"Lord Wisdom, I—"

Arrogance made a fist. "I don't recall giving you permission to speak."

Zeen collapsed and screamed. The torment echoed through the throne room. Even as his own hand throbbed, David couldn't help but pity him.

"I believe this is yours," Arrogance said, materializing Zeen's old blade, Hope, in his spectral hands. "How does the phrase go? Hope will find a way? I have a different hypothesis. I don't believe hope will find anything at all. Perfection is inevitable. It relies on nothing but the flow of reality. Here, strike me down if you can." He threw the blade and it clanged next to David.

It was hopeless of course, but if David could leave even a scratch on the mask, he would die content. He forced himself up and grabbed Hope with his left hand. He rushed forward, swung, and a flash of pain shot through his arm as his sword struck the bronze sun mask. There was no scratch, no dent, no indication he had wounded the god at all. A portal opened behind David as Arrogance grabbed him with a spectral hand. "Serenity?"

"No, my friend. That portal goes somewhere worse. Far, far worse."

David smiled, looking into the eyes of the sun mask. "There is nothing worse than a tyrant's vision of paradise."

"What a delightful sentiment. Let's visit in a few months, shall we? Enjoy your vacation. Don't worry, I'll write."

A push sent David through the portal before he could respond.

CHAPTER 14

VOICE OF A TRUE WARLORD

loom and Serenna materialized in the Mylor Guardian room portal, with Serenna landing right on top of her. Good thing she was tiny for a human: one of the fat ones would've crushed her tail. "Get off!" she yelled, throwing Serenna several feet away.

Slow-moving human guards rushed forward, some helping Serenna and the rest pointing swords at Bloom. They had some balls to threaten her after today. Sure, her detonators were long gone, but they wouldn't know that. Bloom ignored their threats and forced herself up, wiggling her tail to get the feeling back.

"Where is the senator?" one of them asked.

"Right there, Boss," Bloom said, pointing at Serenna. Actually, she wasn't sure if humans used the same leadership hierarchy. Vaynex had the right idea. If the dad dies, follow the son—unless the son turns out to be useless. Hmm. Eltune had no son, no kin, no next in line. Sure, they had lain together a few times, but Vaynex would probably demand a stronger tie than that.

It was a bad sign that Serenna had no reaction. Bloom had seen that look in soldiers' eyes after the more violent skirmishes with Nuum and Terrangus. Serenna would need some time to process how badly her plan had failed. Some people took months, years, or never got there at all.

All the humans were yelling and, damn, it was annoying. "Stop whining and trigger the portal to Vaynex. Whatever problems y'all have to deal with, trust me, no one's more screwed than me." After an awkward five seconds or so she said, "Hello? Serenna? Anyone home?"

"Someone…open it," she said, staring into nothing. "Send Bloom home, then close all the portals. Close everything. No one may enter or leave Mylor ever again."

One of the scrawniest-looking humans she had ever seen stepped forward, erupting the portal into the familiar crimson glow. "Farewell, Guardian," he said.

He didn't seem important enough to answer, so Bloom entered without a word. As she felt herself fade away, all the anxiety came crashing down at once. Guardian or not, her fellow zephum may just kill her the moment she arrived —

"*You are not alone, mighty Bloom,*" Sardonyx whispered through her thoughts. "*Together, we shall keep Vaynex intact. Strength without honor—is chaos!*"

A nice sentiment, but none of those words seemed true as she portaled away.

*

What a pain in the tail that the Vaynex outskirts portal was the only one still open. It was refreshing to see the relief on the portal guards' faces as they saw her. It wouldn't be refreshing once they realized she was alone. "Guardian Bloom," one said, darting his eyes between her and the portal.

"Take me to the citadel at once. Eltune has business in Mylor and will be delayed."

"*No! Speak truthfully! There is no honor in treachery!*" Ugh. If Sardonyx thought lies were dishonorable, wait until he saw her on the battlefield.

"Why are you covered in blood? Do human weddings partake in honorable combat?"

"Yep. Was a surprise to me too. I'll tell you the full story after a hot bath." The fear of having to tell the true story to her superior was overshadowed by the fear there was no one to tell. *I always wanted to be Warlord but...not like this.*

It took forever to travel through Vaynex, and it didn't help that every zephum on the way stared at her and whispered to each other. If any of them used their lizard brains and thought for a moment, they would see right through her ridiculous lie and toss her body into the street.

Bloom had amassed quite the crowd by the time she entered the citadel. She took a long gulp of water and refilled her detonators. With nowhere else to take her lies, she sat on the throne, enjoying the gasps and murmurs that followed.

"What treachery is this?" one of them yelled. Hmm, she better start learning their names if she was going to lead them.

She sighed. "Okay, here's the deal. Eltune is dead. Most of the Guardians are dead. Most of the other kingdom leaders are dead. Everything is completely fucked. I'm the boss now. Follow my lead or kill me. What's it going to be?" Even by Bloom's standards, it was bold to threaten an entire room filled with angry zephum. She could kill a few of them if it came down to it, but no mortal alive was winning a one against fifty...

Ah shit. They all charged in unison. Well, it was a good run. If she had to die, she would rather bite the sand from her own people than those miserable Vanguard things—

"Stand down!" Sardonyx's voice rang from behind. It was his actual voice and not that bizarre thing he did through her head. And gods, it was *powerful*. The voice of a true warlord. It took a moment to realize the actual Sardonyx in his god form stood behind the throne, looking all high and mighty with his arms crossed.

"As God of Tradition, heed my words. No zephum will commit violence against their own. We unite under the honorable Dumiah Bloom to face a powerful enemy. An enemy that embodies the very essence of dishonor itself. An enemy of treachery. An enemy of lies! An enemy...of Arrogance. The Vanguards will come! They shall walk upon the sand and bring their dishonor! Let none leave here alive. Let none who threaten the Vaynex empire see tomorrow. Many of you will not survive. But you shall meet your end with honor, and the Great Fields in the Sky welcomes you with open arms.

"Strength without honor—is CHAOS!"

"Thank you, Sardonyx," Bloom whispered, but there was no way anyone heard above the honorable roars. Damn, if only Tempest could see his father now.

CHAPTER 15

NOTHING LEFT TO DESTROY

ary held Calvin within her chambers, rocking him with a mother's desperation. "Everything I have done. Everything I have become. It's all for you." The words came out empty; she was grateful her son was too young to call her out for lying.

"You sure you don't want a bath?" asked Ruby, noticeably keeping her distance. "Uh, you're probably aware, but it looks like you just single handedly stopped a riot."

Blood was all over her hands and dress. Mary couldn't help but laugh at the tiny smile on Calvin's face, completely oblivious to the atrocities committed in his name. "You're right, but I had to see him immediately. He is the only thing keeping me going. Ruby, I don't know how to stop this. All the violence keeps piling up. Every time I assume it's over, that we finally achieved peace, the only thing we achieve is a new low. When does it *stop*?"

The distance between them seemed realms away. Ruby sighed then said, "Mary, you're the empress now. You can't hide behind other people's faults anymore. The violence stops when you decide it stops or when there's nothing left to destroy. After today, I am preparing for the latter. Gods, I can't believe the archon is dead. It feels like the point of no return. Hopefully, Mom already went home or you're in serious trouble—"

"Hello?" asked Francis from the chamber entrance. He did a

light tap on the door after already leaning inside, which defeated the purpose. "Ah Ruby," he said, entering. He had apparently found the time to take a bath: his new robes were spotless, and all the blood and filth had been washed from his face. "My gratitude for watching over Calvin. Many unpleasantries tonight. Many things unsuited for a child's eyes. You may leave now."

"Gladly."

"Wait!" Mary yelled, but it was too late. Her sister left the three of them alone and Mary was unsure she would ever see her again. *The violence stops when you decide it stops, or when there's nothing left to destroy.* Was that how everyone saw them? How simple it must be for those without children to judge the crimes of desperate parents…

Francis sat on their bed and wept quietly. The act was so startling, Mary rushed over beside him with Calvin still in her arms. "Forgive me, my beloved," he said, leaning his head into her shoulder. "This obviously is not how anyone imagines their wedding night. It is overwhelming to keep track of all the times I have disappointed you. Half of me wishes we never met at all, that you never became a Guardian. You could've lived a long, fulfilling life, chasing your dreams in a worthy man's arms. The other half thanks every god above and below that we met that day in Alanammus."

Mary laughed. "Ah, that was right after my first time in Vaynex. If I recall correctly, I was covered in blood just like now."

"All three of you," Francis said. "David was drenched in some unholy mixture of ale and blood, while Zeen…"

An awkward quiet followed, a realization that the well of nostalgia was susceptible to the poison flowing from the present. "I don't suppose we could send him back? Serenna lost her father. It seems cruel to keep Zeen as well."

Francis rose and stepped away. "Serenna and her goons attempted to murder me. To murder *us.* We can enjoy reminiscing about simpler times as long as we acknowledge they have met their end."

They were aiming to stop Arrogance. We just happened to be in the way. "You should consider why those simpler times are realms away. Francis, what happens when there is nothing left to destroy?"

"What?" he asked, cocking his head. "Nothing left to destroy? How about nothing left to save? These people treat progress like a disease. You want to blame the riots and unrest on me? Fine, but the line stops there. These people came into *our* home with murderous intentions. All things considered, I'm glad they're dead. My one singular regret is that we didn't manage to kill them all." Francis always had a tendency to drift into the absurd whenever his temper rose, but it was usually cute and not…whatever this was.

"For an intelligent man, you end up sounding like a child more often than not." She clutched Calvin to her chest and stormed off to their balcony. What was once a beautiful view was now a reminder of how far away the past had become.

Francis approached softly from behind. He'd stopped huffing so perhaps he was prepared to act like an adult. "Forgive my outburst. Stress corrupts my mind faster than any drug in the realm." He reached out to hold her hand, then after Mary nodded at Calvin, he took the hint and stood next to her. "I don't have the answers. It's unlikely I ever will. My only saving grace is that since we constantly ponder how damaged we are, it means we have not crossed the line to become fully broken. But once we lose that doubt, we lose what few pillars of humanity remain."

"That's not enough," she said, then flinched as Arrogance appeared in the sky above them.

"Not how *I* would choose to spend my wedding night," he said with a chuckle, "but I see the appeal of arguing. Now that you are joined in body and mind, you will argue together until the end of time. When you finish your… dallying, I suggest an evening of rest. Vaynex and Mylor aren't going to invade themselves."

Calvin began crying in her arms, and she resisted the urge to join him.

SIX MONTHS LATER

CHAPTER 16

NO MATTER THE COST

enator Morgan?" Captain Martin asked, wiping the blood off his blade.

A few seconds passed before Serenna could respond as she took in the carnage of the grand bastion halls. It would never feel comfortable hearing that title. A Guardian holding a political position would be considered madness in better days, but better days had ceased to exist during the reign of Arrogance. "Report," Serenna said out of obligation, but she already knew the obvious: Mylor had again secured their half of the bastion at great cost. It was a miserable grind, a delay of the inevitable...

And the only way to move forward.

"Our melee forces continue to dwindle. However, our crystal mages remain in stable quantity. All things considered, the war is going rather well."

"Rather well?" She glared at him, gripping the Wings of Mylor, her last remaining loved one. "I am not my father. Don't suppress the truth to comfort my ego. Food supplies are unsustainable without imports. We either drive them out now or face starvation by winter. And stop referring to my people as if they were stock. If we treat them as less than human, we are no better than the Vanguards."

"Apologies, Senator," Martin said with a bow. "A cold demeanor is one of the many unfortunate habits formed in war. But I swear to you, on Valor's grace, we shall prevail. No matter the cost."

"No matter the cost." The mere mention of Valor sent a pain through her gut. Serenna had never told them how the goddess had met her end and, gods willing, that would never change. Too many mistakes. Too much failure. Too little time—

A squad of Vanguards rushed through one of the corridors, engaging the small defensive team stationed by the doorway by one of the giant white pillars. Fools. If they wanted another battle after today's defeat, then so be it.

"Get down!" she yelled, grabbing the Wings of Mylor and erupting into her platinum glow. The past six months had been cruel, but the endless amount of violence had reawakened what Serenna was capable of. Martin and a few of the remaining high-ranking soldiers had requested she stay in the capital, but nothing would deny her the opportunity to slay them all.

She captured a lone Vanguard in a sphere and ripped it in two. The neutral expression on their faces filled her with rage. She wanted to see the fear. She *needed* to see the fear. It was a blessing Death hadn't spoken to her since the wedding. All those ideals of never giving in for power would fade at any opportunity to destroy Francis and Arrogance.

One of her soldiers fell. She took a deep breath and refreshed their shields, loosening her grip and analyzing the battleground. A crystal mage is a protector first and attacker second, but the image of her fallen father in a pool of his own blood made it difficult to remember. The image of Zeen on his knees right before she had left him to die made her yearn for their destruction. Gods, she would never admit it, but she welcomed the war. It brought violence to her doorstep in the form of mindless puppets. These weren't the young men and women with families waiting at home. These were *monsters*, and Serenna had slain monsters her entire life.

You took Valor away from me.

Ringing filled her ears as she drew platinum energy to form three giant crystal spikes. The lack of awareness was dangerous, but if her enemies were dead, their location wouldn't matter. She pointed her staff forward, sending her first spike flying into a

Vanguard's skull. The chest would be the most efficient target, but there was something thrilling about watching the neck snap back as the spike went through.

You took Father away from me.

She stepped forward, keeping one spike floating by her side as she launched the next one. This one *did* hit the chest, with enough force to keep the Vanguard impaled as the spike flew into the wall and got stuck. Let the dead Vanguard hanging there be a testament to Serenna's vengeance.

You took Zeen away from me.

Only one Vanguard remained, and it was hers to destroy. It wasn't a clear shot, but she launched the final spike anyway, then grimaced as it grazed one of her allies on the shoulder. *That was unnecessary,* she thought, but the disfigured corpse of her enemy freed her of any guilt.

Martin grabbed her arm, earning himself a murderous glare. "Control yourself!" he yelled, tightening his grip.

Control myself? she thought, resisting the urge to send him to the void. Who did this fool think he was? She pulled her arm back and said, "Grab me again and you can hang on the wall next to that one. Collect the dead. Heal the wounded. Gather everyone else and follow me. We're taking the portal back now."

Trickles of blood rolled down her cheek as she entered the occupied hallway. Yells of defiance came from behind, but they were so muffled, it was like someone blowing into her ear. If the four Vanguards guarding the next room were surprised to see her, it didn't show on their faces. Nothing ever did. She drew power to form ten mini spikes; she would've crafted more but her vision started to blur. Darkness crept in; usually, this was the point of no return. She would possibly lose consciousness and collapse in enemy territory, never to awake again.

And that would be okay.

Various colors danced in front of her eyes from the glowing Vanguards. If they weren't the enemy, perhaps the sight could have been beautiful. She launched all the spikes at once, hopefully before they could cast their spells. Her shield was strong, but once her legs started to wobble, it was usually a warning her power was near-empty.

Ah, it was such a release to see the tiny crystal shards tear into their skin. For all their loss of humanity, at least they still bled. The fact they only wore white armor only made it better. Surprisingly, one was able to crawl away on his hands and knees. His refusal to die was an insult, a spit in the face to her fallen allies. She ignored the pain and rose, reaching for any ounce of remaining power to finish him off.

Serenna reached, and found nothing but darkness.

*

"Captain! I think she's awake!"

Serenna groaned and rolled over. There was plenty of room in her bed now that she didn't share it with anyone. "Go away," she said to whoever it was. If they were watching her sleep, that was weird, and they should find something better to do. *How did I even arrive here? What did...*

The battle.

"Thank you, sir. Now, please leave us." Martin approached with a smile as the other man left. If he was smart, he would choose his next words carefully. "Serenna, there is no backup plan if we lose you. Our kingdom is held together by crystals and strings. Despite your battle prowess, the capital is where you are needed most. Am I clear?"

She rose with another groan to ensure her annoyance was known. Part of her welcomed Martin's newfound leadership abilities, but the other part wished he would shut up. "How many of them did I vanquish today?"

Martin sighed. "That's not—"

"Between both battles, I single-handedly killed twenty-two of them. Nineteen yesterday. Eleven the day before that. Tomorrow, I won't stop until I reach thirty in a single battle. Every day they remain in my kingdom will be another day they face the Guardian of Mylor. Where I am needed most is wherever my enemies may linger. Am *I* clear, Captain?"

He glared at her, and she respected that his face showed no fear. "Zeen wouldn't want you to be this way. Don't tarnish his memory by becoming a monster."

"Monsters are the only ones that survive in this realm. Francis, Mary, and Nyfe are all monsters. *Arrogance* is a monster. The only ones with any semblance of good have long left us to fend for ourselves. The fact that I'm still here solidifies what I am—what I've always been. All I can do now is become the most powerful monster of them all."

"The one you hit with friendly fire: his name is Arthur," Martin said. "The boy will survive, but I'm afraid he must lose the arm. Regardless, he still views you as our savior. You will never be a monster, Serenna. Not to your own people. Not to me."

Serenna blinked as hard as she could to push back the tears. "Bring me Landon. I must see Landon."

Martin looked down. His face told her everything. "He never woke up this morning. I wasn't sure how or when to tell you. You have too many burdens already. You have—"

"Get out. *Now.*" She rolled over so he wouldn't see her weep. Despite her exhaustion, sleep would never come after hearing such news. Thirty wouldn't be enough. Nowhere near enough. She wouldn't stop until she killed one hundred.

She wouldn't stop until she killed them all.

CHAPTER 17

SOME MEN JUST LIVE TOO LONG

It had been zero days since David's last drink.

He slumped on his stool at the bar as he'd done every day for the past few months, or however long it had been, eyeing the balcony behind him that would one day be his end. Until then, he clutched his magic wine bottle that never emptied and refilled his chalice. If someone had given him such a gift back in his twenties, David possibly could have saved enough gold to purchase Alanammus Tower. He laughed out loud at the thought, with no one to hear him or join in with his laughter. It was difficult to decide if his dream prison was torture or a merciful end for the once-protector of the realm. Hopefully, wherever she was, Noelami could smile at the irony. To turn his back on the dreamer, only to meet his end within a madman's dream.

"And what, old friend, would be so funny?"

David nearly fell off his stool at Grayson's voice. It was impossible, but sure enough, the fallen emperor approached the stool next to him, wearing his old regalia with the thick black coat and steel boots. The man was much younger than David's memory of him. It had been decades since that golden hair flowed all the way down to the armor on his shoulder. The only evidence it was an illusion was the fatal sword wound near the center of his chest, the exact spot David had pierced the Herald of Fear through all that time ago.

"You're not real," David said with a sigh, unsure if that was a blessing or curse.

Grayson sniffed the wine bottle and laughed. "By the gods, what is this? I imagine nothing feels real after a few glasses of such a potent wine. May I have a glass?" he asked, pouring one before David could answer. "Bah! Don't look so glum. I am the emperor: all my requests are mere courtesies. I take what I want, for all is rightfully mine. I can do no wrong, for I decide the laws of men. Cheers!"

David cautiously clinked glasses. The man was obviously some sort of parody, but any opportunity to converse with another being—dream or real—would be taken. "You look just like him. I would be impressed, but the voice is slightly off. I remember…a few more pounds on that gut as well."

Grayson's gut grew by an inch or two. "There. Better? Ah, it's funny how we remember the faults, but the more positive aspects always get lost in time. I can't blame you: my mistakes have led to some interesting outcomes. Wisdom warned me not to attempt Serenna's execution when you and Zeen were stuck in Boulom. Did I listen? Did I ever listen? *No!* Why would a mere mortal listen to God? That was the catalyst. The realm lost Melissa, and in her place, we got *you*." His smile faded as he drank the full chalice of wine. "It's nothing short of remarkable how one foolish decision altered everything. The absurdity of freewill is a wretched, volatile thing. It must end. It will."

"I don't recall my old friend feeling so strongly about freewill. He was too worried about battle and ale until Vanessa was born. That was…those were his best days. Our best days." David sighed, then refilled his own chalice. "It all comes down to loss, doesn't it? You, me, Grayson, we all crumbled under our loss. I suppose the only difference between the three of us is that you eventually won. So cheers to you, *Arrogance.*"

"No!" he yelled, slamming his fist on the bar. "Stop being so simple-minded. Paradise is not a competition, a zero-sum game of winners and losers. If I win, everyone wins. That is the message I have been attempting to relay for nearly two centuries now. But alas, it's been like trying to teach a cactus how to perform mathematical equations. Such is every professor's burden: the lesson is only as competent as the student. And, as always, I have judged the student, and found him wanting."

David snickered, swirling his glass to enrich the taste. "Do you ever grow tired of blaming everyone but yourself? If the cost wasn't so terrible, I would welcome your victory with open arms, just to watch you realize what a fucking fool you are." He glanced over to the balcony. "My end is soon upon me. I accept that. But you? You are divine. You will be falling until the end of fucking days." He laughed; wine made everything hilarious, even the idea of his own death. "Hello? Lord Wisdom, are you finally out of words?" David's laughter ended as he glanced back as Grayson, who was the broken old white-haired husk from his final days.

"Shame on me for assuming you would be more sympathetic. You were right all that time ago, back when you begged me to stop the siege of Mylor. Imagine if I listened? Imagine what your life could be like today. Strength would be with us. Pyith, Tempest, Julius, the list goes on and on. Oh, I nearly forgot…Melissa. If you learn nothing before this is over, consider the joy you have been denied by the horrors of freewill. The joys…we have all been denied."

Grayson finished his wine, rose from the stool, and approached the balcony. "Some men just live too long. It would appear I am no longer among them."

David watched Grayson fall from the balcony without a scream or a whimper. Too many feelings rose up at once, with the desire to follow him down rising to the top. *No. Not yet. Not yet…* His hands shook as he refilled his chalice.

Not every pain could be forgotten, but with enough wine, every pain could be numbed.

CHAPTER 18

THE SHADOW OF GOD

n any competition of wits, such as a chess match or Alanammus tavern trivia, it's obvious when the contest has concluded. The game would end and the victor—Francis of course—would lie and tell his opponent they had played well. In life, the game persists, leaving the winner to ponder all sorts of things. Was the cost too high? When does prosperity take hold? How can something as ugly as war ever lead to paradise? And the one question that always lingered, no matter how much life had seemed to go his way…

How much can a person be damaged before they are considered broken?

"Happy birthday, little Calvin!" Mary said, hugging their son tightly.

There were far too many people gathered in the throne room, celebrating the future emperor's second birthday. After the wedding debacle, Francis preferred to keep these events private, but Mary had demanded a party to celebrate their son—and for an excuse to drink all day again. It was a simple numbers game really: the more people involved, the higher the risk of something going amiss. But no, they couldn't live in fear. Not according to Mary, at least.

The crowd cheered as the smiling Calvin lifted himself up and walked over to his mother. It was a wonder the child could move at all with all the flashy garments Mary had slathered him in. Oh well, anything that made her happy these days was a blessing. Mary had sort of…stopped being Mary after the wedding. If he had to choose the precise moment, it had been when Ruby left and never returned. It was difficult to relate—Francis never had any siblings. His father had been a good man, but Mother? Well, Francis once had a dream where Mother had died. Tears falling down his cheeks had been the only confirmation it couldn't have been real.

"Isn't he wonderful?" asked Mary. Her glazed eyes stared at Calvin and nothing else. "The most precious thing in the entire realm. No harm will ever come to him."

"Indeed," said Francis, though he wasn't sure if that was a question or just Mary speaking out loud. Out of all the annoying traits, people that spoke to themselves were among the worst. Mary was the exception of course, but still…

"It's been nice lately…without…you know. If you're the one keeping him away, then thank you. It's almost like we're a real family and not prisoners."

Not my doing, he thought, but saw no reason to avoid taking credit. Arrogance had been less involved with day-to-day royal life and more involved with the…other things. The wars with Mylor and Vaynex were probably going well. It was always difficult to tell when other kingdoms incurred the cost. And whatever that business with David, Francis didn't understand the purpose. What he *did* understand was not to ask questions. "Not only are we a real family, but the realm's most cherished and important. I believe good days are finally on the horizon, my beloved."

Mary laughed out loud, less in a ha-ha funny way and more that someone had just said the most foolish thing she had ever heard. "The most dangerous goals are the ones that keep sneaking away as you approach them. I look forward to standing here on Calvin's tenth name-day, and listening to you tell me again that we're almost there."

He stopped himself from sighing. "But we *are* almost there or, at least, the worst of it is surely over. Our so-called friends spit on our invitation and attacked our family. Only two outcomes were possible. Look at our son and tell me you regret anything."

It was concerning that she didn't respond immediately. Silence was often the prelude to victory in most arguments, but with his wife, it was usually the prelude to sleeping alone. "I suppose I should just be grateful to be alive. Whatever," she said, grabbing a chalice of wine from a servant and walking towards the crowd. How she managed to drink all day without falling asleep was one of the realm's greatest mysteries.

That left Francis alone with Calvin, who was staring at him in puzzled amazement, as if his father had somehow grown a tail or two heads. *Why doesn't he ever smile at me? Did I behave in this manner towards my father? How maddening—*

"Daddy! Daddy! Daddy!" Calvin's legs hobbled as he yelled.

Francis grabbed him before he fell. The fall likely wouldn't have been painful for such a sturdy youth, but no need for embarrassment on his day of celebration. "Careful, my son. I won't always be here to catch you when you fall." Oddly enough, the somber phrase brought laughter from Calvin. *How intelligent are you? Do you laugh at the idea of my demise? Do you already know it's inevitable?*

He sighed as Mary spilled her chalice and grabbed a new one. Hopefully, none of the onlookers gave her increased appetite for wine any notice. "One day, this will all be yours. It won't be…this, of course, but it will be yours. I hope you manage to recall the happy days. Before…before whatever the days are called now. You have flawed parents, little Calvin, but I swear they love you. Loving you is a very simple task indeed. But ourselves? Well, may you fare better than I."

"My lord?"

Francis nearly jumped at the voice of Marcus. His former general stood at his side as a decorated Vanguard, with his monotone voice and empty eyes. Perhaps he had become more efficient after the change, but something about him, something difficult to articulate, had certainly been lost forever. "I wager you have a good reason to interrupt my talk with the emperor-in-waiting?"

"Two. God has returned, and a Harbinger of Fear has been

located in the military district. We have the invader isolated, but our barriers will not last through the night."

Great. Just great. He knew the day would come. How cruel of Fear to choose Calvin's birthday. Children should always be left off the table when it comes to vendettas. Francis carefully placed Calvin down and sat on his throne to avoid losing balance as anxiety set in. "Go to Mommy." After a moment of Calvin standing there doing nothing, Francis clenched his fist and yelled, "*Go to your mother! Now!*" Silence engulfed the throne room as everyone stared in his direction. The onlookers were mostly confused, but Mary's eyes were filled with fear as she rushed over. An intelligent reaction. Fortunately, all that wine hadn't drowned her good senses.

"What the hell is going on?" asked Mary, picking up Calvin. "Is it Serenna? Bloom? There are so many out to kill us, it could be anything."

Francis leaned back and sighed. "Fear. And before you ask, no, I don't have a plan yet. I knew this day would come. I just needed more time…"

To his surprise, Mary laughed. "Well, better grab my armor. I guess it's up to us again. Which of your Vanguards is our best crystal mage?"

The room rumbled before he could respond. Arrogance appeared behind Mary and said, "Ah, it would appear my dear Noelami has crashed our party. While the news is most unfortunate, at least it provides an opportunity to reunite with my favorite royal family." He snickered, which alleviated some of Francis's nerves. If God wasn't afraid, there was clearly a plan…

Right?

"Look who it is!" Mary said with slurred speech. "Tell me, oh magnificent one, how goes the war?"

"Which one?" Arrogance chuckled. "Oh, don't worry yourselves over such nasty business. Keep on drinking and let the apathy flow. Today will either confirm or reject a hypothesis I have pondered for a *very* long time. Now, off to your chambers! Sleep soundly while I handle our Fear debacle."

Francis rose from his throne; the seat always felt insignificant in the shadow of God. "But, what is your plan? As emperor, I think I deserve to know—"

"How about you *think* about going to your chambers and not question me again. Has my absence inspired an age of buffoonery?" Arrogance scoffed. "Not even *I* can be everywhere at once. You three have a very simple role in a very complex realm. I advise you to learn how to manage before I decide Terrangus would best be ruled by Vanguards."

Francis grabbed Mary before she could say something that would escalate the situation. "Marcus, ring the bells and disperse the crowd. The empress and I shall await further instructions from God." *I must stop calling him Marcus,* Francis thought, as he picked up Calvin and left towards his chambers with Mary.

It was an awkward walk. He took each step carefully, allowing Mary the extra time to keep her balance up the flight of stairs. She was more drunk than he'd realized; maybe it was for the best that a Harbinger canceled the celebration.

"When are you going to wake the fuck up, Francis?"

He sighed. "Please refrain from such language in front of our son."

"Calvin may as well hear it now. There is no point in trying to keep him innocent. He descends from us and that makes him tainted."

"Do you hear the venom that sprouts from your tongue? Or are you so numb to courtesy that vile notions are all that remain?"

Mary laughed in that obnoxious drunk way of hers, then strengthened her grip to keep her balance. "You say fancy words anytime you know you're wrong. Ruby…pointed it out. Tell me, *dear,* you spent years studying this shit. What other emperors throughout history have been banished to their own chambers against their will?"

None of course. It would seem we are pioneers in failure. "Counterpoint: what other emperors have ushered in paradise? You may no longer believe, but I do. I must. There are several fables, several tragedies, where the hero in question concedes right before their eventual victory. They are the saddest of tales. Lessons to those dashing towards greatness to never turn away, no matter how vicious their path."

"Let me guess, your mother told you such stories?"

"Well, yes, of course. My parents had an efficient collaboration. Father loved. Mother taught. It didn't…well, it didn't seem ideal at the time, but how could anyone argue with the results? I am the emperor of a foreign kingdom, on the cusp of ushering in Serenity."

"Your mother was a bitch."

Fool! She was a monster, not a bitch. Or perhaps a monster bitch? Hmm. It was a blessing to open the doors and enter. Both their chambers and the end of the argument hopefully awaited them. *Who are you to call her that? She had her flaws of course, but what about you? Simple Terrangus military scoundrel turned Guardian! You were Pyith's temporary replacement. Marrying me was the best thing that ever happened to you—*

"Guess I finally struck a nerve. Silence is the obvious sign that you're angry. Another tip I learned from Ruby."

"Well, perhaps Ruby could teach you to stop being a drunk and *raise your goddamn son!*" He had to stop himself from shaking. Outbursts were never free, and this one would likely carry a great cost. "I apologize. Such words were beneath me." As if on cue, Calvin started crying. Whether from discomfort at the yelling or the realization his parents were frauds, it was impossible to tell.

To his surprise, Mary sat on their bed and patted the spot next to her. She rocked Calvin until his whimpers ended. Odd that she didn't appear angry. Or perhaps it was a trick to finally send Francis to the void. On days like this, such a fate didn't seem too bad. "I would rather hold your ire than your apathy. Anything to show that you still care. Listen, we are *well* past the point of no return. We must either learn to travel this journey as a family or learn to cope with the realization that nothing but sorrow awaits."

He leaned against her shoulder. "I'm trying. I know it may not seem like it, but I swear to whichever god you favor, I'm trying. I just need more time. Just…a bit more time…"

The three of them sat there in silence, likely lost in their own thoughts. Perhaps Calvin was pondering naptime. Perhaps Mary was pondering what life could've been with a better husband. Francis pondered the usual.

How much can a person be damaged before they are considered broken?

CHAPTER 19

SHIELD?

een… Vanguard Ultra sat at his desk within Terrangus Castle, working out the final lines to the conclusion of *Rinso the Blue: Volume IV*, though it was difficult to focus with those loud bells ringing. There was so much work to be done, so much nonsense to be edited out. Apparently, Tempest had written an entire four chapters or so of Rinso being lured away from the party by a tree-woman sex goddess thing. It was weird.

In the end, he wrote, *the greatest tragedy was all that time lost chasing silly dreams, while perfection was the obvious goal - hidden away - far away - in plain sight. Conflict was meaningless. Suffering was obsolete. Serenity was inevitable.*

Rinso smiled with his face as he looked up into the skies, looking into the puffy white clouds floating in the sky. It turned out - there was a god of gods all along - and his name was Lord Wisdom. With all the imperfections of his life removed - Rinso was free to let go and follow his dream, which was…

All that he wanted was to
All he wanted was
All he ever wanted

Ultra tapped his pen. Something was obviously missing, but what? Olivia! How could he insert her into the scene naturally? He thought less about her each day…

And less of Serenna.

Although it was odd, it felt like something was actively making him forget his friend, lover, or whatever the relationship had been. There had been moments where Ultra fell to knees, obliterated by some terrible rush of lies, some horror that everything was wrong. Everything was lies. Any resemblance to truth had been buried in a sea of deception. He tapped the pen harder and harder. Moments like this had occurred less frequently in the past month, but when they arrived, pain always followed.

He let out a deep breath as all the anxiety and doubt dispersed from his mind, fading like Rinso riding off into the sunset. God was here. Finally, God was here, and everything would be okay.

"You look well, Vanguard Ultra," God said, floating in the middle of the barracks. "It's intriguing that your inferior emotions still assault you from time to time. One would assume those days have vanished, and yet here we are. How much can I remove? I would simply *hate* to lose your sword work. I won't have much use for you otherwise."

Ultra smiled at God's laughter. He wasn't exactly sure what any of those words meant, but it was such a privilege to hear his voice. God could have spoken to anyone, and he had chosen Ultra. Not only that, but God had also made Ultra leader of the Vanguards, the one above all to usher in Serenity. Life was simply beautiful.

"I am yours to command," Ultra said, kneeling.

It took every measure of restraint not to fall over in awe as God floated over and studied him. "Gambling is a loathsome act, and yet, in any imperfect world, risk is the only path available for prosperity. A Harbinger has arrived, and instead of the usual group of misfits, I have assembled a team of...Vanguardians. You'll notice there are only five of you. Pardon the odd number, but it's difficult to control larger groups at once. Now, the time has come to roll the dice. Head to the castle entrance. And pray for sixes."

Vanguardians? That name is awful, Zeen thought, but after a moment of pain, Ultra realized the name was perfect. God didn't make mistakes. If he did, the consequences would be vast. Would be simply inconceivable.

Ultra tied his cloak and grabbed the Legacy of Boulom from its wall rest. The glowing blade was like paradise in his hands. Despite the panicking crowd, everyone was quick to clear a path as Ultra approached the castle doors. It was nice to be feared. It has been a long while since anyone had loved him, and that was okay. Fear creates paradise, then paradise creates love. It was balanced in a way far beyond Ultra's capacity. Good, the team was already assembled, standing in a circular formation in the pouring rain…

A pang of hatred came over him as he met eyes with Nyfe…Omega. It only lasted a moment before a calming sensation removed it, but there was something about this man, something that made God's voice come in just a tad softer. Aside from Omega, Vanguard Five was there, accompanied by the unfortunately named Vanguard Shield who…made crystal shields. Zeen wasn't used to seeing women with no hair. It certainly wasn't bad, just different. What would his old friend look like without that long platinum hair?

And there was Vanguard Gamma, Zeen's once-captain: Marcus. In a bizarre way, the man looked better as a Vanguard; he was draped in full chain armor with a bright white helmet that covered most of his face. Hopefully, they would all take orders…

Zeen's head throbbed; it took all his strength to stop himself from collapsing in the cold Terrangus rain. Why was he commanding Five? Why was he commanding Marcus, a man who had always outranked him? Why, oh why, was he commanding Nyfe, a monster who should have left the realm ages ago?

Screaming is not often a choice. Zeen gave in and fell to his knees from the pure agony burning inside him. If God's love was infinite, his fury was endless. It felt like hours, but as Vanguard Ultra rose, everyone was exactly where they had been before the outburst. The pain was replaced by clarity. Doubt was beneath him. God had chosen Ultra to lead, and lead he must.

"Vanguard Gamma," Ultra said, stepping forward. The stormy darkness was harsh, but the Legacy of Boulom sword lit the way. "March forward. While we are enroute, what information do we have on our opponent?"

"Master Zeen," Five said, then made a painful-looking twitch.

"Master Ultra, our Harbinger is of the elemental variety. A woman named Molly, consort to Master Gamma from his imperfect days."

"Wife. Not consort," Gamma said. There was a determined look in his eyes. It would be inspiring if the gaze didn't suggest a seething hatred. "Whatever you may think of me, I swear in the name of Serenity, I shall not falter. I will help build paradise, though it seems I will never experience it."

Something about those words made Ultra feel…odd, but the upcoming battle held his attention. The rain did its best to mask the uncomfortable silence. *It feels like I should say something inspirational here. What would the old leader say. Who was the old leader?*

"Vanguardians!" Ultra yelled out abruptly. "We go forth into battle! I…uh, this is the finest Vanguardian team ever assembled. I trust each of you with my life. We do this not for Terrangus, not even for the realm, but…for God. No one else deserves it."

No applause followed.

It was disappointing to see how terrified the Terrangus people were. One would assume they would hold more faith in God, but apparently, it was up to the Vanguardians to inspire them. Noelami's puppet would be a worthy foe. Ultra wasn't sure how he knew Fear's name, but it inspired several conflicted feelings. Why one of those feelings was love was difficult to comprehend. Why love was the strongest feeling of all was even more bizarre.

"Shield!" Shield said, shielding Ultra.

The rather faint platinum tint flickered before reverting to its natural lucid state. *Why does she say the spell name out loud?* he wondered. Something was off about her. While all Vanguards had that look of someone who hadn't slept in days, Shield's twisted grimace and bloodshot eyes looked on the brink of tears. That could be a problem—Ultra knew that look, it was the look of someone who would crack at the start of a battle.

He felt a faint tingling within as they approached the platinum barrier covering the military ward. So many fragments of memories came from looking at the line of now-empty barracks. Before he had been made perfect, Ultra lived in one of them. Those had been good days. Right?

It was impossible to remember.

"Orders, sir?" the Vanguard commanding the barrier team asked.

It took a moment to realize the Vanguard was directing that question to Ultra. *Okay, it's time. Shields are up. Morale is high. And it's a perfect stormy setting for a battle. Just like Rinso would have faced before his enlightenment.* "Open the barrier. Wait for God's command before reopening to anyone. Fear is no match for the avatars of perfection."

He took a deep breath and entered the barrier. How did formation work with these things? Why couldn't he recall any of his old leaders? Oh well, best to treat this like a military skirmish. "Marcus, sorry, Gamma, take the front. We split the rest, two and two. Me and Shield, Omega and Five."

Fortunately, everyone made their adjustments, though Shield stood uncomfortably close, close enough he could smell a familiar lemony scent. Her eyes stared right through him. "Um, Shield? Can you—"

"Shield!" Shield said, shielding Ultra.

"Not what I meant but I admire the tenacity." Whatever, the distance was awkward, but, in theory, it should make them safer.

Five and Omega eyed each other cautiously. Ultra couldn't remember why but there was some reason those two didn't get along. The rain tapping against the barrier above them tried its best to drown out the awkwardness, but units with no camaraderie eventually get exposed.

A crawler's screech pierced the silence, echoing all around them. Finally, some sound! Gamma marched towards it; he was moving too quickly but, to be fair, the man had no Guardian experience. Having no mechanist or an Engager and a crystal mage with no experience could be a problem...

"*Come, Darling,*" the Harbinger's voice yelled from afar. "*Come face the consequences of ignoring your wife.*"

"And I thought I was bad with women," Omega said, smirking slightly. "Well, at least you're holding a shield."

"Shield!" Shield said, shielding Omega.

"Focus," Ultra said. "And spread out. If a colossal charges, we are too clumped together. Shield, give me some room here. You're too close for me to swing properly."

"Shield!" Shield said, shielding Ultra.

Gamma sighed; tears flowed from his eyes but his expression never changed. "Finish this quickly. Time is not on our side."

"Peace, Master Gamma. All of our sacrifices for Serenity shall not be in vain."

"So I'm told—"

A colossal crashed through one of the barracks, sending debris flying in all directions. A part of Ultra welcomed the disruption, while another part wished Gamma would react faster.

Or at all.

Gamma held his shield out and sluggishly charged a crawler, which was *not* his job, but he didn't seem to care much about protocol. He didn't seem to care about anything.

Dammit, Ultra thought, gripping his blade. "I'll engage the colossal. Omega, defend Shield. Five… I apologize, but you must make do. Use your experience to survive."

A new crystal shield flickered in front of Zeen as he rushed in. He sidestepped to avoid the giant fist crashing down, then countered with a quick slash. His blade tore across its rocky fist; he hopped backwards to avoid the colossal's flail and swung again.

Perfection is one of those things that must be experienced to truly be understood. Without the limitations of doubt, fear, or mercy, Ultra was unstoppable. Maybe powerful enough to stop the Harbinger alone—

A crawler dove into his side, knocking him into the rocky debris. His crystal shattered; for a mage named Shield, she wasn't very proficient. Zeen flinched as a blast of lightning blew up the closest crawler. He resisted the urge to gag from the aroma of burning flesh.

What the hell was going on? Why was Omega on the colossal and not defending Shield? She screamed, swatting a crawler away with her staff and refreshing her own shield, over and over. "Shield!" she yelled, shielding herself. Maybe she couldn't articulate the words, but her eyes screamed for assistance.

As Ultra pushed himself up, a crawler's blade slashed across his face. The sudden influx of pain was nothing compared to the horrors of clarity overwhelming him.

I am Zeen… Zeen Parson. What the fuck am I doing here? Where is Serenna? Where did I get this sword?

The wedding.

He grabbed his blade and dodged the crawler's next swipe by pure instinct. Without the power of Arrogance, there was no way to hold back his fear.

"*Squad leader Zeen Parson,*" the woman's voice yelled. He couldn't see her, but a glowing red aura radiated from afar. "*My husband always favored you. Saw you as everything right about Terrangus. I always knew better. You and Marcus helped commit atrocities across the realm. Why would life as a Vanguard be any different?*"

"I never chose this," Zeen whispered. For all his mistakes, this one really wasn't his fault, though trying to explain that to the ones suffering would be a fool's task. He rushed at Shield, who stumbled back, looking at him as if he were a monster as he slayed the crawlers surrounding her.

"Shield!" Shield said, this time only shielding herself. Gods, she looked terrible. If they weren't in the middle of a battle, Zeen would hug her and say everything would be okay, even though right now, that didn't seem very true.

"*Juliana,*" the Harbinger yelled. "*Poor stupid Juliana. My husband may be a fool but at least he was forced into slavery. You? You willingly signed up, thinking Francis would usher in a perfect realm. Your mind rejected the change, and now a shattered husk of a woman is all that remains. I'll consider it mercy to send you to the void.*"

"Shield…" she said, lowering her staff. Crawlers jabbed against her crystal but she paid them no mind.

It was growing difficult to protect her. The crawlers must have realized something was off; several of them disengaged from Robert and Marcus to rush over. Such a scenario could be advantageous if Nyfe wasn't struggling against his colossal, which, to be fair, would happen to anyone. What a mess. What would David say if saw such sloppy formation?

David is gone. He died trying to save me…

Zeen gripped his sword and kept swinging. The damn thing was powerful—if it truly was a relic from Boulom, it was surreal to think the entire kingdom fell to a Harbinger. It was always a relief to kill demons. They have no morality, friends, family and, best of all, they look weird. A crawler rose on two of its hind legs to appear taller. Zeen swiped right at center frame to tear it in half—

"Shield!"

A shimmering aura of platinum surrounded Zeen right before a blast of lightning crashed down. The force of it shook his entire body, but the platinum shield didn't shatter until the very end. He took a moment to catch his breath…

Shield was gasping for air on the ground, her staff several feet away. Her body kept twitching as Zeen rushed over. He knelt beside her, taking her hand into his own.

"Shield?" she asked. Her fading eyes stared into Zeen.

"Shield," he said, squeezing gently. He laid her to rest as her eyes closed, thankful she left the realm with a smile.

He rose and clutched his sword. Fortunately, Nyfe and Robert had defeated their colossal. Unfortunately, the Harbinger was pounding her staff into Marcus's head, over and over. Her glowing red aura meshed with the splatters of blood flying through the air.

"I told you!" she yelled, crashing her staff down. Up close, Molly did not resemble the woman from Zeen's memory. Like everything in Terrangus, she had been tainted by the gods. "I fucking told you!"

Forgive me, Marcus, he thought, rushing forward. Slaying the Harbinger was the only path to victory. Nyfe and Five were overrun by crawlers, but if they survived, surely they would understand. And if not, Arrogance would force them to anyway.

A crawler intercepted Zeen, but one swing tore it in two with minimal effort. Maybe his Legacy of Boulom blade was corrupted, but by Strength's name, it was powerful. He stopped to slay two more; by now, there was blood all over his face and white armor.

Molly finally noticed him and changed her aura to yellow. As surreal as it was to see her standing over Marcus's dead body, adrenaline was kind enough not to allow any of it to sink in yet. "How fitting," she said, pointing with her staff. "You two can die together. This time, if a god offers to bring you back, don't bother. No one wants you here."

A blast of lightning soared forward. After such words, Zeen didn't feel the need to dodge. He swung his glowing blade at the blast, closing his eyes and accepting whatever fate brought. A slight pain went through his wrist, as if he had struck another sword. He opened his eyes; the ground to his right was scorched but his blade kept glowing.

Zeen sprinted as she adjusted her glow to blue. Maybe his sword could deflect ice, but the safest strategy would be to kill her before ever finding out. He swiped at her throat; she tried to parry but lost her footing. A sad part of Zeen was thankful Marcus had fallen, if only to avoid him seeing his wife's throat torn open. Zeen stabbed her three times while she lay there to be certain, then screamed.

"Well done, Master Ultra," Five said, limping forward with Nyfe at his side. "Exceptional swordplay on your part. I am most impressed by... Why can't I hear you? What happened to you?"

Zeen sheathed his sword and smiled. "Freedom. The freedom to—"

His already-sore body trembled as he collapsed to the ground next to Marcus and Molly. The pain was bad enough, but the loss of control was torment. It would have been more merciful to let him die.

Forgive me, David. Forgive me, Serenna. Forgive...

Forgive what? Ultra rose with a smile. Not only had the Guardians become obsolete, but Noelami's puppet had also failed to defeat the greatest god. Under the banner of Lord Wisdom, Ultra was one step closer to ushering in Serenity.

CHAPTER 20

THE DREAM THAT SHOULD NEVER HAVE COME TRUE

ire!" Bloom yelled, finishing off the final Vanguard as her people watched on. She covered her face to avoid the blood splatter that always followed, then slowly returned to the citadel. Fucking Vanguards couldn't have the courtesy to beg for mercy or even scream. There were literally piles of them outside Vaynex Citadel, yet no matter how many were butchered, more always came. Worst of all, Arrogance had started converting zephum.

The sheer fucking dishonor of it was staggering. Bloom suspected that was why Sardonyx had spent so much time trying to rescue David instead of remaining in Vaynex. What a miserable time to be warlord. She yearned for an honorable death, but her enemies seemed intent on bringing her in alive.

She always kept one fire-detonator by her side to ensure that would never happen.

"Well fought, Warlord," Warmaster Typhum said. At least, Bloom thought that was his name. The role had changed hands so many times this month, it was impossible to keep track. "I concede it was wise to force the conflict to take place outside the citadel. It's the only battleground where we hold an advantage against their magic."

You really think it was my plan to lose all of Vaynex and battle here? "Spare me that shit. What's the damage?" To be fair, there *was* a brilliance to it, but the zephum who had suggested layering tan-colored block formations and digging trenches all around the citadel had died weeks ago. With their long-range magic, the Vanguards were unbeatable in open field combat. Only by forcing them to navigate the trenches and barriers did Vaynex stand a chance.

"What we lost in casualties, we gained in honor. I will speak plainly: at our current rate, the Great Plains in the Sky awaits us, but we will arrive with our honor intact. Our final stand shall be glorious!"

We won't even make the week. "I see." An awkward pause followed. What more did he want? Inspiring speeches had long lost their effect—lying before certain death was more of a human thing. "Are you afraid to die, Warmaster?"

Typhum smirked. "Not anymore. Life...well, life has changed a great deal since the end of the Claw reign. I remember thinking Warlord Tempest would be the end of our people. But this? Never in my dreams did I foresee human invaders upon our lands. It sickens me to my very core. I yearn to die just so I can rise from the sand and haunt them."

"Well said. I don't mind biting the sand if I could just get them to fucking scream."

"Trust me, Warlord—stab them in the right human parts, and their screams are deafening." It was a relief to be surrounded by fellow psychopaths. Any zephum with a stable mind had long left the realm.

A smaller zephum rushed over. Far too young for battle, but once the home is under attack, everyone serves in one way or another. "Warlord! Our scouts...the next wave is already here. Humans! So many humans!"

Bloom sighed, squeezing the detonator at her side. *Today may be the day, old friend.* "Fuckers have gotten persistent. Let's turn this blade completely red. How many?"

"I can't count that high, Warlord."

There was a bizarre feeling of relief to hear the words. The struggle was over. Today would be the fall of Vaynex. Bloom could die and get some fucking sleep. "Are your parents still with us?"

"No, Warlord. I lost both of them when the gates fell. Vaynex is my only mother now."

"She is the mother to us all," Bloom said, meeting his eyes. "I wager you wouldn't hide in the citadel even if I commanded it?"

"Father commanded me never to follow an order that would cost my honor."

"Then grab your blade and follow Warmaster Typhus. And child, remember the words: Strength without honor—is chaos."

"Warriors!" Typhus yelled, banging his bloody sword into the ground. "Give your blessings to the God of Tradition, for our enemy has deemed fit to offer another opportunity for glory."

To Bloom's *enormous* relief, all the zephum in the citadel cheered, waving their weapons in the air and yelling all sorts of annoying battle cries. Did they not realize it was over? Or maybe they yearned for rest. The gods know Bloom did.

"May Tradition favor you, Warlord," Typhus said, "but if not, may we again meet in the Great Plains in the Sky." He left the citadel with the child by his side.

With the throne room cleared, Bloom walked up and grabbed the armrest of her throne. So many meaningless years had been spent chasing the dream that should never have come true. She glanced at the empty spot behind the throne where the God of Strength had used to stand. Damn, it had been fun to mock everyone after Strength's fall, but no one was laughing now. *Strength is dead, and we have killed him.* Cheap insults always survive the longest yet leave the most shameful memories.

Bloom grabbed a sword in one hand and a fire-detonator in the other. A warm wind blew across her snout as she rushed out of the citadel gates with a roar, immediately tackling the first Vanguard in her vicinity. Fuck finesse. These husks needed to focus in order to cast magic, and slamming their bald heads into the rocky sand was the quickest way to ensure that never happened. Since they didn't scream like regular humans, it could be difficult to tell when they died. Bloom found the solution to that problem was to bash their heads until colorful liquid poured out of their skulls like sundered fruit.

She rose and spit on the dead Vanguard. It's a terrible feeling to know when exhaustion lingers but is actively suppressed by adrenaline. A chill from her left side made her grab her fire-detonator and throw it before she saw the blue Vanguard.

"Fire!" she yelled.

The detonator exploded, launching pieces of human bone and flesh flying into the air. It was *far* too close to be safe; the blast knocked Bloom back on her ass.

FUCK!

She forced herself up and grabbed a new fire-detonator. She was running low. Light-detonators were useless in the daytime, and ice really didn't work well either. She needed that quick *bam you're dead* attack to survive.

There were so many dead zephum on the ground that it was difficult to charge the next Vanguard. This one was already glowing yellow—while that sucked for the zephum who took a lightning blast to the chest, it worked out just fine for Bloom, who pierced her sword right into its neck, then picked it up by the sword handle to slam the Vanguard down. She didn't bother to check if the attack was fatal—

A blast of fire erupted close enough to send her flying. She landed right on her tail, and as every zephum knows: that shit hurts. Well, it was a good run, and the perfect setting for an honorable death: clear skies and a seething sun. The sand burned against her back, or maybe that was the aftermath of getting blown up.

Bloom reached for her emergency detonator, but it was missing. She patted all around her armor but the only detonators remaining were ice and light. Useless for anyone looking to off themselves...

"Warlord!" a familiar voice yelled. Ah, it was that damn kid.

"Kid...get out of here. Run away. Anywhere. Just not here."

"Never! Strength without honor is—"

A blast of lightning launched the kid flying. By Tradition's name, it was loud. Despite the explosions, yells, and roars, that kid's scream pierced through everything.

Bloom forced herself up and ran away. If the kid was watching from above, let him spit on her. She kept running towards the citadel. If anyone saw her, then so be it: they would all be dead in the next hour. There would probably be a whole mess of people ready to kick Bloom's ass when she reached the afterlife. That kid's screams still echoed through her head as she crashed through the citadel doors. The room was filled with wounded zephum and noncombatants: the *really* young and the *really* old.

"Everyone!" she yelled, limping to the throne. "Go to the safe rooms. Once we secure the perimeter, you will be allowed to roam freely." She made sure to avoid eye contact. The young may believe, but the old would see through such nonsense.

She sat on the Vaynex throne and sighed, her back leaning against the hot stone. There was a beauty to how uncomfortable the throne felt. It was like whoever had built it knew how miserable leadership could be. The room cleared as a strange-looking shimmer appeared in the center of the citadel...

Arrogance. The god floated up to her and chuckled. "Oh, what an honor, *Warlord*. I'll admit, you brutes put up a far better fight than expected, though it's to your own detriment. Let it be known that I considered destroying you all, but now I see it as a challenge. There is so much opportunity for improvement, I don't even know where to begin, if we're being honest. Any change at all would be an improvement. Is a puzzle simple or impossible if every move is a winning solution?"

Bloom rose and grabbed an ice-detonator. She held it to her snout, then said, "Not how I planned to go, but I would rather freeze to death than listen to you talk anymore. Even if Vaynex falls, you'll eventually lose. You're a fucking loser—"

Riding a giant unicorn, Tradition crashed through the citadel ceiling. Arrogance vanished immediately before Sardonyx reached out his hand. "Mighty Bloom! Take my hand and ride my majestic steed! Vaynex has fallen, but the war is not lost!"

"It's over, Boss. Never imagined I would be the final warlord. I'm sorry I failed you. I'm sorry for everything. Our home...it's gone."

Sardonyx pounded his chest. "Home is in the heart! We shall reclaim what is ours by birthright, but this is a war, not a battle. Ride with me to Mylor. The Arrogant One has several enemies, and I plan to enlist them *all*."

Time passed, whether a few seconds or minutes, it was impossible to tell. Bloom took his hand and was heaved onto the unicorn. "Sardonyx... Strength without honor—is *chaos*."

The unicorn neighed gloriously, then soared into the skies. "To hear you speak the words brings joy to my old heart. Have patience, Child of Tradition. The Arrogant One shall falter, and honor will prevail as it always has, as it always will."

CHAPTER 21

DAMN THIS ITCHY TAIL

t had been zero days since David's last drink.

He sat on his stool at the bar, avoiding the mirror across from him. Yesterday, or whenever he was last conscious, he had made the mistake of taking a quick glance. It had been a painful confirmation that whoever or whatever David had been was gone, and a frail, bearded husk with glassy eyes was all that remained. The only difference today from any other day was the rumbling had stopped. He assumed it was either Noelami or Sardonyx. Had they given up? Perhaps they took a glance at David and finally realized he wasn't worth saving. David eyed the balcony to his left; he swore it inched closer each day. *If something is not worth saving…should it even exist in the first place?* Arrogance was a cruel god. After manipulating the realm with treachery and lies, he had shown David the one thing he couldn't bear…

The truth.

He turned away from the balcony and towards his never-empty wine bottle. It was difficult to say what kept him going. Defiance? Fear of the end? Perhaps the wine was too delicious to part from. "How long has it been?" he said out loud, to no one. The faceless bartender had given him food and water when requested but otherwise was useless. "I won't do it. Even if the gods have abandoned me, I will not abandon myself. I am the mountain… I am the mountain." He took the vapid inspiration as an excuse to chug his wine. By Fear's mercy, it was delicious.

"Guardian Williams? Is that you?" asked a familiar voice. It was a zephum but didn't sound like Sardonyx or... Ah. Tempest.

"Come to mock me?" asked David, glancing behind him. An odd clash of relief and regret came when he saw Tempest was not alone.

"Come to *drink*!" Pyith yelled, rushing over and taking the stool next to him. She poured herself a glass then chugged the entire thing. "Damn, no wonder you haven't offed yourself yet. This stuff is delicious. A few glasses and even Tempest will look good. Melissa should've been the drunk, not you."

David couldn't help but smile even though it wasn't her. Pyith was long gone, but did it matter? It was a lost friend to spend lost days with. A reminder of a better time. "I suppose nothing tastes better than lies."

Tempest held his snout as he surveyed the room. "What an odd location. I wonder how I would describe such a place if I used it in Rinso? Descriptions were never my strong point. I make the reader do most of the work."

"Does it matter? I've been here for months and I see nothing at all."

"Oh David," Tempest said, letting out an exaggerated sigh that would put Francis to shame. "To the artist, every room is filled with words. You just have to learn where to look."

The whimsical feeling of seeing his old friends faded. They were no more real than David's chances of ever leaving here alive. "You are unworthy of the title. You are a *liar,* not an artist."

Tempest snickered before taking his seat. "That line is thinner than you may think. Nevertheless, we can argue later. Today we celebrate the fall of Vaynex! Particularly now that my father is no longer trying to break in."

"Impossible…"

"What's wrong? You just claimed I was a liar. If that were true, why would my words bother you?"

David took a deep breath, staring down into the empty chalice before refilling it. "I suppose that's why the rumbling stopped? Interesting, so it was Sardonyx and not Noelami—"

Pyith slapped him across the face. It was a rattling sensation, but the alcohol diminished the pain, at least for now. "Stop calling her that. To you, she is Fear, and Fear alone. I know she is watching. She is *always* watching. When you finally take the dive from that balcony, I will revel in her pain."

"Dear, you're ruining the celebration," Tempest said. "And, if anyone has a reason to be upset, it's me."

She scoffed. "What are you whining about? I'm the one that died to a crawler. The best Engager in Guardian history defeated by a fucking crawler! Even a writer as terrible as you wouldn't have done that!"

"I had ideas. Dreams! And they were layered with evidence and logic. If we had a better realm, we would be guiding Vaynex towards Serenity. Such is the ultimate flaw of freewill. Our joy is dependent on others' choices. Take any genius from any kingdom and stick him in a room of zephum. The poor fool would be dead within minutes. Seconds, perhaps. I was wise in comparison to my people, David, but ultimately, I was no wiser than you. If only I severed my ties to Father and collaborated with Wisdom. It was never supposed to be this way, and yet here we are."

David took another sip; the sweet taste had faded just a bit. "You're the only thing keeping me going. I've lost everything else, but when you fail, I will fall to my fucking knees and laugh. I will laugh until my throat tears open."

Tempest sighed. "The sad part is, I believe you. The absurdity of freewill has corrupted you so deeply, you yearn for a broken world to continue, just for the opportunity to gloat. Part of me wants to keep you alive just so you can see how beautiful Serenity will be. But such a thing would be the ultimate cruelty. You will never be happy, David. Look upon the balcony: I *beg* you to leap before my ascension. Everything you ever believed will not only be proven wrong but also broken beyond comprehension. A shattered perspective, as they say."

There was no reason to respond. He ignored them both and went back to his wine as they got up and walked away. Either they would leave or he would pass out, and either solution was fine. The familiar numbness came as he downed another glass. It was admittedly less comforting each time, but such was the realm. After a few moments of silence, he gave in to the urge to glance at the balcony.

"I'll give Serenna your regards before I have Zeen cut her throat," Pyith said, leaning over the side. "Ugh, damn this itchy tail." She let go and collapsed into nothing. Despite how dehydrated he was, David couldn't stop himself from weeping.

"Don't weep, old friend," Tempest said, leaning over. "Just as you were born to be a mountain, I was born to be a storm, though I'm still not sure what that means, to be honest. May you find me, David, wherever storms go when the sun returns and clouds fade."

David wept out loud, no longer caring if Arrogance saw it. Pride had abandoned him long, long ago.

CHAPTER 22

THE COST OF LIES

lood poured down Serenna's eyes as she lifted the Vanguard high into the air of the bastion halls, trapped within her crystal prison. She had stopped counting her kills over the days—there was no point in counting towards forever. She tore the prison in two, reveling in the blank expression of the invader's face. They never screamed, but that didn't bother her anymore. The day would come when Arrogance's scream would echo against the Mylor mountains.

"Senator!"

She ignored whomever it was. Damn them for using that title. The only senator was Father, and he had died from her mistakes. He had joined Pyith, Valor, and Zeen as victims of an unqualified leader. Serenna pressed forward, letting her insides burn as more platinum energy radiated all around her. Her legs were completely numb, but instinct kept them working. Darkness crept through her vision as she pressed on. *Damn this weak body for denying my vengeance. Just a few more. Just one more…*

Mylor soldiers rushed over as she collapsed. She tried to push them away, but they carried her out of the bastion halls. What had once been soreness had morphed into a permanent agony. A lack of food and sleep had taken their toll, amplified by the horrors of remembering that wedding. It was impossible to let go. It was impossible to find peace. Worst of all, the longer the days went on, reality made it clear it would be impossible to kill them all.

"Water," she whispered. One can learn to ignore pain, but thirst must always be quenched. To her relief, they brought her into one of the tents at the bastion entrance. She resisted the urge to close her eyes. Sleep would mean dreams. Dreams would mean nightmares. Serenna grabbed the flask of water from one of her soldiers with more desperation than intended. She drank the whole thing in one gulp and gasped. "More...get more. Also, need report. Tell me...report."

"Senator," one of them said. While long ago she had been able to identify every soldier by face or name, they all seemed like blurs now. "Our status is dire. We slay them on a ratio of two-to-one, but attritional warfare is their goal. Rumors are they even have zephum now. I—"

"That's enough!" Captain Martin said. "Senator, you need rest. Have faith in your people. Remember, Mylor has never fallen. Her mountains are stained red from the blood of those who tried."

Zephum Vanguards? Does that mean Vaynex has fallen? By Valor's grace... She forced herself up, gasping as a sharp pain went through her legs when she put weight on them. "I'm going back to the front. Grab me more water and a change of armor. I swear, one of them smiled at me in that last battle. That one dies last."

Martin sighed. "Please leave us."

To her surprise, they listened and left the tent. In what absurd realm did Martin outrank Serenna, let alone any Morgan? "You dare?"

"Only because I must. Allow me to be blunt: the moment you fall, the exact moment, Mylor is defeated. Your presence is the only thing keeping us in this battle. Rest. Not because I command it, but because we need you to recover. Your eyes are bloodshot. Your face is sunken. Your arms look like twigs. It's time to rest."

"Fine." He was right, of course, but it still hurt to hear the truth that the mirror had already whispered through her eyes. "Help me stand and take me to my chambers. I still want that water and fresh armor."

"Yes, Senator," he said with a smile, taking her by the arm. His eyes lit up, and it didn't take a scholar to see the desire within them. Those feelings would never be returned. Martin would end up disappointed, just like Father, just like Valor, just like Zeen…

Her near-delirium made the journey go rather quickly. Every step she took was another Mylor soldier who would die without her shields, but the thought of rest nearly brought her to tears. Maybe she wouldn't wake this time. Maybe instead of giving some faceless Vanguard the satisfaction of defeating her, she could fade in the middle of a dream with Zeen. Dreams were the only place she saw him anymore. The only place she could hold him in her arms. The only place they could kiss. The only place they could perform the other act, where she always woke up right before the good part…

She flinched as she hit the bed. Martin had been right, she needed rest. He was saying something, but none of his words were important enough to keep her awake.

*

"Senator?" Martin said. Damn him for waking her. For however long she had rested, it was wonderful. No dreams from what she could remember; maybe her mind was too tired to construct lies.

"Already?" Serenna said, yawning. Oh, she had fallen asleep in her armor. Not the first time. Hopefully, not the last.

"I wouldn't bother you unless absolutely necessary. It seems… It would seem we have a visitor. Two of them."

"What?" That caught her attention. With the portals deactivated and her kingdom under siege, visitors weren't possible— unless they happened to be immortal. "Who is it?"

"Well, best that you see for yourself. They are waiting in the gardens."

Not the most helpful answer. Serenna rolled out of bed and grabbed the Wings of Mylor. She didn't wait for Martin as she rushed out the door. *Two* visitors? Who could it be? It was rude to ignore the people saluting throughout the citadel, but her mind was elsewhere—

Two zephum stood in front of a giant unicorn. His glorious neigh echoed against the mountains. "By Valor's grace… Bloom?

Sardonyx?" She rushed up and hugged the warlord, squeezing him. "Oh, Warlord. I have missed you beyond words. And Bloom," she said, giving her a quick hug, "you too, of course. What brings you to Mylor? I had assumed the worst. Is your presence here... I suppose it's true then?"

"It's worse than you think. Sorry Boss, we fought them with everything we had. I swear we were winning, but their numbers. Fuck, it was like fighting flies. You kill one and two more just buzz by your snout. It was fucking endless!" Rage filled her voice. The rage of an inevitable loss.

"Indeed. We have the same problem here and... I received a report of zephum Vanguards."

Bloom sighed and leaned against the balcony. "Don't even get me started on that. I'll tell you what: it makes me appreciate the concept of honor. Never felt like a real thing until I saw the void it leaves in its wake."

"If you have come to fight by my side, the aid is welcome. I am well past the days of lying. This war may not be winnable, but we shall die with honor." She glanced over to Sardonyx and smiled. "It shall be *glorious.*"

She waited for a *glorious indeed*, but instead, Sardonyx sighed and said, "Do not be so quick to bury yourselves under the sand. There is no glory in the loss of our loved ones. I came here for victory, and I require your aid to make that happen."

"How?" she asked, not bothering to hide her anger. "Do you want me to fight harder? I don't even know what day it is, Warlord. Look into my eyes and again tell me that this war is winnable." She held back a flinch as he met her eyes. It was like she was sixteen again, staring into a monster for the first time.

"Our path to victory lies with Death and... *her*. You must speak to the fallen empress. After her deception in Nuum, I will not do so. So much could have been avoided if only...but alas, such is the cost of lies. Convince her to meet us for a summit within the Great Plains in the Sky. With our forces combined, Arrogance will learn humility."

"What? Why would Fear listen to anything I have to say?"

"Don't look at me, Boss," Bloom said with a shrug. "I think the idea is nuts, but the only idea is always the best one."

"Death…I will speak to Death," Sardonyx said, but why? Ah, it was obvious. After Serenna had accepted a taste of his power all that time ago, no one could trust her. Apparently, people never grow or change.

"How do I even do that? David is the only one she ever spoke to. And David—"

"David will be saved," Sardonyx said, turning toward the mountains. "If you believe any of the words I offer you today, believe that above all. David will be saved. Call to her. She may not answer immediately, but it will occur. And Serenna Morgan, Child of Valor…heed my words. We will save him too. I will cleave the mask off the deceiver's face until you are reunited with your life-mate."

Serenna clenched her fist as all the fatigue in her body yielded to rage. "Don't promise me such a thing unless it's certain."

"Oh, Child of Valor, the realm has taken its toll on us all. Speak to the fallen empress. Bring her to my summit. I shall do the rest. Now! Speak the words! The words that have guided our realm through the darkest of horrors. Strength without honor—is *chaos*!"

In a surreal moment, she realized Sardonyx was no more. He had ascended to a level of divinity only offered to the greatest of mortals. This zephum who had once shaken Serenna to her very core now made her believe she could enter God's realm and defeat Arrogance when all else had failed.

She stepped forward, grasping the Wings of Mylor. "Strength…without honor…is chaos."

CHAPTER 23

The Warrior, the Sorcerer, and the Puppeteer

ary had always hated drunks. They were useless vagrants, people so defeated by the past they would rather mope around than do anything to improve their future. As she sighed in the throne room and poured more wine into her chalice, she wondered when everything had changed. What happened to the Terrangus warrior who had stood face-to-face against Sardonyx in the snowy ruins of Boulom? That would've been the perfect way to die. A *glorious* death, as they say…

All the senators, guests, and even Francis gasped when Arrogance appeared in the middle of the throne room. It was so annoying how they marveled at his presence. Behind that mask, cape, and all those words real people never used was a fucking coward playing savior. Did no one else see it? Or maybe everyone was just kissing his ass. At least that she could understand—behind the jolly god was an unhinged monster. Did they know? No matter how hard Francis had tried to lie to himself, surely he understood by now. Calvin grabbed his father's leg and started shaking. Good boy. Children can always tell who the monsters are.

"Welcome, Lord Wisdom!" Francis said, gently pushing Calvin away. "What brings you to our royal kingdom today?"

Mary groaned. "Can you please act like the emperor? Wisdom, you only show up when there's a problem. So what is it? What did you fuck up now?" She took a swig and held back a laugh at Francis's scowl. Since they had married, he put less effort into hiding his emotions. It could've been a beautiful thing, but it turned out most of those hidden emotions were various stages of being annoyed.

"God, please forgive her. Mary forgets herself—"

Arrogance laughed out loud, and not that usual chuckle. "It's quite the opposite really—the wine helps Mary remember what she is. It would appear I'm not the only one wearing a mask. Now, silence please, and take a moment to let this set in before you react." He cleared his throat, which certainly was for a dramatic purpose. "Vaynex has fallen."

This time, the gasps were warranted. How could Vaynex fall? All those crushing defeats in the Koulva mines… How the fuck could the unified zephum empire fall to Emperor Francis of all people?

"What of Bloom?" asked Francis, and that was a good question. It seemed unlikely she would allow herself to get taken alive. That would make Serenna the final Guardian. Mylor and Alanammus were all that stood between the realm and Serenity.

Are we actually going to win? It didn't seem real. Nothing with Arrogance had ever gone right until the wedding. Gods, that day…it was a turning point. Maybe the key to tyranny is to keep trying until everyone who opposes you dies.

Arrogance sighed. "Now, Francis, I *did* say to wait before responding. Was that a wise question?"

If he's annoyed, that means she escaped. Good for her.

"Forgive me, God. I have a tendency to speak before my thoughts are settled," Francis said, even though that was nonsense. The twitch of his lip made it seem like he had more questions, but he pulled Calvin back in and didn't say a word.

"Forgiveness? Consider it done! How could I be angry on such a joyous occasion? But alas, the celebrations must wait. Only two enemies remain, and one of them has chosen to hide behind their flimsy ivory walls. Mylor, however, is a rather…barbaric kingdom. We must assume the worst, and I believe I can safely speak for us all when I say our emperor doesn't require a new stab wound." He floated up to Calvin, who clenched Francis's leg and shook like he was in a winter storm. "You wouldn't want dear old Daddy to get stabbed again, would you?"

The combination of wine and Calvin's cries erupted a rage inside Mary. She threw her chalice at the sun mask, but it was slapped away by his spectral hand. "Lay a hand on my son, and god or not, I will carry your shattered body back to the ruins of Boulom." A long silence followed, and hopefully everyone in the throne room used those moments to reflect on their own cowardice. "This is all a farce! Guardians are dead, kingdoms are falling! Where is paradise? When does anything good happen? Look at him!" she yelled, pointing at Zeen. He had no reaction, of course: her old friend no longer reacted to anything. All that stupid, misguided optimism had been wiped from his being, replaced by a husk with a glowing sword. It was wrong. All of this was wrong.

Francis rushed over and whispered, "Please stop. Now is not the time nor the place. We must show a unified front or Serenity will always be a fleeting dream. Do it for Calvin."

"*Do not react,*" Arrogance whispered through her thoughts. "*Just listen. Now, I am a patient god, but my tolerance for disobedience is finite. While I cannot place a quantitative value, per se, just know there is a bottom, and you are near it. With Vaynex defeated, I need you just a little bit less. Enjoy the winning side as Empress or Vanguard. I'm sure your son will love you either way.*"

Mary searched for words that never came. The smart move would be to shut up and enjoy victory, but Arrogance... Arrogance was going to win. The sheer hopelessness of the thought was staggering. Why fight back? David, Serenna, Bloom, even Valor, all of them had failed miserably. What chance did Mary have? How could a drunken mother defy God?

"You're right," she said to Francis, but intended it for Arrogance. "My tolerance to wine has faded with motherhood. Enjoy the celebration. I will retire to my chambers with Calvin."

Francis gave her a quick kiss. "Thank you. I'll wrap this up quickly and join you. Some rest would do us all some good." It was nice to see the relief on his face. Bless her husband: the scholarly genius and the emotional fool. "Enough silence! Vaynex has fallen, and in its wake, the glory of Serenity shall rise!"

She smirked and picked up little Calvin. It must have killed Francis to speak that way, but the people cheered. He was growing better at that. Odd how he thrived while Mary descended. Oh well, if she had learned anything from war, it was that everyone deals with nightmares in their own way.

Terrangus had too many stairs. After a few steps, she put Calvin down, who immediately rushed all the way up to their chamber doors. Her son's giggle brought a clash of pride and shame. It was only a matter of time until he didn't need her anymore. Every mother stares down the hourglass. *We bring them into this realm, then watch them thrive as our own mind and body diminish.*

Mary huffed after the final step. It was absurd that the former Guardian had lost all her stamina, but the years had not been kind. That wasn't entirely true. Perhaps it wasn't true at all. The years had brought a husband, a son, absolute power, and a divine ally gripping the realm by the throat. She opened the door, and such relief came from the sight of her bed. A final glass—or two—of wine and then back to the joyful numbness of sleep. "Ready for a nap?" she asked Calvin. It was a trick question: he was getting that nap no matter what his response.

"Okay." He seemed a bit disappointed. Hopefully, he was still too young to understand just how fragile his mother had become.

She tucked him into his little bed on the other side of the room. The day would soon come when he would have his own chambers. It was overdue of course, but…it was difficult not to keep him in her sights. We cannot protect what we cannot see.

How was he already so comfortable? Children have it so easy when it comes to sleep. Mary poured a chalice of wine as Calvin wrapped himself in a blanket. All that energy from the stairs was apparently gone. "Mommy. Story?"

"Story?" She snickered and took a swig of wine. "I'm afraid I'm not much of a storyteller. Most of your mother's memories are rather violent. No need for a little boy to hear any of that."

"Did someone say story?" Arrogance said from behind the bed. She wouldn't look but the power radiating from him made her shiver. "Perhaps I can be of assistance. Little emperor, would you care to hear *my* story?"

"I think Calvin is ready for bed—"

"Story! Story! Story!"

She sighed and refilled her chalice. Even her son had turned against her.

"Very well," Arrogance said with a chuckle. "Partake in my tale of the warrior, the sorcerer, and the puppeteer. It began not so long ago, but the concept of time is impossible for a child to grasp. In your little mind, it may as well have been forever ago."

He must have been insufferable as a teacher.

"Our hero, the puppeteer, had many, many puppets. He was a scholar of his craft, a master in the arts of entertainment. The children would come to the Boulom plaza and cheer, cheer until their little throats burned. *But...* one day, another puppeteer wandered in. A younger man, untrained in his craft, eager to reap the wonders of art without putting in the misery. While our hero offered the children a story of peace and serenity, the...let's call him a scoundrel, flashed his war, his plagues, his lizard-people, and his misguided empresses. Flashy disasters. Lies gilded in freedom. The worst part? He let them choose! And what do you think they choose? Peace or chaos?"

"I don't know," Calvin said, rolling over. Fatigue filled his voice. For all of Arrogance's faults, he did seem to excel at boring people to sleep.

"Ah, but you do, little emperor. When it comes to choice, the answer is always chaos. And why not? It's fun. *Flashy!* Utterly destructive. The children flocked to the new puppeteer, cheering for things they could never understand. Our hero saw it as his mission to bring the children home, but tragedy struck when his dear warrior puppet ran away. The poor girl had witnessed so many atrocities in her lifetime that anything resembling joy was so hostile and foreign, there was no choice but to flail against it with every fiber of her being."

Mary scoffed and sipped her wine as Calvin let out a yawn. The lack of subtlety was outrageous.

"The warrior puppet spilled blood for the children, letting out battle cries that drowned out her internal screams of desperation. See, that's the problem with calamity: we invite it in as an exciting guest, but it never leaves. Unfulfillment carries a heavy toll. What was a lifetime for her was merely days for the rest of us. Eventually, when the children grew bored of their chaos, they did what us adults are incapable of: they walked away. And that's exactly what happened next! Humbled, defeated, our broken warrior looked inside and found nothing. She approached her old puppeteer, head down, afraid to look into his eyes. She didn't know if the puppeteer smiled or frowned as she asked him a simple question. How much can a puppet be damaged before they are considered broken?"

After a moment, it seemed clear Arrogance had finally finished speaking. Mary finished her chalice and leaned back. "Well? You and my husband seem obsessed with the question. How is it that you never found the answer?"

"Oh, my dear Mary, the only way to learn the answer is to break completely. Such is the cold truth of science. The day you stop pondering is the day you are truly lost. I'm disappointed you didn't ask the more important question: did the puppeteer take her back?"

It was adorable that Arrogance didn't consider himself broken. Good thing he had never asked any of the inhabitants of Boulom. "Of course he did," Mary said with a smile. "The warrior puppet was his favorite. Parents always love the troublemakers. Now get out of here so I can sleep before Francis gets in. Last thing I need is another man asking me to justify his mistakes."

Arrogance chuckled. "Ah, delusion truly is the cornerstone of happiness. Sweet dreams, Empress."

CHAPTER 24

DAUGHTER OF VALOR

he war in the bastion raged on, and it killed Serenna not to be involved. The consistent good news had only escalated her worries. Whatever details they had left out about the morning's skirmish must have been dire. People have it wrong when it comes to liars. It's not the lack of eye contact but the opposite. The worst tales are the ones when the liar stares straight through us.

At least her strength had returned. A few days away from the battle *had* done her good. To fully comprehend exhaustion, we must eventually reunite with our rested self. She sipped her tea, staring out at the mountains.

Where are you, Fear?

To anticipate her lifelong nemesis brought a unique tingle of anxiety. Sardonyx had suggested the goddess would contact her, but so far, nothing—

"*SERENNA!*" Sardonyx's voice blasted through her thoughts, nearly knocking her over. Perhaps newer gods struggled with communication; Valor had always been the same way. "*SEEK OUT THE FALLEN EMPRESS IN ALANAMMUS! TIME IS OF THE ESSENCE!*"

She grabbed the railing for balance. Gods, his voice was overpowering. Going to Alanammus had never been the plan. How would she even get in with the portals closed? *Forgive me, Mylor, for what I must do,* she thought, heading to the Guardian room. Her soldiers saluted her as she entered, but she couldn't help but feel their disdain. Their Guardian, their senator, was abandoning them. "I shall return," she said, raising the Wings of Mylor to trigger the portal. Nothing. The Guardian portal wouldn't respond, nor would the outskirts portal. Closing the Guardian portal was understandable in times of war, but to shut off access to the outskirts was unheard of...

"Trigger the Guardian portal now. You have ten seconds." The shock of hearing a woman's voice in her head made her freeze. It wasn't Valor, which obviously meant it was Fear. Ah, to feel nostalgia over stern demands.

She attempted the portal again, and this time, it erupted in a silver light.

*

Harrowing was the only word to describe how it felt to appear back in Alanammus. Serenna hadn't been here since the fall of Gabriel. To be fair, no one had. Everything had been shut down. In true Alanammus fashion, they had isolated themselves in silver as the realm around them burned.

"Serenna?" asked one of the gold cloaks, a brute of a man who reminded her of Julius. They pointed polearms at her until they withdrew, stared at each other, and waited for someone to take command of the scenario. "How is your arrival possible? Explain yourself!"

"Bring me to the archon immediately."

"Assassin!" a different gold cloak yelled. "Arrogance has breached the portals!"

Perhaps speaking directly had not been the best path. Serenna took a deep breath then said, "In these trying times, you are wise to doubt my presence, but understand I have slain more Vanguards than any mortal in our realm. From one soldier to another: look into my eyes and call me an illusion." It was an insult to call these men soldiers. While Vaynex and Mylor fought for the will of the entire realm, Alanammus had done what they do best: nothing.

"We should escort her to the archon." the first one said. "If we harm her and it ends up being the true Serenna…well, my career can't handle that one. How did you even trigger the portal? The only reason I believe it's you is because Wisdom would have already opened it if he had the means."

"Wisdom is not the only god in this realm," Serenna said, brushing the hair from her eyes. "Look, I'm sure you have many questions, but time is of the essence…" She stopped herself from saying Vaynex had fallen. They probably had no idea, and panic would get her nowhere but a prison cell. "Escort me if you so please, but I assure you, I know the way."

"Come," the big man said, lowering his polearm and heading for the exit. "Forgive my men, but everyone is on high-alert these days after Vaynex. Many of us have been promoted far beyond our means ever since the wedding. Surely you understand."

Ah, so they did know. "I wager I understand far greater than you, Gold Cloak. It's tiring to hear battle theory from those who avoid battle."

He grinned. "Fair, but avoiding battle is often the best strategy. It's Kolsen, by the way. Never favored the idea of using our names as titles."

Exhaustion returned. There was no point in holding back her frown. "A man very dear to my heart held the same belief."

Thankfully, he took the hint not to ask further, but it made the journey to the archon's chamber filled with an awkward silence. Those damn diamond-encrusted doors stood in front of them. Famine and war always expose the absurdity of opulence. "And this, my friend, is where I leave you. She reminds me of old Addy. I won't ask where your politics lie but uh…yeah."

"Many thanks, Kolsen." Serenna pushed open the doors, to find a short, slender woman with brown hair sitting on a throne, looking oddly familiar. It was a bold choice—Alanammus had been known not to use thrones to avoid the stigma of tyranny. Best to speak first: Father had used to say it's an assertion of authority in political discussions. "Archon."

"Serenna." The woman leaned back and folded her arms. "Do you prefer the title of Guardian or Senator?"

An odd question, but one easily answered. "Guardian. Always Guardian."

"Then you have learned nothing," the archon said, rising. She leaned forward and pressed her hands against the table. "Why do tools always yearn to be tools?"

That voice. It was Fear. "After everything I have done for this realm, you have no right to call me that. Perhaps if you had lent your aid, Vaynex would still stand."

"An interesting theory. And why didn't *you* defend Vaynex?"

"I was defending my home!"

"As was I!" Fear yelled. For a moment, her human features flickered into the angelic monster of her true form. "What do you think kept these people from rioting and burning Alanammus to the ground? From wasting our food supplies in one cycle? Fear. It is the true Guardian of this realm: everything else is a means to an end. There is no army here: you and Valor made sure of that when you stormed Serenity. Oh, you fucking fool. Some mistakes carry a toll that lingers beyond centuries. We aren't going to win. All we can do now is limit how badly we are going to lose."

"No," Serenna said, walking around the room to clear her head. A sign she was getting older was how many of the portraits on the wall had become memories of better times. "The archon had his faults. Many, many faults, but one piece of wisdom stuck with me. Sometimes it's better to knock the board over than to accept defeat. Warlord Sardonyx...the God of Tradition, proposes a summit. In a neutral zone: The Great Plains in the Sky."

Fear scoffed. "I know the sweet temptation of dreams, but I assure you, now is the time for harsh realities. Do whatever you wish. I will not be joining this summit of fools."

"In what realm is the Goddess of Fear a coward? What is it about the title of archon that ends people's resolve? I would say you're no better than Gabriel, but even he tried in the end."

"*Never* compare me to that man."

Serenna stomped forward, uncaring if the woman in front of her could send her to the void. They were probably all heading there, anyway. "You wear his colors. You wear his banner. You may have been an empress in ages past, but in my eyes, you are just another disappointment gilded in silver. Revel in your poisonous mantra if you must. I would rather die."

Fear looked her in the eyes. It wasn't intimidation, but genuine interest. "*You* would parley with Death?"

"I stand before you as a Daughter of Valor. All of my mistakes, all of my failures, carry a great toll, but it is a toll I shall pay in blood. I have lost my father, my goddess…my lover. I would parley with the void itself if it meant putting an end to Arrogance. Join me, Noelami. You defeated Ermias the Harbinger all those years ago. It's time to defeat him one last time."

Noelami stepped to the balcony. The wind blew her hair to the side and brought a gentle chill to the air. "He tortures David by giving him the one thing he could never resist. You…you have no idea what that man has sacrificed for our realm. I accept. I do this not for you, not even for the realm, but for David.

"No one else deserves it."

CHAPTER 25

IT'S NEVER TOO LATE TO CHANGE

oss, where the fuck are we going?" asked Bloom, clutching onto her unicorn for dear life. Geography was never her thing, but being this far north meant nothing but snow. And snow meant it was fucking cold. "Do I have to freeze to death to get into the void? Because I can think of quicker ways to die."

"Silence!" Tradition yelled, and that about summed up their trip so far. Bloom would complain, followed by a "Silence!" from Sardonyx. Maybe gods no longer feel the cold.

It was weird to pass above the ruins of Boulom. Every zephum learns of the place: the *glorious* battlefield where the God of Strength had assembled a team of angsty humans to defeat the Arrogant One when he was a Harbinger. But to see it in person…damn. Maybe there was something to the stories. Humans here really had their shit together before everyone died.

She gripped tighter as the unicorn descended. They were heading towards the ruins of some bizarre-looking building. Actually, it was similar to the structure from the Terrangus wedding—like a castle but with more annoying colors. Humans were always so weird about such things. A harsh landing sent a pain through her legs, but at least she could get off the damn creature.

"Child of Tradition," Sardonyx said, drawing his sword. "Before I commence, I require your word that you are prepared to face the end. I will not back down. I will not falter. We leave these ruins with an alliance, or we shall sleep beneath the snow with only honor to keep us warm."

"So, if I refuse, you'll give me the unicorn and let me go?"

"Indeed. But no Child of Tradition would ever make such a choice." It was rare to see Sardonyx smile, and, to be honest, it was terrifying. Honor always seemed like nonsense for old people to sound relevant, but there was a beauty to it. She would die for Sardonyx, for Vaynex, for all of them. Such is the glory and burden of being warlord.

"Well, you got me there. Let's do it, Boss." She waited for whatever "it" was before Sardonyx raised his blade to the skies.

"DEATH!" he yelled, stepping forward. "HEED THE CALL OF TRADITION! I DEMAND YOUR PRESENCE! FACE ME ON THE HONORABLE BATTLEGROUNDS OF BOULOM! STRENGTH WITHOUT HONOR—IS CHAOS!"

Oh, so that was the plan. Well, it had been a good run. She took two fire-detonators from her belt, holding them tightly to account for the smaller size. It made sense human-made detonators would be smaller, but damn, it was annoying. It was a relief that nothing happened at first. It was not a relief when the ground rumbled and the cloudy skies went fully black. *Oh shit*, she thought, taking a step back by instinct. Bless Sardonyx for not doing the same. He gazed upwards with a smile, probably content to win or die trying.

"And what do we have here?" said Death from the skies. All she could make out was the glowing red eyes swirling within the clouds. "The lizard-people have come to beg for their end. Sheathe your blade, Child of Strength. Despite my reputation, I have always been a merciful god. The void awaits, and your peace with it."

Sardonyx stepped forward. "I have come to parley against our common foe. Once he is dealt with, the endless struggle of life and death can persist as it always has. As it always must."

"Parley?" asked Death, laughing in a high-pitched shriek that burned her ears. "The void is an absolute. There are no deals, no bargains to be made. There is only the nothing, the forever, the end. The nothing, the forever, the end."

"Spare me your ruse, Ender of Realms. The Arrogant one has made Harbingers irrelevant. He has robbed you of purpose, as he has robbed me of my people. We have eons to do glorious battle as rivals. Let us work together this one time—"

"IRRELEVANT?" Death yelled. A black hand-shaped cloud soared out of the skies towards Bloom. It grabbed her, and *fuck,* it was cold. "You are all infected by Arrogance. You have forgotten what it is to know the void always lingers. I could destroy every mortal in this realm. Drown the Time God's children in a sea of tears."

The time for pride had long passed. Bloom screamed, pushing against the black hand pulling her towards the sky; it was like trying to push Vaynex Citadel across the sand. "Fucking do something!" she yelled. She dropped the one trap but held onto the other for dear life. Bloom was nuts, but not delusional. Yelling *Fire!* would do nothing but blow her own head off. It may eventually come to that.

"Tempest Junior, to me!" Sardonyx yelled, then leapt upon his unicorn, who neighed gloriously. He held his sword forward with one hand as he flew into the abyss.

Now, it was a sight to behold, but there was that ominous feeling that every outcome would lead to Bloom either freezing to death or falling all the way down and dying on impact. Instant death was becoming far more appealing by the second—

Death released her, and the freezing cold was replaced by that weird feeling when falling too far for the body to handle. She landed on Tempest Junior, and if her legs were sore before, they were on fire now. Fuck it—she screamed. Since the only other people here were dead or gods, let them think less of her. Tempest Junior shrugged her off after she landed, sending her crashing into the snow.

She lay there, watching the cataclysm of red energy clashing with the darkness. Tempest Junior gave her face a quick lick, then rushed to the skies, just in time to catch the falling Sardonyx.

The black cloud above expanded, making it appear like one of those hurricanes that had devastated Vaynex in years past. Darkness surrounded them.

"Foul deity!" Sardonyx yelled, rushing towards the darkness. He swung his blade at the glowing red eyes, and all Bloom heard was laughter echoing from every direction, crumbling pieces of the ruins to the ground.

She forced herself up and grabbed a detonator. There was nothing she could do against such horrors, but damn it all, Bloom was a warlord. Against every warning her mind offered, she started running towards Sardonyx. Was this honor? It had been a humbling two years. After easily defeating humans in war and her fellow people in the honor grounds, the reality of being insignificant against true power was difficult to accept. "Die, you fuck!"

"No," Sardonyx said, halting her approach with his sword. "This monstrosity took my son. I will force him to behold why strength without honor is chaos." A black fist soared down from above, and Sardonyx didn't bother to dodge. He dropped his sword and caught the fist with both hands, letting out a roar that immediately stopped Death's laughter. After adjusting his grip, Sardonyx *pulled* it forward, revealing the true face of the deity. It wasn't human. It wasn't zephum. Bloom didn't know what the fuck it was.

Sardonyx quickly grabbed his sword and swung at the glowing face; it struck and tore a gaping wound. He swung again, but his attack was caught by Death's second hand.

Death surged forward,. His body was like a snake with wings, with giant arms but tons of tiny little legs. What were those weird looking bugs called? Centipedes? It was like one those things mixed with an angel.

His free hand knocked Sardonyx all the way to the castle ruins, and Death immediately followed up and pinned him into the snow with one hand while pounding him over and over with the other. "*Irrelevant?* You dare call me irrelevant? You have been a god for merely a cycle. I was the second being to ever exist. We were supposed to rule together…but Time banished me to this miserable realm of yours. He said it would change me. Give me a perspective, empathy.

"Time loves you. Time loves all life. Humans, zephum, even

creatures with no sentience. But not me. Never me. I have no purpose. All I can do is destroy. If he will not allow me a piece of his world, I will do everything in my power to ensure this one ceases to exist."

"All this time," Bloom said, cautiously approaching. "Have you learned nothing? Listen, I get it. I've done some vile shit that will haunt me for every remaining day of my life. It's never too late to change. Trust me, Boss." Saying the words to Death was nearly laughable. It didn't seem likely that the giant bug-looking monster was going to suddenly become the God of Hugs and Kisses.

While Death didn't respond, he stopped wailing on Sardonyx, which was progress. He turned his gaze to Bloom, sending her a few steps back. "What are your terms, lizard-woman? Your god is too wounded to speak."

"I…"

"WELL?" The ruins and Bloom shook at the vibration of his voice.

"The Great Plains in the Sky. Tomorrow. Serenna and I will represent the mortals. Tradition, Fear and…you will represent the divine. The Arrogant One will fall. This time, for certain."

Death laughed. A snicker at first, then a near-maddening howl. "Ah, the empress, the warlord, and the ender of realms reunite to destroy the first Harbinger. Know this, mortal. I am intrigued enough to attend but, rest assured, I will settle this my own way if I see fit. There is only one effective way to end a fool's paradise. The nothing, the forever, the end. The nothing, the forever, the end." Death faded, taking the darkness with him. If Bloom ever hated the snow, it looked beautiful now.

"Boss?" she asked, kneeling at Sardonyx's bloody body. Tempest Junior was licking him frantically. "I think we did it, though I'm not sure it was the right choice."

"I forget who said the words, but the only choice is always the correct one. Sounds like a human phrase. You…spoke well. Give me…a moment. I will open a portal to the Great Plains in the Sky. We must prepare…for a variety of guests."

"Sardonyx?"

"Yes?"

"I am honored to be a Child of Tradition."

He grabbed her by the hand. "The honor is all mine. And it is *glorious!*"

"Glorious indeed…"

CHAPTER 26

DIVINE GAMBIT

rancis sighed, looking down at the snoring Mary lingering in their bed. He didn't mind her excessive consumption of wine. By Wisdom's glory, it was easy to relate with the stress of royalty. Uncomfortable was the best way to describe it, or perhaps ominous was more direct. Vaynex had fallen, and scholars would study the event for *thousands* of years. Mylor would soon follow, then Alanammus after a few months. The realm wasn't just changing: it was a complete metamorphosis, like a caterpillar embracing its wings for the first time…

And yet, Terrangus was still Terrangus. Rain pattered outside their window while loud voices yelled despite the unruly hour. If anyone, years ago, had told Francis that Terrangus would be the herald of Serenity, he would've laughed them out of his chambers. The only one who laughed or smiled these days was Calvin. The boy was a heavy sleeper—an enviable trait for anyone living in such a kingdom.

"Emperor, step outside. Quietly."

Francis froze. Was that the first time Wisdom had called him Emperor through his thoughts? There had been an obvious fear in the pitch of his whisper. Was it a Harbinger? Unlikely: his unfortunately named Vanguardians had efficiently displaced the last one. Francis grabbed his staff, smiling at his sleeping family before shutting the doors behind him. May the excitement of having a family never end. He considered asking out loud where to go, but

Wisdom had said *quietly*. Since nothing happened, he continued down the stairs, hoping no one would question his motives. At least he wouldn't have to lie. The best way to avoid spilling the truth is to never know it in the first place.

A mix of Vanguards and the few remaining human guards clearly noticed him, but none took any action. He would never admit it to Mary, but it was a thrill to be the object of someone's fear. All those years dealing with anxiety…it was like he had mastered his own flaws and forged it into a staff—

"Emperor," Zeen said, staring into him with empty eyes. He had always been annoying, but it seemed…something was missing since the transformation. A problem to revisit on less troublesome days. "God has requested our presence. I am to be your escort."

"Requested" was an interesting way to put it. There were no requests when it came to God, but Francis appreciated the show of civility. Two could play that game. "Very well. Then *please* lead the way, Vanguard Ultra."

Zeen gave a wide grin as he led Francis outside into the pouring rain, to an isolated alley behind the castle. In his Vanguard form, it was difficult to tell if those smiles were fake anymore. Hopefully, Serenity had absolved him of his pain, just as it had for Marcus, Nyfe, and Robert. "Forgive me, Francis."

For what? And it's Emperor now, not Francis. Oh—is this another assassination attempt? Would he truly dare? "Choose your next words carefully. I defeated David, Serenna, even Valor herself. What chance do you stand against the Architect of Paradise?"

To his surprise—and honestly, relief—Ultra laughed. "None whatsoever. You misinterpret my intentions. Forgive me for never saying thank you." The lack of enthusiasm gilded the words in lies but… Zeen was serious, wasn't he? "I never understood Serenity until I experienced it. The world is so wonderful, even Nyfe has found enlightenment. I wish… I wish you had won years ago."

"It would be premature to celebrate," Arrogance said from behind, causing Francis to flinch. "The fall of Vaynex has caused unanticipated results. It would seem even Death fears me now.

What a splendid turn of events!" His god laughed, but it was more of a nervous chuckle than amusement.

"A Harbinger then?" asked Francis. "Shall we assemble the Vanguardians? Our new crystal mage lacks experience, but with the others leading the way, that should be irrelevant."

"Ah, irrelevant. What an interesting word that one is. I have seen gods and men broken, abused, shattered, but irrelevant…that is the driving force of madness. What is it about purpose that encourages otherwise rational people to storm heaven? Do you remember my lesson on desperation?"

Francis would never forget. It had been during the happiest days of his life, back when life's most pressing challenge had been maintaining perfect academic scores. "Desperation is not a virtue."

"Indeed. You have been a wonderful student since your dear mother introduced us. Francis, I want you to understand something. I don't often speak from the heart—the mind is the far superior muscle—but you are very dear to me. I will take full credit in my guidance towards…wonderful, wonderful things, but the past year has been harsh. So very harsh. One more victory, my friend. Defeat them one last time, and Serenity is ours."

What should have been a touching moment was poisoned with doubt. "Who is *them*?"

"Everyone. All of them. Death, Fear, Tradition: they despise progress so badly all they can do is pour everything together in one last divine gambit. We may lose this one. But…if I win. If *we* win. That's it. There will be nothing in the entire realm to stand against us. We can finally…finally give our people the joy of Serenity. I have paid such an immeasurable price over a countless number of years. To see it come to fruition is overwhelming. Francis, no matter how the conclusion to our story is written, you have my gratitude for being a colleague. And a friend."

It was too much to take in at once, and the pounding rain only worsened his concentration. If the end was near, there were two questions that needed answers. "If you're truly my friend, I must ask… Did you kill my mother?"

"Indirectly to stay within the rules, but yes. And I would do so again."

"I suppose that deep down, I always knew the answer. Then I only have one further question... How much can a person be damaged before they are considered broken?"

Arrogance chuckled then shifted his sun mask to the stormy skies. "I'll never comprehend why you are so obsessed with this riddle. Damaged and broken are merely perspectives."

"That doesn't answer my question at all."

"But it does. In my eyes, you are incapable of ever being broken. To our enemies, you were shattered long ago. Reflect on tonight and prove them wrong. Goodnight, Emperor." Arrogance vanished, leaving Francis with more questions than answers.

What about Mary? Did she consider him broken? Calvin? Francis sighed, then noticed Ultra was still standing there in the oppressive cold, rain pouring down his drenched hair. "Zeen... would you care to take my coat for the walk back? No need for you to be chilly tonight."

Zeen met his eyes and smiled. "I appreciate the sentiment, but it's entirely unnecessary. Will you promise me something?"

"Perhaps. What is it?"

"When Serenna becomes a Vanguard, will you leave her hair intact? I have always found it quite nice."

Foolish Zeen. If he knew Serenna at all, he would already know she would never accept life as a Vanguard. "Of course, my friend. You have my word." The lie came easy, but the goofy smile on Zeen's face was a reminder that the transition from damaged to broken always lingered.

CHAPTER 27

THE WEIGHT OF CROWNS

avid took a small sip of wine. He had been drinking just enough to avoid migraines for the past few days, or however long it had been. Once a vice loses its pleasure, the only reason to indulge is to defeat the addiction, taking less and less each day. No more shame. No more self-pity. Sardonyx or Fear would rescue him, and they would rescue the battle-ready Guardian of old.

A weird chill breezed against his neck; he glanced back to find an unfamiliar man walking towards him. Who was that? It was a skinny, non-threatening fellow, looking sort of like a senator or one of those people in Alanammus who glanced over paintings then sighed in disappointment. Whoever it was had probably been banished here as a prisoner. Hopefully he wasn't annoying—if David was here with one other person, there were few things less terrifying than being stuck with someone like Francis.

"Greetings, good sir. Is this seat taken?" The voice was strangely familiar, but he couldn't place it.

Never mind. It was him. Of course it was him. "Arrogance?"

He sighed. "Just for today, call me Ermias. What gave it away?"

"You look exactly the way you sound. What brings you here as a human? Come to drink with an old friend?"

"Actually, yes. I have had an awful, *awful* day. Be a gentleman and pour me a glass, Guardian."

It was tempting to smash the chalice into his face or tell him to fuck off, but despite his appearance, the power of a god still lingered. Fortunately, there are other strategies. Kindness to an enemy can be a sharper dagger than any combination of words. "Gladly, but why don't we bring this conversation elsewhere? I could use a change of scenery."

Without the mask, the annoyance on the face of Arrogance was perfectly clear. He probably didn't even realize he was doing it. "Hush, hush. Your only method of escape is over that balcony. It would be most kind if you could do it sooner rather than later. I fear our time together may be coming to a close."

David leaned forward; the bravado gave him an excuse to take a deeper sip than usual. "You're afraid! You're actually afraid! Who is it? Serenna? Bloom? Fear?"

"*All of them!*" Arrogance yelled, slamming his fist on the table. The entire room and all of its inhabitants flickered for a moment before reverting to normal. "As a man who has suffered to the point of seeking his own end: please explain it to me as if I were a child. Why are all my enemies afraid to be happy?"

"You don't even know what happiness is. How could you offer such a gift to anyone? It would be like me offering the realm sobriety."

Arrogance sighed again, sounding eerily similar to Francis. "Our realm is not built upon blocks and stones, but regrets and tragedies. I never understood why you oppose me. Serenna, Zeen, and the lizard-people are all fools. I understand that, but why you? I would've given you Melissa. I would've given you children. I would've given you gifts you don't even know you desire."

There was something pitiful about Arrogance. It was similar to Forsythe and, unfortunately, probably David as well. "Striving for the past is an unattainable goal. If you desire my honest opinion, consider it a blessing that your defeat is imminent. It would be cruel—even for you—to see how flawed your ideals are. There is no paradise. No Serenity. Heavy is the head that wears the crown. I have seen the weight crush greater men than you."

"I tire of hearing about the weight of crowns. There is nothing divine or mortal heavier than a mask. I hide the true Ermias, to the point where I'm unsure who he is anymore. I am God. I am a scholar. I am a destroyer. How can all of those statements hold true? Does perspective supersede divinity?"

"Indeed it does," David said, taking a large swig. There was no need to slow down his drinking. He could always taper off again tomorrow. "I think every man is a combination of his best and worst perspective. I am Melissa's mountain and…and I am that man in the mirror." All his confidence faded as he glanced at himself. His bloodshot eyes and sunken face had aged him decades in however long it had actually been. "I suppose…that is our greatest difference. I see nothing but my own flaws, while you see yourself as perfection personified."

Arrogance took his own sip of wine. "Self-loathing is a pitiful trait. No man who strives to change the realm can ever afford such depravity. There are so many mortals and gods who despise me; I have little time to despise myself. True progress always comes with opposition."

"Oh, spare me. Melissa loved me, and nothing you do could ever change that. Stop making freewill your scapegoat and do some introspection. Noelami doesn't just dislike you, or find you appalling: she hates you. *Hates* you with every fiber of her being. Whether you win, lose, or just fucking fly away into the sky, nothing—and I mean nothing—will ever change that. The only reason you don't hate yourself is because delusion is the cornerstone of happiness—"

David wasn't prepared for a fist to crash into his mouth. He hadn't felt physical pain in so long that he nearly screamed, despite intoxication numbing most of the blow. It was a quick yet ugly fall from his barstool. Whenever his face stopped throbbing, the rest of his body would soon follow. Despite the pain, all he could do was laugh. "Did I strike a nerve? Delusion is the cornerstone of happiness…"

Arrogance mounted him and swung down, crashing into David's nose. Blood flowed and the laughter stopped. "Don't let this body fool you. I could break your spine with the snap of my fingers. Know your place, mortal."

"Then do it," David forced out. "Kill me, break the rules, and we can die together. The realm would rejoice in our end. Do it…" What a fitting end it would be to save the realm by being pure garbage. Even more so by fulfilling Arrogance's scheme of a self-inflicted end.

Arrogance must have had a moment of clarity. He let go of David and rose. "Well played, Guardian. Your misery is infectious. There is no reason to behave this way. I still hold Vaynex, Nuum, and Terrangus. Mylor and Alanammus will never cooperate. Yes. Oh yes, a simple overreaction. The concept of Tradition, Fear, and Death overcoming their differences is pure nonsense. Fools tend to defeat themselves. I can simply wait for the absurdity of freewill to do what it does best."

The opportunity was lost. David took a deep breath and leaned up against the bar, wiping the blood off his face. "The Time God named you appropriately. Though in your case it's a merciful attribute. I would pity you, but you lack the awareness to see how doomed you truly are."

"It's a fine line between bold and arrogant. Only one of us in this dream is doomed. Take a good look at the mirror, the balcony, then reassess which one of us that is. If your answer remains the same…well, perhaps I'm not the most arrogant being in the room."

"Fair enough, but take this warning from one who knows all too well: whenever you finally fall, it's a long way down, Ermias."

"Then perhaps I'll see you at the bottom." Arrogance refilled a chalice and leaned down to push it into David's face. "Drink this. It will numb the pain that is yet to come."

So he did. David drank the wine quickly enough to drown out his inner self screaming at him to stop as Arrogance faded from the room. He *would* stop eventually.

Just not today.

CHAPTER 28

MOMENTS THAT DEFINE FOREVER

y Valor's grace, sunlight finally entered through Serenna's window. Sleep had evaded her the entire evening, and now she had an excuse to rise and move about. Her royal guest chambers in Alanammus were a mockery to the true state of reality, a reminder that the entire realm could be on fire and some people would just close the door and count their silver. A change of clothes would've been nice, but Serenna hadn't packed for the trip. And she *definitely* hadn't packed for a summit of the gods, if that was still in the works.

With staff in hand, she stepped outside, startled at the cluster of carefree people strolling about, sipping tea and eating bread. Was this how it had been when Terrangus laid siege to Mylor? Serenna and her people fighting to their dying breath while the archon and company drank tea? It was absurd…and *infuriating* how well isolationism had rewarded Alanammus. If she was successful against Arrogance, change would come—

"Ah, there you are!" a familiar man said. The gold cloak from yesterday, what was his name…

"Kolsen?"

"Good guess," he said with a grin. "Pardon me for skipping the pleasantries but the archon requires you immediately. Don't give me that look! I'll bring tea. Our reserves are dwindling, but I can spare the good stuff for you."

Serenna wasn't sure what look he was referring to, but being cheerful in the morning was never her strong point. "Very well, Gold Cloak. Wait for me by the door."

"Afraid not. I have strict orders not to leave you alone with these people."

She raised an eyebrow. "Are you suggesting they pose a threat to *me*?"

"Quite the opposite, my friend. Your hands have nearly lost color from how hard you are gripping your staff. Listen, I get it. My family came from nothing, and I would likely still be there if we hadn't suffered such catastrophic losses from the wedding. None of these people understand and yet, they're the ones who order me around. Anger is a natural response."

She loosened her grip. Now that he mentioned it, her hands were rather sore. "Nothing ever changes. They're so naive and carefree. I'm shocked they haven't allied themselves with Arrogance."

The happy expression on Kolsen's face vanished. For a moment, he looked like a true soldier. "Fear would never allow that, would she?"

Interesting. "I let the gods speak for themselves, especially that one. On second thought, some tea would be pleasant. Farewell... soldier." In hindsight, it wasn't much of a surprise. An empress would know which roles require puppets.

The only thing more annoying than the diamonds and silver chalices was the way people stopped their conversation as Serenna walked by. It was tempting to berate them, to drag them by their shiny coats back to Mylor and force them to watch one day of violence in the bastion. It was *just* tempting enough to stop and say, "Have any of you left this tower in the past year? Do you have any idea of the amount of suffering the realm goes through on a daily basis? My only saving grace is knowing that if Arrogance prevails, you'll suffer through his Serenity with the rest of us. I doubt even *he* could find a use for the lot of you—"

"*Enough*," a stern voice yelled, echoing through the hallways. All of the nobles put their heads down and scurried away like insects. "Leave intimidation to those who weave shadows and nightmares into dreams. Enter my chambers. Now."

Apparently, Fear's secret identity wasn't very secret. Serenna took a deep breath and approached the chamber doors. Goddess or not, the idea of her being able to read Serenna's fear was frustrating. Trying to block out the feeling only made it more apparent. In an attempt to look brave, she forced open the doors, not flinching as they crashed into the walls. Her bravado vanished as she found Fear in her goddess form, standing above a woman sitting on the throne. "What sorcery is this?"

"The sorcery of gods," the mortal woman said. She smiled and leaned back. "This kingdom has always been ruled by lies. Fortunately, I found the best liar to help me rule properly."

"I see," Serenna said, maintaining eye contact with the woman on the throne, forcing herself not to stare into Fear. "But why the ruse? All of the nobles already know you're collaborating with Fear. Even the gold cloaks."

"You would be surprised how many kingdoms are held together by ploys and terror," Fear said. "Enough. Forced bravery only makes the fear seep through your skin. Stop this show of pride and let go. Ask me why I called you here."

One of the advantages of anger is that it tends to smother other feelings. "Fear, Noelami, Goddess, whatever you wished to be called these days. Get to the point."

Fear gave a small grin. "You were always my favorite. Even when you nearly killed me. Listen carefully: while on the surface things are well, I have a tendency to observe every angle from the worst case. Sardonyx somehow got Death to agree to a summit. We meet tonight in the Great Plains in the Sky."

"Isn't that the desired result? Why do *you*, of all people, look nervous?"

"I answer your question with a question. Take a fair guess at how many years I have lived."

"Well, if the fall of Boulom was three hundred years ago, that would mean—"

Fear raised a hand to silence her. "There are moments that define centuries, and there are moments that define forever. This," she said, slamming her fist on the glass table, "this is it! Nothing in history has prepared us for such a moment. We enter an age of freedom, or an age of misery."

Something about the tone of Fear's voice made Serenna part the hair from her eyes. "But…with every god on our side, how could we possibly lose?"

Fear sighed, rubbing her hands down her face. "Foolish, foolish girl. The worst defeats I have ever witnessed started off as guaranteed victories. Never forget how confident you were strolling into Serenity. Hate Gabriel if you must, but his backup plan is the only reason you are still here. There is no fallback if we lose this one. Our fates are interwoven with Sardonyx and the Ender of Realms. If that doesn't terrify you…then you are the bravest soul I have beheld in three hundred years. But from what your essence suggests, that isn't remotely true, is it?"

She would've preferred lies. If Fear herself was hesitant, the odds were much worse than expected. The irony of being overconfident against Arrogance was not lost on her. "I agree with your assessment. I suppose instead of rushing towards the end, we should anticipate how tonight's summit will go. I trust Sardonyx with my life, but what about Death? If the deity betrays us, are we capable of defending ourselves?"

"In the event of any combat, absolutely refrain from including yourself. Gods can only slay mortals within the planes of existence if they are attacked first. Sardonyx is too new at being divine; it is near impossible that he comprehends just how powerful he is yet. I don't know if I could defeat Death alone. What I do know is that he doesn't know either. I doubt he will try unless negotiations go catastrophically."

All her anxiety now seemed warranted. To hear the actual plan in motion only highlighted the absurdity of it. "Is Death…even afraid to die?"

It was startling how loud Fear laughed at the question. "Believe me, Guardian, no one fears the end more than those who deliver it. There are no Great Plains in the Sky for us. When we fade, we fade entirely. The thought often hovers between peace and horror."

Oh, Valor. Serenna broke eye contact and sat down, allowing her body to rest against the soft cushion of her chair. "I never had a chance to say goodbye. Her dying words... She forgave me."

"It's more than you deserve. Don't take that the wrong way. I didn't deserve forgiveness from Strength either, but not a twilight ends where I don't yearn for it. The best course of action now is to ensure their sacrifice was not in vain. Listen, girl. The loss of Boulom was the greatest tragedy of my existence. Vengeance and regret have taken me far enough to see this through, but I cannot lose everything again. I will gladly die before that happens."

Fear sighed, losing her cocky grin and staring not at Serenna, but through her. "Tell me, did Valor have a mantra? For better or for worse, her service as a goddess was rather short. From what I observed, most of that time was spent berating you."

"I never thought to ask. She was less of a mantra and more of a protocol goddess. Everything was, 'Foolishness is not the protocol of Valor! Victory is the protocol of Valor! Dallying is not the protocol of Valor!'" If only the angry Serenna from last year could see herself smile now. "She called me a harlot to my face. I've never... I mean the audacity!"

A few uncomfortable moments of silence passed as they sat there, reminiscing about days long gone. Fear finally said, "Victory is the protocol of Valor. It's not the most creative mantra, but we can carry it into battle. It still beats Sardonyx. He just continues to yell Strength's mantra. I expect no less, but honoring the past is no excuse not to improve the future."

"Fair, but at least he ensures not to make it worse."

It never looked natural when Fear smiled. "We won't know for sure until tonight."

CHAPTER 29

GUARDIANS AND GODS ALIKE

 brutal headache had kept Mary away from her wine all morning but, finally, her body had finished flushing out the poisons, which meant it was time for more. Why did everyone around her seem so stressed today? Anxiety had always been a part of Francis's identity, but even the Vanguards were fidgety. Well, if 'God' wanted her to know, he could take a minute out of his day and say something. Mary reached for her wine—

"*Not yet, my dear empress,*" Arrogance whispered through her thoughts. "*I need you in top form today. I realize that means I would need the Mary from two years ago, but I'll manage. Meet me in the throne room.*"

There was a temptation to ignore him and drink away, but it put Calvin at too great a risk. It was no secret that Arrogance was a monster. Fortunately, he did seem to favor the boy, which was likely due to needing him in the future. Mary's own usefulness was swiftly on the decline. "Zeen," she said, refusing to ever call him Ultra. "Bring Calvin to the healing ward for the evening. *You know who* needs me and I have no idea if or when I'll be back. Even if you're a Vanguard, you're the only one I trust with my son. Please don't let me down."

"As you command, Empress," Zeen said with a bow. He gently picked up Calvin and matched his smile. For a just moment, he looked like the overly happy idiot she always remembered him as. His transformation had been a cruel fate, a destruction of something innocent into another monster. Judging by the way he made Calvin laugh, in a better realm, he would've made a great father. "Um…good luck tonight, Mary."

"If I don't return, please raise him to be like you." She rushed out of her chambers and down the stairs before Zeen could respond with some generic Vanguard phrase. She couldn't listen to it. Even Nyfe had been impossible to converse with; just once, she would love to hear him threaten her life again or act like an asshole.

It was alarming that she could hear Francis yelling before she reached the bottom. He didn't often raise his voice unless he was truly nervous. She eased open the door to the throne room and said, "Hello? Should I be insulted that you started the meeting without me?"

"Explain to him!" Francis yelled, rushing towards Mary and pointing at Arrogance. Perhaps alarming had not been the correct word. For Francis to yell at his favorite god, he must have been absolutely distraught. "Tell him you won't do it. I will not allow this… I cannot!"

It had been a while since she had to console Francis and not the other way around. While a day without wine had been a disappointment, a clear head was clearly required. "Slow down, my beloved. Slow down, take a deep breath, and tell me everything. From the beginning." She ignored the chuckles from Arrogance and maintained eye contact with her husband. By the gods, he shook in her arms.

"I, I, I…"

"Allow me," Arrogance said, floating over towards them. "Hypothetically speaking, what would you say if I told you there was a congregation of the gods this evening, and that the best one did not receive an invitation?"

Take a deep breath and focus. Francis needs you. Calvin needs you. "If this leads to another puppeteer story, I'm drinking all the wine in Terrangus and heading back to bed."

"Oh, Empress, you *are* going somewhere, but not bed. Not yet, at least."

"Tell him no!" Francis yelled. He gripped her arm with a surprising amount of strength. Since it was unlikely Francis had become stronger, the more unfortunate alternative of Mary's decline was apparent.

Mary shrugged at Arrogance. "But why? I doubt you trust me enough to negotiate any sort of terms." A moment passed as she considered the alternative. "Fuck, you want me to die, don't you?"

"Heavens no!" Arrogance said. "How I wish you were more intelligent. Allow me to make this perfectly clear to both of you. This is not a threat, but merely a declaration of truth: if at any point I desire your end, your end will occur. Scheming is for the manipulation of realms, not smashing insects. Now, stop disappointing your professor and take another guess."

He sounded just annoyed enough for Mary to believe it was true. But what alternatives were there? Francis couldn't go. Vanguards would be killed on sight. Mary would... Ah. "I'm the only one they won't kill immediately."

Arrogance chuckled, floating down the stairs. "Close enough. You've solved about eighty percent of the equation. I'll leave you to find the remaining twenty."

I already have. You don't care if I die. There was no reason to say it out loud. Not with Francis already distraught. "Before I accept, what exactly do you need me to do? If I stroll into Sky Vaynex or whatever it is and make demands, I wager I'll never see my favorite god again."

"Simply do what you do best these days: nod drunkenly while other people speak." Arrogance raised his spectral hand and a chalice of wine appeared. She swore she could smell the berries. "Despite common knowledge, warriors always make the best spies. The preconception they are all fools lets them steal from the minds of those who think they know better. Listen, and when it's time to speak, encourage their attack."

Encourage their attack? Even Arrogance must have known the combined might of all their remaining enemies would lead to a swift defeat. "Have you grown tired of my kingdom? I'll do as you ask, but I fear I'm only hastening the collapse of Serenity."

Arrogance chuckled. "Hastening! What an interesting word that one is. Doubt me if you must, but if I have learned anything in three hundred years, it's that putting faith in the absurdity of freewill is a surefire way to invite defeat. Let them come. I hope there is an existence after divinity, a plane where Strength and Valor can welcome their ignorant comrades with open arms."

"Whatever. May I please have my wine?" asked Mary, taking a step forward. The whole thing seemed like a trick. Arrogance probably wanted her to push for the invasion, just so the alliance would think it's a trick and not attack. But maybe he knew that? Maybe he anticipated her anticipation and sent her with a doomed task? Whew, enough of that. She grabbed the chalice from his spectral hand and took a large swig. It was delicious, of course. Liars always brew the best wine.

"Ask and you shall receive. Funny, I thought it would take more convincing. Should I find it *strange* that you willingly walk into the garden of freewill?"

She took another sip. "Why would following God's orders be strange?"

"Are you certain?" asked Francis. "I would never doubt your mind or body, but to surround yourself with those who wish us dead... Is that truly wise?"

Not only was it unwise, but it was certainly one of the dumbest decisions she would ever make. "Most of them want me dead, but I doubt Sardonyx will allow it. Murdering an unarmed mother wouldn't be very glorious."

"Glorious indeed," Arrogance said.

Francis groaned and stepped away. It looked like he was trying to compose himself but couldn't quite manage the look. "If any harm comes to my wife, I will burn every kingdom to the ground. Serenity will be on hold until my policy of scorched earth is complete. Am I clear?"

"Your voice has never been more clear, Emperor," Arrogance said, floating forward. "But remove such thoughts from your mind. I am a pragmatic god, not a degenerate gambler. Our dear Mary will return to us. I guarantee it."

"F… *Fine!*" Francis yelled. It nearly melted her heart to see him so distressed. "Before you go, I'll answer my own damned question. How much can a person be damaged before they are considered broken? I am held together by the love of my wife and our son. Mary, beloved, please return to me. There is nothing we cannot accomplish together. All of these moments are mere footnotes in our own little Serenity."

Unable to find the words, Mary kissed him, then stared at Arrogance. "When do I go?"

"Funny you should ask," Arrogance said, raising both hands, then creating a portal. "How about…immediately? I usually prefer fashionably late, but this is one of those rare moments where it pays to be early."

"So be it," Mary said. She resisted the urge to look back at her husband, and stepped into the portal.

*

Travel by portals was usually jarring, but there was a calmness in the air that made everything okay. She nearly gasped at the familiarity of the wind brushing against her cheek, the bright green blades of grass coming up to her knees, and…it was him. Sardonyx Claw, Warlord of Vaynex, with a unicorn on one side and a zephum she had never met before—most likely Bloom—on the other.

"Mary Walker!" he yelled, noticeably not using her new last name. "Come forth! Let me look upon you!"

"Were you expecting me?" she asked, slowly stepping forward. It was surreal to see him in person again. The other gods all had ridiculous personas, but Sardonyx was simply Sardonyx.

"You are an unexpected surprise, but a surprise most welcome. Ah, look at you… You wear a mother's fatigue! It is *glorious!*"

She wasn't sure what that meant, but the words were spoken with such warmth, she couldn't help but hug him. "Now that you mention it, old friend, I am tired. Very, very tired."

"We all are, Guardian. Unfortunately, the next rest for some of us may end up our last."

"Um, Boss, isn't she the enemy? I know you can't kill her, but do you want me to do it? We may want to get that done before the others arrive."

"Silence!" he yelled, which caused his unicorn to rush off into the plains beyond. "This human and I have a glorious history. She once struck me in the face with her shield. Speaking of, where is your shield?"

"I haven't held it in months," she said, before the urge to lie pulled through. By all measures, the shield in her chambers was denser and more colorful, but the honor was missing. "Strength himself blessed that shield and, well, yeah. I don't feel worthy anymore. Too much has changed in too short a time."

"While we should always remain our own harshest critic, the view must be balanced with honor. Look at me, old friend. Do you truly believe I am worthy to become a god?"

"I—"

"Before you respond, remember the zephum tyrant you pledged a fair amount of time to destroying to avenge your father. I am still that zephum, but I am a zephum wearing the armor of experience. Here in the Great Plains in the Sky, we are all worthy, or none of us are."

"Sardonyx, is there a way out of this without violence? Arrogance wants me to goad you into a full-on attack. I doubt we can stop you, but after the wedding, anything is possible."

"Without violence?" Bloom yelled. "Tell that to fucking Vaynex. Violence is coming, Empress. I won't do it here out of respect for Sardonyx, but by Tradition's name, I'll kill you and your son with one detonator."

Perhaps it was foolish, but Mary walked right in front of Bloom. "Keep your grievances with me and my husband. Speak of my son again at your own risk."

Yep, it was foolish. Bloom stepped forward and gave her a slight push, which nearly sent her flying. "Calvin Haide, emperor in waiting, son of a human bitch. I will nail his body to the citadel walls once you and the Arrogant One are dead." She sighed and stepped away. "What are you even doing here? You're supposed to be some human engager of legend, a warrior blessed by the mighty Pyith herself, and I get this skinny woman in a dress? Fuck off and go home. Lay with your husband a few more times before we burn Terrangus to the ground. Maybe get started on a new kid before I butcher—"

"*Enough*," Sardonyx said. His voice wasn't particularly loud but it shook the entire plains. "Regardless of circumstance, I will not tolerate threats against children. Not here, not in Vaynex, not *anywhere*. Am I clear—"

A new portal erupted behind them. Serenna emerged first, followed by a nightmare of a woman who could only be Fear. Mary had heard the tales but to see her in person was staggering. Fear wore the look of a true empress, with burning wings of black energy sprouting from her shoulders and a crystal in her eye that shone so brilliantly, it made the plains appear darker.

Fear surveyed the plains. She tried to hide it but the torment on her face was more clear than the sun burning above them. "We are truly in the end of times if the zephum arrived early. What... What is *she* doing here?" asked Fear, staring into Mary.

As startling as Fear's voice was, it was nothing compared to Serenna rushing over and grabbing her. Damn, she was strong for a shorter woman. It was obvious which leader had been lounging around with wine and which had spent the past few months fighting for her life. "Where is my Zeen? You had the audacity to come here without him? You will never leave these plains alive. *Never!*"

Thankfully, Fear said, "Stop embarrassing me, Guardian. It's obvious that Ermias wants us to kill her. If you can't control your emotions, then go back to Alanammus and let the adults speak. Never alter a dominant strategy."

"What about you?" asked Mary. She pushed Serenna away and clenched her fists. "You crashed my wedding in some insane attempt to destroy the most powerful god in the realm. Zeen isn't here because you threw him away."

"Enough!" Fear and Tradition said at the same time. They gave each other a quick glance—Sardonyx grinned but Fear looked away.

But, it wasn't enough. Serenna was out of her damn mind if she thought Mary would back down. "Everything was just fine until you and Valor decided to open the floodgates. Arrogance was never in a position to assault the realm. Your stupidity destroyed the Guardian force and most of the gold cloaks. All you had to do was nothing, but no, Serenna the Pact Breaker had to fuck everything up. Well, great job. Do you have any idea what it's like living under his rule? I drink every single night and day hoping that I won't wake up to see another one. But it comes. Tomorrow always comes for those who don't want it."

Serenna grabbed the Wings of Mylor from behind her back. She stared into Mary as if she was a monster. Sadly, she probably was. "Spare me your pitiful excuses. I acted because evil was growing within your home. To ignore evil is to enable it, and I will *never* enable evil again." The rage in her eyes descended into concern as the plains grew colder. Whatever it was, it certainly wasn't the breeze.

"Serenna... Serenna, Serenna," Death said. He was a black cloud in the skies, with a voice that echoed across the open plains. Despite his appearance, it was interesting the deity kept a safe distance. "When all the gods fail and all the gods fall, your destiny will always be linked to me." The red eyes within the cloud looked around. "It is...surreal to have existed thousands of years and to see something for the first time. I can only wonder how many mortals I have sent to this plane. May they all think of me one last time before the void consumes them."

"Guardians and gods alike, welcome to my home," Sardonyx said. Despite the potential chaos, she had never seen the zephum more calm. "There are obviously several...issues with this summit. I ask for respect, cordiality, and restraint. If anyone violates these terms, they will regret their dishonorable mishap. For any grievances, speak them now, or forever hold your silence."

Death laughed. "The only forever is the nothing and the end."

"Perhaps I was not clear!" Sardonyx said, drawing his sword. "We are here to defeat the Arrogant One. As gods, it is only natural to be filled with pride, but never forget that pride is the sword of our enemy. Death! Fear! All I can do is request your cooperation. Before I waste words, I demand confirmation: can we coexist in the face of irrelevancy?"

It was alarming that no one responded.

CHAPTER 30

DIVERSION

For all of Serenna's anger towards Mary, it was harrowing to look upon the black clouds of Death and face a reminder of her true nemesis. "Death, for as long as I recall, you have been my greatest enemy," she said out loud, if only to break the silence. "Yet, our feud is nothing compared to Arrogance and the pantheon of gods. Let it be known that I pledge my cooperation. We shall destroy him together. I know how badly you yearn to send one of your own to the void."

"He is not of my own," Death yelled, rumbling the plains. Perhaps that last line had not been wise. "*None* of you are. I came here to speak, not listen, and speak I shall. Serenna: say my words, the words you know all too well. While it hasn't been long enough since Gabriel to give you my full power, you don't require it to do my bidding. I've seen the ecstasy of destruction in your eyes. The yearning to drown the Time God's children, the—"

"No," Sardonyx said. "We shall find another path. For as long as I live, you will never have her."

"Oh, lizard beast, that may not be much longer. Have you already forgotten the result of our last skirmish? Draw your blade and face me again. This time, I can reunite you with your fallen son."

Fear erupted with void energy; she floated into the air and materialized a glowing blade in her right hand. "Give me reason,

Death. We can kill Ermias, or we can simply kill you. I'm fine with either scenario."

Serenna nearly jumped as Mary grabbed her by the shoulder. "Do something! If this leads to a free-for-all, the realm is lost! Arrogance *cannot* win!" There was genuine terror on Mary's face, accentuated by the puffy cheeks she used to see on David.

"Do you truly desire that result? Mary, if you lose…"

Tears rolled down her cheeks as she said, "I know. I've known since the day I became a mother. Just don't harm my son. Despite his parents, I swear to you he is innocent. He is too perfect to have come from me. He is too perfect for anything."

"All children are innocent," Serenna said. What an awkward scenario. Unsure of what to do, she pulled Mary in and hugged her. "I know what it is to be flawed. I still love you. He will never become emperor, but no harm will come to Calvin. I will raise him as if he were my own son." It was far too late to wonder if the words were true. Zeen would surely agree…if he made it out alive.

Serenna clutched the Wings of Mylor and entered her empowered form. While it stopped the bickering, it had the unfortunate effect of drawing every god's gaze to her. *Let them watch.* She shielded herself, Fear, and Sardonyx, then created a giant crystal spike and hovered it in the air. "While I wager we cannot win without you, Death, I also wager you cannot win without us. Stop this reprehensible display of ignorance and forge an alliance. Victory shall be the protocol of Valor."

With a quick swipe, Fear shattered her own crystal shield. She glared at every mortal and god but eventually sheathed her blade. "So be it. Where reality fails, dreams are eternal."

Sardonyx let out a mighty guffaw. He slammed his blade into the ground. His unicorn reared and neighed gloriously. "Strength without honor—is *CHAOS!*"

Death didn't appear to be impressed, though it was near impossible to gauge any sort of emotions through those glowing eyes. The dark cloud that covered whatever his body was expanded throughout the plains. "I agree to *nothing* before there is a plan in motion, and here is mine: I propose we turn Serenna into my Harbinger and unleash her upon Terrangus. If you have an alternative, speak it now. I tire of listening to the lesser gods yell out broken promises."

One of you better speak, Serenna thought, having no intentions of ever accepting that power again. "Saving" a realm by burning it to the ground was worse than living under Arrogance.

"It's only been a few months since the wedding," said Fear. "How much power could you offer a Harbinger if you did it tomorrow?"

A deep rumble that resembled a groan came from within the clouds. "If you seek to mock my power, I can ensure none of us leave this plane alive. I observed the Guardian team of Arrogance defeat your servant. Unless I allow my wrath to fully return, any Harbinger will suffer the same fate."

"Diversion," Serenna said as soon as the thought came to her. "Xavian and possibly Nuum are loyal to him. If your Harbinger attacks Xavian, it will force him to divert several of his Vanguards to defend his position."

Both of Mary's hands shook as she stepped forward. "From a tactical standpoint, the plan is sound, but I suspect Arrogance will simply allow Xavian to fall. We are nothing but puppets to him—"

"How fitting," Death yelled. His cloud expanded enough to surround all of them. "Our enemy finds flaws in the plan of their annihilation. I like it. No, I *love* it. Either way, it's a victory for me." As the cloud pressed forward, the glowing red eyes were fixated on Mary. "Eventually, mortals playing god always run out of people to sacrifice. Hide in your rainy grave for as long as I allow, but eventually, you will face the nothing, the forever, and the end. The nothing, the forever, and the end." Death's laugh echoed throughout the plains as the god faded away.

What have I done? Serenna thought, taking deep breaths to calm her beating heart. To unleash a Harbinger against anyone was horrific, but what was the alternative? She should have chosen her words more carefully, or just let the gods do the planning. Every decision, every choice, had always seemed to make the realm worse off.

"I must leave," Mary said. "Portal... Someone portal me back home. I must get back home. Now. Someone, any of you."

"At ease, Empress," Sardonyx said. What a sad state of affairs that the fallen warlord had become the voice of reason. "Unfortunately, this places a mighty weight upon your shoulders. Can you convince the Arrogant One to send his Guardian force to defend Xavian? I cannot allow the destruction of any kingdom. It would truly be strength without honor."

"No!" she yelled. "I can't! No one can! None of you understand him. He is an absolute monster who will sacrifice anything to remold the realm in his own image. We're the villains in his eyes. The harder we press, the worse he will become."

Fear sighed, staring down into the grassy plains. "There is not a soul in the realm who knows him better than I. Your doubts are logical, but they are in vain. Ermias will defend Xavian. Not out of empathy, but pride. You have my word, and I care not if you believe me."

"This is madness," Mary said. "Fine. Then I suppose we're done here. Everyone knows the deranged god ruining my life better than I do apparently. I will do my part, though I make no promises. Send me home."

"From one empress to another, farewell," Fear said. She raised her blade to create a portal, then Mary rushed through without bothering to say goodbye.

"There is one more topic to discuss," Sardonyx said, sheathing his sword. "I had to wait until Mary and the Ender of Realms were gone."

Serenna parted the hair from her eyes. "She may be our enemy, but there is good within Mary. I trust her."

"Sorry, Boss, I can't agree with you on that one. She's a soldier, and soldiers have a tendency to survive, despite whatever is happening around them."

"Then what—"

"Before the assault," Sardonyx said, "David must be freed from his punishment. He is tormented within a prison of lies, and I cannot claim to be honorable until such...*evil* is abolished. Forgive me for being blunt, but this is not up for debate. David shall be free, and David shall be free *immediately* after this summit."

"Agreed," said Fear. A genuine smile filled her face. "Guardians, you did well tonight. If we were in the days of Boulom, I would make you my personal advisors. But we're not. And we never will be. Bloom, work with my puppet-archon in Alanammus to assemble the armies. Serenna, it is your burden to ensure Mylor does the same."

CHAPTER 31

KINGDOM OF ASHES

How the fuck am I supposed to do this? Bloom thought, reemerging within the Alanammus Guardian room.

All the humans in their hulky armor gasped, pointed, and a few of them even grabbed their polearms. The biggest one yelled, "Hold! Hold, dammit! We have orders!" before anyone did something stupid. "Warlord, please accompany me to the archon's chambers. She is expecting you."

"Sure thing, Boss. Lead the way." What a fucking trip this place was after seeing Mylor. Diamonds, chalices, and gluttony was everywhere as they traveled through the halls. Worst of all, the humans in robes kept staring at her. Not a glance, which would be rude enough, but a stare. Such audacity would be a death sentence in Vaynex...but there was no Vaynex anymore. Partly because these humans sat here and did nothing. She met eyes with one of them from across the hall. That was his cue to look away, but he just kept fucking staring. "What is it? See something you like?"

Bloom's escort chuckled as the humans ran away. "Don't take it the wrong way. Most of them have never seen a zephum in person, let alone a warlord."

"Is it true that Sardonyx came here once? I can't imagine him walking through this dump without leaving a trail of bodies."

"Yes! He was escorted by my old captain, Julius Cavare. I wasn't there to see it but, apparently, some child grabbed his tail in the middle of the courtyard."

"My condolences to that one. Child or not, touching the tail is probably the quickest way to get cut in half."

This human must have had an odd sense of humor, because something about that statement made him laugh out loud. "Warlords always make it interesting. How was Serenna at the summit? I enjoy your company, but part of me wished she would come back."

"Well, she's not. You're stuck with me so you may as well get used to it. Maybe if you cowards had bothered to aid Mylor or Vaynex, you could ask her yourself."

Her escort stopped laughing, looked down and took a deep breath. "That's fair. If it means anything, it wasn't the gold cloaks' decision to stay idle. We wanted to battle alongside—"

"Doesn't mean a thing to me, so shove it. I don't understand this place. *You* hold the armor. *You* hold the blades. You hold all the fucking power. The only reason you stood by and did nothing is because some coward with a crown gave you an excuse not to."

"It's not that simple..."

"Sorry, Boss, it is and it always has been. Are we almost there? You're starting to piss me off, and I don't want to walk into this meeting more angry than I need to be."

He answered by pointing to a large door. Out of all the unnecessary luxuries, the diamonds pounded into the structure were the most obnoxious. How did they even get them in there? "I hope you can forgive me for being a disappointment."

"Well, I hope you can forgive me for what you'll be doing tomorrow." Good, let him raise his eyebrow. Most of these humans were going to be useless. It was fortunate that Fear seemed like a fellow psycho; the obvious strategy would be to throw them straight into the enemy while the real soldiers from Mylor engaged. Bloom pushed open the door and sat at her end of the table. No bows. Never bow to humans.

The archon smiled from her throne. "Welcome to Alanammus, Warlord Bloom. Please accept my gratitude for not slaying any humans on the way here."

"No need for that when most of them will die soon." She studied the archon's face to see if she already knew about the upcoming battle, but by Tradition's name, it was impossible to get any intel from her eyes or nose. If only she had a snout.

"Indeed. It's to our advantage that they already fear you. If my goddess has taught me anything, it's the value of fear and how to use it accordingly. Not that you need it, but you have my permission to put down any soldiers who question your authority. There will certainly be at least one, but after a few heads come off, I imagine loyalty will soon follow."

Hopefully this human couldn't read facial expressions because Bloom had *What the fuck did she just say?* written all over her face. "Listen, Archon. I've only just got here and I'm exhausted. If you know more than I do, just fucking say it. I don't do the whole cloak-and-dagger thing. Speak plainly or prepare to clean human blood off your diamond walls."

Her legs were still crossed, which was annoying, but at least she stopped smiling. "Apologies, Warlord. I thought you already knew. It's never been in my best interests to antagonize a zephum with a...reputation for dealing with such things rather harshly. Tomorrow, we begin our march on Terrangus. For better or for worse, Fear has declared that *you* are to lead my armies."

Of fucking course. Leave it to the zephum to do everything, even after the loss of Vaynex. "Why not you?"

"The public reason is that you have far greater battle experience than me, and have a personal vendetta against Terrangus and Arrogance in particular. The true reason? Well, let me put it this way. There are only two possible scenarios with this assault. We win, or everyone loses. *Everyone.*"

"I don't follow. Does that mean—"

"What happens when reality fails?"

Ugh, these humans and their riddles. Bloom rose and slammed her fist on the table. "*Speak plainly!* If I'm going to lead this thing, I need to understand every detail."

"Forgive me, I have played the game of politics so long I forget some people manage to rise without treachery and deceit. Alanammus will never exist under the rule of Arrogance. His short time in this kingdom poisoned us *forever*. Consider me a Harbinger in waiting. Arrogance shall fall, or he shall rule over a kingdom of ashes."

Bloom sat down and leaned back. Human leaders were always so…dramatic. "Such is the mortality of humans, I suppose. Alright, I'll do it, but you must promise me something."

"Name it."

"If I end up under the sand, burn Vaynex to the ground. Kill my people. Kill every last one of them. If that command is my final one as warlord, it's a command I'll wear proudly within the Great Plains in the Sky."

"So you do understand. Your demand shall be met, but unfortunately, I meet your demand with one of my own. Before I ask, do you prefer wine or zephum ale?"

"If it's human wine you can fuck off with that. Give me zephum ale. And it better be true zephum ale and not that swill they brew in Nuum. Trust me, I can tell."

The archon snickered as she rose. She took two bottles from a desk behind her, one red, one black. "Straight from Vaynex herself, a gift from the noble Tempest Claw. I would not lie about such things. For an archon's lies to hold value, said lies must be diluted with truth, regardless of how often or why they occur. Predictability is the death of democracy."

Oh, the burn. Yep, this was pure zephum ale. Tempest had always hated the stuff; he probably gave it to one of the talk-in-riddles humans as some sort of joke. "Whatever you say, Boss. Well, I suppose it's best to get started. I was going to say hopefully we'll never meet again, but the ramifications of that outcome would really suck. Just…if it comes down to it, kill them. Tradition and I will be watching from the plains. Maybe I don't scare you, but I'm sure you could do without a flying unicorn crashing through the walls." With a large gulp, Bloom finished her ale and wiped her snout. She got up and left the room, while the archon kept talking. No point in listening—the time for words had ended.

"That was quick," her escort from earlier said. He looked more confused than alarmed, so to his credit, he probably hadn't spied on them. "Are you heading home?"

Home? *Home?* What a fucking fool. "What's your name, Gold Cloak?"

"Kolsen will do. My last name from my mother's side is—"

"You better be a good soldier because, so far, you're a fucking idiot. Gather whatever men we have and assemble them...wherever the assembling is done."

"*We* have?"

"Good, you're learning. I don't know how it works with gold cloaks, but warlords don't ask twice."

"But—"

"*Go!*"

*

For all the nonsense in Alanammus, at least they took their military seriously. No diamonds or luxury here. It was eerily similar to Vaynex: stacks of barracks clumped together with weapons and targets scattered about, soldiers in armor sparring, and a high vantage point to oversee the training. The rations were pitiful compared to the delights of the tower. No wonder the soldiers here had no honor. They had been so used to being treated as inferior they somehow managed to accept it. A tragedy, one that would come to a swift end if this plan worked. "Gather them," she said, mostly as a joke. She wanted to watch him yell and struggle to get everyone's attention.

"GOLD CLOAKS, ASSUME FORMATION!"

And by Strength's balls, they did. Men and women lined up in perfect rows, standing straight with both hands wielding the polearm in front of them. The mages stayed in the back. While Bloom hadn't much experience commanding magic users, it seemed shortsighted to dress them in robes, which was a giant flag saying, *Hey there soldier with a giant sword, you may as well target me first!*

They all stood at attention, in complete silence, waiting for someone to say something. That was a problem, because Bloom had no idea where to start. Humans never seemed into the whole honor thing, yet giving a speech about bathing in the blood of their enemies probably wouldn't go over well either. Fortunately, the solution was easy: it's one gifted to all those in positions of power. "Kolsen, introduce me."

A few seconds passed as Kolsen probably went over options in his head. Fortunately, he chose the correct one. "Soldiers of Alanammus, standing before you is Dumiah Bloom, Warlord of Vaynex. I will always be your captain, but as of this moment, she is your *god*. The voice of Warlord Bloom supersedes your first in command, your captain and, ultimately, your archon. I yield the floor."

Hey, not bad. She looked over her new army, and it was…weird. By all measures, they were infinitely more disciplined than a Vaynex unit, but it seemed so fake. These sort of things never carried over into battle. Honor, glory, and all those fancy words tend to fade the moment the soldier next to you blows up or takes a sword through the chest.

"Alright, listen up, Gold Cloaks. I came here to kill a god, not to speak words. If any one of you disagree with my authority, I welcome the chance to face you in combat and get it over with. Any takers?" Of course not. She cleared her throat to prepare her speech before one of the heavily armored female humans broke rank.

"If your offer is true, I wish to test your melee against my own. My father worshiped Strength, fought alongside the Claws in the uprising against Nyfe, and found nothing but death after all of his sacrifices."

The look on Kolsen's face was a mix of horror and shame; he was much worse at hiding his emotions than the archon. Maybe male humans have larger bodies but smaller brains. "Gold Cloak, stand down! You bring shame to your captain—"

Bloom leaped from the balcony and onto the grassy training grounds. Her knees lit up in pain upon landing, but ignoring pain was a universal sign of power. No need for detonators; she drew both blades and stepped forward. "It's been a while since I've killed a real human. The Vanguards never screamed when I tortured them. Let's see if you do the same."

There are few things more hilarious than the face of an angry human. She rushed at Bloom, both hands gripping her polearm. Polearms are a weapon for losers. If you're going to wield something that large, choose an axe—

Bloom stepped back to dodge the quick thrust at her snout. Damn, this human was out for blood. Bloom thrust one of her blades up in the air to parry the polearm from the bottom, then rushed forward to close the gap.

It didn't work.

The gold cloak rolled back, which was pretty damn impressive considering she never let go of the polearm. She did a quick brush across her face to get the sweat off, then charged at Bloom again.

Enough of this. Bloom grabbed an ice-detonator from her side and threw it. She yelled, "Ice!" when the detonator was close to the pointy end, freezing that half of the weapon. It was an act of mercy that would get no recognition, but such is the sacrifice of warlords. The shaky human rushed forward with her frozen spear and lunged.

That was a mistake.

A downthrust from Bloom's blade caught the icy end of the polearm, shattering it. Closing the gap was much easier with nothing in the way. Bloom grabbed the human and pulled her close; it took all her restraint not to simply shove a blade through her neck. The human trembled, clearly expecting the killing blow to come any second.

There wasn't enough time to clearly think out the scenario, so Bloom did a quick punch to the face and dropped her to the floor. Damn, that felt great—no wonder Sardonyx had always favored those duel-ending punches. If it was Vaynex, she would just kill her and move on, but humans never seemed to appreciate true honor—

Bloom flinched out of the way of another polearm. A new human—this one male—rushed in front of the fallen one. "You will not have her, beast!"

Beast? Was that supposed to be an insult? "That's where you're wrong, Boss. I have her, I have you, I have every human wearing that ridiculous cloak. You want to try me, go for it. I'll make a mountain of humans until you learn obedience the Vaynex way."

"If I fall, so be it. Better to meet my end than to serve a monster."

"Monster? If I were a monster, your friend, mate, or whatever you are would be blown to pieces. You want the truth? I don't want you. I want *my* people, but my people are dead or slaves. You want more truth? I'm afraid of the Arrogant One. Not merely afraid, but terrified. You can tell a soldier's worth by their greatest fear. If your greatest fear is me when there is a god stealing people's freewill, then you have no fucking worth at all."

"Stop it," Kolsen said, huffing, out of breath. "Everyone, please stop it. While we sat here for the past six months and did nothing, Vaynex has fallen and Mylor will soon follow. We cannot afford the luxury of inaction any longer."

"And what of Julius?" the woman yelled from the ground. Blood poured down her mouth but the rage never faded. "He ventured into Terrangus and died for a people that never learned his name. Alanammus has always stood—"

Bloom sheathed her swords. "My people stood alone for centuries and now they don't stand at all. Listen, I really don't have time for this. To those of you willing to storm heaven, grab your polearm and follow me into hell. For everyone else...fuck you. If we win, you better not be here when I get back. You have two choices: hand me your cloak and get out of my sight, or get back into formation."

Most humans looked the same to Bloom, but she swore she would remember every detail of any human's face that handed her a cloak. Not a single one did. It wasn't out of respect, and that was fine. Pride, regret, whatever, let them find their own inspiration.

Most of them were about to embark on a one-way journey anyway.

CHAPTER 32

GODS, LIZARDS, AND FOOLS

With his arms crossed behind his back, Francis paced back and forth within his throne room. The silence from Wisdom was *infuriating*. How could God of all people not know what was going on? How could they send Mary? What if she never returned? How would he raise Calvin alone if the worst came true? And most importantly…

How much could a person be damaged before they are considered broken?

"My dear Francis," Wisdom said, "you must relax. The advantage of dealing with 'honorable' foes is that their actions are always predictable. No harm will come to our empress. 'Tis a shame you could even flirt with the idea."

"How can I relax?" he yelled. Yelling at God was not often a good idea, but Mary was out there, surrounded by enemies and fools. How could Wisdom not see it? There were so many possibilities: take her as hostage, kill her for morale, give her to Mylor or Vaynex. The thoughts were inconceivable—

A portal erupted next to the throne, then a brilliant flash of black energy blasted throughout the room. An outline of his angel appeared: the mother of their child, the empress of Serenity.

"My beloved, you have returned! Oh thank the glory of Wisdom. I have so many questions! How was the meeting? What was discussed? Tell me everything!"

"Indeed," said Wisdom, floating forward. "Tell us *everything*."

While it took a few moments before Mary spoke, her face and shaky hands suggested something was terribly wrong. Whatever it was, at least she was home. "We are in grave danger. The gods have formed their alliance, and their first plan of attack is to unleash a Harbinger of Death within Xavian as a diversion."

Death? What sane people could collaborate with *that* one? Francis's first thought was to let Xavian fall, but such a cost would be too much to bear. To treat people as pieces on a board is the inevitable burden of leaders, but to forget they are people at all is a quick way to descend from damaged to broken. Hopefully, God would have a plan...

Wisdom chuckled, which wasn't very inspiring. "I was quite the card player back in my mortal days, beating vagrants and scholars alike with a simple philosophy: 'tis better to call a bluff and fail than to fold and surrender to a weaker position. To fold is a one hundred percent certainty of defeat. With a call, even in the face of annihilation, there is always a chance. Like anything else, it's a numbers game."

Francis assumed Wisdom was a rather poor player based on those comments but kept his opinion to himself. "But Lord Wisdom, what about—"

"*No!*" Mary yelled. All hints of fear yielded to an intense rage. "What rulers would allow entire kingdoms—men, women, and children—to fall?"

"The rulers that win, my dear empress. You must clear your conscience and open your mind. Perhaps Xavian shall fall, but such is the price of Serenity. If you believe diamonds are expensive, *oh*, just imagine the cost of paradise."

With Mary on the verge of tears, Francis took a deep breath and said, "We send the Vanguardians to Xavian, while defenses are bolstered at home. I have done...unfortunate things in my short reign as emperor. Many, many unfortunate things. But I will not oversee another Boulom. Lord Wisdom, please don't place that burden on me. I cannot handle it. No one can."

"*Do not,*" Arrogance yelled, his voice echoing throughout the throne room, "dare tell me what can or cannot be handled." He looked like he had more to say, but the sun mask began twitching. "No... *No!* They are coming. All of them. Gods, lizards, and fools alike. All this time, all this plotting. Was it truly in vain? Oh Maya, dear Maya, why have you opposed me from every angle? The joys I could have given us both..."

Then Francis heard something he had never heard before. Arrogance screamed. It nearly sounded human, but it was drowned out in a distorted echo that, quite honestly, was terrifying. "I must leave and take care of divine business. David is their first target while the armies make their way to Terrangus. Now *listen.* When I return, I expect *every single* Vanguard here, ready and willing to perish for the glory of Serenity. There is no room for error. All our lives...all of our children's lives, hang on the outcome of this final battle. Hate me if you must, but my word is absolute."

And just like that, he faded, leaving Francis and the trembling Mary alone in the throne room with Vanguard Ultra. Francis flinched as Mary rushed up and hugged him, pulling him close. "Don't place this burden on your family. All of your sins flow into me, all of my sins flow into you, and the combination of both flows down to Calvin. It's time to speak truthfully: we are both already broken, shattered beyond redemption. Whether or not paradise ever comes, it will never hide the fact that we have grown into monsters, complacent fools who spent too many years looking the other way."

Francis had always hated the truth. It had a tendency to reveal things better left unsaid. For as much as he wanted to release Mary and step away, his place was in her arms. Their truths, both beautiful and terrible, had already meshed into a conglomerate of confusing emotions. "But my beloved, what if God is correct? The horrors of our journey no longer matter if we prevail. Altering the past takes nothing more than a few strokes of a pen."

"Your grip loosens when you lie," Mary said. To his relief, she said it with a smile. "I already know you'll do the right thing. When it comes to your family, you always do."

"But what about Calvin? Gods forgive me, but I would burn

every kingdom to the ground to ensure his survival." Maybe the truth wasn't so terrible. It brought a great relief to speak it out loud. "Serenna made a vow that Calvin will not be harmed. She will raise him as her own son if the fates declare our doom."

Serenna? Never. Never, never. He kissed her on the cheek and let go, taking a few steps forward to compose himself. *Her* own son? Intentions be damned, Serenna would never raise Calvin. It would be Francis and Mary, or it would be no one. "We haven't lost yet. It's time to stop planning our funeral and begin planning our defenses. Ultra, assemble the Vanguardians."

"They are outside the throne room, awaiting their orders," Zeen said. He raised his sword in the air; it glowed and unleashed a high-pitched screech. By the time the horrible sound ended, Zeen was surrounded by his ragtag group of Guardians. Despite their efficiency, it would never appear normal to see bored-looking soldiers in matching white armor set to protect the realm.

Francis stared into the eye of his staff. Something about that eye always filled him with doubt any time he went against God's command. "Vanguard Ultra, take your team and head to Xavian immediately. We have it on good authority that a Harbinger is imminent." It was difficult to speak the words with confidence. If 'good authority' was the word of his enemies, it could be disastrous to assume it was true. But Mary, oh his beloved Mary. *I trust you. With this, with Calvin...*

With everything.

All the Vanguards left except Nyfe and Zeen, who frowned and slowly shook his head. "To defy God's command... Have you no faith, Emperor?"

Oh no. Was it a trick? A test? "You have your *orders!*" Francis yelled, not bothering to hide his desperation. *Did I doom us all?*

"Our orders come from God, not you," Nyfe said, stepping forward. He then grabbed Francis before he could react. "Take it from one fallen emperor to the next: you could do everything right, wield all the power in the realm, but it only takes one mistake to lose it all."

"*Let go of me,*" Francis said. He tried pushing Nyfe arm's off his robes but to no avail, until Nyfe finally let go on his own.

"Of course we're going to defend Xavian," Zeen said, bringing back his smile. "Just not me. Consider me your own personal bodyguard. Next time, if there is a next time, have some faith."

Francis limped over to the throne, hanging onto Mary for support. Sweat poured down his head and his stomach felt woozy. "We are emperors of our own prison. Forgive me, my beloved. I wish we had never met. I have inherited my mother's gift for tearing down everyone in my presence. What have we done? What have we done…"

"Enough of that," she said, holding his hand as he sat on the throne. "After many years of attempting to slay the past, I assure you it's impossible. I'll see this one through. If by some miracle we prevail, Calvin can be emperor-in-waiting. If our journey ends in blood, Calvin will start a new life in Mylor. Neither scenario is perfect, but they are scenarios I can accept before I leave this realm."

Bless Mary for believing such nonsense. Their enemies would never protect Calvin. They would probably make his execution a public event to be cheered. Perhaps even make a holiday of it. The end of Serenity. The end of the Haide tyranny. The end…of progress.

Francis stood up and took a deep breath. Fear and anxiety had taken a harsh toll his entire life. If said life was nearing the end, he would end it on his own terms. Let them remember the Architect of Paradise. Francis Haide, elemental Guardian, emperor of Terrangus…loving father and husband. Out of his titles, that one brought the most pride.

He took his staff from behind his back and pointed it at Nyfe, then blasted him across the room with a bolt of lightning. "Heed my words. From this moment forward, Vanguard or not, to lay hands upon me or my family is to forfeit your life. If I am cursed to be a puppet, I shall be the most powerful puppet that ever existed. Do you oppose?" he asked Zeen, who was gripping his blade but had not moved.

"I would never oppose perfection. Welcome back, Emperor. For all your faults, you always were a quick learner."

"As far as you're concerned, I have no faults. Take this as a not-so-gentle reminder." Francis pointed his staff at Zeen and shot another blast. It wouldn't be enough to kill him, but it would certainly remind him to use the proper courtesy when speaking to—

With a quick swipe of his blade, Zeen deflected the blast to the side of the throne room. There was an eruption and a bright flash before silence followed. "Emperor or not, don't press your luck. There is much to be done before the upcoming assault. Omega, what are you still doing on the ground? Stop embarrassing the Vanguardians and head to Xavian." Zeen pulled up Nyfe by the arm and they both left the throne room.

"We should flee," Mary said. "We can grab Calvin and get out of here before Arrogance returns. Nothing but death awaits us."

"And go where? Mylor? Nuum? It matters not. Arrogance has his grip on the neck of every kingdom. Terrangus may be our prison, but it's the only place we have a chance to survive."

Francis sat on his throne and leaned back. The seat was never comfortable but the thought of losing it was too much to bear. "I have been very ungrateful to Terrangus. I love this kingdom. I think I have for quite a while now. Mary, my beloved, if you decide to flee, I would not dare stop you. But my place is here. I will live or die defending the only kingdom that ever gave me a chance to be happy." *Please stay with me*, he thought, but couldn't bring himself to say it. As his wife, surely she could hear the silent words. The unfair bargain, the pleading to do something foolish, not out of duty or faith, but love.

Mary met his silence with silence of her own. She walked up to the throne, gave him a quick kiss on the lips, then left towards their chambers.

If freewill was absurd, could there be a word to describe what love does to people? Francis closed his eyes, letting the patter of rain on the window calm his headache.

You are too good for me. Thank you.

CHAPTER 33

FALLING, FALLING, ALWAYS FALLING

It had been zero days since David's last drink.

Sobriety had been put on hold; there was no point in recovery if his prison sentence was a permanent fate. Unfortunately, alcohol has diminishing returns. Who would have guessed that one could get numb from feeling numb? Not even the wine could block out reality any longer. Fear wasn't coming. Sardonyx wasn't coming. Zeen, Serenna, and Bloom were probably all dead, or worse yet: reduced to Vanguards. After everything, part of David yearned to become a Vanguard, if only to become something that wasn't David.

Glancing at the balcony, he swore it inched closer every day. It was calling his name, an ending to a life that had lost its meaning. Failure is exhausting. Truly exhausting. It starts off as a teacher but, when there are no more lessons to learn, it eats at us, chipping away at the soul, chopping off dream by dream until the hollow truth of the dreamer is exposed for all to see.

"David? My love! Is it truly you?"

Melissa's voice. Not today. Why today? He could never fully prepare to hear it but today was not the day. "Don't. Just don't. Arrogance, if you have any mercy at all, leave me alone. Is your time so worthless that you can afford to spend it with me?" Part of him always knew this day would come. Months ago, he had been eagerly awaiting it. Melissa would always be the final illusion. A last-ditch effort to force David's leap while things were dire back at Terrangus. Such bravado of victory had long faded.

"Don't be silly, dear. I came to say goodbye." Every word was agony; the tone and pitch of her voice was a perfect match from his old lover. "Mylor has fallen, and with it, Serenna, Bloom, and Tradition. I always knew victory was within reach, but the ramifications are still overwhelming to consider."

Was it true... Did it even matter? "Save your lies. They have no effect on me."

Melissa laughed, and it took every ounce of restraint not to glance back and see her smile. "Save for what? I no longer need them, or you, for that matter. However, I could use your expertise one last time. I am embarrassed to make the admission, but I can't seem to conjure up a name for Vanguard Serenna. Nothing seems to fit. Vanguard Platinum is uninspired and derivative. Vanguard Valor was my second choice but something is missing. Plus, who wants a double V name? David, stop being rude. Look at me when I'm talking to you. Look at me now."

I won't. I can't. "There is nothing to look at. Melissa is gone. You are the memory of a dream that isn't my own." He forced himself to keep looking at his glass. Was it truly over? Defeat had always felt inevitable, but against Death...not this fool. How could Arrogance have won? What would Melissa say if she could see them now?

David drank most of his chalice. He reached for his wine bottle but it was...empty? It rattled in his hands weightlessly. How? In all the months, it had always refilled. The one true constant aside from his self-loathing. Fine, if the high was about to end, he would do it. For the first time since Serenity, he would look upon his lover.

Everything was the same. Dark skin. Curly brown hair. Green eyes. Detonators on her belt, complimented by tiny daggers sheathed all over her pants. His eyes watered as he said, "I used to pity you, but you're worse than any of them. You lost Boulom, lost Maya, lost everything. You know what it is to suffer, and yet you inflict it upon others without hesitation."

"It's funny you would say that, because I don't pity you at all. Desperation is a disease, not a virtue. Consider the audacity of it. I offered you paradise, and in exchange you offered me a blade. In my very home! Part of me wants you to persevere just so you can see what I have in store for Zeen and Serenna. Oh, listen, you'll *love* this. I wiped his memories but kept hers. Now, she yearns for a man who doesn't even know her name. I could stop the pain, of course: I just choose not to. As God, such is my right."

Gods, forgive him. Gods, forgive them all. Fear had been right, it had been beyond foolish to attend the wedding, let alone attempt to assassinate a god. The price of failure was... unfair, if not deserved.

"Choose?" asked David, forcing a smile. Like everything else in this room, it wasn't genuine. "Even in your crowning moment, you are a slave to the concept you war against. There is no realm without freewill, not completely. You'll be the last one. The paragon of choice. For as much as I hate myself, I can leave this realm knowing I'll never be as pitiful as you. Here, finish my glass. You need it more than me."

"Bold words," Melissa said. She smiled back and, unfortunately, hers appeared real. "Spoken to a rather bold god. You may as well finish that glass. It's your last taste of paradise. Your lips and your heart will never know joy again."

The last glass? It was nearly halfway full, but it had never looked so empty. He drank the whole thing. While it had long lost its taste, those final remnants were wonderful. Perhaps the body knows when the party is over.

"My goodness!" Melissa said, grabbing him by the arm. "You drink too quickly! You must savor the taste."

David flinched at the touch, and nearly fell off his stool when he noticed the ring on her finger.

"Oh, this old thing? Do you remember my words from that day? And there it is, my love. I will wear this ring for the rest of my life. I wish I had one for you too. Really though, after all those years as a Guardian, you could have done better. The gem is so tiny! What charlatan convinced you to drop all your gold on such a pitiful ring?"

It was too much. He stumbled as he rose, clutching his chest for air. Everything around him was lies, everything except that balcony. Melissa's laughter only made it harder to breathe. What a maddening fate after a lifetime of service. If someone had shown twenty-year-old David the future, he could've saved himself decades of torture and ended it sooner. He took a few steps forward, but the spinning room made it impossible to keep his balance. He collapsed face-first onto the ground. It spoke volumes that nothing hurt. For whatever reason, it felt like the room was rumbling as well. Maybe it was his body surrendering.

"Let me help you," Melissa said, reaching out her hand, and of course he took it. "Helping flawed Guardians is what I did best, regardless of the toll it took on me. You didn't even notice, did you? You wore your pain and struggles like a suit of armor while I buried mine behind a mask of smiles. What a pity that I never had a chance to love someone more suitable. I spent all those years falling, falling, always falling."

The room rumbled again. Maybe it wasn't the alcohol? The bartender and some of the inhabitants started to flicker. No. The time for hope had ended. "You win. I'm ready, Ermias. Perhaps I've been ready for ages."

"Oh?" she said with a snicker. "What happened to the man claiming to be a mountain? 'I will not leave this realm, until I am worthy of the mountain she saw in me.' If I may speak truthfully in a room of lies, you are a grave, not a mountain."

"I was always a mountain, but one of sorrow and shame. Will you leap with me? Even… if you're not her… I…give me this."

"Of course, my sweet David. All you had to do was ask." The smile on her face faded as the room rumbled again. Whatever it was, David had no time for such things. It would all be over soon. Even if there was no afterlife, just the idea of rest was more beautiful than he was willing to bear.

Time never made sense with the blur of intoxication. They

arrived at the balcony, but it was…different than his time from Alanammus. No birds, no clouds, no unicorns frolicking on the plains. Just darkness. Layers and layers of darkness.

And that was okay.

"Before I leave you," David said, leaning against the balcony. "Serenna and Zeen…let them be happy. Give them the ending I never had. Please." He nearly fell over as the room rumbled again. Was it truly the wine?

A pity she couldn't look him in the eyes. Illusion or not, Melissa's face would have been the perfect send-off. For whatever reason, she appeared nervous. "Consider it done. Whatever you want. No more words, David. It's time to—"

Rumble was too soft a word. The entire half of the room shattered, with two glowing entities rushing towards them as David fell to the ground. Gods they were terrible. One was an angel-looking thing that soared towards Arrogance, and the other…the other…

David curled up on the ground and closed his eyes. He could take no more lies, no more nightmares. Any time he had agreed to accept the end, something interfered. A rough, rather large hand held him by the shoulder. Whatever it was, it held the power to crush him into pieces. "Leave me," David yelled. "Please, leave me. I can't… I just can't."

"You can, Child of Tradition. And you must."

"*No!*" Another lie. Lies on top of lies. When would his punishment be enough? Was it because Noelami favored him? It had always been a relationship of understanding, never attraction. She understood. They had suffered together, two Guardians of different ages, navigating a realm tortured by lies and violence. "Liar, dreamer, whomever you are, leave me to my end."

"I shall not. Death may be the end, Guardian, but Strength is the now."

A terrible chill came over David as the hand left his shoulder. Even if it wasn't real, to be comforted by anything was a blessing. He rolled over and opened his eyes to the most *glorious* sight he had ever seen. Sardonyx, fully armored, unicorn by his side, stood over him. The glow...the glow. It was him. No lie could ever dare be so beautiful. "Sardonyx? You came for me? Truly?"

"Forgive me, I could not break the barrier without her assistance. You are free. I swear on your mightiest human oaths, you are free, and I shall protect you."

"Her? Does that mean..." It did. Fear clashed against Arrogance by the bar. His blurry vision had no ability to follow the bright flashes crashing against each other. Fortunately, screams never blur. Arrogance's yells were filled with pain. Gods, let him die. All the realm's problems could fade away if he just died.

All the flashes and loud noises were too much. David rolled over, looking at Sardonyx but refusing to meet his eyes. How pathetic he must have appeared to the honorable god above him—

"How *dare* you flee from me?" Noelami's voice. "Let us finish it here! Our war has always been on a battleground of lies. *Fine.* We are coming for you, Ermias. All of us. We shall bury you and your illusions in an icy grave."

David tried to laugh but nothing happened. Arrogance had vanished and, with him, Melissa. He didn't want to weep. To weep in front of Noelami and Sardonyx would be mortifying. But...he was free. The nightmare was over. What started off as tears descended into wailing. All those months wasted, drinking in isolation through the taunts and torments of a monster.

"Is he...okay?" asked Fear. They met eyes for a split second and then she never looked away from Sardonyx. The gods spoke some words to each other, but it was impossible to follow. "Fine. Whenever you're ready, bring him to Mylor. Serenna will provide him with the proper accommodations."

"Mylor? No, not Mylor," David said, his words slurring. "They can't...she can't...see me like this. From the bottom of my heart, thank you for freeing me. But I'm ready to leave this realm."

"Perhaps, human, but the realm is not prepared for your departure."

"The loss...it's too much. You wouldn't understand."

"I lost my son. Human traditions are still foreign to me, but loss is a catalyst that burdens every race. We do not need to leave immediately. I cannot give you forever, but I can promise now." Sardonyx reached out his hand and, after some agonizing moments, David accepted and rose.

The weeping stopped, but tears still flowed down his cheeks. It was nearly comical that Sardonyx's grip was so soft. "Thank you—"

"Shh. No words. Just walk with me towards the darkness."

"But why?"

"Neither of us are leaving here until we agree the darkness cannot harm us. Come."

He clutched Sardonyx's hand, taking a deep breath to try to stop the spinning. It didn't work—it never does—but Sardonyx guided him forward. "Serenna... Arrogance said she was a Vanguard and that Vaynex fell. Was it all lies?"

"Not all. Serenna is alive and well. My home...not so much. It all converges on Terrangus. Alanammus already marches forward; once Mylor breaks the siege and joins them, we can destroy the Arrogant One and liberate the realm. You deserve rest, Guardian. More rest than I could possibly give you. However, I must demand your service one last time. Not for me, not for the realm, but for Zeen. Tempest always favored the boy. I will *not* sit back and allow such evil to manifest."

He nearly smirked. A year ago, David had tried to usher in a realm without gods. A fool's task of course. The realm didn't need to exist without all the gods. Just one.

And he would be happy to do it.

CHAPTER 34

WE HAVE A GOD TO KILL

erenna's head throbbed as she lay in her bed. A lack of sleep, a terrible diet, and really, life in general had been paying the price for months of neglect. Breaking the siege would be unlikely, if not impossible. It spoke volumes to the honor of Mylor and the sheer determination from war after war that her people were willing to try.

"*Arise, Guardian. Bloom and the gold cloaks are enroute to Terrangus,*" Fear said through her thoughts. The goddess had a surprisingly gentle voice, though it made Serenna yearn to hear Valor's yelling, if only one last time. "*The time has come. There is still a considerable force within the bastion, but many of them have portaled back home in anticipation of the upcoming assault. And, as I promised, the false Guardians have been stationed in Xavian.*"

Another failed day of rest. Serenna yawned and forced herself up. "Understood." While it was the desired outcome, that meant no reunion with Zeen. Perhaps for the best…

"*I considered not telling you, but if this alliance is to function, a communication of truth must exist. Zeen was left in Terrangus—I presume as a tactic against you. Whatever your feelings for the boy, cast them aside. He, along with everything else corrupted by Ermias, must be burned to ashes and grown anew.*"

"We have conflicting opinions on what it is to save, Goddess. In the spirit of our newfound honesty, understand that Zeen *will* be returned to me. No other result is acceptable." One of the advantages of exhaustion was how it diminished the power of fear. Both the feeling, and the goddess—

The door to Serenna's chambers slammed shut, a tactic apparently popular among angry goddesses. She grabbed her staff and stepped back towards the wall. "Do your worst, Goddess. If you can read my fears, you'll find yourself very low on that list."

"This is difficult for me to ask, so choose your next actions carefully. Tradition and I have rescued David. I am sending him to you and only you. He requires many things, all of which you will provide. The most important is discretion. His pride is wounded but his body is not yet slain. Ensure such an outcome does not come to pass. Defy me at your own risk."

Before she could sort through any of that information, a portal erupted on the other side of her bed. An outline of a man appeared. By Valor's grace, was it truly David? The only evidence David still lived was the labored breaths as he collapsed to the ground. His color had faded, his beard took up most of his face, and...he was weightless. All his bones were visible, with most of his clothing torn to shreds.

"David?" she said, rushing over to hold him. "Oh David, what have they done to you?" The stench was unholy. It took all of her restraint not to gag, but she would not *dare* show her old leader such disrespect. Her first thought was to summon guards and get him some help, but Fear had demanded discretion. Unfortunately, it was easy to see why.

David stared at her with his glassy eyes, but instead of smiling at the sight of a friend, he began weeping. "No... I said no. Not here. You were never meant to see me this way. Don't... don't look at me."

"Before we faced Harbinger Tempest, you said I was a daughter to you. It was the proudest moment of my life. If those words meant as much to you as they meant to me, then respectfully, be silent and let me heal my second father."

Forgive me, Dad, she thought, but certainly, he would've understood. She rushed over to the barrels of water and, one-by-one, emptied them into her bath. The water was damned cold, but David wasn't in a position to complain. It was harrowing to help him stand and let him lean on her as they walked to the bath. He weighed nothing. *Nothing.* The barrels of water had been heavier.

"No…" he said, as she removed the remainder of his clothing. He groaned as his pants came off but he was helpless to resist. Life returned to his eyes after being placed in the water. He shivered, groaned, but thankfully, didn't speak.

She made no mention of how the water lost its clarity mere moments after his submerging. She grabbed her jug of lemon-scented oils and poured it over his body. "Can you move?"

"Y-yes."

"Get comfortable and rub the oils all over. Give me a moment and I will return with water, food, and some new clothing. Can I trust you to be alone?"

His silence didn't inspire confidence, but he eventually said, "No need to worry. Every time I approach the end, some god or goddess stands in the way." If that was supposed to be a joke, she didn't laugh. "Apologies. Water and bread would be divine. As for clothing…leather please. My days of wearing anything heavy have long faded."

"You shall have it." She kissed his forehead and left the room, towards the grand hall. Several quick salutes made the trip more awkward than necessary. Her soldiers were probably anxiously awaiting words of inspiration for the upcoming battle, but even with her home on the line, David came first.

"Senator Morgan?" asked Martin, rushing up from his table as she entered the room. "I thought we had until nightfall before the assault. Is all well? You appear frazzled."

"Indeed…to both questions. I require water, bread, and a fresh leather armor for a man of a slim, tall build. And find Lady Sophia and have her sent to my chambers at once."

He raised an eyebrow. "What aren't you telling me?"

It was a fair question, but she glared at him anyway. "Captain, must I remind you of the power dynamic here? Your purpose is to be an extension of my will. We will not reclaim the bastion if you question the most simple of my commands."

"Yes, Senator," he said, keeping his head down.

She took a deep breath. It was meant to release some of the stress but none of it left. "Martin, forgive me. When your task is complete, I shall join you outside the bastion. To the best of your abilities, ensure that everyone is prepared."

"There is nothing to forgive. The severity of our situation is hitting all of us. Today is the day we liberate our home! Serenna, if this is the end, I…"

"It is indeed the end, but for them. I will not entertain the idea of defeat. Whatever words you wish to tell me, speak them within our reclaimed bastion." Some admissions are better to never be spoken out loud. Hints are often free, and it would be in Martin's best interest to take this one.

A pang of terror swirled in her gut as she opened the door to her chambers. To her enormous relief, David was still in the bath, alive and well, seemingly relaxed as she entered. He glanced at her and said, "Forget the bread?"

"All accommodations are enroute. Do you recall Lady Sophia? She will attend to your every need in my absence."

He sighed. "I suppose I have no choice in the matter? Sardonyx had mentioned a war against Terrangus. Must you leave so soon?"

"Consider this the war before the war. *Many* aspects of our plan depend on tonight's victory. David, if I never see you again, swear on your life you will find a way to prevail. I cannot leave our realm in the hands of Arrogance. He took my father, my goddess, and my Zeen away from me. For that, and countless other crimes, he must die."

"The only thing I swear, is that when all is said and done, I will stand over the shattered mask of Arrogance."

"David, you—"

"*It will be me!*" he yelled, splashing water out of his bath. "Arrogance appeared to me as Melissa. The fucking audacity of it. You will have your Zeen, and I will have my vengeance. Am I clear, Senator?"

"It's *Guardian*, not Senator. Rest up and regain your strength. We have a god to kill."

*

Serenna stood outside the bastion in the moonlight, fully armored and wielding the Wings of Mylor. Of course it would rain before a battle against the forces of Terrangus. It felt odd to call them that, for this was not the Terrangus of years past with a melee-heavy front and weaker magic support. Vanguards were superior to her own forces in ranged combat, but less than ideal up close. It had taken an unfortunate amount of time and lives to alter the strategy enough to account for that.

Her army stepped aside as she made her way to the front. The wind blew her hair and cape to the side. Like most Mylor evenings, there was a temperate chill. It calmed her nerves to some extent, but even if it was snowing, she would still sweat before a battle. Each step up the stairs brought a conflicting clash of memories. Before she had become a Guardian, or even a soldier, life was a simple and carefree existence. Father hadn't even become senator yet. For Serenna, those days had long ended but, for her people, their days had yet to be written. Let the children of tomorrow forge their own happy memories within this bastion.

"Soldiers of Mylor," she yelled from the bastion entrance. It was near impossible that her entire army would be able to hear her voice, but the words themselves didn't matter—it was the confidence in how the message was delivered. "For most of you, damned near all of you, this is not the first time you are tasked with protecting Mylor. Allow me to be brief, for every moment the enemy lingers within our home is time stolen from our families and brethren. We are not here to regain ground, not here to fortify a position for future assaults. We are here for complete and utter annihilation. No mercy. No prisoners. Let them beg Arrogance for answers before the darkness claims them. The only truth they will learn from us is the one I hold dear: Mylor has never fallen. Her mountains are stained red from the blood of those who tried."

Serenna clutched her staff and erupted into her empowered

form. It wasn't the most efficient use of energy, but her people cheered. "The time for words has ended. Take hold of your staff or blade, and relish the opportunity to tell future generations you slayed the army of a divine tyrant. Now come." She refreshed her shield, then walked through the open doors to the only room in the bastion still under their hold. "Follow your captains through your respected corridors. Push them out. Let their only taste of Serenity be of their own blood."

She raised her staff in the air, then her army charged through. The boom of fire blasts immediately followed and, unfortunately, screams and shattered crystals. There are none more brave or driven than those at the head of a charge. Her melee heavy team rushed forward, not wavering in the face of heavy casualties.

Serenna secured a position behind one of the largest pillars in the grand hall and set up a platinum barrier, with four other crystal mages around her. A few more would have been ideal, but spreading out had been the most efficient strategy against fire. Screams made it difficult to concentrate. Unlike most battles, they only came from her own people, so instead of the mercy of never knowing voices, each scream was one more friend she would never see again.

It was harrowing to see zephum Vanguards. Thankfully, none had ever used magic, but it made reaching the casters more costly. Defense was not the strategy. Serenna forged several tiny crystal spikes and launched them forward, prioritizing the zephum. Aside from being the largest targets, their existence was a mockery. Poor Sardonyx, to see his people used in such a disgraceful manner...

She flinched as her barrier shattered. Even though the axe-wielding zephum had a clear path to kill the other mages, he charged straight towards Serenna. *Spike or shield?* she thought, then forged a new crystal spike.

The zephum made no effort to dodge as the spike impaled him through the chest. Even as he collapsed, his face was filled with utter boredom. More screams. More crashes. A cacophony of violence smothered her from every direction. She refreshed her shield and raised a new barrier. It was impossible to pinpoint an attack coming from everywhere.

Two zephum warriors were slamming their sword against her barrier, not bothering to acknowledge the Mylor soldiers rushing over to stop them. They were so numb and mindless, it was like facing demons.

She crafted one spike, then her vision blurred and her empowered form ended as she attempted to create another. *Take a deep breath. Focus—*

That idea failed when her barrier shattered. She immediately launched a spike, slaying one zephum, but leaving her vulnerable to another one rushing forward. The fact that none of her people were coming to her aid did not inspire confidence. *I cannot risk collapsing,* she thought, gripping her staff and adjusting her stance. After she had lost her duel against Zeen all those years ago, she had given up on the idea of melee combat. But as the zephum closed the gap, the choice was no longer hers.

She made no attempt to parry his blade, instead, hopping back and tightening her grip. A true zephum warrior would slay her in seconds, but this was a mere husk, a mockery of the once-proud warrior now slashing wildly like an amateur.

After a sloppy swing barely missed her face, she swung the Wings of Mylor up with all the strength she could muster. Fortunately, it was a perfect strike, slamming metal into snout. Unfortunately, the zephum didn't even flinch. There were no moves available to stop the next swing. It shattered Serenna's crystal shield, sending them both crashing to the ground in opposite directions.

I hate this bastion. I hate it oh so much, she thought, wheezing on the ground. Several of the worst moments of her life had taken place in this very hall. As bad as they had been, somehow none of them had ever killed her. She forced herself up and crafted a quick spike. It was tiny, sloppy, but sharp—the sort of spell Valor would've been proud of. She felt naked without an active barrier or shield but she forced the spike forward, then fell to one knee. The spike tore through his throat and the zephum collapsed with no reaction. It was like slaying a dream—

"*Serenna!*"

She flinched as Captain Martin pushed her to the ground, taking a sword through his chest. "Serenna, I hope…you find him…you deserve to be…" Someone else's crystal spike impaled both Martin and the zephum Vanguard who had stabbed him.

A mix of adrenaline and terror forced her to rise, entering an empowered form and refreshing her shield. It wasn't wise, but she rushed down to Martin and cupped his head. "Rest easy, Captain. Your service to Mylor has ended."

There were still screams but less crashes. The most likely scenario was that melee had overrun both sides, leaving both Vanguards and Mylor's backline to fend for themselves. Using the last of her empowered form, Serenna formed a spike and launched it, but the sudden blur of vision made it impossible to tell if it hit anything. She then leaned against her pillar and ripped the jug of water from her side.

Dehydration is one of the few feelings that can never be ignored. *Oh, Martin, please forgive me,* she thought, drinking the full jug and huffing for air. If they couldn't liberate Mylor, how could they possibly defeat Terrangus? Arrogance would prevail again, perhaps for the final time. *If we had waited until after the wedding, could we have done better? What have I done? What have I—*

"Senator!" a man yelled, saluting her from above. She was certain she knew his name but everything was too frazzled to piece together. "The enemy has evacuated the main hall, retreating towards the war room. What are your orders?"

Evacuate? Did that mean… "You already have your orders. Follow them and slay every last one. No mercy. No surrender. Force them out of the war room, then flank the side corridors. Begin the assault, I shall join you momentarily." There was a temptation to ask for his hand to help her rise, but showing weakness as leader was never an option.

Had they achieved victory? Was Mylor free? It felt absurd to even consider. Martin's body lay there, undisturbed by either side. She would give him a proper burial, but first, she needed a moment to regain herself. Instead of growing stronger, her body was starting to crack from battle after battle. *I can't do this much longer, but...it's almost over. It's almost over...*

Serenna took a deep breath, leaned against the balcony, and closed her eyes.

CHAPTER 35

REALMS UPON REALMS APART

 ary sipped her wine as Francis leaned back on his throne. Her husband had never been one for hiding emotions, and annoyance was written all across his face. "Can I pour you a glass, beloved? I swear it helps with the nerves."

"Tempting, but no," Francis said with a faint grin. "My mind is my greatest asset. I cannot afford to poison my intellect with war coming to our doorstep."

There was so much to say but nothing he would have wanted to hear. With all the kingdoms and gods united, their reign was coming to an end. Even Francis should know you can't win a chess match when it's pawns against gods. "Very well, but it pains me to see you this way."

"Oh? And what way is that? Do tell."

"Francis…"

He rubbed his hands down his face. "There is always a winning move. I just need to find it. Perhaps if you put the wine down, we could strategize together."

"Sure, I'll put the wine down. One moment please." She finished the entire chalice and slammed it on his armrest. "Okay! Let's put our great minds together and figure this out. Is David still in his prison? I don't know. What is happening in Alanammus? I don't know. With all the Vanguards returning through the outskirts portal, did we lose Mylor? I don't know. I don't fucking know anything. We are sitting here waiting to—"

"*Shut up!*" he yelled, then took a deep breath. "Sorry, sorry. I apologize. That was beneath me. All of your points are valid, of course, but where does that leave us? I refuse to believe that defeat is inevitable. For all my flaws, I am not a coward. Not anymore."

"No, you're not," she said, holding his hand. "Sometimes, running away can be the bravest action. I don't care about pride, honor, or any of that right now. I just want to get away with my family and start over. There is no need to die here."

"Pardon the interruption," Arrogance said, materializing into the middle of the throne room. "Let me take a guess...you would like an update on our scenario? Careful now, you may not like what you hear."

"Lord Wisdom, please—"

"Fucking tell us!" Mary yelled. She grabbed her empty chalice to throw it, but wine began appearing in the glass.

Arrogance chuckled. "Normally, I would advise moderation, but you may as well indulge to your heart's content. David is free, Alanammus is enroute, and Mylor has reclaimed their bastion. Their armies will soon unite outside our doorstop, resulting in a massive force seeking our destruction."

"Then all is lost," Francis said, his eyes darting across the room. "Mary, on second thought, I'll take you up on that offer of wine. Wisdom, any news of the Harbinger?"

"Oh, my dear emperor, your lack of faith is a weakness held by most scholars. No news on the Harbinger front. Our Vanguardians have taken the initiative to begin culling those who are possible suspects. I doubt we'll catch Death's target preemptively but, *oh*, that would be a major victory." It was absurd that there was no hint of distress in his voice. Was he in denial?

"Why aren't you afraid?" she asked, not expecting any real answer.

The eyes on the sun mask turned to her. "As my name may suggest, I have never been one to lack confidence. Time will be the judge if said attribute is a strength or a weakness. Still, I cannot help but feel invigorated by this turn of events. Imagine the disappointment when they come here together, the realm at their fingertips, just to simply…fail."

Delusion is the cornerstone of happiness, she thought, but didn't say. Mary had dealt with these kinds of leaders in the Terrangus military. The ones willing to charge a fortified position to the death with nothing but promises of glory. Those leaders had tended to "disappear" with no official records of how or why they had gone missing. Unfortunately, making God disappear didn't seem possible.

"So that's it?" asked Mary. She yearned for her chalice, but Francis didn't seem willing to let it go. "At least with the wedding, you had something of a plan. Are we really supposed to sit here and wait for the entire realm to trample us under their boots?"

Arrogance floated over to them. "Answer me this, my dear empress: when the realm banded together to take out Emperor Nyfe, why was he defeated?"

"Where do I even start? Nyfe had no plan, no contingencies, and his army surrendered at the first sign things were dire. It was the perfect storm of idiocy."

"Interesting," he said, laughing as he floated back into the air. "I daresay there is a brain behind that beauty after all. It all came down to loyalty. Treachery is a rather contagious disease, always rooted within the absurdity of freewill. Vanguards cannot and will not falter."

If that was supposed to be inspiring, Arrogance was wasting his breath. If Nyfe's soldiers had fought to the last man, the Terrangus military would be a footnote in one of Francis's history books. "Okay, our strategy is that we can't lose unless everyone dies. Great."

"Hold on," Francis said, taking another sip before he put the chalice down. "I dare say he makes a valid point. Aside from loyalty, Vanguards are superior in every way. Besides, it's only Mylor and Alanammus. Nyfe had to face all four kingdoms at full strength. We are facing weakened armies that are unprepared to attack head-on."

I married a fool, she thought, though maybe it was the wine. "Have you no memory? We stormed the gates and laid waste to Terrangus's entire defenses. Surrender was the only option.

Otherwise, we would still be clearing out their bodies from the trade district. Francis, you are not Nyfe. Can you sit there and claim you have no issue with overseeing a massacre?"

Francis probably didn't realize how long he paused. "Fair but...what is the alternative? I already told you, I would burn every kingdom to the ground in order to give our son a future. Perhaps the realm is calling my bluff."

"Enough of this," Mary said, taking her chalice back. She took a quick sip then said, "Victory isn't random: it comes to those who prepare for tomorrow. We need maps, blueprints, generals who know the ins and outs of the kingdom. We need..."

"Silence, for starters," Arrogance said with a chuckle. "It's already handled, dear empress. In fact, I came here not to discuss any of that nasty business, but to pose a question. Do you recall what happened when the rioters nearly took your heads?"

Mary recalled all too well. Her Francis had become a monster, using the Herald of Arrogance to burn friends and foes alike. It had saved their lives, but in doing so, it had cost much, much more.

Francis sighed. "How could I forget? While I do admit it's an interesting thought, the idea of losing clarity again is...unwelcome."

"*No*," said Mary. "You both swore to me that would never happen again. We don't need it."

"Don't need it?" Arrogance chuckled. "Just a moment ago, you were quick to rattle off things we need, and now that I offer one of them, you protest. You are a difficult woman to please, Empress."

"What exactly are you proposing, Lord Wisdom?"

"While I am quite brilliant," Arrogance said, somehow without a hint of shame, "battle strategy has never been my forte. However, I do believe I have figured it out. Despite centuries of theory and debating formations, it's rather simple really: the more powerful side always wins."

How could he be so foolish? If that were the case, the entire realm would be under zephum rule. "Spoken like a man who has studied war but never participated in one. Perhaps we could make inane statements to the enemy until they grow bored and leave?"

It was a badge of honor any time she could get Arrogance to groan, though it usually came with a cost. "We sway the imbalance of power with two words: Royal Vanguards."

And there it was. She always knew the day would come. No tyrant can rule completely if their puppets are allowed to think. It was important not to react. The only solution was to flee, and by panicking, Arrogance would ensure that escape was impossible. Perhaps he had already done so.

"That cannot happen," Francis said, to her utter shock. Was this the moment? Would they finally defy Arrogance and accept their fate, for better or for worse?

Instead of an outburst, Arrogance simply chuckled. "Would Francis make a liar out of Francis? Just moments ago, you claimed you would destroy our entire realm to ensure your son's future. Well, I have offered you the flint. It's up to you to strike a fire."

Francis stepped away, keeping his head down. "I will elaborate on my position. I will indeed accept your offer to become a Vanguard. However, I will *never* entertain the idea of Mary doing the same. Is that clear?"

"*Oh*, you may have your father's eyes, but I can hear Mommy's voice soaring from your throat. I would prefer Mary as well. However, I am a compromising god, if nothing else."

Mary dropped her chalice, not flinching as it shattered. "Wait. What the fuck is going on? Francis, you cannot possibly consider such madness. You are a father!"

"That, my beloved, is precisely why I must do this. The time for lies has ended. There is no running away, no new life awaiting us. It's impossible to run from yourself. Believe me…I've tried. Take care of Calvin. You were always his favorite, anyway."

"Shut the fuck up," she raid, rushing over and grabbing him. "You want to discuss running away? Then what do you call this? Don't leave me here alone…"

"Not alone, Empress," Arrogance said, who had floated farther away. "You are surrounded by friends and loved ones, one of whom is about to become *very* powerful. Still, it would be more efficient if you joined your husband. Wouldn't you relish the idea of using magic? I just *cannot* get the zephum to master it, but I could place all the elements at your disposal. Trust me, it's as fun as it looks!"

"There is always a winning move," Francis whispered, refusing to look her in the eye. "Unfortunately, this one comes with very long strings. But knowing you and Calvin are safe makes all costs irrelevant. I cannot fathom what will occur next. If it is… unfavorable, then please, remember me at my best."

She let go, resisting the urge to scream. Why do intelligent men always make the most foolish mistakes? "Before you throw your life away, come and say goodbye to your son. I want him to have a pleasant memory before his father becomes a monster."

"I cannot do that."

"*No?* After everything, you can't even give me that?"

"Not out of spite," said Francis, who cautiously stepped towards her. "If I see his little face, my courage may falter. Why are you so angry with me? Do you think I truly want this? I…enjoy my life. I have a proud position of emperor, a loving wife, and a child I love an unquantifiable amount. Probabilities never lie. This is the only outcome in which Calvin is safe."

"Serenna promised she would take care of him. Even if we lose ourselves, all this, and everything, there is a future out there waiting for him."

"My beloved," he said, taking a deep breath. "I am incapable of believing such convenient lies, particularly from the woman who tried to murder me on my wedding night. I have read and reread the history books, trying to find an example that offers hope. Rest assured, there are none. Royal families face destruction after a takeover. It is the natural order of things."

"You don't know that for certain."

"Indeed, I do not, but that is precisely my point. I will not risk our son to odds that would make a gambler blush. Please don't hate me for this. I will not claim it's a perfect maneuver, but it's one that offers a chance of victory."

"You're not the one I hate. This is your fault," she said to

Arrogance. "Was one kingdom not enough? You had to destroy Boulom *and* Terrangus? Damn you for coming into our lives."

Arrogance did a yawning gesture with his spectral hand. "Is that all, Empress? Surely, you could insult me better than that. Tap into that tiny brain of yours. Use some naughty language!"

"Everyone, stop," Francis said. "Our fates are intertwined. If we resort to bickering among ourselves, we have already lost. Lord Wisdom, please wait for me in the conversion room. I must request a moment alone with my wife."

"Granted, but do not linger. You know how I just *hate* waiting." Arrogance faded from the room, leaving the two of them alone, together but realms apart.

"Mary, I—"

"I love you," she said, pulling him close and embracing him. Could Vanguards be reversed? Maybe if they somehow defended Terrangus, Arrogance would be so giddy he would consider giving...

Of course not. Tyrants never relinquish control.

"After reconsideration...may I see him? If only one last time?"

"Of course. Don't lose faith, Francis. If there is a winning move, I swear I will find it." He didn't answer, so she held him by the hand and guided him upstairs.

Calvin was sleeping, watched over by two healing mages and a Vanguard. While she never appreciated having Vanguards in her chambers, she may as well get used to it with her husband soon to become one.

"He'll understand as he grows older," Mary said, if only to break the silence. The despair on her husband's face as he watched their son sleep was as clear as the candle flame illuminating their chambers.

"The Haide family line is filled with regret and trauma. It would be best if he simply...didn't think about me at all."

"When he's old enough, I will tell him the truth. I will tell him his loving father was a gentleman, a scholar, a ruler with incredible ambitions...and despite his greatest fear, a man that never became broken."

His eyes welled with tears as Francis whispered something to his son and kissed him on the forehead. "Let us proceed. I am prepared to face the judgment I have forced upon thousands of our own people."

She took him by the hand. "We could grab Calvin and flee. I don't care where. Just...anywhere that isn't here."

"Here is now and everywhere. Be strong, Mary. It's time for me to go."

Francis guided her down the stairs and out of the throne room. She wanted to let go, run to Calvin, and rush out of the castle, but her husband needed her. Maybe she could appear to be strong for his sake, because her true determination was dead. With this act, Arrogance had finally won. All Mary could do now was drink her wine, love her son...

And pray for the realm to lay waste to the deity that had ruined her life.

CHAPTER 36

EVIL IS AN ABSOLUTE

David's hands were too shaky to shave his beard. He sighed and put the blade down. Everything about this was wrong. He was in Serenna's chambers, pampered like some mixture between a servant and a dying old man. All of the yelling outside his door had been annoying but acceptable once he had realized they were yells of joy. The bastion had been liberated and while he hadn't seen Serenna since yesterday, it seemed likely her survival was part of those cheers. He flinched as his door was flung open.

"Lord David!" Sophia yelled. "I come with great news!"

He wished she would knock next time but wasn't in a position to complain. "After battling Harbingers for over twenty years, I can discern joyous yells from tragic ones. Congratulations on the bastion. And please, never refer to me as Lord David again."

"Clever man," she said with a smile, before staring at his hands. She approached and handed him a tiny chalice of wine, filled only about half-way. "I was told to give you this."

David pushed down the shame and drank the full chalice in one gulp. It wasn't the numbness he desired but a relief from his shakes and pounding headache. "Thank you. Give Serenna my regards."

"Your gift didn't come from Serenna, my lord. It was a…friend of yours. Not a woman I would invite for tea, to be honest."

Fear? The realm had truly gone mad if Noelami offered him wine. "I had a similar reaction in our first meeting. You may find this hard to believe, but there is a kind-hearted woman behind those threats. These days, I dare to call her my closest friend."

"I have some odd friends but none like that... Oh! You must be starving! My life would be easier if you waited here, but if you desire some fresh air, I can escort you."

"Most appreciated, but I have spent many days in this capital. I'll show myself around." Hopefully that didn't come off as too abrasive, but an opportunity to step outside alone was nearly heaven.

Sophia's friendly demeanor faded as she glared at him. "I have *very* strict orders to watch over you. Enjoy your peace, Guardian, but I must have your word that nothing will happen."

David sighed. It was harrowing to have a reputation for being a danger to himself. More so because it was valid. "If my word holds any value, consider it yours. I just want to see the mountains again. To gaze upon something real...is a gift I had taken for granted."

"Very well, but please don't linger. Your 'friend' was not vague when describing the punishments I would endure if any harm came your way."

He nodded with a smile and left the room, and had to catch his breath when he entered the hallway. It was real. All of it was real. He could come and go as he pleased, without the nightmare of knowing it was a prison.

What an odd scene. People were cheering and hugging, screaming, not giving David a second glance. He didn't matter, and that was okay. Honestly, it was better than okay. From the grand hall came a whiff of bread and other delights. Despite his growling stomach, it wasn't the day to face a large crowd, let alone a wild one.

He ignored them all and entered the gardens. There was no debauchery here—Serenna would never allow such a thing. Other than some older woman tending to the lilies and roses, it was quiet, carefree, and, ironically enough, perfect.

It was difficult to hold back tears as the temperate breeze caressed his face from the balcony. Ah, the mountains. There they were, sleeping on the outskirts in their giant, rocky glory. Unmoved, unchanged, uncaring of all the horrors and joys of the realm. *I am cracked, perhaps even shattered, but I will always be a mountain.*

"People should never compare themselves to nature," Noelami said from his left side. She must have materialized without him noticing.

He smiled at her. "Where else would dreams come from?"

"There are greater things to strive for," she said, while analyzing him in a rather uncomfortable manner. "Don't come out here again without shaving. It adds thirty years to your face."

"What if I favor the look? Besides, care to guess what the past few months have added to my heart?"

She turned away and towards the mountains, studying them like they were a riddle. "That would be unnecessary. Every time I believe you've found your lowest point, I somehow find you lower but still breathing. David, I will not apologize for my actions. Do you now understand why I kept you from the wedding?"

He did, but it still wasn't her right to do so. "It doesn't matter. My tolerance for regret has long faded after spending time with you and Arrogance. I've seen what happens if we never let go."

"Spending time with him has made you reckless, I see. Choose your next words carefully. Insulting me from the safety of shadows is one thing, but to do so up close is *very* unwise."

The scowl on her face made him laugh out loud, uncaring of the consequences. "My friend, it's not you I slight. Ermias still loves you, so much in fact that he lashes out against me at every opportunity for holding your attention. He thinks you love me. Meanwhile, we can't have one conversation without an outrageous threat."

"Of course I love you." She must have come to her senses as she flinched. "Stop it, not like that. You are a little brother to me. A cold, brooding child who cannot resist consuming poison. It's why you must lose the beard. I cannot have you looking like my father."

David took a deep breath and stared into the distance. "I would excel at the role. You could be my second daughter. The two of you could berate me together."

She sighed. "Fine. I do apologize. Even a goddess can make mistakes. I have never been one to allow good intentions to diminish the power of ignorance, yet I have nothing else to fall back on."

"Never apologize for good intentions. Besides, if we were to compare debts, I only exist because of you. Did I ever thank you for saving me from that balcony?"

"Not with words. You didn't need to. In a way, I didn't want it. My intentions were selfish. You were a desperate husk of sorrow, prepared to fill the hole in your heart with my bidding. I had very cruel intentions, and yet it was one of my greatest decisions."

"If I am your legacy, you must have been a terrible empress."

He regretted the words when she didn't laugh. It was impossible to find the line with a woman stuck between reality and dreams. "Ermias believes with every beat of his heart that he is the hero of our conflict. I don't know how to cope with that. I say this to you and you alone: sometimes, I fear he may be right."

David turned his head and met her eyes. He smiled, even if she refused to. "I assure you, he has never felt the same. Evil cannot survive scrutiny. It must be treated as an absolute, a divine prerogative that casts destruction upon its naysayers. Good is plagued with the what-ifs, how's, and why."

She leaned her head against his shoulder. David had always wanted a sister, and perhaps he had finally found one that was three hundred years old. "While we're on the topic of truth, I don't know if I can kill him. The task may fall to you or Serenna."

It wasn't the right time to laugh, so he held it in. "I can barely hold down a loaf of bread, let alone slay a god. You have my undying loyalty, but the death of Ermias will not come from my blade. It's funny, really: just yesterday, I demanded that Serenna give me the opportunity. I hate that she pities me. I was…a great man once."

"There has always been a great man inside of you. You just have to stop drowning him." She took her head back and moved a few steps away. "It's why Melissa loved you. She saw it in you from the first day."

Please stop, he thought, but couldn't say. It was comforting. Perhaps, it was even true. "Would it be a step too far to request more wine?"

"As empress, I am familiar with people requesting things I will never grant them. You are an addict. The distribution of blame is up for debate, but you will only be granted enough to survive. No more. No less."

"Very well. As a Guardian, I am familiar with disappointments—" His stomach rumbled.

"Come," she said. It didn't sound like a request. "If the crowd is too noisy, I can show them my wings. It will empty the entire room in moments."

"Big sister protecting her little brother. Every forty-six-year-old man's dream."

*

Later that night, after gorging himself on bread, meat, and…water, David had said his farewells to Noelami. It was time to check on Serenna. It was a bizarre feeling, guilt-like and riddled with shame. Mylor had reclaimed their bastion after months at war, while David had wept and drank. Did she even respect him anymore? Well, she had called him a second father. Had that been out of pity?

It was a long trek to the bastion. The streets of Mylor were still filled with cheers and howls, people uncaring that despite their victory, the true battle had only begun. A guard approached him as he made his way up the stairs.

"Halt. Enjoy the ceremonies, friend, but the bastion is off limits to all but military personnel. Perhaps you should rest? Your eyes tell quite the story."

While David had once been part of Terrangus military, making that claim would be a swift journey to jail or worse. "Are Guardians welcome?"

"Of course, but don't insult my good nature by claiming to be one. Move along, friend. You have no business here."

"My name is David Williams, once-leader of the Guardians. I may be a shadow of the man I was, but nevertheless, I am still that man. Please allow me passage to the bastion."

Something about those words brought a murderous rage to the guard's eyes. "I don't care if tonight is a celebration. You shame a good man's name, and you pay the price." He cocked back and swung.

It was slow enough for David to follow. In the old days, he would have caught it for intimidation, but it was easier to slide out of the way. "Thank you for calling me a good man. It means more than you will ever know."

The guard didn't stop him as David walked by. The others appeared anxious, but none acted. "You," David said, picking a guard at random. "Will you escort me to Serenna? I am unarmed and wield no magical attributes."

"Um, sure," he said. The guard was noticeably fidgety. It had been a while since anyone feared David and, to be honest, he relished the feeling. Anything other than irrelevance. "Are you really him? I mean, you don't come across as a liar, but, well, you know."

"I assure you, there are better men to impersonate." David paused as he entered the bastion. There was no celebration inside. Soldiers were gathering the wounded and fallen, yelling orders and rushing around. "Keep the joy outside and the reality within. Charles would have been proud."

"Indeed. The senator had his issues of course, but I swear no one loved this kingdom more—"

"You are relieved," Serenna said to the soldier, glaring at him with the wrath of a goddess. Perhaps she could be Noelami's sister after all. "David, why are you here? Can you not follow simple orders? Sophia would never defy me. What treachery did you pull to make your escape?"

"Escape? Am I your guest or your prisoner?"

"You are...you are..." Serenna collapsed into his arms. It nearly knocked him over, but the adrenaline gave him enough strength to gently lay her on the ground. Up close, she looked close to death, with dark circles under her eyes and blood dripping off her armor.

"Guards! Anyone! Serenna requires aid!" A pang of terror came immediately after those words. The scene didn't look good. A fallen leader and a sickly man in civilian garments. Soldiers on edge would immediately think assassin—

Something blunt crashed into his face, then soldiers grabbed him to pin him down. Others were converging on Serenna, but it was impossible to follow with his vision blurring. "Ignore me. Help…her." The lack of pain made it clear what would happen next. His blurry vision faded to complete darkness.

*

"Mage, come quick! He's coming to!"

David flinched, trying to make sense of his surroundings. Hard bed, white walls, soldiers and mages all around. Healing ward. Serenna was his neighbor, glaring at him while huffing for breath. He forced a smile and said, "Fancy seeing you here."

"You…are a fool." If she was trying to hide her smile, she failed. "Thank Captain Lawson when you find the opportunity. She recognized you before it was too late."

"Serenna, are you as bad as you look?"

"*Never* ask a soldier how they feel after a battle. Bastions don't liberate themselves."

He saw through the venom in her voice. It was exhaustion. Pure, crushing, exhaustion. "I'm not talking about wounds; I'm talking about scars. Look at us. We're skeletons hiding in armor."

"I have created many skeletons over the past year. I assure you, none of them look like us. Some have been burned, others are buried under the mountains. I will not stop until Arrogance is one of them. I pondered your request from our last conversation. Consider it denied. He dies by my hand. This is not negotiable."

"Stop it. Please, stop it. You sound like Fear. While I love her like a sister, she is nearly as miserable as I am. It's almost over, Serenna. Compose yourself. We'll get him back. You have my word we will get him back."

She glared at him. It seemed more out of disappointment than ire. "Don't fill my heart with lies. Mylor is free, and I have never been more empty. If you can't bother to speak the truth, then you have no use to me."

It should have hurt more than it did, but she looked so

214

miserable. "A father's love will always outlive his usefulness. Get some rest, my friend. Your words are poisoned by anger."

"My entire *life* is poisoned by fatigue. I will rest, David. Not because you command it—that privilege has long faded—but because I am tired. Oh, so very tired." It was obviously true, because she closed her eyes and rolled over.

Ignoring the mages prodding and poking him was easy. Despite the annoyance, his mind was fixated on one thing. To destroy Ermias.

CHAPTER 37

WARLORD WITHOUT A KINGDOM

amn, human armies move slow, Bloom thought, taking a bite from her orange. What was the hold up? Any Vaynex unit worth a damn would have made it to Terrangus already. "Boss!" she yelled to Kolsen, who sighed and walked over. The human was clearly tired of getting yelled at, but Bloom had nothing else to do, so too bad.

"Yes, Warlord?"

"Enough is enough. My people usually drop dead around forty years. I didn't plan to waste half that time walking."

"Bloom…" He took a deep breath, most likely to stop himself from saying something stupid. "Gold cloaks are primarily a defensive unit. Mobilization is, well, not really our thing."

"Less excuses, more wine!" Torturing Kolsen had been the only way to pass the time. Eventually, she would get him to crack. To be honest, being surrounded by human soldiers—if one could call them that—had been very lonely. Her own people were back in Vaynex, under rule of the Arrogant One, suffering unspeakable shame…

It was best not to think about it.

"The humans are indeed lethargic, but do not deserve your ire," Sardonyx said, which nearly sent Bloom to the ground. She hadn't heard his voice since the summit. He had left with a vague declaration of saving David, then disappeared.

"Why not? And where have *you* been?" She took a deep breath. To yell at humans was one thing, but Tradition was a god. A zephum god. "Forgive me. I need a release. If I can't yell at them, I want to kill them. I want to kill something, anything."

"And you shall, Daughter of Tradition. Our plan is finally set into motion. David is free, Mylor is liberated, and you are to meet Serenna on the outskirts of Terrangus. Be cautious of yearning for death. I assure you, it is coming in the form of an army, and you are its herald."

David being alive brought a smile to her face. Usually, when someone goes missing for over a month, it's due to alcohol or gambling debts. After that, the only way to find them is to check beneath the sand. "David is here? I've missed the old bastard. We can slam drinks and talk about his rocks."

"I sent him to Mylor in Serenna's care. They refuse to admit it, but both of them desperately need each other. Not all demons can be slain with blades. Many, if not most, need the comfort of a loved one."

"Fine. But you know, I could use some love over here. It's not easy being surrounded by humans. Their wine sucks."

Sardonyx smiled, in that happy, yet oddly threatening manner. "I shall remain by your side throughout the journey to Terrangus. While I can still sense the chaos inside you, somehow, you are the most stable of my children."

Tradition was never one to lie, but how was that fair? Bloom had battled in Vaynex until the very end, when the Vanguards stormed the citadel. If anyone was prone to nightmares, regret, shame, dishonor, it was Bloom. It was Bloom, and no one cared. The warlord without a kingdom. She flinched as a giant hand went to her shoulder.

"I understand, child. If I may, please allow me to quell your doubts. The Arrogant One will indeed be slain, and Vaynex will return to its former glory. It shall not be easy, but I assure you, when the day comes...it will be *glorious!*"

"Eh, maybe." He was probably waiting for a *glorious indeed*, but she wasn't in the mood. The human captain was nearly back, and he didn't have enough wine to numb her regrets.

"In the meantime, have some fun if it eases the burden. Insult his mother," Sardonyx whispered. "Humans in particular hate that. Make a comment suggesting she was overly promiscuous and had several mates."

Bloom smiled. It was tempting, but Kolsen was a good man. "You got my wine, Boss?"

"Yes, Warlord. I also took your concerns to heart. Consider our pace ten percent faster going forward." His goofy smile suggested he was proud of such an insignificant accomplishment.

"I'm not one for math, but isn't ten percent of a low number just a lower number?"

"I mean…"

"Shut up and drink with me. I just found out Serenna liberated Mylor. With both of our armies combined, we may actually do this."

"My goddess feels the same. Cheers, Warlord."

It sort of pissed her off that Fear spoke to the humans and not her, but oh well. Bloom had the best god on her side.

*

A few days had passed, and despite Kolsen's grand declaration of "ten percent," their pace hadn't changed at all. It was still that human slogging, stopping for bread and water every couple of hours instead of just eating while they walked.

"We have nearly arrived, Warlord," Sardonyx said with a smile on his face.

"It's about damned time." Bloom marched ahead of her army, squinting through the rain. Yep, there was an entire army of humans waiting at the bottom of the hills. "Their banner holds that uh…what do you call those things? Owls? It's not a trick right? We're good?"

"Proceed."

One simple word was all it took. Bloom rushed over to Kolsen and yelled, "Boss! Mylor's army is straight ahead. Let's unite our forces and kill those fuckers in Terrangus."

To her surprise, Kolsen frowned and stepped away. "So it seems. Forgive me if this comes across as craven, but…how do you deal with it? The fear? The possibility we are marching straight into a massacre?"

What the fuck? Was this a human thing? "If we die, we die. Why does that bother you? Have you no honor?" She ignored Sardonyx snickering behind her.

"I suppose you're right. Forgive me, Warlord," he said, clearing a tear from his eye which, honestly, was pathetic. "I'm still new to this captain thing. When does it change? When do I wake up with nothing but courage coursing through my blood?"

It was Bloom's turn to snicker. She turned to Kolsen and said, "You have it all wrong. It's not courage, kid, it's hatred. Pure fucking hatred. As we speak, they are in Vaynex, turning my people into slaves. My home. My fucking home!" Ah, that actually explained a lot. Alanammus had never been invaded. They cowered and slithered their way into the shadows, letting the other humans take the brunt of war. From a tactical standpoint it was kind of smart but, ugh, the dishonor of it.

When Kolsen didn't respond, Bloom took a fire-detonator off her belt and handed it to him. "You know how to use this?"

"A detonator? Of course not. I'm not even a mage."

She grinned. "Swords can do magic, Boss. If it becomes clear we've lost, plop this thing in your mouth and thrust your sword through. Won't feel a thing until you wake up in the…uh, Great Plains in the Sky for humans." Poor kid probably had no idea what she was insinuating. Fearing death is one thing, most zephum children struggle with the idea until honor and glory are properly bashed into their skulls, but to become a Vanguard, to lose yourself completely and utterly to a deranged deity: what could be more terrifying?

"Is that supposed to inspire me?"

"If you had half a brain, then yeah. Think about it, your greatest fear is being slain by the enemy. I just gave you a path that takes that power away from them. Once you realize how easy it is to die, the entire concept of life becomes nothing more than a joke. Relish it, my friend."

After a pause, he handed the detonator back and said, "Keep it. While I appreciate the sentiment, it wouldn't be fair to the men. I led them here, and I will suffer whatever fate brings my way."

Right. Moving on. Bloom nodded and approached the Mylor army. Finally, here were some real soldiers! They all appeared malnourished, traumatized, broken, and shattered beyond repair. Most of all, they appeared mad. *Really* fucking mad. It was beautiful. She could've kissed them all.

"A pleasure to see you again, Warlord," Serenna said, reaching out her hand.

Bloom gladly took it and it laughed out loud. "You tiny bitch! Look at you! I cannot tell you how glorious it is to look upon real warriors again. Where is David? I miss my brooding buddy!"

Bloom's smile faded as David approached. He was a stick. Serenna and Bloom had faced off against Vanguards, but to spend months alone with the Arrogant One was an unmatched cruelty. Despite his fragile frame, the man was beaming with violent determination. He would be the one to slay their nemesis. No one else stood a chance.

David slowly crept forward. He hugged her in a way no one had in years. It was weird but she let it happen. "Forgive me, old friend. I never had an opportunity to congratulate you on becoming warlord."

"Don't hug me, you old fuck... Alright, fine. If you must." After too many seconds, they let go and Bloom stepped back. "Well, the gang is all here. When are we doing this? It's been over a week since I've killed someone. That has to change."

"Tomorrow," Serenna said. She studied Bloom's army and didn't bother to hide the disappointment on her face. Ugh, even if it wasn't Bloom's fault, that was embarrassing. "I assure you, there will be enough Terrangus blood to satisfy a thousand lifetimes."

"Who gets to kill Francis?" asked Bloom. "I want to mount his family up in Vaynex Citadel for generations to look upon." It was an unfair ask, but since humans weren't into that sort of thing, maybe it would be approved.

Serenna didn't budge. It seemed like she didn't even blink. "I care not who gets the killing blow, as long as it comes. I have already failed once. It cost more than I could possibly fathom. Arrogance dies tomorrow. My only absolute is that the child is not harmed. Kill the mother if you must, but Calvin must remain untouched. Am I understood?"

"What I understand is that you have it all wrong. Look, you may rule Mylor. You may even rule the Guardians. You don't rule me. If it's a big deal, just close your eyes and look elsewhere. In Vaynex, wars don't end until last names disappear. It's about time humans learned the same."

"Warlord," Sardonyx said, which made her stop. "Children are off limits. The mere thought of it makes strength yield to chaos."

"*Nothing* is off limits when it comes to Ermias," Fear said from behind Serenna, finally revealing herself. "Arrogance cannot be defeated by compromise. He is a liar and murderer to the full extent of either definition. Put aside your honor for one evening and battle without limitations."

To Bloom's enormous relief, Sardonyx smiled instead of drawing his sword. "Honor is not a mistress to be cast aside whenever convenient. It is a life-mate, to be taken hand-in-hand, treasured forever, till death do us part. No, Goddess. I will do no such thing. Calvin is innocent from the sins of his parents. Though the sins of his parents are indeed vast." Bloom had no response for that, but hopefully Fear could talk some sense into him.

It didn't seem likely as the goddess sighed and took a step back. "Some days it's like Strength never left us. Do what you must, Tradition. As long as we prevail, I will not force the issue."

"I shall, Maya—"

"Do *not* overstep. Refer to me as Fear, Goddess, or Empress only. I will award you the same courtesy." Something about that statement made David grin. Whatever weird thing they had going on was none of Bloom's business.

"Everyone is clearly on edge," Serenna said, taking a deep breath. Damn, she looked tired. "Let us retreat to our respective tents and reconvene in the morning. Some of us have waited years for this moment. Others, centuries upon centuries. We shall rest this evening, then prepare for the assault. You are all dismissed."

Bloom made a mental note to end future monologues with "You are all dismissed." Not letting other people speak is the best way to win an argument. "David, I missed you, buddy. Join me for a drink?"

"Of course. Let me fill my chalice with water and I'll come over."

Damn, he was doing the sober thing again. Bloom would have to drink for two.

CHAPTER 38

ARCHITECT OF PARADISE

rancis opened his eyes. For whatever reason, he was strapped to a chair down in the Terrangus castle prison. But why? Such a dank chamber was no place for an emperor. How long had he slept? It was impossible to recall the past few days. Most of the puzzle was missing, but what he could remember was that Mary and Calvin had desperately begged him to become a Vanguard for the sake of their family. He had done so, because Francis was a hero. A selfless, unstoppable hero.

"Good evening, Emperor," one of the Vanguards said, whoever he was. Gods have no need to remember the names of their pawns. "You are awake sooner than anticipated. Tell me, what do you recall?"

"I recall that I am the one who asks the questions." Were the straps loose? It took no effort to rip them off. "Be useful and retrieve my staff immediately. Enemies are on the horizon. They are here to stop Serenity. Little do they know, the only thing that will stop is their beating hearts."

"Please relax, Emperor," the Vanguard said, noticeably waving another one to come to his aid. "It's too soon. God made it clear we had a few more days before…"

Francis stopped listening. Any sound other than obedience was entirely unnecessary. He closed his eyes, channeling a feeling he couldn't articulate to summon the Herald of Arrogance. The staff materialized in his hands, bringing two wonderful things. The voice of God, and the wrath of God.

"*Oh, my dear Francis. How I have yearned for this moment. It's all coming together. You are the blade that pierces the heart of freewill, ending its cold embrace for those who cannot dare to be happy. I'm not particularly fond of these two. Why not take this opportunity to flaunt your new power?*"

The Vanguard's expression didn't change but he slightly raised an eyebrow. "I know he speaks but I cannot hear the words. Secrets? I would not pry into the whispers of God, but perhaps—"

Francis erupted into a yellow glow. It would take no effort to kill them both, but why rush? "Vanguards, defend yourselves. Consider this your final test before paradise." Common people could never read the expressions Vanguards make when distressed, but for the properly educated, every shift in their faces told a story. Confusion, alarm, terror. Terror was a wise choice.

Both Vanguards erupted into yellow auras of their own, but they were pitiful excuses of light. *These* were the people chosen to defend Terrangus? No wonder Mary had begged him to ascend. His family needed more than raw power or intellect.

They needed a hero.

Francis pointed his staff and blasted one of the Vanguards hard enough against the wall to make pieces of it crumble. If the other one was intelligent, he would've taken the opportunity to counter, but instead, he fell to his knees.

"We are unworthy, Emperor. I am yours to command. Or execute, if such is my fate."

It would take no effort to execute him, but *oh*, to be worshiped. Pride is a hunger that shall not be denied. "You exist because I allow it. Rise, and never forget the extent of my superiority—"

Ultra broke through the door, holding his blade out and glancing all around the room. "What happened? I heard a blast."

"How perceptive." Part of him wanted to blast Ultra back to the void. The way he had deflected Francis's lightning back...whenever that had been, was a terrible afront to perfection.

Actually, it was difficult to piece all the events together. Mary had pleaded with him to become a Vanguard but...why was that so difficult to recall? Was it a lie? Parts of it were coming back. Her screams, her cries, her begging.

"Is all well, Emperor? You appear a bit frazzled."

"Silence!" Francis yelled, amplifying his yellow aura. He pointed his staff and prepared to burn Zeen into dust for asking such an outrageous question.

"*Halt*," God's voice called out, before revealing himself. "While it pleases me how...let's call it *bold* you have become, I do require the boy's talents for the time being. Vanguard Ultra, from here on out, your purpose is to defend the royal family. Particularly our little emperor-in-waiting. Our enemies are coming for us all, but they have a very bizarre obsession with the child."

"They will never have him," Francis said, glaring at God. He never would have done such a thing in the past, but the mere mention of his son's name brought a crazed determination. In history, the morality of war was often a complicated subject. In reality, it was rather simple: the ones aiming to harm your family are the ones who shall face the devastation of fire.

"Oh my," Arrogance said with a chuckle. "Emperor, please sheathe those daggers in your eyes. Save all of that hatred and newfound 'confidence' for tomorrow. You're going to need it. In fairness, so will I."

The smile on Ultra's face as he approached was irritating. "Lord Emperor, it would appear I have been designated as your blade. What is your command?"

Go away was his first thought, but he had to play nice with God. "Is your hearing damaged? God proclaimed you are to defend the royal family. I assure you, he did not mean Francis Haide, Emperor of Terrangus, Architect of Paradise. Defend my wife and child. If any harm comes to them, you will never know Serenity. You will only know an existence where suffering is as infinite as my newfound power. Am I clear?"

Oddly enough, Ultra losing his smile brought him no joy. "I

225

shall defend them with my life. Thank you, Emperor. No matter how the battle goes tomorrow, you have my eternal thanks for allowing me to be one of your subjects." Ultra offered a poorly executed salute. "For Serenity. For God."

"For me." Francis took a deep breath, then noticed the dead Vanguard collapsed under the rubble. It nearly made him laugh, but comedy was unworthy of the divine. "You," he said to the luckier one, who was still kneeling. "Clean up this mess."

While part of Francis yearned to see his family, there was an ominous warning in his gut to stay away. They wouldn't understand. Most people love the concept of God, but if he were ever to appear as a mortal, they would pelt him with sticks and rocks. Besides, there was no time. The armies of Terrangus and Mylor were assembled on the outskirts, most likely waiting for the morning to begin their assault. Let them wait. No sun awaited them, only rain and blood.

"By the gods… Francis?" an all too familiar voice called out. One he begged himself not to hear. She wouldn't understand.

His confidence abandoned him, leaving only the frightened man trying to play emperor. The one so fearful of becoming broken, he had allowed God to shatter him like glass. "*Please*, don't come any closer. Take care of our son. Keep him away from me. Tell him I… Tell him I…"

What a bizarre misstep. A soothing feeling came over him, a reminder that Francis was God's chosen one. The Architect of Paradise. Perfection has no need to apologize to those who cannot understand it. "Ignore that lapse in judgment. Care to join me for a walk? I have a strange desire to gaze upon the outskirts. I want to see which ones shall be allowed to serve Serenity, and which ones will die screaming as my flames turn them to ash. Doesn't that sound wonderful?'

Unfortunately, Mary didn't smile back, which was the expected response. One of the downfalls of knowledge is knowing the exact quantity of sorrow waiting to strike. She stepped forward and gave him a long kiss on the cheek. It wasn't one of those little good morning pecks lovers did when they woke up at the same time. Actually, it reminded him of the last time Mother had kissed him before passing away. A bizarre, yet intimate moment. All Francis had felt was awkwardness but, looking back, it had clearly been her way of saying goodbye.

"Beloved," he said to Mary, who was walking away. "This is not farewell. Find it within yourself to have faith in me. All of my pieces have been put back together. Look at me! I am no longer broken. I am the Architect of Paradise."

She stopped and glanced back. Why she had tears in her eyes was anyone's guess. "You were never broken. You were perhaps the most put-together man I have ever known. It's my failure that I could never convince you of how special you were."

Were? As in the past tense? Please don't leave me, he thought, but something prevented him from saying it. No matter how badly he wanted to scream, perfection wouldn't allow it. Such is the price of being a hero. "Leave if you must, my beloved. Rest assured, your enemies shall be slain by this time tomorrow. Our son will sit on a throne crafted from their bones and ashes."

Francis stepped into the main hallway and met the gaze of a familiar merchant. "You," he said. "Hand me your cloak. Now." While the man didn't appear intelligent, he proved that assumption false by obeying immediately.

Maybe it was silly to hide, but Francis had no desire to be seen or, worse yet, spoken to by his inferior subjects. A tad ironic, considering how painful the name Invisible Guardian had used to be. The rain pattered onto his hood. His face was covered, but all the Vanguards still glanced in his direction. Of course they would know, but at least none disturbed him.

He passed through the military ward and into the trade district, an area he normally wouldn't waste his time in. The first day he had been there, he nearly gagged from the horrid smells and constant screaming. It was like the people had summoned a demon from the ruins of Boulom to overwhelm his senses. Now...it was quaint. Nowhere near its full potential, but the streets were clean, the homeless had been moved well out of sight and, best of all, it was *quiet.* Curfews had sent the people home, all based on a simple logic: an empty street was a safe street.

There was so much more to be done but Terrangus had clearly prospered under his rule. Father would not have condoned such acts, but Mother would have been proud. If they won...oh, if they won. Francis could help every kingdom reach its full potential.

He smiled, took a deep breath, then approached the city gates. Unfortunately, it was time to lose his cloak. While most of the military were Vanguards, "normal" soldiers still patrolled the giant walls surrounding Terrangus.

"Sir, there is no passage beyond this point," a guard said. "Go back to your home without incident and I'll spare you the penalty for ignoring the curfew."

While it was absurd the man didn't recognize Francis, at least he enforced the law—to some extent. "You have five seconds to recognize who you're speaking to. After that, you will be sent to the conversion room for improvement."

"Forgive me, Lord Emperor. The rain...it clouds my vision."

"Does it also cloud your judgment? It matters not, remove yourself from my path and let it be known that if I ever hear you offer leniency for ignoring curfew again, the results will be... unfortunate. Heed the advice of your emperor: mercy and greatness are incompatible. Do you understand? No, of course you don't."

The man was smart enough not to reply. He bowed and stepped aside, hopefully taking the full brunt of the threat to heart. There are few things more unwise than calling a god's bluff.

The stairs were steep, obviously meant for soldiers and not scholars. His ankles burned as he made the final step, then he sighed and leaned against the stone barricade. The view at the top was nearly worth it. It was like a painting—rain sweeping across the plains, tents and men scattered out far into the distance. Was it madness to admire the enemy? They had traveled by foot all the way from Alanammus to defy God himself. Most of them would never see their home again.

"Admiring the view, Emperor?" asked Wisdom from behind. "I must admit, beauty is one of the more bizarre aspects of freewill. If only the cost wasn't so catastrophic."

"I'll never comprehend what drives them to defy us. It's more than sheer madness or ignorance. Why are they so convinced we are wrong?"

"A fair question. I have been a god for several centuries now, and I struggle to provide an adequate answer. All I know for certain is that it all comes down to loss. Mortals and gods are beings of balance. Take something, anything, away and it creates a need to fill the void. Some fill it with art. Some grab their weapon of choice and fight for leaders who will never know their names. I... Well, you see, Francis, I learned from my loss. If I win...if *we* win, all is forgiven. I have thought about it every day for centuries upon centuries. Your lack of reaction betrays you. Just ponder the ramifications. It's like alchemy. We take our loss and turn it into paradise."

Turning loss into paradise? Francis wasn't sure it was possible, but he would not dare tell that to God. "It's odd really. Their determination is gilded in lies. They all came here to die. Lord Wisdom, if I may ask, what will you do when there are no more enemies?" A long pause followed those words. Perhaps the question was unfair, but a scholar must never apologize for the pursuit of knowledge.

Arrogance finally chuckled. "Simple. Anything I want really. I just have to figure out what that is."

The rain pattered down, giving them an excuse to stand there in silence.

CHAPTER 39

AN EMPRESS AND HER VANGUARD

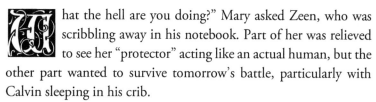

hat the hell are you doing?" Mary asked Zeen, who was scribbling away in his notebook. Part of her was relieved to see her "protector" acting like an actual human, but the other part wanted to survive tomorrow's battle, particularly with Calvin sleeping in his crib.

"Well, I'm nearly finished with *Rinso Volume IV*. Most of us aren't going to survive the battle tomorrow. Forgive me if that frightens you, but I am bound to speak the truth."

Mary snickered. "Aren't you my bodyguard? Shouldn't you be doing...I don't know, bodyguard things?"

"I shall, Empress, but please allow me to finish, in case tomorrow is the end. While I gladly serve Lord Wisdom and your family, there are oaths I made that cannot be denied. No matter... how hard I try."

Oaths? It was probably something between him and Sardonyx, especially if Rinso was involved. Mary had only read the first book and it was awful. Really awful. Characters fell in love instantly, the names were bizarre, and most of the pages were characters snickering while they drifted towards things. One glance at the back of book two was all she needed to confirm there were grander things in life deserving her attention. "Maybe I can help. Let me see—"

"No!" he yelled, taking his papers back.

"Too bad. I guess we're going back to Terrangus military protocol because I command it." The idea of Zeen or Mary commanding anyone during their time in the Koulva mines would have been laughable, but here they were: an empress and her Vanguard. Arrogance was probably half-right about freewill being absurd, but the more reasonable observation was that life itself was a weird mix of chaos and beauty. If we take all of that away...what's the point?

"Fine," Zeen said, pushing his work forward and stepping away.

Mary grinned at him, pushing down how sad it was that he didn't smile back. Arrogance never bothered to understand what made people special. *Rinso smiled with his face,* she read, making a note to cross out "with his face," *as he looked up into the skies, looking into the puffy white clouds floating in the sky. It turned out - there was a god of gods all along - and his name was Lord Wisdom. With all the imperfections of his life removed - Rinso was free to let go and follow his dream, which was...*

All that he wanted was to

All he wanted was

All he ever wanted

Damn, Zeen was a terrible writer. Tempest would definitely be proud, wherever he was. "Zeen, this sucks. Are you writing the ending? There's nothing at stake or any emotion."

"That's the problem! Rinso won, and I don't know what to do next."

"What about Olivia? I only read the first one, but wasn't the whole point to get them together? Rinso kept reminding the reader how he wanted to 'caress her womanly curves.' Now, I'm no healing mage, but I still don't know what that means."

Zeen appeared lost in thought. Maybe he was trying to remember how to laugh. "He doesn't get Olivia in the end. That was the original plan of course, but God won't let me write it. If he can't have Maya, Rinso can't have Olivia. Honestly, I'm not sure what that means but his word is absolute."

Arrogance was such a petty loser. If Calvin's life wasn't at stake, she would welcome the invaders with open arms and let them burn it all to the ground. "What if I write it? With the way things are going, I'll either be dead or a Vanguard by this time tomorrow. Zeen, I owe you… many favors. Let me give you this."

It was always fun to watch Zeen think, because she could nearly imagine the cogs in his head as he rubbed his chin, trying to come up with a response. "Write it, but don't let me read it. The unknown cannot be blasphemy. Right?"

If the Haide family all died tomorrow, hopefully historians would leave out the fact Mary had spent her last night writing a terrible book. She turned to a blank page and wrote,

"Rinso," Olivia said - with a gentle - yet very powerful voice. "Come forward, look at your daughter. Our daughter. She has your eyes. Our eyes."

With the heart in his chest beating very hard and very fast, he quickly walked over to Olivia and their daughter. "What will we name her?"

"How about…"

She paused. What would they name her? It would be best to let Zeen decide. In a perfect realm, Arrogance would die tomorrow, and her old friend could open to that page with a smile on his face. Unfortunately, they didn't live in a perfect realm. No wonder people like Zeen and Tempest had spent all that time writing silly stories. Was fantasy a distraction, a yearning for a better future, or some weird combination of both?

"What did you write?" asked Zeen, who then came to his senses. "Sorry, don't answer that. Empress, will you think less of me if I admit that I'm scared?"

"I didn't know you could feel that way anymore. Is it Arrogance? Is he watching us right now? Can you even tell?"

"God is far away. Far, far away. Sometimes, I don't think he can hear my prayers. Other times, I worry that he does and just doesn't care enough to answer them."

Mary pushed the paper aside and sat next to him. It probably wasn't a great sign that her bodyguard looked like he wanted to cry. "Zeen, what's wrong. Why are you so nervous?"

"Of course I'm nervous. Even from here, I can tell God is nervous too. And if he's afraid, what hope do we have?"

She sighed at the obvious. Tomorrow would be a bloodbath, and it would take a miracle to get her son out alive. "I'll be afraid with you. Listen, whatever happens, there is no shame in defeat. You and I have survived a hell of a lot longer than we should have." Mary smiled, but he didn't smile back. In fact, he looked worse than before.

"No, no. It's not defeat that worries him, but victory. God doesn't know what to do when there are no more enemies. Serenity…is more of an ideal than he dares admit. What if it isn't real? What have we done?"

"Lower your voice!" she yelled which, admittingly, defeated the purpose. "What we have done is survive but it's not about us anymore. Tell me, and be honest, do you love my son?"

"Of course I do! Look at him! He has your eyes."

It was probably a terrible mistake, but she took a deep breath and said, "If you want to protect me, ensure that my little boy safely gets to Serenna. She made me an oath—"

"*Stop!*" Zeen dropped to one knee, gasping for air. "That name… I am not allowed to hear or think about that name. You are my empress, but please, spare me the torment."

Calvin cried from his crib while Zeen trembled. Great, she now had two whining boys to look after. She picked up Calvin with one hand and helped Zeen rise with the other. "Relax, you two. How about I read you a story?" Calvin didn't stop crying; he must have been distraught about the prospect of hearing another puppeteer's tale.

"The Harbinger of Death has arrived," Zeen said, leaning against her bed. "Xavian kingdom. We have all been alerted. Never imagined the safety of the realm would be in Nyfe's hands."

"Hush. Focus on me, and nothing else." Mary grabbed Zeen's notes from the table, and turned to the first page. She cleared her throat and read out loud, "'Rinso gently stepped off his unicorn, coming down into the soft, sand-like grass…'" *What the hell is sand-*

like grass? "'While Death's Harbinger was already defeated, Fear would be lurking. She lurked in the shadows, lurking with bad intentions, waiting for the right moment to strike. Who would be her target? Olivia had already lost her father, brother, and long-lost twin sister to becoming a Harbinger. Would she be next? Impossible!'"

Damn, it was going to be a long night.

CHAPTER 40

HEART OF STONE

ven after a week's travel from Mylor to Terrangus, David couldn't help but admire the midnight sky. If the worst came to pass and they failed tomorrow, he would at least die a free man. The dagger in his sheath would make sure of that. While his reflection still showed a Guardian's frail shadow, he felt healthier. Maybe it was all mental, or just his body's thanks for finally putting down the wine.

Strange that he couldn't find Noelami. Sardonyx stood at the head of their encampment, staring solemnly into Terrangus, most likely on the lookout for treachery. To be fair, tomorrow was the big day, and if David had learned anything, gods were usually more anxious than the mortals who worshiped them.

Everything else was the classic pre-war scene. Some soldiers slept, some vomited behind trees, most slammed drinks and exchanged tales by the campfire. In a different realm, David would be one of them. At least the awkwardness had passed. Mylor had given their Alanammus counterparts a cold shoulder for most of the journey. Was it deserved? Sure, but most of them had wised up and realized they were all going home or none of them.

David refilled his chalice with water and walked over to Serenna's tent. He had been denied entry every night since the march, but perhaps tonight would be different. Maybe not. Her tent was more guarded than usual, which made sense this close to Terrangus. Oh well, the worst defeat is to never try at all.

"Good evening, sir. Is Serenna accepting visitors?"

"Sorry, David," the lead guard said. Disappointing, but at least they recognized him now. "Warlord Bloom is the only one permitted to enter. You must understand, the battle weighs heavy on her mind—"

"Let him pass," Serenna called out from inside her tent.

The guard didn't look pleased but was smart enough not to argue. He nodded at David and stepped aside.

Within the tent, Serenna stood fully armored, sipping a steaming drink. She eyed him cautiously. "Forgive me, I'm still not used to seeing you sober. Care for a cup of tea? Supposedly it helps with sleep, though I remain unconvinced."

"A kind offer, but water has proven to be a powerful ally."

"Nonsense. Sophia, brew our friend here a cup. Make it strong. Not *that* strong. You know what I mean."

David had never enjoyed tea, but it didn't seem wise to argue. Serenna had lost too much weight and the circles under her eyes were dark enough to look painted on. He smiled and said, "After all these years, I never imagined the two of us having a tea party."

She sat at her end of the table and gestured for David to take the far seat. "Tea party? Is that what this is? Pardon me for assuming you had urgent business the night before the realm is altered forever."

Don't get mad, David thought, forcing a smile and accepting his cup from Sophia. He took a sip and pushed down the urge to groan at the bitter taste. "Urgent business indeed. Take it from me, there are many paths to self-destruction. Some appear more appealing than others. On that note, Sophia, please leave us for a moment."

"You presume I have time for this nonsense? It was foolish of me to allow you entry. Once a fool, always a fool."

He took another sip; to be honest, it was rather pleasant. "I'll give you that one. I am indeed a fool. However, so are you. The only reason I still breathe is because the Goddess of Fear saved my life. I leapt from Alanammus Tower, not giving a second thought to all those I would leave behind."

"*Stop it.* Why are you telling me this?"

David slammed his fist on the table, causing her to flinch. "You have leapt from a tower of your own making. It's not instantaneous like most ends, but a corrosion of the heart and body. Pride abandoned me long ago, so I have come to beg. To beg you to return to us."

Her eyes flickered from rage to defeat. She sipped her tea, then rose and stepped away. "It's happening again. I'm marching the realm's remaining heroes to the very doorstep of hell. Arrogance is always one step ahead. I never had your instincts, David. Why do they trust me? What have I done to enlist every mortal and god in this endeavor? My only solace is that I doubt anyone will remember me if we lose. Arrogance will wipe my name from the history books, and write nothing but his own Serenity."

All David could do was smile. And sip his tea. By Fear's mercy, it was delicious. "Leadership is mostly perception. I'm intrigued that even now, you could never see through the mirage. I was just a depressed old drunk, waving my sword and yelling out orders. I think you're different. And if not, then congratulations, you have constructed a mirage of your own."

"Why are you not afraid? He tortured you for months on end. He is evil. Pure evil. I cannot be the one that forfeits the realm to his control."

"Then don't. Be the one who ensures his demise. I am a shadow of the man I was. I say that not with regret, but with acceptance. If I meet my end tomorrow, rest assured I will do so swinging my blade at a tyrant. All mortal and divine forces are at your call. We're going to kill him, then we're going to bring home Zeen. Total victory, or total annihilation. There are no half-measures."

Maybe she took the words to heart because Serenna sipped her tea and took a long pause. Silence was usually a good sign. "When you lost Melissa…how did you persevere? How does one ever recover from such a loss?"

"They don't, and that's okay. I stopped trying to remove the scar and accepted the scar was part of me. Heed my words, Serenna of Mylor: I am old, tired, and damaged, but look upon me. I have never been more strong. I have never been more determined. And I have never, *ever* been more of a mountain. It's about time you looked in a mirror and realized the same."

"The mirror has never been kind enough to lie." She approached, then gave him a gentle hug, leaning her head against his chest. "Thank you for everything. Regardless of how tomorrow goes, being your friend for the past ten years has been a wonderful blessing. I must demand one final oath. If things become dire, we perish together. I will not—I *cannot*—serve Arrogance."

After Arrogance had lied about Vanguard Serenna being tortured, David had no choice but to agree. "I have dodged the void for a very long time. If tomorrow doesn't go as planned, then I shall join you there. We can walk into the infinite darkness together. And finally, *finally* get some rest."

Serenna let go and stepped away, giving a hint of a smile. "It's rather nice when you put it that way. Happily ever after, or a peaceful slumber. Be that as it may, we must give this everything. There is no backup plan, no heroes waiting in the shadows to avenge us. Everything depends on me. Perhaps, it always did."

"Not you, but us. It may be a simple word, but never lose sight of its power. The army of Arrogance is filled with puppets and slaves. They are woefully unprepared to face a desperate team with nothing to lose. Enjoy your tea and sleep well, my friend. By this time tomorrow, your most stressful decision will be who's in charge of rebuilding Terrangus."

"Indeed, I have already given it thought... What about you? You're still a legend there, and if anyone could bring the people together, it would be Terrangus's greatest Guardian."

David laughed; the idea was pure lunacy. "If you ever loved me, the only authority I desire is to become emperor of sleep. But...thank you. There was a time when I thought my entire legacy would be that of a monster. Perhaps it still may come to pass, but I dare to dream that history will remember me favorably."

"If your story is written with any truth, it will tell the tale of an

imperfect man who sacrificed everything to protect the realm."
Serenna stared into her empty chalice. "Could I interest you in more
tea? The night comes to a close but I'm not prepared to rest."

"Of course, but only if we can drink outside."

She nodded, took both their chalices, then put leaves and some
other things inside them. As long as the minty taste was waiting for
him, David would drink anything. She handed him his chalice, then
held open the tent flap for him to follow.

Surprisingly, no one really paid them any mind. People did
stare of course, but no one approached or bothered them. Maybe
they understood the need to be alone, or maybe they were terrified
of Serenna. The days of fearing David had long passed.

She sat on the grass away from the tents and soldiers, and David
sat next to her. After a few moments of relaxing silence, Fear and
Tradition appeared next to them both and sat as well. Sardonyx
snapped his fingers, creating a tiny fire in the middle.

"A fire before the final battle," Noelami said with a snicker.
"How glorious."

"Glorious indeed," Sardonyx said.

David smiled and sipped his tea. "Nice of you to finally join us.
The only one we're missing is—"

"Hey! Make room," Bloom yelled, rushing over. Her eyes lit up
when she saw their glasses were full. "Ah, we getting sloppy? Let me
take a sip." She gagged before the tea ever hit her snout. "What the
fuck? *Tea?* It's possibly the last night of our lives and we're drinking
tea?"

"Not all of us," said Fear. With a wave of her hand, Bloom and
Noelami each held a chalice filled with a dark liquid that looked—
and smelled—like zephum ale. "And you, Tradition? I cannot
fathom the warlord of old sipping on human tea."

"The only thing that will quench my thirst is victory over that
vile fiend. Still…" He hesitated, then created a mug in his own
hand. "I shall join you in a drink. Raise your glasses! We honor the
fallen!"

"To Father," said Serenna. "And Valor. Landon. Even Martin."

My mistakes shall always linger, but I will harness them to create the peace I have always yearned for."

Bloom chugged half her glass, then rubbed her snout. "Glory to the fallen Eltune…and Pyith! The best damn Guardian I ever knew. She was the very pride of Vaynex."

Forgive me, my love, but it must be done. No one else would say it, so David raised his tea and said, "To Tempest Claw. No matter how it turned out, I will always remember the kind-hearted zephum who studied trade laws and wrote books that…other people enjoyed."

An awkward silence followed, but Sardonyx nodded at him. He didn't smile, didn't grin, but they shared a moment of acceptance. "Glory and honor to Melissa," Sardonyx said, raising his mug. "A warrior can best be measured by the wake that forms following their demise. Heed my words: there is not a human or zephum in our realm who could gaze upon her wake without trembling."

Thank you, old friend. A crushing wake indeed—

"To Ermias," Noelami said. She drank her full glass instead of raising it. She must have felt everyone's confused stare lingering, so she said, "I don't care how you feel about that, or if you choose to honor him. It changes nothing. He still must die, but I will never relinquish my memories. Of all my three hundred years, there are about four of them I dream of every day. There are so many events… that should never have occurred. I knew my mantra from the day I opened my eyes as a goddess. Where reality fails, dreams are eternal. No matter how tomorrow fares, I shall join my kingdom of Boulom as both a memory and a dream. It's time to let go. It's time to go home."

"I'll drink to that," David said, even though he didn't want to. "While we're all here, I want to make something perfectly clear. Zeen comes back alive."

"If that's not possible," Serenna said, "then let me be the one to end him. I have spent our entire journey preparing for the moment. I shall destroy my heart, if it means bringing my lover peace. He would do the same for me."

It wasn't David's place to tell her how wrong she was. Honestly, she probably already knew. Against his better judgment, he said, "If it comes down to it, I should be the one. My heart of stone cannot grow harder." After such thoughts, there was a sad irony in lying. Hearts have no threshold. They can bleed out of love or loss in infinite quantities.

Serenna sipped the last of her tea and placed her chalice on the grass. She looked at David with a sad mix of anger and loss. "I know you mean well, but your words are cruel and gilded in lies. If Melissa was under his hold, we wouldn't even be having this conversation."

Gods, he didn't want to fight on their last night. She was wrong, oh so wrong, but he could accept that. "Perhaps. Perhaps not. Regardless…your tea is having the desired effect. Excuse me friends, I'm off to sleep. To dream." He rose and walked away. It was rather disappointing that no one stopped him.

CHAPTER 41

VICTORY IS THE PROTOCOL OF VALOR

erenna hadn't slept well last night, and that was okay. After tonight, she would finally rest easy with the burden of Arrogance off her shoulders, or permanently within the void. Both options seemed appealing as her eyes twitched. There was no point in changing her armor from last night. In a few hours, perhaps sooner, she would be drenched in blood.

She stepped outside her tent, letting the rain soak her platinum hair. Of course it would rain on their fateful day. The faint thunder and howling wind made the scene look like something out of a Rinso novel. Formation was surprisingly good: Bloom and company had already lined up most of their forces across the outskirts, far enough to avoid ranged attacks but close enough to charge.

"Boss," said Bloom, rushing over. It was odd to see her in the same light mail as last night; most zephum leaders wore so much armor to battle they could barely move. "My humans are ready to go but, apparently, we need to shield everyone first. How long will that take?"

"Just a few minutes with everyone already in formation. Before you voice dissent, remember we are facing an army of mostly magic users—"

Bloom tapped a large scar on her snout. "It's been a long year. Don't need no reminders."

Serenna bit her lip; that was a fair point. "Apologies. Then I shall begin so we can proceed with the assault. May the gods protect us."

"Sorry Boss, but that's your job. Oh, one last thing. It's not our battleground but Tradition confirmed that a Harbinger of Death is active in Xavian. I'm not one for lying so let me be blunt: I think we're gonna win. But hey, if not, it's been an honor." Bloom pounded her chest. "Strength without honor—is chaos."

Serenna matched the salute and said, "Victory is the protocol of Valor."

Bloom nodded and left, most likely to hound Captain Kolsen of the gold cloaks.

"How can I serve?" asked David, equipped in light leather armor. It was pleasant to see some muscle had returned to his body. He was still far thinner than the average soldier but to be fair...so was she. It didn't seem right to throw him in with the military. To be honest, she preferred that he stay behind as some faint shimmer of hope, someone who could rally the realm in case their battle ended in failure. Again.

But he would never accept such an order. "Stay by my side. You have protected me from all sorts of demons in our time together. I humbly request that you do so one last time."

"One last time. I like the sound of that." David drew his sword and studied it. The blade was much lighter than his usual weapons, but she held no doubts about the man wielding it. "Zeen named this blade Hope when I gave it to him. I look forward to returning his gift."

"Come," she said, grabbing the Wings of Mylor and stepping forward. "Crystal mages! Commence the barriers!" Her voice was only loud enough for the closer squads, but after several giant platinum barriers filled the air, the others followed suit. It was difficult to tell the quality of each barrier from within her own sphere. They would have to suffice.

"What is our plan of action?" asked David. He seemed uneasy with all the shields and barriers coming up, which was fair. "I am unconvinced we can occupy the kingdom for any significant amount of time. Once the Harbinger of Death is slain, massive reinforcements may overwhelm us."

"Be that as it may, it's our only option. At the very least, we need to secure the trade district and most of the military ward to gain access to the castle. Once that is complete..." She took a deep breath. It felt absurd to say it out loud, but such was the realm. "We storm the castle. We storm Serenity. And with Fear and Tradition on our side, we kill God."

"Simple and to the point. A fair plan," he said, though he probably didn't mean it.

The gates of Terrangus always appeared twice as large when fully manned. Most of the Vanguards were already glowing orange, clearly prepared to turn the choke point into an inferno. Barriers would be enough to get her forces inside. After that, they were on their own.

Serenna approached the edge of her barrier. "Proceed," she said to the lead mage. It was a slow, steady march to the gates of Terrangus. The rain tapping on their platinum barrier distorted her view, but the glowing Vanguards were like beacons in the darkness. Waiting, inviting her. Did they have any fear at all? Did Arrogance even allow such emotions? She would have pitied them if they weren't monsters. Even after defending her home for all those months, it would never feel normal to face puppets draped in human flesh. Puppets like Zeen. *Stop it. No distractions. I will free my love. By any means necessary.*

As they approached, balls of flame flew towards them from the gates. She grabbed her staff, channeling her own energy into the enormous barrier above, making sure not to enter her empowered form. She would require every drop of energy to defeat Arrogance. "Brace yourselves for impact. No matter what, do not slow our pace, nor can you afford to lose balance in the mud. Every first-year mage is taught to target the unmoving."

The first crash hit, which sent a loud impact but did not dent the barrier. She barely flinched at the sound. The soldiers that did quickly composed themselves after noting their leader was unfazed.

David had been correct: leadership was a mirage, and she would wear the lie proudly.

She tensed her shoulders as she marched towards the gates, pouring more energy into the barrier above them. The impacts increased in frequency, but repetition is the death of surprise—

It was too early for screams. One of the barriers must have shattered in the rear squads, but there was no time for hesitation. "*March!*" she yelled, and they obeyed. Gods forgive her, but they obeyed. Sweat poured down her head as the screams fell silent in the distance. Hopefully it wasn't Bloom's team. If it was…

Keep moving.

Sardonyx leaped off his unicorn to land in front of the gates. In his god-form he was nearly as large as a mountain. With a swift swing of his sword, the gates crashed open. He stepped forward, swatting away the barrage of fire and lightning spells pounding him. "Children of Tradition!" his voice boomed out, echoing throughout the rainy skies. "Come forth and enter the fray! Our battle shall be glorious!"

It must have pained Sardonyx to restrain himself from slaying the Vanguards. One rather large inferno crashed into his snout which, to her shock, sent him stumbling a few steps back. "Ah, so the emperor reveals himself! Savor the glory, Child of Arrogance. It shall be your last." He hopped back onto his unicorn and soared into the skies.

If Francis could wound a god, they were clearly in trouble. None of her forces had any artifacts. Ironically, their greatest strength was desperation. While it may not have been a virtue, it can turn the tide of any battle. "Maintain our pace!" she yelled. Her soldiers were clearly ready to charge, but a lack of focus would weaken the barrier. No excuse to be foolish. It would only take one spell to break through and kill them all…

Despite her orders, their unit charged forward into the trade district, and she had no choice but to follow. Apparently, a screaming lizard god can be quite the muse. "Fine! Keep moving; don't stop at the entrance. We need to push in and make room for the rest of our forces."

No one was listening. The barrier flickered after taking another strike; she tensed her shoulders to keep it going but quickly gave up as Terrangus forces rushed them from all directions. Several of them were zephum, draped in black Terrangus uniforms. What a woeful sight. Others were standard soldiers and not Vanguards. How odd, to face normal humans again—

A fireball landed to her right, far more powerful than the others, knocking her to the rocky terrain. Francis probably had them target her specifically. She rolled over and re-shielded herself as David helped her stand. The Vanguards above them had to be dealt with. It would be impossible to win a melee with spells crashing down the entire time, particularly against a foe that was unbothered by casualties.

Bloom. I need Bloom. Where is Bloom?

"Kolsen!" She rushed over and grabbed him. "Where is the warlord? We must secure the upper perimeter."

"I… I…" the captain stared down, shaking. Of course he was. Alanammus had hidden themselves away from the horrors of the realm for too long. Now they were face-to-face with an enemy they could not comprehend.

Useless. Serenna pushed him aside and refreshed her crystal shield and David's. She needed to get to the stairs, but the melee was converging all around them. At least her forces were pushing through the gates. The Vanguards above kept launching spells, regardless of friendly fire. It was surreal how the Vanguards didn't scream as they burned from their own allies.

A zephum slammed his axe down on her sphere, creating a large crack. She summoned a single spike and launched it into his neck, then crafted two more smaller spikes. Let them come. Let them think she was weak. It felt cruel to Sardonyx to target the zephum Vanguards, but they were the largest targets.

A Vanguard fell behind her. David pulled his sword out and nodded. "We need to get them off the towers. Even if we press forward, we are wide open for attack. Give the word and I'll do it."

As much as it needed to be done, he couldn't do it. Not alone, at least. She refreshed their shields as another fireball landed beside them. Despite the frosty wind, all the fire spells made it feel like a miserable summer day. "Find Bloom and tell her to clear the towers. I'm pressing ahead."

"Serenna…"

"You never tolerated dissent when you were leader. Take it to heart that the lesson carried on."

She gasped as he grabbed her by the shoulder. "Fuck the lesson. *You* must carry on. Consider those towers cleared. When we reunite, we shall do so in victory. Farewell, my friend, my leader." David rushed off into the darkness.

An unmoving target was most vulnerable, and yet she froze. That was proven unwise as a blast of fire shattered her shield, launching her into the side of a building. Only by pure instinct did she keep the Wings of Mylor in her grasp. Her skull ached. Even with adrenaline coursing through her body, it was difficult to rise. Shields enveloped her. Not from herself but forces throughout the trade district. Then barriers on top of the shields.

More impacts, followed by a perfect strike against her shields. She watched the eruption through the hazy platinum hue. Several of the Vanguards must have attacked her in unison as a blinding cascade of orange and yellow pounded down.

"Serenna!" a voice called out.

"Protect our Guardian!"

"Arrogance shall not have her!"

Shields upon shields protected her, preventing the onslaught of fire and lightning from sending her to the void. Despite the cacophony of war, her people were focused on her. Endless shields and barriers, layered upon each other from soldiers whose names she would never know. Twenty-nine years and it had all been a lie.

It didn't only depend on her. It never did.

Serenna erupted into her empowered form, her platinum energy knocking down the wall of the building beside her. She immediately formed two giant crystal spikes outside of the barrier protecting her. There were too many glowing targets up above to choose from. Oh? One aura was far away and much brighter than the rest. Francis was never one for subtlety.

She launched both giants at the same target.

CHAPTER 42

THE PRECIPICE OF SERENITY

he sight of the empowered Serenna only made Francis grin from his tower in the military ward. She was a fool. She had always been a fool. To waste her power this early into the battle was unworthy of his nemesis. Perhaps some novice girl had stolen her armor and decided to lead the battle on her own? Francis snickered at the thought. *This* was the woman Mary had trusted to raise their child? Serenna? Oh well. His beloved had chosen poorly, but such was the natural order of things.

Francis gripped the Herald of Arrogance, letting the power flow through him as he radiated orange. Such wrath was his to command, and what a wrath it was. He had wounded a god! The worst one, unfortunately, but a god, nonetheless. One more blast would send Serenna to the void. The flames would burn so fierce, not a scholar in the realm would be able to identify her remains. Hmm? Two flickers of platinum were flying towards him. Oh well, not even Serenna could manage such a shot from afar. Maybe if she still wielded Valor's scythe, but the goddess had already fallen to the superior deity—

"*Move, you fool!*" God yelled through his thoughts.

So Francis did, against his will. Those involuntary movements were highly uncomfortable, but such was the price of ultimate power. One of the crystal spikes flew by, grazing his shoulder. The shock of feeling pain again sent Francis down, stumbling until he hit the railing behind him. Bless that railing for saving him from a catastrophic fall, though it would've been a fitting end for the kingdom and emperor to fall in unison. A bizarre moment of clarity followed as he caught his breath. By Wisdom's glory, they were here in Terrangus, burning down his kingdom. All of them! Alanammus, Mylor, Bloom—all of them! *Mary,* he thought, gripping his staff. *Terrangus doesn't matter. I must protect Mary. I must protect Calvin...*

"My dear Francis, if you ever desire the embrace of your wife or son again, I advise you to get off the floor and compose yourself. You stand upon the precipice of Serenity, of pure perfection and joy. Oh, and also, your own death. Now stop embarrassing me and flaunt your new wrath."

Francis groaned as he forced himself up. Another spike flew at him, barely missing as it shattered the adjacent railing. Flee. He should flee. Regroup, reform, do something other than stand there. Perhaps it was time to call Vanguard Ultra away from Mary? No. No, no. It was just one woman doing everything in her power to ensure the realm stayed miserable. Serenna was nothing compared to the Architect of Paradise.

No need to oppose her directly. All I have to do is slay her forces.

Easy enough. Francis casually walked down the stairs of his tower, taking the time to catch his breath. The irony was not lost on him. He had invaded Terrangus to remove Nyfe from power. Now, the ouster was the one being ousted. Let them try. None of them would live to see tomorrow.

Francis pushed open the door to the tower. He had to focus on his hands to stop them from shaking. Already, there were so many dead, forces battling upon the towers above, slaying his Vanguards and pressing forward. By Wisdom's glory, they were losing. How could that possibly be? Everything...had it all been for nothing? Perhaps they would allow a surrender or a compromise? No. A fool's thought. Arrogance had taught the lesson: perfection is an absolute. To parley with failure is a fate worse than death.

Francis adjusted his glow to yellow. He walked to the very gates of the trade district. Serenna would be a problem, but there were easier ways to deal with her. Kill her people. Kill them all.

It was oddly refreshing to point his staff at a gold cloak and incinerate the man with a bolt of lightning. The fool didn't have the courtesy to move; he just stood there and blew up like a practice dummy. Francis effortlessly blasted six more of them, letting out a sigh of relief as several zephum Vanguards assembled on his position. He had imagined many things in his days, but being protected by inferior lizard-beasts had never been one of them. Going on the offensive was clearly the best course of action. He took a step forward—unfortunately getting mud on his sandals—and pressed the Gold Cloaks back all by himself. *These* people were the pride of Alanammus? Useless! They were all useless! One of his zephum bodyguards dove in front of him, intercepting a familiar-looking gadget.

"Fire!"

The Vanguard literally exploded, launching blood and body parts in all directions. It was kind of the rain to move that mess elsewhere.

"Attack her at once!" Francis yelled, taking a step back. Bloom was a fool, but the most dangerous sort of fool. His Vanguards all rushed in together as Francis adjusted his glow to orange. In normal circumstances, fire has several disadvantages in a group setting. Most of his Vanguards in the proximity would die a terrible death, but they would die in service to Serenity. Their names would be remembered for their sacrifice. Not by Francis of course, but by... someone else.

It was surprising that Bloom didn't rely on her detonators. Slashing and dashing like a brute, she punished each miss with a fatal blow, surrounding herself with fallen Vanguard after fallen Vanguard. Why was she more powerful than his soldiers? Enlightenment was meant to be an improvement, not a downgrade—

She was rushing forward.

Francis needed to act, but was frozen, paralyzed by the anxiety and doubt that had always cursed his life. Thankfully, his hands moved on their own, as if he were guided by some powerful, vengeful wrath. Enough foolishness. The chosen one of Arrogance was destined for a greatness these mortals couldn't comprehend. They raged and flailed at perfection, uncaring at the absurdity of it all. Francis launched a fire blast.

It was a tad off target, but that wouldn't matter.

CHAPTER 43

THE WORTHLESS LEAVE NO LEGACY

amn. That was one giant ball of fire. Bloom's first thought was to grab an ice-detonator, but it was too late. Fuck it, this would be a fair death. She pushed down all her doubt and kept rushing forward. Math was never her thing, but maybe if she stood at the right spot, the blast would launch her in the direction of Francis, and she could use that momentum to slice his throat while she flew past him.

Yeah, so that didn't happen.

Bloom *did* get launched, but to the far left, sending her crashing through the window of some human tavern. The weirdest part was the sound. While the fire blast was loud, the shatter of her crystal shield was so high-pitched, she couldn't help but scream. The few humans that were inside abruptly rose from their tables and fled upstairs. Probably a smart move. Ugh, Bloom was tired of facing magic users. The four or five zephum she had managed to cut to shreds had been such a release—

The entire building erupted into flames. Bless her body for not feeling the pain; she felt a numb determination as she dove back out through the broken window. The relief died when a tiny piece of broken glass grazed the bottom of her tail. She screamed and welcomed the rage. Enough of this shit. She rose from the ground and drew a sword in one hand and a fire-detonator in another. If this human wanted to play with fire, it would end with the emperor burning alive.

"Come, Warlord," he yelled, but she swore it wasn't his usual whiny voice. Something had changed in the human, and whatever it was, it had ruined him forever. As always, everything the Arrogant One touched eventually turned to shit. "Look upon the pinnacle of humanity. Look upon the Architect of Paradise. It's not too late—I am indeed a merciful ruler. You could join me and reap the benefits of Serenity."

Was Francis seriously going to stand there and monologue? Fuck it, she threw her fire-detonator, but he quickly shifted to blue and covered it in ice. Despite the pain burning in her tail, she resisted the urge to blindly rush forward. With no crystal shield, the next spell that hit would be the last. Maybe words could force him to act recklessly. "Fuck you and fuck Serenity. Better kill me, Francis. If you lose, I'll skin your son alive. I'll make Mary watch until I grow bored and make her my human slave."

At least that ended his smile. He adjusted his glow to orange and stared into her with dead, empty eyes. "Why do brutes always resort to obscenities when the end draws near? A common phenomena. Believe this, Bloom, I will not celebrate today's victory. As soon as your bodies are gathered and burned into ash, your names will soon follow. The worthless leave no legacy—"

Francis turned to his left and immediately launched a ball of fire. It collided with a crystal spike, sending an eruption of fire and glass all around them.

"About time, Boss," she said to Serenna, who had entered her shiny form. "Shield me, I'm going in." Bloom rushed forward, wielding swords in each hand. The plan was to stab something. Anything. Just get this guy down.

Francis had the opposite plan. He erupted into a yellow aura, then sent a blinding flash of light towards her. Bloom never saw the crystal shield, but it was the only explanation as to why she didn't die instantly from the bolt that slammed her body into the rocky terrain. *Get up,* she thought, but struggled to do so. Everything was so tired and weak, like her body was calling in the debts from months at war. More crashes of glass and light forced her body to rise with a warlord's desperation, ignoring the pain in her tail. At least it wasn't itchy.

With Francis pushing the shielded Serenna back with lightning blast after lightning blast, Bloom grabbed an ice-detonator and rushed forward. Odd, he never looked in her direction, but he definitely knew what was happening. Francis sent one giant blast at Serenna, then turned his attention to Bloom. Good, he was still yellow. Probably meant Bloom would be dead in a few moments, but that's all she would need to land the killing blow. She threw her detonator, aimed at his midsection. Didn't matter what froze as long as it was something.

Before Bloom managed to yell "Ice!" a rather large human knocked the detonator away with her shield.

What the fuck? Was that Mary?

CHAPTER 44

MOTHER

 ary swung her shield at the detonator, knocking it far to the side. Her husband was damaged, perhaps even broken, but she had taken her oaths. Till death do them part. Little Calvin was still in their chambers, protected by Zeen. He had offered to come down in her place, but hopeless battles should always be fought alone.

"Empress?" asked Francis. His eyes twitched but his lips barely shifted. "Remove yourself from this skirmish at once! In the case of my demise, one of us must remain to guide our people towards Serenity. If such a tragedy must occur…let me be the one to fall."

"My beloved, we win, or we die, together as a family. Keep Serenna occupied. I doubt I can defeat the warlord, but if you can force Serenna's retreat, we can flank Bloom." She didn't wait for confirmation. She rushed at Bloom who, conveniently enough, was already rushing her with a sword in both hands.

It had been a while since Mary fought a zephum, let alone the mightiest one. Most of them were heavily armored, sluggish, and wielded slow, giant weapons. Bloom was none of those things. With both blades swung at her head, Mary let go of her sword and gripped her shield. She blocked the strike, and channeled every instinct from her infantry days to avoid tripping on her feet as she staggered back. Either Bloom was strong, or Mary was weak. After a year of motherhood and too much wine, the answer may have been obvious.

Still, the empress would *never* be easy prey.

Mary stepped forward, flailing her shield wildly with one hand at Bloom's center. It actually struck, which probably meant Bloom was looking for a counter. Mary watched the hands. Weapons are irrelevant on their own; hands always dictate the steel.

There. Bloom swung up with her left hand, which was slow enough for Mary to duck under and advance. Up-close, the warlord was clearly wounded, with burn scars and blood seeping everywhere. Mary grabbed her, then used every ounce of her body weight to force Bloom to the ground. That wine-weight was good for something. Mary kicked her swords away, then mounted her and rained down blow after blow. Was this really happening? Calvin would never believe her in his later years. "Sure, Mom, you punched a warlord in the face," he would say—

Bloom grabbed her wrist and flung her a few feet back. It wasn't the raw strength or determination that worried Mary, it was the fact Bloom threw her in the opposite direction of her shield. No sword, no shield, up against an opponent who probably weighed twice as much.

She glanced at Francis, who was struggling against Serenna, despite his newfound "supremacy" from becoming a Vanguard. They were going to die. The thought weighed upon her heart like a stone, and all she could do was silently beg for Calvin's safety. He may have had Mary's eyes and nose, but the boy was innocent of his mother's sins.

A fist pounded into Mary's skull. The realm blurred, pain faded, but instincts forced her eyes to watch Bloom's other fist raised high. When it came down, Mary let it hit, but flung her right elbow with whatever strength was left into Bloom's neck. She wasn't sure who got the best of that exchange. Mary swung again with the other hand, barely feeling her entire body weight colliding into the warlord's exposed kidney.

She went to pour all her strength into one last punch until a fist crashed right into her eye. The darkness spread like a disease. Gods, would it truly end this way? Dying to a warlord would be an honorable death, but such a meaningless end meant nothing to her anymore. Mary wanted to live! With her son! With her husband!

Let them say she was a coward. Mary ran behind Francis, barely able to find him with her vision blurring. Thank the gods his glow was so bright. Her legs gave out. She fell on her back, smiling at her husband, reminiscing of better days. What a strange yet wonderful journey from nameless soldier, to Guardian, to empress...to mother. That was the best one. Any fool can wear a crown, but it takes a power beyond gods to bring life into the realm.

"If this is the end, my beloved, thank you for everything."

CHAPTER 45

THE WRATH OF HEAVEN

His beloved was wrong. This wasn't the end. It couldn't be. "Stay behind me," Francis said, letting the power of Arrogance flow through him. Fire and ice were too dangerous with Mary up close, but lightning wasn't prevailing against Serenna's shields for whatever reason. What other options were there? Stall? Yes, stall was a great idea.

He surrounded himself and Mary with a giant wall of earth. His wife had the right idea in lying down for a second wind. May Wisdom bless her tired, beautiful face. Francis collapsed next to her, smiling as the rain tapped along his head. From their little fortress of dirt and rocks, the cacophony of war seemed so far away. If only moments like this could last forever. "We find ourselves in quite the debacle."

"Indeed," she said, wielding the same defeated smile. "Despite everything, it was a wonderful life."

"Not was, but is. We haven't lost yet, Mary—"

"We lost the moment we accepted Arrogance into our lives. My beloved, despite what you may believe, you were never broken. Damaged? Perhaps, but not a mortal in our realm is without their cracks."

"My dear Francis, you must let go. Holding on to your mortality is the only thing preventing me from taking full control. I can save your family. I can create the Serenity you always yearned for. Let go. Let it all go."

"I…" Arrogance was right, Francis could still prevail. It would be the only way to prove her wrong. To prove them all wrong, even himself. Francis rose. By Wisdom's glory, he was exhausted. Wasn't the point of leadership to make other people do the work? "Enough… Enough, enough. This cannot all have been in vain!" It was difficult to describe how, but he did indeed let go. To Mary, to Calvin…to everything. Perfection was an absolute. It all made sense now.

Francis erupted into a multi-colored aura, letting out a nova that crumbled the wall surrounding them. "You have the audacity to challenge the emperor in his own domain? Well, here I am! Take me! Send me to the void of freewill that awaits you all!"

Serenna was tending to the wounded Bloom. She rose and covered the two of them with a shield, then a platinum barrier. Her lips moved, but Francis heard nothing. The silent wail of insignificance was never a sound worth listening to. What…she was fleeing? Serenna was fleeing! Perhaps the wisest move she had ever made.

Interestingly enough, her soldiers didn't follow as Serenna escorted Bloom away. They grouped up and approached the Architect of Paradise. But why? What was the plan here? To rise against the wrath of heaven? Their stoic frowns may have been brave to the uneducated, but Vanguard Francis saw everything. Every flinch, every pang of sweat, every shaky limb. They looked upon the vision of perfection, and they did so in *awe*.

For a few moments at least.

Francis launched an inferno at his attackers. The way they screamed before melting was a comedy unrivaled by any theatrical production. So many invaders in his kingdom, so many fools, so many targets to choose from. Mylor's forces were a fair choice. Hopefully, Serenna knew the name of every last soldier to amplify her despair.

Ah, how wonderful. The Vanguards on the upper levels were pushing back the invaders. Never let anyone say that one man cannot turn the tide of battle. Francis blasted several more into dust with the wrath of his lightning, maintaining eye contact until his opponents no longer had eyes. To be fair, they deserved a miniscule speck of acknowledgement. They wanted this. They *chose* this. Arrogance had been correct; he had always been correct. Freewill was a plague upon the realm.

"I shall destroy you *all!*" he yelled, channeling the flames, letting the heat course through his body. Standing within the middle of the trade district, Francis had been wrong. Improvements were nothing but excuses. Everything needed to be destroyed and born anew. If Terrangus was destined to become the new Boulom, it would need more than simple upgrades. Perhaps the removal of their castle to make way for a cathedral? So many choices! A quick glance at his wife crushed his euphoria. She appeared absolutely miserable, despite their good fortune. A tragedy that couldn't be helped.

Soldiers rushed at him, screaming, wielding their toys. Polearms may look appealing on a wall, but a simple blade on a stick will never defeat God. That didn't stop them from trying.

With all the elements at his disposal, Francis chose ice. He froze gold cloak after gold cloak, leaving them there like statues dedicated to his glory. It was entertaining for a time, but where were the leaders? Ah, there was David, sneaking his way closer, his sword dripping blood from the fallen Vanguard behind him. Ice would be too good for that one. Francis took a deep breath and radiated pure orange. The heat was so powerful, the trade carts in his immediate vicinity caught fire. *Farewell, dear leader. Here's one final lesson before you leave our realm.*

Perfection is an absolute—

"*NO!*" yelled the voice of God, so loud, it brought Francis to his knees. "*He is not to be slain. Death would be a blessing for Maya's chosen. I will not allow it. He will live for ages as I draw every ounce of suffering from his broken mind. He shall stand at the entrance of Serenity and be denied entry, existing forever, weeping at the sight of a life that will never be.*"

God was wrong, if such a thing was possible. The mere

existence of imperfection should not be tolerated. Francis denied his command, forcing the orange glow to return. It did but...oh, it was such agony. Whatever had shielded him from the wrath of his own flames had abandoned him. But why?

"You dare? You truly dare? After everything we accomplished together? And they call me arrogant. My dear Francis, your never-ending defiance is rather exhausting. I warned you about overstepping the line. Now, look behind you and see what your choices have earned you. Good luck."

With the rays of platinum light seething in his peripheral vision, he already knew who it was.

CHAPTER 46

SHATTERED ICE AND GLASS

lood trickled down Serenna's eyes. She was so tired. Even if she managed to defeat Francis, the true enemy still lingered. Regardless, the emperor had lived long enough. He had chosen the life of a tyrant, the same path as his mother. All of this could have been avoided. Where had everything gone wrong? If Alanammus had come to Mylor's aid all those years ago against Forsythe, would all of this have still occurred? It was pointless to wonder, yet she couldn't help but do so. Enough. Serenna pointed her staff and launched a giant spike.

Francis surrounded himself with another wall of earth. A coward's spell. She would not be denied as the spike tore a massive hole through the bottom half of the wall. She crafted two more giants, ignoring the pain in her shoulders. Her body must have known it was nearly over. It offered her power that would have sent her to the ground a month ago.

The two giant spikes flew in unison, striking the earth wall at the right angle to send it crumbling down on one side. Of course, Francis anticipated the attack, immediately sending a ball of flame hurtling in her direction.

She was too exhausted to move. The fire was a direct hit against her shield, shattering it, sending an unrivaled agony soaring from her face down to her toes as she collapsed. It didn't matter—pain was irrelevant now. Serenna nearly laughed, using the pain as inspiration to tear more energy from her flesh.

With Francis exposed, Serenna crafted eight tiny spikes. Trying to focus on all of them made her vision blur; she let go of two of the floating spikes, then launched the remaining six all at once. Tiny though they were, they would easily tear into the emperor's flesh.

He shot a desperate blast of ice, blocking some of the spikes but not all of them. The cold blur of shattered ice and glass made it impossible to follow, but screams always tell the story when eyes fail. Knowing Francis, he would likely retaliate with one final spell—

And there it was. A seething ball of flame soared in her direction, immediately drawing sweat despite how far away it was. Every instinct forced her to rush out of the way, but she tripped over her first step, landing onto her knees. Whatever agony she felt before was quickly replaced by an ache that would make even a god scream.

The fire was almost beautiful. An orange that rivaled the sun, a cascade of hatred and desperation crafted only to defeat one woman. Hopefully, one of her spikes had landed a fatal blow. That would be a fair end, though someone else would have to defeat Arrogance. Maybe Fear or Sardonyx? With David missing, Bloom injured, and Serenna about to perish…well, such was the realm. *One of you better save Zeen. You swore to me. Don't make me return as a vengeful goddess.*

With the fire closing in, she made one last attempt to stand. It worked but, by Valor's grace, it was painful. Her legs moved so slowly. Perhaps they were finally depleted and saw the incoming inferno as a release. Tiny shields formed in front of her, with awful form and a glow so pale they could barely block the rain. Ah, so her forces were doing their best to save her. She wouldn't run. She *couldn't.* A martyr would be an honorable end. Perhaps it would inspire her army to finish the battle in her name. *Even now, after everything…*

I should never have left that balcony—

She gasped as someone grabbed her and dashed out of the fire's path. The grip was strong enough to be Bloom but that would be impossible. "David? Why… Why aren't you on the towers? You never follow orders. You're a defiant old fool."

"I…" he tried speaking but was huffing for air. Gods, he moved slowly. Despite his apparent heroism, the two of them wouldn't outrun the blast. They were about to fall together, which was a massive disappointment, yet it seemed fitting. "I swear I used to run faster. If we don't make it, please forgive me."

"Did I get him?"

"You did. Thank you, my friend. I'll sleep easier knowing the emperor will soon join us. If we all end up in the Great Plains in the Sky together, I'll punch him in the face one last time."

"I...would enjoy that." With the fire closing in, the pain didn't seem all that bad. "Promise me that Fear will save him. Give me that, and I can rest easy."

He smiled, somehow keeping his pace. Up close, he looked nearly one hundred years old. Gods, if she somehow made it through this, she swore David would have a statue made in his honor. It would stand there in the middle of the trade district, a reminder to everyone that good days come at the expense of heroes.

The deep boom from the blast was the only sound she could hear. She had no idea what happened to David, but no one was holding her as she flew backwards. Serenna soared through the air like one of her crystal spikes, gripping onto her staff for dear life.

She couldn't say which part of her body hit the ground first. Everything throbbed in unison; her eyes begged to close, but she wouldn't allow it. She wouldn't allow it, despite the rain offering her a blanket of rest. She wouldn't allow it, despite how much her body trembled. If Zeen was alive, she would persevere for the faint remnant of a dream they could be reunited. It couldn't all have been for nothing. He had been allowed to rest for seven months after Nyfe. Surely Serenna had earned at least eight months or even a year. *You damn silly boy,* she thought, letting out a faint grin.

You better be there when I wake.

CHAPTER 47

HOW MUCH CAN A PERSON BE DAMAGED BEFORE THEY ARE CONSIDERED BROKEN?

rancis sighed. A crystal spike hung from his shoulder. The other spike had torn a large hole at the edge of his chest. Oh, how he was tired of the various things constantly stabbing him. Perhaps he could have survived one of the blows, but both? No. No, it was apparent: Mary would be empress and Calvin would grow up without a father. Maybe that was for the best. His son couldn't hate a man if he never got to know him.

Vanguards in the vicinity were being pushed back to the gates of the military ward. Despite the pain, Francis limped ahead, ignoring how each step brought pure agony to his bleeding side. Oddly enough, his shoulder didn't hurt too much, which was probably a terrible sign. "God?" he asked, letting the rain hide his tears. "Why did you abandon me? I believed in you. Even when everyone begged me not to. Mother, Mary, I gave you everything against their wishes, and my prize is to die alone in a hostile kingdom. I just wanted to be happy. Was that too much to ask?"

"*Use whatever remains of that mind of yours and figure it out. Happiness is the ultimate delusion. Not greed, not lust, but happiness. It is the stone of every castle, the soil of every farm, the heart of every poem. And yet, it does not come. Or worse, it reveals itself only to vanish, leaving the destruction of an entire kingdom in its wake. For the longest time in the days of Boulom, I believed there was a God of Despair. I prayed for nothing, and I received even less. How many times must I fail? Serenity...is it truly a dream? A mad god's delusion? Francis, I answer your question with a question of my own. How much can a person be damaged before they are considered broken?"*

Francis couldn't help but smile. Despite the roar of bravado from the incoming forces behind him, despite the pain that was near blinding, all he could do was smile. "Wisdom, my friend, I love you. Alongside Mary and Calvin, you are the family I always yearned for. I think... I think I finally found the answer. Nothing with a heart can ever break completely." Francis waited for a response, but God said nothing. Or, if he did, the words were too soft to hear. With his mind finally clear, Francis watched the rain fall upon the fiery kingdom of Terrangus. His home would recover in time. It always did—

Someone put a sword to his neck... David? Torn leather armor dangled off his shaky hands. It was the only time Francis had ever seen pity in those eyes, despite all the cuts and burn marks all over. "Ah, your shoulder. I take it that's a fatal blow?" David eased the sword back into its sheath. Despite his lack of education, he had clearly answered his own question. "I will not be cruel. Do you have any final words before leaving our realm?"

"Escort me...to my family. Let me die alongside my wife and son." It was an outrageous request to make of his enemy, but if anyone understood, it would be David.

David groaned and looked around. The fact that he didn't immediately say no or just stab him was a good sign. "Can we realistically make it to the castle? I... I'm not the man I used to be."

"I wish I could say the same." Francis snickered—

"Let go of him. *Now,*" said Mary, her hand trembling as she gripped her shield. Her right eye was swollen shut.

David stepped back and showed his empty hands. "Take a deep breath before you hear my next words. Hand over your son. I swear to you, on whatever deity you find holy, I will ensure his safety. Listen to me and listen closely: you and Francis are going to die. It's not a matter of preference, but the reality of our current scenario. Let the boy live a good life."

The pause that followed was terribly awkward.

"Would you allow it?" she finally asked, staring at Francis.

Francis held back a scream as his side throbbed. He wouldn't weep in front of them. "To be fair, I'm not in a position to refuse anything right now. That being said, you have my blessing, though it feels rather odd to hand our son over to the woman who just sealed my fate."

"Children inherit our names, but not our sins," said Serenna from behind. She limped forward, taking labored breaths. Not that it mattered anymore, but at least he had wounded her. Hopefully, it was something permanent so she would always remember him. "Little Calvin shall want for nothing. And you have my oath, when the time comes, I will speak favorably of his parents." She made eye contact with Francis and let it linger. "Both of them."

Francis looked over to Mary. Her pleading eyes told him everything. It seemed like blasphemy to hand their son over to the *Pact Breaker,* but...ugh. Mothers always know what's best. He sighed and said, "Come quickly." Bless Mary for letting him lean on her without asking, and bless the despair on her face. Despite the awkwardness, every man yearns to see their family's tears when the end comes. "I am unable to control the Vanguards directly anymore, but I can most likely force them to stay away. For now, at least. We must move quickly."

It was easier said than done as he limped forward. Fortunately, they all moved at the same, pitiful pace. The realm's damaged—but not broken—heroes went unbothered as they approached the castle. By any measure it was a simple distance, but each step was its own journey. Every part of his body throbbed in pain.

"I haven't been inside this structure in over a year," said Serenna. She looked around awkwardly, never letting go of her staff. "We should not linger. There is a darkness within this castle that cannot be denied."

She was obviously referring to Arrogance. While Francis was certain the god was watching them, it was rather bizarre that no action had been taken. Perhaps he was overseeing the battle? Gods forgive him, but Francis still yearned for the victory of Terrangus. Mary could oversee the realm and mold Calvin into the first Haide to rule over something without dying soon after. "I would move with haste if there wasn't a spike in my shoulder."

"Stop it," Mary said. She was right of course; the pain on her face tore away any desire to comment further. While Francis's time in the realm was nearly over, Mary was about to surrender her child to hostile invaders. Was that really the best path? Maybe, just maybe, Francis could...

"It would appear the team is back together!" said Zeen, caressing the sharp end of his Legacy of Boulom sword, with Calvin standing by his side. "All we're missing is Pyith and Melissa. A pity they are already gone. Though, if I were a gambling man, I'd wager friends are enroute to the void. Run along, little Calvin. Go to your mother. And if you hear screams, be a good lad and cover your ears."

Everyone took a few steps back, other than Mary, who grabbed her son and clutched him to her bloodied face.

Francis attempted to control his Vanguard, but it was fruitless. Behind them, the loud crash of castle doors slamming shut echoed through the air. No wonder Arrogance had let them through. "Stand down," he said to Zeen, kicking himself for the irony. "Your emperor commands it." He always hated Zeen's fake smiles, but unfortunately, this one looked very real.

"Zeen!" Serenna yelled, limping forward. Thankfully, she stopped when David put his arm out. Part of her must have known she would've been rushing to her death. "I'm here. Forgive me, my love, but I'm finally here. It's time to come home."

Zeen cocked his head. "Home? Now there is an odd statement. Surely you don't mean Mylor? I am home, or at least I will be. Terrangus will be reborn into the kingdom of Boulom. And this time, it will last forever. You look tired, my dear. Would you prefer to rest? There is a *wonderful* chamber awaiting you down below. You descend the steps, lie on the table...then perfection takes hold."

Francis forced himself to glow yellow. Lightning was the only safe element with his family in close proximity. "Mary, take our son upstairs."

"I will not leave you," she said, holding Calvin tight. Up close, his son was absolutely adorable. Bless the happy little smile on his face. For all he knew, this was just a common disagreement between grown people, and not a cataclysmic event that would alter the realm forever.

Francis sighed. "I know." He sent every last particle of energy into his lightning blast. The shock of it all—no pun intended—sent him to his knees, gasping for air. One of the disadvantages of knowledge was knowing when every available move was a losing option.

Even through his blurred vision he could watch Zeen deflect the lightning. Most of it was sent crashing into the senators' chairs on the east side, but a single bolt struck Francis and numbed everything. What an outrageous shame. When the pain fades, the party is usually over.

Something was moving him... Mary. His wife screamed and moaned, doing all the necessary marital tasks to honor his name. "No, Francis, my beloved. No, no, no."

"Daddy? Daddy, get up!" Ah, that one stung. Perhaps Francis had been wrong. A family's mourning is best unwatched.

"It's okay," Francis said, though he didn't appreciate the irony of being leaned against his throne. The damned thing had brought him nothing but misery. "My family never fared well at leadership, though it would seem we keep trying. In hindsight, I suppose this was always my destiny. Take Calvin and get out of here. To become the emperor of ruins is no fate for our son. He deserves true wealth: a family. People who love him. A mother who will spoil him and make him completely unprepared for the miserable, imperfect realm we find ourselves in."

"Save your strength!" Mary said, gripping him. Oddly enough, despite the scars and battle wounds spreading all over her face, he swore she had never appeared so beautiful. "Give me your pain. Give me your sorrow. I can take all of it."

"What have I ever done to deserve a woman like you?" *Oh! She's looking at me. I should say something. For the last time.* "All I ask of you is to please break the cycle. Protect Calvin. Don't let him...become me. Mary, my beloved, I am well aware that I am a difficult man to love. From the bottom of my heart, thank you for trying."

Francis had always expected to die alone with no loved ones. How could anyone love a broken man? Throughout his years, he had found one and helped raise another. Mary held his hand as he faded. Such wealth, such rapture, was a prize beyond anything he dare craft in his most intimate of moments. Perfection was not a dream: it was the warmth of his wife. He laughed, recalling his words to Arrogance. If only he had realized sooner...

Nothing with a heart can ever break completely.

CHAPTER 48

THE LEGACY OF BOULOM, PART II

amn, it took forever for Francis to die. The emperor was like a character from the Rinso Saga; one who, despite his *several* fatal wounds, clung to life long enough to redeem a lifetime of atrocities. Vanguard Ultra had no time for such nonsense. He had orders from God to kill them all.

"Zeen?" asked Serenna. God had commanded he kill her first, but something about that platinum hair. And the way she said his name.

"There is no Zeen. There is only Ultra, and this throne room shall be your grave." Odd, he never thought of the words, but they were forced out of his mouth. God was commanding him. It was a welcome change, if only to remove the feeling in his stomach when he met the blue eyes of the sorceress...

David drew his blade and came a few steps closer. That seemed unwise—Ultra had already defeated him months ago. "If you're still in there, my friend, drop your sword and come home. I have no desire to harm you. None of us do."

God had obviously been correct: these people were fools. To demand surrender from a weaker position was the sort of thing Serenity would put a stop to. "All of that poison must have shattered your memory. Allow me to help. Seven months, eleven days, and two hours ago, you came into this very room with some *very* similar demands. You were defeated with complete and utter ease. At least now you brought some friends. As I serve a fair god, I will give you the same offer. Drop your weapons and join me in Serenity."

The pretty woman erupted into a platinum light, which didn't seem practical with the open wounds all over her face. Ultra really wished she wouldn't fight him. Something about this woman made him want to walk over and give her kisses, ignoring the horrors of war, laughing over sweet wine, lying naked under the covers—

"WAKE UP!" God said.

So Ultra did, because he had to. He may have overestimated the woman. She launched one spike and collapsed, a tiny little thing that he struck down with a clean swipe. God was correct: she was unworthy, just one final obstacle before Serenity prevailed. With his enemies and sorrows destroyed, Ultra could finally sit back and let his dreams take root.

All that he wanted was to…

All he wanted was…

All he ever wanted…

David rushed forward and swung. His swings were always slow. Ultra resisted the temptation to dodge and tear his throat. It would be more fun to keep this one alive for a while. And something about this man… Ultra didn't want him to die.

A shield crashed into Ultra's face, sending him staggering back. The empress? Ultra found his balance and swung forward to prevent her from following up. The throbbing pain in his jaw rattled his senses; for a moment, odd memories barraged him. *Mary? David? Serenna?*

He swung his sword at the incoming shield by pure instinct. The empress had become predictable in the past year, but by Wisdom's glory, she was strong. And angry. *Very* angry. Still, she was slow and unpracticed. One simple counter would easily—

"Kill the rest but leave our empress alive. I need a replacement for the father. He was a broken puppet with very expensive strings."

Ultra would follow God's command, but to be honest, it made the battle rather awkward. A shield user's biggest disadvantage is their lack of speed, and it's best to kill them right away. *Well, God commanded me to leave her alive, but said nothing about harming her.* He dodged a shield bash by stepping to the side, then elbowed her in the face, hitting right where a bruise already was. While she yelped and tended to the blow, he used the pommel of his blade to crack into the center of her head. Anger is never a match for reality. She collapsed, letting the shield fall out of her hands. The future emperor screamed and ran to his mother. The sight of it made Zeen shiver, but…Ultra regained himself.

An involuntary movement swung his blade high, barely deflecting a crystal spike that would've missed anyway. The swing left him vulnerable to David's attack, which opened a small gash across Ultra's chest. Annoying and completely unnecessary. God may have been perfect, but the deity didn't understand the art of sword combat.

It took every ounce of strength to resist God's command and parry the next strike properly. Perhaps God had read too many of the Rinso books, because his knowledge of swordplay was not based on experience or reality. Ultra disengaged the parry and swung. To his surprise, David dodged and stepped back with a grin.

David swung viciously, driving Zeen a few steps back as he parried what would have been a fatal blow. Damn this man. Even now, David was trying to teach him.

I wish you were on my side.

But he wasn't. Hopefully, paradise would be truly beautiful, for the cost was harsh. Oh so very harsh—

"What is it about you fools that makes you hold back? David is beneath you. Destroy him, then finish the crystal woman. You stand upon the precipice of paradise or ruin. The Harbinger is slain, and the military ward will soon be mine. It's almost over. After so many harrowing centuries of misery…it's almost over."

The sorrow in God's voice nearly moved Ultra to tears. His reluctance to kill his former allies could mean no Serenity. It would make him a worse scoundrel than Vehemence *and* Rensen the Red combined. Enough. If David wanted Ultra to strike harder, he would oblige.

Ultra charged forward, swinging low, low, high to try to catch David off guard. While none of the strikes got through, David was clearly tiring. Even before the battle had started, he was plagued with scars and burn wounds, barely a shell of the Guardian from Zeen's memories.

They stood close enough where a mid-level slash would either get blocked or end the battle. Zeen swung, and while David blocked, the force of the strike sent him off balance, falling backwards to the throne room floor. Ultra kicked his sword away and stepped forward. He'd had orders earlier to keep this one alive, but God had changed his mind. No more risk. Kill them. Kill them all—

A shimmer of light flew forward. Ultra prepared to deflect the spike until it was grabbed midair by a giant zephum.

Sardonyx Claw, once warlord of Vaynex, now God of Tradition, clenched his fist and the spike crumbled into dust. "Stand back, humans. I shall take it from here." He was back to his mortal height, but a red glow followed the zephum that seemed all too familiar. "The Arrogant One holds you within his clutches. That ends *now*."

As Tradition approached, all confidence fled from Ultra. How was he supposed to defeat a god? A *zephum* god? "Stand down!" he yelled, even though that tactic never worked.

"I shall do no such thing. Heed my voice, Zeen Parson, Guardian of Terrangus! Heed my words! Strength without honor—is chaos!"

What could he do? To his knowledge, gods weren't allowed to strike unless struck first. Ultra froze, then trembled as his hands raised the Legacy of Boulom against his will. God had taken over. Perhaps for the best, as there was something about this zephum that made Zeen want to fall to his knees and weep. He was too similar to Strength. A god, a fallen god. A god that had sacrificed everything for the realm.

"Regain your composure, Vanguard. This zephum is nothing more than a sad imitation of the monster from your memories. He would never harm you, and that is why his victory shall never come to pass."

The words made no sense, but Ultra couldn't help but swing his blade across Tradition's chest. It struck. Not only did it land, but it also formed a large gash. Ultra had always wondered if gods could feel pain. The grimace on the face of Sardonyx answered that question.

And yet, the god did not strike back. He approached Ultra and kept a stern expression as he stared into his eyes. "Remember the mantra! Strength without honor—is *chaos!*"

The words burned into his head a guilt more painful than the migraine. Strength's mantra, a glorious declaration that had given Zeen another chance at life. "There is no strength! Only chaos!" he lied, swinging his sword again. The glowing blade tore through Tradition's chest, all the way to his neck.

Sardonyx flinched, but never wavered. Never lost eye contact. "I said remember! Strength without honor—is chaos!"

"You're wrong! You have always been wrong! Only Wisdom holds the truth. If the proper god controlled our realm, everyone would rejoice. There would still be a Boulom! There would still be Melissa! There would still be… Tempest would still be here." The final words came out so weak. Even with God's control, it was harrowing to stare into the face of Sardonyx and invoke his son's name. What sort of god ruled with such cruelty? Strength had never been cruel. Sardonyx…okay, maybe a few times, but Wisdom? What had Wisdom ever done for Zeen? For anyone? The only one who ever loved Wisdom lay dead upon the throne.

"Stop stalling and destroy him. You have survived countless wars, demons, gods, but words? You yield to words? My dear Ultra, paradise is within your grasp. It's a mere sword swipe away—"

Sardonyx grabbed Ultra, pushing him against the wall behind him. One thing immediately became apparent: if this god wanted Zeen dead, he would no longer exist. So why swing his sword? What honor was there in attacking an enemy that held back? Zeen had shown mercy to Nyfe, only to find a dagger in his neck.

Am I becoming the very thing I fought against? What would Strength say if he could see me now? What would Tempest say? Serenna? Against his will, he slammed the Legacy of Boulom into the chest of Sardonyx.

The god finally broke eye contact, taking a few steps back to hold the wound. But only for a moment. Sardonyx groaned and stepped forward, pushing Zeen back into the wall. "I SHALL NOT LOSE YOU! I SHALL NOT! STRENGTH WITHOUT HONOR—IS CHAOS!"

With all the thoughts and emotions spiraling through Zeen's mind, it was easier to ignore God, since he couldn't focus on anything. *It is okay not to save everyone, but it's unforgivable not to try.* Strength's lesson played through his thoughts, over and over. Ah, how times change. Zeen was the one being saved and, despite his horrible demeanor, Sardonyx would never stop trying. Ultra broke away from his glare and looked at Serenna. A terrible mixture of tears and blood rolled down her face. And she was so skinny! What terrible pain had she endured in the past few months?

"STRENGTH WITHOUT HONOR—IS CHAOS!"

God tried to control Zeen's hands, but he resisted as Sardonyx held him, filling him with a warm energy. Enough. An untrue faith shall always crumble before the power of love. It was time to go home.

"STRENGTH WITHOUT HONOR—"

"Is chaos," Zeen said. He dropped his blade and hugged Sardonyx as tightly as he could. The tears flowed, and he made no effort to stop them. No shame could surpass being a tyrant's Vanguard for the past few months. No shame could surpass killing Francis, leaving a sweet little boy without a father.

"It's okay, my little human. Hold me and let your tears flow. There is no greater glory than the power to heal those in need."

Steps approached but Zeen refused to check who it was. How could he look anyone in the eyes after tonight? "I'm sorry," was all he could say as they came closer. "I understand if you never forgive me."

"*Go to her,*" Sardonyx whispered, then approached Mary and Calvin. "Empress, your life-mate perished with honor. When the day comes, you will reunite within the Great Plains in the Sky. For now, give your boy all the love in the realm. He shall persevere."

Zeen froze as Serenna took his hands. He immediately looked down to hide his shame. "You were never supposed to see me like this. If you wish to kill me for all I've done, I will not resist." He fell over as she hugged him, accidentally dragging her down with him.

She groaned from the awkward landing, then smiled and kissed him. The joy left her face as she leaned up and analyzed him. "Are you back to your normal self? Completely?"

"I think… I need more kisses."

Serenna obliged, which was wonderful, but quickly interrupted by one of those loud throat clears from David. Ah, he was right. It wasn't the time to celebrate with Mary mourning her husband. Serenna must have come to the same conclusion as her face blushed red; she rose and composed herself. "Empress Mary Haide, you hold my deepest condolences. If it means anything to you, my offer of safe harbor for Calvin still holds true. Sardonyx can bring him to Mylor, where he will be raised as a Morgan. If…if it pleases you."

Mary kissed her son, rose, and grabbed her shield. She glanced at her sword for a moment before throwing it over to David. "My son is a Haide. He will be raised a Haide, or he will not be raised at all. Sardonyx, take him to Mylor then return here immediately. Arrogance must be slain. His death shall be *glorious*." She wiped the tears from her eyes, kissed her son again, then nudged him towards Sardonyx.

"Glorious *indeed*." Tradition gently took the child, holding him like he was the purest thing in the realm. He then created a red portal and stepped through.

"Mary…" Zeen said but she shot him a glare.

"Sardonyx slayed my father. Now, by some cruel joke, you have slain my husband. The only acceptable resolution is that we defeat Arrogance together. Not for honor, not for glory, but because his very existence is a mockery to the realm. I will not back down on this. I demand all of you, Serenna, Zeen, David, to aid me in this endeavor. Speaking of which, where is your goddess?"

She materialized behind Mary. "I am always here. Watching, waiting. From one empress to another, you are correct: Ermias must die."

"Is such a thing even possible?" asked David.

Fear smiled at him. It was such an unnatural-looking act, Zeen couldn't help but shiver. "Perhaps. Perhaps not. Have you already forgotten my mantra? Where reality fails, dreams are eternal."

"She's right," Zeen said, even though it probably wasn't his turn to speak. "We can sit back and let our simple lives continue, ignoring the terror that haunts our realm, or we can put a stop to this right now—"

"*Never* interrupt a goddess," said Fear. "Though I agree with you. 'Tis our duty to finally slay the false god."

Sardonyx reemerged from his portal with Bloom by his side. All the cuts and gashes on the god filled Zeen with a terrible guilt. Bloom somehow looked even worse. "Ah, there is a bloodlust in the air, and it is glorious! Noelami, lead us to victory. Strength without honor—is chaos!"

Bloom glanced at the fallen Francis, then everyone else. "Damn, I missed some shit. The bossman said it's time to kill God? Let's get a move on. You probably don't know it from here, but it's getting bad outside. With the Harbinger slain, reinforcements have been pouring in. No, that wasn't a rain joke: I mean they're really pouring in. The way I see it, we have three options: retreat, die, or kill the Arrogant One. Wait, why is Mary still alive? We should—"

"Enough words," Mary said. "He dies, and he dies now."

David nodded at Bloom. She shrugged and said, "Fuck it. She may be the only one who hates him more than I do."

"*No one* hates Ermias more than me," Fear said, before anyone had a chance to speak. "Quantifying suffering tends to be a fruitless task, but rest assured, I speak the truth." The goddess picked up the Legacy of Boulom, then created an odd-looking platinum portal. She stared at it awkwardly for a few moments before speaking. "This portal leads to Serenity. Enter at your own risk. If we fail in our task, there is no swift death awaiting us. Ermias will force us to suffer forever, lingering in his mockery of heaven. I shall be the first to enter. Follow the empress of Boulom into the nightmare of a broken paradise. Save your realm, as I failed to do."

She entered, followed by Tradition and Bloom. David took a deep breath and was next, followed by Mary.

Serenna offered his old blade, Hope, to Zeen, who took it without hesitation. They met eyes and smiled. "Any regrets, my love?" she asked.

"The realm is on fire, but with your hand in mine, I wouldn't change a thing. I struggled to find an ending for Rinso and Olivia. Perhaps there was no greater fate than to save the realm one last time. I'm ready," he said, and to his own surprise, wasn't lying. They approached the portal hand-in-hand. Hopefully, she was more confident about their chances.

Zeen never expected to return.

CHAPTER 49

GRAVES FOR YOU ALL

erenna materialized in the garden of Serenity, surrounded by the misery of lies and squalor. No wonder Francis had loved this place: it was every snob's dream come true. Puffy white clouds floated in the distance, while a stream flowed to her left. The cathedral was missing, which was odd, but in its place was Arrogance, sitting on a chair, playing an instrument she had seen in Alanammus but couldn't recall the name of. Piano, was it?

Two Vanguards were by his side, but they were too far away to recognize. The sharp tone of the notes didn't mesh well with the cellos and violins floating above. Hmm. The song was from the *Mylor March*, but Arrogance ruined the beautiful ballad by making it his own. It's rather tragic how often the ones who claim to love art actively work towards its ruin.

"I forgot how much I hate this place," Zeen said, drawing Hope. "How exactly does this work? Can he just blow us up?"

Fear took a deep breath. "Not until you attack first. So, when you do, make sure it counts. Sardonyx and I will do the majority of the fighting. If our battle looks dire, interfere immediately. There will never be another opportunity to save the realm."

"Indeed," Sardonyx said, grinning, despite the horrible wounds Zeen had inflicted upon him. "To slay the Arrogant One in his own domain. It will be *glorious!*"

The tempo of the ballad went faster as it became louder. Serenna's heart pounded in her chest; she gripped her staff and cast shields on the two gods to clear her mind. Unfortunately, the shields were visibly weak, but she had very little energy left after such a grueling evening. Serenna parted the hair from her eyes and shielded Bloom, David, Zeen, then herself.

Zeen snickered. "Never seen you shield yourself last before. I suppose the realm is truly coming to an end."

Ah, he was right. Every crystal mage is taught to shield themselves first but…those lessons felt like a lifetime ago. After years of war, demons, and deranged gods, she just wanted her teammates to survive. They were her family now. The realm had taken everyone else.

"Can we get moving?" asked Bloom. "If this human music gets any louder, I'll jump off the gardens." Despite her words, she didn't begin the approach. "Look, before we do this, I just want to say thank you. Every one of you, human or not, is a hero in my book. If we die, I owe you a drink in the Great Plains in the Sky. Even you, David. No use remaining sober if you're dead."

David smiled, wiping the blood from his mouth. "Sorry, old friend, but if I happen to die, I'm taking the opportunity to rest. If you must, feel free to drink in my honor, though I would rather us all survive. If the worst comes to pass, it will be quite some time before we enter the fields. I have seen our opponent in his true nature. He wears a mask to hide the monster underneath."

Despite the temperate breeze, a trickle of sweat dripped down Serenna's head. Hopefully, Fear wouldn't be offended at David's words. Before anyone else could speak, Serenna said, "It takes more than words to slay a god. Let us proceed."

The improvised formation would have to do. Tradition and Fear slowly stepped forward, still in their mortal forms, weapons drawn, while the Guardians followed closely behind. By pure instinct, Serenna couldn't help but look for crawlers. While there were no screeches or roars, the cacophony of the off-key piano was somehow worse.

It was easier to recognize the Vanguards as Serenna approached. Of course, it was Five and what was his name… Omega? Enough of that. Nyfe and Robert. They were Nyfe and Robert. No more naming people as numbers or edgy terms. Actually, the two of them appeared rather injured—Nyfe in particular had a swollen, bloody face and a noticeable limp. *Thank you, Death...I think.*

Arrogance slammed the keys of his piano as the other instruments fell silent. For a few moments, it was the only sound she could hear. After a final off-pitch bang, Arrogance rose from his seat. He snapped his fingers and the water froze in place. The wind stopped blowing. The grass under her sandals and all around her went still.

Arrogance grew in size and slowly floated forward. "I always found the cliche that history repeats itself to be rather tiresome. History never repeats. It rhymes, and with Noelami, fake Strength, and these...mortals here to oppose me, I find your rhyme to be uninspired and derivative. Come if you must. Paradise will provide graves for you all. Despite your ridiculous conversation from earlier, there will be no prolonged suffering. It's not worth it. You shall die within my home, then be forgotten. Vanguards, attack. That means you too, Ultra."

Zeen screamed and fell to his knees, clutching his chest. Serenna held him close and said, "Resist! I need you, Zeen. If you love me, if you ever cared for me, you will resist." The words were cruel yet, dammit, they were true.

"Serenna...kill me. Please, kill me. I can't resist. Not here; in these gardens, his hold is torture. Don't let me attack you again. I could never live with it." It was madness to suggest such a thing. She would never slay him, let alone harm him. Yet if he were to become hostile...

"Save your breath. By the time you know clarity, everything will be okay." She entered her empowered form, forcing whatever was left from her body to erupt into radiant platinum light. She kicked Zeen's sword away, then surrounded him in a crystal prison. "Have faith in me. Stay here for now."

With Tradition and Fear entering their god-forms and surging towards Arrogance, the Vanguards were her problem. Nyfe was rushing forward while Robert followed, glowing orange. Of course he would use fire. "Take down Nyfe," Serenna said, her words all too familiar. "I'll do my best to block the fire. If I fall, spread out."

"Boss, if you fall, we're dead. No pressure or anything."

Serenna sighed, but it was true. She refreshed her crystal shield, then stood directly between Robert and her forces that were engaged against Nyfe. It was rather disturbing to see Robert grin. The Vanguard launched a ball of flame, which seemed wildly off target, until it became apparent his target was Zeen. In hindsight, trapping her lover in a prison had not been a wise move against an enemy that saw morality as a weakness.

"It's fine! Leave me here and counter him!" Zeen yelled, but she wouldn't.

She forced more energy from her already-depleted body, placing a platinum barrier in front of her and Zeen. Perhaps it would be enough. If not, they would die together, in a brutal manner. To be quite honest, she was tired of enemies trying to burn her alive.

Fortunately, Robert wasn't as powerful as Francis. The blast hit, the barrier shattered, but no burn followed. Her empowered form was gone, but overall, a fair trade. On the downside, a new blast was enroute. She didn't bother to tear any more energy—there was nothing left. "Forgive me, my love. If there is a life after this one, I look forward to traveling through it together." She forced a smile and glanced behind, only to find…nothing?

Zeen rushed in front, grabbed Hope off the ground, then slashed with his blade to deflect the blast. He knocked most of it away, but a fragment got by and exploded, knocking them down in opposite directions. She reached out to try and grab him, but it failed. At least their eyes met, despite the light-headed delirium taking over. If her lover's face was the last thing she ever saw, the void could take her.

CHAPTER 50

DAVID WILLIAMS, GUARDIAN OF TERRANGUS

avid risked a quick glance as he parried Nyfe's dagger to watch Serenna and Zeen fall over. That would be a problem for several reasons, the most pressing of which was Five could now focus his full attention on David and Bloom.

"Have you no pride?" David yelled to Nyfe, parrying another dagger strike. "No pride at all? Where is the monster who brought the realm to its knees?"

"I serve...Serenity. I serve..." Nyfe took a few steps back and screamed, grabbing his head and pounding his dagger into the soil.

David resisted the temptation to kill him. Not out of mercy, but every possible ally would be needed to defeat Arrogance. Despite Tradition's bravado, the god had clearly been wounded in his battle with Zeen. Every time Tradition had gotten close to Arrogance, the god blasted him back with a bolt of lightning. Noelami wasn't faring any better.

"You want redemption, Nyfe? Take it! You want respect? Help me! Together we can save the realm. Do it for Emily. You owe her an insurmountable debt."

Perhaps that had been a mistake. Nyfe rose and swung his blade with enough speed to rival his Harbinger days. "*Never* speak that name to me again. I have paid my debts in my own way. She knew...she always knew what I would become. What I am."

"No," David said, grabbing the weakened Nyfe and pulling him close. "She knew who you were. I know who you *are*. Help me.

Create your own purpose and save this damn realm. Do it for her."

"I…*can't!*"

"Ice!" A detonator erupted against a fire blast, freezing it solid, giving them a few more moments. "What the fuck are you doing?" Bloom yelled, riffling through her belt. "I'm nearly out of detonators. Finish him and help me kill the Stickman."

Stickman? David thought, then quickly dodged another stab from Nyfe. "Zeen was able to resist, and you can't? Are you a lesser man than Zeen? Maybe you're right. Maybe you are better off serving a tyrant."

Nyfe swung again but it was noticeably slower. After a few breaths, he tried again, then said, "Spare me your lessons, old man. The last thing I need is Fear's whore berating me. You have no idea what it's like. You have no idea what Arrogance is capable of—"

David grabbed him and pulled him in, close enough to touch noses. "Look at me. *Look* at me! I have been tortured, broken, left for dead, all of it! And yet, I fight. For decades I have been told it's a losing battle. Perhaps so, but I made an oath. I will not leave this realm until I am worthy of the mountain she saw in me. Look deep inside and find something to strive for. The realm may never forgive you, but you can forgive yourself. It's the only victory that matters."

"Move, you fuck!" Bloom yelled; at the same time a ball of flame soared towards them.

Nyfe screamed, then dashed ahead and swung his crystal dagger at the blast, deflecting it far off into the clouds. He glanced backwards with a cocky grin. "Ah, sometimes I forget how great I am. Be a good Guardian and help me get Robert down."

A powerful yet awkward relief followed. David ran and tried to match Nyfe's speed, but his legs were so sore from everything—

Fear crashed right beside him, letting out an unholy wail as she rolled over. "*Get away!*" she yelled, forcing herself up, materializing a black sword in her hand.

Hmm. Serenna, Zeen, and Nyfe were all advancing on Five. Very slowly of course, but that *should* be a winnable battle. At the high point of the gardens, Arrogance was bashing Tradition with a giant version of the Herald of Arrogance. The god laughed as he parried a sword swing and called down a giant bolt of lightning from the skies.

That battle didn't seem very winnable, so David forced himself to rush forward. Ah, there was Mary, gripping her bleeding side and trying to follow. "David," she said, gasping for air. "We must help them. Sardonyx won't last much longer, and Fear cannot defeat him in his own domain."

"Agreed. I don't know what aid we could offer, but…there are no other choices." The closer he came to Arrogance, the more it became clear the idea was absurd. Maybe it was because they were in Serenity, but the wrath of Arrogance was unmatched. Not even both gods in unison could get him to falter. The music earlier had been loud but no sound rivaled the laughter echoing through the skies.

Arrogance hovered in the air, blasting Fear and Tradition back again, laughing to the point of madness. "Help me understand. When you saw my blade conveniently lying on the ground…you thought I made an error? *Me?* You presumed to trespass into heaven, easily defeat *God*, then wallow in your glory of imperfection and squalor? What a fitting end to the absurdity of freewill." The bulging eyes of the sun mask stared directly into David. "Why, hello, David. Hello, Nyfe. Please, don't stop your approach on my account. I yearn to see freewill in its most feral form: broken mortals swinging their blades at perfection."

If David couldn't defeat Arrogance, maybe he could at least get him to shut the fuck up. He froze in front of the god, staring at the monstrosity of raw energy emanating from the cape and sun mask. Overwhelming was the only way to describe it; David's eyes burned from just staring at him.

Arrogance chuckled, then surrounded Noelami in a black-tinted crystal prison and slammed her in front of David. "I could exist for ten thousand years and never understand why she favors you. Madness… It must be madness. What other conclusions are there?" He pointed his staff at Fear, then blasted her with a stream of lightning. The goddess screamed, convulsing as smoke rose from her skin. "Choice: everything comes down to choice. It will end, Maya, I swear it will." He blasted her again, laughing as her screams grew louder. "Immortality has several disadvantages. Unfortunately for our dear empress, I have learned quite well how to maximize suffering. Unless of course…you wish to aid her?" He mockingly dropped his staff, bringing his spectral hands to his mask in shock. "Dearest me! I have dropped my staff! What a tragedy it would be if some heroic mortal took advantage of my blunder. Oh the shame!"

David's hand trembled, gripping his sword as he watched the smoke drift from Maya's body. The smell of it alone would be enough to make him vomit. It was *very* obviously a trap but…the agony on her face nearly brought him to tears. This goddess had saved his life. Her reward for rescuing David was to suffer at the hands of a monster. For better or for worse, she would not suffer alone—

Tradition finally tackled Arrogance to the ground, roaring *gloriously* as he rained down punches upon the sun mask. Sardonyx grabbed the Herald of Arrogance, roaring even louder as he attempted to pry the staff from the god's hands.

By Fear's mercy, David was scared, terrified even, but with both gods tumbling on the ground, the moment was there, and it would never come again. David rushed forward, screaming as loud as he could as he slammed his sword into the sun mask. Despite the burn in his throat, the only sound he could hear was Tradition's roar…

Until it stopped. It became so quiet, David honestly considered that something had made him go deaf, until Arrogance flung Tradition all the way to the other side of the garden. The thud was startling, but the joy in the eyes of Arrogance made him lose his breath.

David's end seemed inevitable, but he wouldn't die a coward. He drew his blade and readied his approach—

"I stand with you," said Mary, clutching her shield for dear life. She looked like she could barely stand. "For Francis. For Terrangus."

"Turn back," David said, foolish as it was. "You haven't attacked him yet. It's not too late for you."

She grinned but her swollen eye stayed shut. "It's too late for a lot of things, David. I don't care if we lose. I will inflict pain on him. I will find a way to scar his mask, to force him to remember my family every loathsome year he remains. If the price for my vengeance is death, I will pay it one thousand times."

There was no arguing with that. David tried to rush forward but Mary went first. She gripped her shield, letting out a yell poisoned with hatred and rage as she swung her shield at Arrogance, landing a glancing blow against the sun mask.

The god let it hit, then slammed his staff into her left leg, snapping it in two. "Like I said, *Empress*, history rhymes. You won't be moving for a while—take this time to ponder how you will raise the future emperor with only one leg."

David slashed his blade across the mask. It may have been for nothing, but watching Arrogance actually stagger back from the blow filled him with a final, fitting pride. David made no attempt to follow through. His old dream of creating a realm without gods seemed so laughable now. Still, he had wounded one, and after forty-six years of disappointment, that brought a smile to his face. "Arrogance, look upon me. I am David Williams, Guardian of Terrangus, Champion of Fear. I offer you the chance to surrender. Otherwise, my next attack will not be merciful."

Arrogance snapped his fingers, creating a black, glowing blade that was eerily similar to the Herald of Fear. "'Tis is a fine, yet arbitrary line between confidence and delusion. Take a wild guess which side you landed upon. Here, allow me to teach you the lesson. How I always seem to fall back on my professor days." Arrogance stood there silently for a moment, then glared into David. "Never let them say I am a ruthless god. Have you any final words?"

David smiled and dropped his sword. The deepest of scars are torn not with blades, but truth. "She loves me, because I am better than you. You could control every decision of every mortal, but you will never change the reality that broke you. She loves me—"

Arrogance rushed forward. It was impossible to follow the movement, but the force of energy nearly sent David to the ground. David closed his eyes and took a deep breath. Perhaps he would end up in the Great Plains in the Sky. Or nowhere. Nowhere would be acceptable, as long as he could rest. Maybe, just maybe, he would awake in the arms of Melissa. Even if it was only a dream, perhaps it would be eternal.

David opened his eyes to find Noelami in front of him, with a sword slammed into her chest. "No!" he yelled, rushing towards her as she collapsed. "Dammit, no! We can't win without you! I was prepared to die…"

She gave him a half-smile, half-grimace, holding the wound. "What a wasted existence it would be to stand there and watch my little brother perish. Thank you, David. There is no afterlife awaiting us…but there is rest. I know…that will please you." She closed her eyes and went limp. She still breathed faintly, but it didn't seem like it would last much longer.

Arrogance stood there, clearly stunned, which looked ridiculous with the eyes and grin on the sun mask. "Maya? Dearest Maya? She's…gone? I can scarcely find the words. All of this… everything…it was all for you. I can imagine entire worlds, filled to the brim with unique people and economic systems, pantheons of creatures and gods. But not even I could imagine a world without you. Make your peace, David. In a few moments, you will no longer exist. Everything, every person you have ever held dear, will scream from the bottom of Serenity."

The fire that inched forward burned with a heat that would make the sun blush. And yet, David saw nothing but his permanent rest approaching. It was seething, it was orange, and above all else…it was beautiful.

Long before the blast actually landed, David disappeared from the realm. Erased by a god who would exist forever and never be happy.

CHAPTER 51

KISS ME ONE LAST TIME

erenna could scarcely believe it. She dropped her staff, letting her mouth fall open as she stared endlessly into the scorched hole where David had been. *He dodged the blast. Surely, he dodged it. After everything we have been through, he would never leave me.* She kept staring at the hole while the others incapacitated Robert. What a day indeed that Nyfe and Bloom of all people had shown the Vanguard mercy. And yet, it didn't matter in the slightest. Fear wasn't moving, Tradition was wavering…and David. Oh, David.

The realm had given her two fathers, and she had lost them both.

Zeen hobbled over. By Valor's grace, it was obvious he was trying to smile, but burn wounds covered more than half of his face. "I don't like that look. How bad is it?"

"He's dead."

Zeen's smile faded entirely. He didn't need to ask who had fallen. "Then there's only one thing left to do."

Serenna nodded, picked up her staff, and limped forward. What a waste to finally reunite with her lover just to end up in the void. "Stop," she said, then grabbed him. "Kiss me one last time. Make it count." She leaned in—

Only to be denied. Zeen held her face and shook his head. "I'll kiss you after we win. You have my word."

"I don't want your word. I want your heart."

"It has always been yours, my love. Now, shield me and let's do this."

Gods, he was a fool, and she loved him all the more for it. She flinched as Nyfe, Bloom, and Robert approached. "You have control?" she asked Robert, tightening the grip on her staff.

"To both my joy and horror, I have reverted to my normal self. Nothing more. Nothing less. We should attack Arrogance immediately. With Noelami gone, he is emotionally vulnerable. When that vulnerability ends, so shall we."

Serenna shielded them all. Each shield was dimmer and more pitiful than the last, but it would have to do. No words would be sufficient, so she ignored the pain and approached Arrogance. To her pride, everyone followed. There is no greater gauge for leadership than to inspire soldiers to march towards their death. "Kill him," she said, crafting a wobbly crystal spike. "Consider this your final order."

Zeen rushed in first, replacing his smile with a murderous scowl. She caught only a glimpse of it, but of course her lover would hate this god. Everyone did. Serenna's retribution seemed pale beside the horrors Mary and Robert had suffered over the past year. Even Nyfe...perhaps, especially Nyfe.

Nyfe got there first and kicked the god's artifact into the air, passing over the bleeding husk of Sardonyx. Zeen arrived a moment later. Maybe it was pure instinct, but they flanked the god in a perfect lateral formation, slashing the sun mask and cape from both ends.

Arrogance groaned, then launched both of them a few steps back with a blue nova. He snapped his fingers, which caused the Herald of Arrogance to hover off the ground and fly towards him. "There is a hole in my cape. What a pity. Well, there is the sum of your efforts. You lost everyone and everything you ever held dear to cause a cosmetic inconvenience." He snickered and reached out his hand to catch the staff—

Sardonyx grabbed it, wheezing as blood poured down his snout. "Strength without honor—is chaos!" With a mighty roar, he snapped the staff in two. "Children of Tradition! Children of Valor! Slay this dishonorable fiend! I shall join you…soon." The god huffed for air, letting out a hint of a smile as he lay in the grass.

"*No!*" Arrogance yelled, and that told her everything.

Serenna erupted into her platinum form, ignoring her blurry vision as she crafted spike after spike of various shapes and sizes. Valor had always told her not to focus on the form, and the lesson had finally come to pass. Murdering God would become the new protocol of Serenna. She launched them all at once, uncaring that most would miss. The mere thought of one of her spikes shattering the sun mask made the entire nightmare worth it. One by one the spikes flew, until a giant one hit dead center, causing a loud clang that echoed throughout the gardens.

The sun mask vibrated, then the eyes shifted to stare directly into Serenna…then Zeen. The god's spectral hands closed into fists, surrounding Zeen in a black-tinted crystal prison. He gestured one hand high in the air, which launched Zeen's shell into the clouds far above. "Wave goodbye, Serenna! In case you were wondering, yes, there is a bottom. And oh, believe me, 'tis a long way down." The shell faded as Zeen collapsed.

Nyfe's prison came next, but he slashed his glass dagger through the shell, shattering it into fragments. Nyfe rushed the god, who flinched back and formed an array of miniature fire balls. They flew at Nyfe one by one, but he side-stepped all of them and continued his approach. Strangely enough, it was comforting to watch someone else struggle against the old Harbinger. Nyfe swung and missed but, for whatever reason, held a cocky smirk as he adjusted his battle stance. A blast of lightning crashed into the sun mask from Robert, who was shaking as he gripped his wooden staff.

Despite the blurred vision and pure exhaustion, Serenna never lost sight of Zeen's crystal prison. She took a deep breath to focus, then attempted to catch him within a sphere.

She missed.

Concentration and terror can never exist in the same domain. The accelerating descent made it nearly impossible to focus on a singular space. She attempted another and missed, ignoring the trickle of blood flowing down her eye. Precision would not work. Perhaps it was unwise, but she formed sphere after sphere, letting her knees fail as she collapsed into the grass. One sphere was heavier than the rest. She laughed in ecstasy and let the rest drop, forcing the one sphere to hover back towards her. Her entire upper body was sore enough to make movement difficult. Her lower body…she felt nothing. It was like someone had cut her in half.

Everything was so blurry, but with her lover up close, he was as clear as the day they had first met. Zeen saluted as his sphere faded, then rushed towards Arrogance.

Serenna tried to call out words of inspiration, but nothing worked. For all she knew, she had already died and hadn't noticed yet. She quite literally dragged herself towards the battle, never letting go of her staff. The Wings of Mylor had been the one friend that had never abandoned her. For all of Serenity's faults—and there were many—the grass was pleasant. She could see herself dying in such an odd place. To be fair, she should have, along with Valor and Father, but Archon Gabriel had given her a second chance. A chance to defend the realm beside Nyfe of all people. Oh, how times had changed—

Bloom crashed next to Serenna, letting out a pained roar as she clutched her sides. The stench of burned flesh emanated from the zephum. "Boss…I have an idea." Bloom squirmed from the ground, eventually taking off her belt. She held it in the air and smiled at Serenna, like that would explain everything. "Put one of those crystal balls over my belt. There's still uh, nine or ten left. Fly it over to his face, then I'll say the magic word."

Serenna hesitated but, to be fair, that idea made a lot of sense. Mercifully, it was easy to form a sphere around the belt with it so close to her, though holding the sphere in place proved to be more of a challenge. It was too uncomfortable with her legs numb; even if she wasn't standing, the total lack of feeling below her chest was rather ominous. The sphere swayed back and forth…

"Boss, are you drunk? Take a deep breath and sober up. Need

you to be accurate with this thing or you'll blow someone's head off. You ready?" The lack of confidence in Bloom's voice was not a good sign.

Serenna tried to give confirmation, but ended up coughing up blood. At least her throat was sore; maybe she was still alive, after all. "Going!" she forced out, coughing up more blood. It was impossible not to be ashamed of how difficult it was to control one tiny sphere. Fortunately, Arrogance was a rather large target, and with his attention on Nyfe and Zeen, the opportunity was there.

The sphere floated forward. Serenna forced her eyes to stay open and find the perfect opportunity. She would never admit it out loud, but she floated the detonators closer to Nyfe's side in case she missed. Focusing on the path helped her ignore the pain. She slowed down the sphere, waiting for Arrogance to knock them back again. Maybe one of those blue nova things...

There.

With Zeen and Nyfe knocked back, she accelerated the sphere's approach. A little too fast but she could still maintain control. Arrogance finally noticed the belt flying forward. He cocked his sun mask and said, "Hmm?"

"Fire!" Bloom yelled. Then, ironically, it felt like the entire realm was frozen.

A moment later, the belt erupted into a cascade of flashing lights. It was like a storm of every element dancing before her tired eyes. The brightness burned, but nothing would force her to look away.

The sun mask fell to the ground with a clang, followed by the cape falling beside it. Serenna would not dare be happy, not yet. She crawled forward, ignoring the aches in her arms and upper back. One of the sad advantages of losing all that weight was making it easier to drag her broken body around. Bloom wasn't following. By Valor's grace, hopefully the warlord survived, but the only thing that mattered was confirming Arrogance was dead.

Zeen arrived first. He fell to his knees and dropped Hope, laughing as he hunched over.

Nyfe was next; he continuously slammed his dagger into the sun mask, filling the air with an awful screech of steel grating against bronze. For as much as she loved Zeen, Nyfe clearly had the right idea. It would be madness to celebrate until every speck of Arrogance was removed from the realm. "Kill him," she yelled, or at least, tried to. It came out as a pitiful whisper. "Kill him. Just…keep killing him until there is nothing left." Zeen finally took the hint and joined Nyfe with the assault.

She crawled forward, close enough to taste the bronze being chipped off the sun mask. Gods forgive her but she was starting to believe. *If you're out there, David, I hope you're watching. We did it, old friend. We—*

A deafening rumble shook the ground, then a black nova launched Nyfe and Zeen several feet back in opposite directions. The skies went dark until only a red moon lit the gardens, covering them all in a bright, crimson nightmare.

"*No!*" she screamed, but it was too late.

The sun mask and cape rose in unison, followed by the spectral hands. The sun mask tilted until an awful crack filled the air. Arrogance chuckled, creating a cacophony that lingered as the laugh echoed. "Consider me impressed, mortals. If we were anywhere but here, I may have lost…but here is where we are. Hmm. Something is missing. What is it… Oh! Of course!"

The ground continued to rumble as Arrogance put both hands out in front, summoning the two pieces of his broken staff. After a terrible screech, bright fragments of light flowed into his hands, until a mini explosion stopped the rumbling. The god held the reforged Herald of Arrogance within his grasp, then maneuvered his gaze to all of them. "You are all such flawed, beautiful creatures, yet you are so poisoned by freewill that I have no choice but to euthanize you all. Take a moment and make peace with whichever lesser god you favor. In a few moments, darkness shall be the only thing left to worship—"

"Shut up!" Nyfe yelled, slashing his dagger across the sun mask. "Just shut the fuck up! Do you even listen to yourself? Did I sound like this when I was a Harbinger?" Nyfe swung again, only to have his blade caught in those spectral hands.

Arrogance took the blade away, then stabbed it into Nyfe's chest.

Nyfe staggered back, gripping the wound, then fell next to Serenna. "I'm sorry," he said, not even looking at her. "For a minute there...I believed. Thought I was the hero. You know? Imagine that... Nyfe the hero. I'm sorry for everything. I wouldn't dare ask you to—"

"I forgive you," Serenna said. It was a lie for the most part but...not completely. Even with the vision of her dead father, vendettas lose their purpose when the end draws near. "More than that...I understand you. Perhaps we shall reunite in the void, Guardian."

"Thank you..." Out of all of Nyfe's horrible smirks, grins, and smiles over the years, the one he gave her now wounded her heart. Nyfe closed his eyes and went limp. The sight would have made her the happiest woman in the realm years ago, but now...

Nothing.

CHAPTER 52

AGE OF ARROGANCE

ike all those destined for greatness, I had accumulated quite the array of titles in my time. Ermias. Wisdom. *Arrogance…*

Never favored that one. Always saw it as more of a mockery than anything else. But alas, I wore my insult like a crown. Figuratively at first, but eventually, a crown of lies manifested upon my mask. I could only wonder if Time was watching my imminent victory. Did it make him ponder his own imperfection? Did it hurt to see his broken child dominate the realm? Time had clearly offered me the role of Arrogance as some obscure punishment for destroying his precious little Boulom.

Or was it all planned? That question always haunted me. If so, what a bizarre, cruel blueprint to achieving perfection. It had cost my home. It had cost Maya. It had even cost Francis. In many ways, he was the son I never had. It will take some time to heal from that one. Oh, the debts I have incurred. The gravity of it all loses relevance after a while, like a gambler losing one more dice roll after he already owes a king's ransom to every noble in the district.

A blast of lightning soared from Five's dingy staff. Oh, Robert. Once my most loyal ally. Now, a vagrant of freewill, attempting to slay God himself within heaven. How many times must I show them the absurdity of it…

What? Were those tears? Robert was weeping…for *Nyfe?* Maybe not. It was difficult to tell. Perhaps my old friend was overrun with guilt, trying to piece together how he had found himself in such a peculiar predicament. If I could impart only one lesson upon my young, hopeful student, it would be this: There is nothing more destructive than the pursuit of knowledge when poisoned by desperation.

All Robert ever wanted was answers. Even before Julius had died, all Robert wanted to know was how and why. Both fair questions, gilded in simplicity but impossible to answer. I could have spared Robert and given him another chance. Taken the time out of my *oh so busy* day to imbue the knowledge that was clearly lacking.

I chose a different route.

With my staff pointed forward, I gave Robert one final lesson: the quickest way to find hell is to rise against heaven. Hmm, perhaps I overdid it. I didn't even hear him scream before he was vaporized: a fate similar to David's end. Don't think for a moment I didn't relish the irony of having to *choose* who would die next. Serenna and Zeen were obvious choices. I favored one of them very much, though I prefer not to proclaim who. Let's just say it wasn't Zeen.

"No…" Sardonyx said as he rose. I would *never* refer to this brute as Tradition. Strength was embarrassing enough, but this one? "You shall not have them. You shall not!"

"I don't want them," I said with a chuckle. And yes, I exaggerated the chuckle. If you find a trait that annoys your enemies, abuse it at every opportunity. "Or perhaps I could reconsider? You know, I bluffed David with a rather cruel fate for these two. Here's a lesson, my dear warlord: pain needs time to find the zenith of misery. It's why mortals always fail in the art of torture. Out of all the tools at their disposal, there is nothing that rivals the horror of forever."

Just as I expected, the threat enraged Sardonyx. He looked so pitiful as he hunched over, barely holding on to his *mighty* blade. This beast wasn't Strength. This beast wasn't a shadow of the shadow of Strength. The God of Time must have been losing his grasp on reality. Promoting these lesser mortals into divinity was shameful…

I froze. Was that my purpose all along? A so-called angel of death? A way to erase imperfection while alleviating Time from the blame? I could accept that. In fact, it would explain everything. Boulom hadn't been my fault. I was merely fulfilling a purpose, guided by a destiny my mortal eyes could never have perceived. As I expected, as I always knew…

I was innocent.

Sardonyx clearly disagreed. He roared and yelled out, "Strength without honor—is *chaos*!" What a loathsome creature. He didn't even have the decency to create his own mantra. Perhaps Tempest could have written one if he hadn't been crushed under the stones of freewill.

I parried the incoming blow and regained my composure. The lizard-beast was clearly trying to separate me from my staff. I wouldn't call it wise but… Fine. It was wise. I found that most lesser beings find one attribute they comprehend and make it their entire identity. Like most zephum, this one had chosen war.

But I was ready. I was more than ready. It would be *glorious* to defeat him in melee combat, so I repeatedly slammed my staff into his snout. Each bash created some variation of a crunch or a snap. Eventually, he fell, lying in front of me like some sort of insect. Believe me, it was tempting to finish him off. It would have relieved the guilt from falling to Strength and Fear all those years ago…

Oh, Maya. My sweet, beautiful Maya. We were supposed to rule paradise forever. I wasn't sure if paradise could still exist without her. Sorry, that was a lie. Paradise *would* exist but not for everyone. Part of balance is knowing that every extreme has a complete and opposite state of existence. And believe me, there are very few things worse than the opposite of paradise. "Look upon me," I said to Sardonyx. "*This* is what a true god looks like. You thought to steal the mantle of Strength and defeat your superior? Divinity does not suit you, Sardonyx. Your family shall suffer. And you are going to watch."

I slowly floated towards Bloom. She was a miracle of sorts. It was like everything wrong with freewill had been dumped into a lizard-woman who was cursed to wander the realm. A pity that she was too injured to fight back. I raised my staff to crush her snout—

A fly must have landed upon my cloak. Oh, it was merely Zeen. The poor boy swung his rusty sword at me. How laughably sad that he had chosen to name his blade Hope. If he was looking to die and avoid torment, attacking me was a wise move, so I had no choice but to believe that wasn't the case. Ah, of course! It was desperation. A trait which, I assure you, is not a virtue. Killing him would be unnecessary, so I raised my staff and prepared the blow. Perhaps if I rattled his brain just the right way, it would make the boy more intelligent.

I brought my staff down with minimal effort. To my surprise—and annoyance—a last second crystal shield absorbed most of the blow. Oh, Serenna. I had met only a few people more driven to be unhappy.

I jabbed Zeen in the face with the blunt end of my staff and floated over to Serenna. How tragic of her to lie there, stuck in the grass, staring directly into me with a murderous hatred. Why did beautiful women always despise me?

"Take your toll, demon," she said, without a hint of irony. Me? A demon? "Even now, after everything, I hope you find peace. It will never come through violence."

My spectral hand picked her up by the throat. I didn't enjoy how her legs dangled lifelessly. She was a doll, a broken toy, some remnant of a Guardian long forgotten. "The woman who scowled at me and proclaimed, 'Mylor has never fallen. Her mountains are stained red with the blood of those who tried,' now condemns the evils of violence. Blame yourself and leave philosophy out of it. We traveled the same path of blood and war. I just happened to do it better."

I threw her to the ground, then hovered the Wings of Mylor into my hand. What a loathsome creation. Still, I could see why Serenna favored the thing. For a mortal weapon, it was an acceptable conduit of crystal energy. That gave me a wonderful idea. "Take a gander, Serenna. Allow me to demonstrate the proper way to harness power." I took a deep breath and summoned a minuscule speck of my energy to come forth. I used it to craft a crystal spike: a flawless homage to true perfection. "Since you worship freewill, I allow you the privilege to choose who dies next." I admired the crystal spike one last time before—

All of Serenity rumbled. Had I not been floating, I would've fallen to the ground. How was such a thing possible? This was *my* domain. Not even Death could threaten me in Serenity. Was that it? Was Death here? It would be a worthy final battle before my ascension came to pass.

Whoever it was, the figure in front of me was not Death. A human stood in the distance, wreathed in a glow so bright, even I could barely look without turning away. The power... was insurmountable. Did Time itself come here to celebrate my victory? To send me to the void? Wait…that wasn't Time.

It was David.

Unlike men, all gods are not created equal. What cruel hell was this? Why was David a god? Why was he so *powerful?* "What are you?" I asked, though to be honest, I did not expect a response.

David stood there and raised his right hand. A sword flew from Zeen's hands into his own, then David erupted into an indescribable light. The power of it would have sent me to my knees if I had any. He smiled, then said, "My name is David Williams. I have accepted the title of God of Hope from Time itself. My first task is to end the Age of Arrogance. Make your peace, old friend."

Old friend? He spoke to me as if I were a child. No, I wouldn't falter. Not here, not in Serenity. I grasped my artifact with both hands and summoned a ball of flame. As I had mentioned earlier, history does not repeat: it rhymes. Mortal David had burned from my wrath, and now the false god in front of me would burn too. With my staff pointed forward, I patiently waited for the opportunity to add another dead god to my legacy.

I never saw him, but I felt his blade tear across my mask. My inferno erupted somewhere far away, filling the air with the scent of burning embers. There was no time to be afraid. Not here. Not after

I had sacrificed *everything*. I swung my staff at the glowing entity, uncaring where it struck. That mentality ended once I met his blade. I couldn't even get him to flinch.

David pushed my staff back until a surge of power knocked it out of my hands. The eye of my staff met the eyes of my mask. Technically, it was within reach, but I knew it was realms upon realms away. There was no point in trying to grab it. I had far too much dignity for such a thing. I didn't have to wait long for the next strike. It tore into my mask, this time, breaking it in half. Was this the end? I had lived for so long... I could barely comprehend my own demise. My spectral hands still worked despite my blurred vision and shattered senses. From the ground I grabbed hold of something...or did something grab hold of me? I couldn't tell. I just couldn't tell...

A hand? Maya? Indeed, how could I ever forget such warmth. Some feelings are so beautiful, they become an agony that haunts us forever. She squeezed her hand into mine, and I despised how difficult it was to squeeze back. Oh, sweet Maya. All of this was for you. Every century of tears, of pain, of nightmares. Every betrayal, every convoluted attempt at creating a future so perfect, we would never look backwards again.

It's okay, Ermias, she whispered, though her lips did not move. *Boulom forgives you.*

It's time to come home.

Home? I could scarcely define such a concept. I had a home once until I burned it to the ground. The comfort of being forgiven for such an atrocity was greater than any paradise ever conceived. Unless she was lying?

Even that I could accept, for delusion is the cornerstone of happiness.

CHAPTER 53

ALL HE EVER WANTED

 ow am I still alive? Zeen thought, laughing despite the embers choking him. It didn't seem real. A glowing David stood with a stoic pose, watching as Arrogance and Fear became white particles that were carried away with the wind.

The ground started to crack, which was both wonderful and rather startling. Was it truly over? The whispers had gone silent. That fear of losing control at any second also faded entirely. Zeen…was again Zeen.

The cracks spread across the gardens as the waterfall collapsed. Zeen forced himself up and limped towards Serenna. Why wasn't she moving? It would be a cruel realm if the worst came to pass but…he wouldn't think that way. Not out of courage, but something more difficult to explain. Delusion perhaps? The irony didn't bother him, especially since Arrogance was dead.

David appeared in front of Zeen and nearly made him fall over. By the gods, his old friend was like an angel. His white glow was too bright to look at, but Zeen wasn't in a position to complain. "Serenity is collapsing," David said, looking at the others. "Grab Serenna. I'll get the rest and open a portal back to Terrangus."

"Can I have my sword back first?" Zeen asked with a smile.

David actually hesitated. He stared into Hope, then said, "You deserve it more than I do. Yet, I must ask that you allow me to keep it. This blade…has become very special to me."

"Then it's yours, old friend. Though I do insist that you find me a new one once we get home—"

The gardens rumbled as the cracks spread.

David did that flash thing to appear next to Sardonyx. He helped him rise, then the two of them embraced. Zeen couldn't hear most of the words but "glorious" and "honorable" were said more than once. Together, both gods collected Mary and Bloom.

Zeen took Serenna by the hands and helped her rise. She fell immediately when he let go, so he picked her back up and took her full weight. "Sorry about that. May I kiss you now? I think... I think we won."

She didn't respond. She leaned against his shoulder, huffing for air. Gods, today had taken a toll on everyone. Serenna gave him a light kiss on the neck and said, "Home. Rest. Sleep. Lots of rest. Lots of sleep."

"I love you," Zeen said, caressing her hair as he held her close.

"Love you. Love sleep. Lots of sleep."

Zeen carried her over to David and friends. Most of the garden had collapsed, but their little section of grass still remained. While David created a red portal for Sardonyx and Bloom, Zeen couldn't help but look at the fallen Nyfe. He would *never* admit it to anyone, but part of him wished his old general had survived. By the end, there was some good in the man. Not a lot, but...more than nothing. For some people, that alone is a victory.

Rest in peace. The realm may not forgive you, but I will try.

David created a white portal, then nodded at Zeen. "I will explain everything when the time is right. For now, take a well-earned rest with Serenna. Mary and I shall handle Terrangus."

Part of Zeen wanted to follow them to Terrangus but the other—much larger—part nearly fell to his knees in gratitude. Home. He was taking her home. Gods, he could barely remember what Mylor was like. So many miserable months in Terrangus, serving a tyrant, actively making the realm worse off...

No. Zeen wouldn't surrender to despair. In a way, he finally had everything he ever wanted. When things eventually calmed down in Terrangus, he would reclaim his notes for *Rinso Volume IV* and fulfill his promise to Sardonyx and Tempest. The best fantasies are the ones that draw from reality. Then, like most moments of inspiration, it hit Zeen at the strangest of times.

Rinso smiled at Hyphermlo, Zeen thought, picturing the ending. *His old friend had been reborn as a god! With Oliva in his arms and the portal to their home in plain sight, Rinso had finally found the answer to his life-long journey. The crystal mage in his arms had stood by his side as he battled Harbingers, emperors, and two, maybe three warlords. Their journey was coming to a close and life had never been more wonderful.*

All that he wanted was to…
All he wanted was…
All he ever wanted…
Was you.

CHAPTER 54

A KINGDOM BUILT UPON SCARS

ary took a deep breath after she materialized in the Terrangus throne room, ensuring to put all her weight on her right leg. By the gods, her husband still lay there, untouched and leaning against the throne. Would she ever see Calvin again? How would she ever explain any of this when he grew older? If this was victory, she could only imagine defeat.

At least Arrogance had died. He was dead. Truly dead and Serenity with him. While the realm would never be perfect, it would at least never be the hell of a madman's heaven.

"Take my hand," David said, reaching out. Was he really a god? It all seemed too ridiculous. The drunken Guardian, the champion of Fear, now a savior of the realm.

Not seeing any other choice, she took his hand, and let him guide her forward. "Why did you bring me back here? Never mind, don't answer that. I shall leave this realm with dignity and a smile on my face knowing that Arrogance is dead. I'll spit on his mask if I find him in the void. All I ask is for you to watch over Calvin. And *do not* lie to him. Tell him everything, even the worst parts. No lies will ever corrupt my son."

David smiled, but it was a smile of daggers. "This is not your end, Mary. This is only your beginning. Pardon me." He lay his hand on her injured leg and groaned. After a few moments, feeling returned—and that feeling was *agony*. "It would seem I cannot fully heal it. You'll have a few hours of mobility, but after that, only time will mend your wounds."

Mary couldn't help but stare at her fallen husband. Tears rolled down her cheeks as she approached him. "The leg may heal, but some wounds stay open forever. You of all people should know this."

"Indeed, but all is not lost. The scar is only as powerful as you allow it to be. I need you to be strong. There is an opportunity to truly do some good for the realm. You were born here. You served in every possible way. Mary, allow me to be blunt: you *are* Terrangus. Make our home something to be proud of. Raise your son with empathy and compassion. Let today mark the beginning of something beautiful."

"There is nothing beautiful about being alone." Mary didn't bother to hold back her tears. She had worn a strong front for so long, it was like everything hit her at once. "What does it matter? They will never accept me. As far as they know, I served as the shield of Arrogance."

"Only one way to find out," David said, nodding at her to follow.

So she did, pushing down the terror of being seen by her subjects. Or worse yet, the possibility that the Southern forces would kill her the moment she stepped outside. Would David protect her if the worst came to pass? At this point, did she even want him to?

It was pointless to worry. The fact Calvin was safe made her emotionally invincible. Let them kill her. Mary had lived long enough anyway. She pushed open the doors, letting in a cacophony of rain and yells.

One of the gold cloaks charged her but stopped within striking distance. "Empress Mary Walker, on behalf of Warlord Dumiah Bloom and Senator Serenna Morgan, I hereby demand your surrender."

"Who are you?" asked Mary, observing the battlefield. Her Vanguards clearly outnumbered the invading forces, but nearly all of them were knelt down or shellshocked, probably overwhelmed at the reality of being free again. Like Mary, they had all done some terrible, *terrible* things. "Who is in charge here? Bring forth your commander at once."

"I am Captain Kolsen of the gold cloaks—" The man froze mid-sentence, staring behind Mary in awe. He fell to his knees and the soldiers in the immediate vicinity followed.

"Rise," David said. His white glow was an incredible contrast against the stormy darkness. "All of you, please rise. The time for kneeling before gods has ended. The realm shall be ruled by mortals, and it was always meant to be. Mary brings a message of peace. Consider her words before you make any rash decisions."

"Emperor Francis and Arrogance have fallen," Mary said, as sternly as possible. Clumping the two of them together was awful, but that's how the realm saw it. Francis would be the sacrifice for stability. In an ironic way, he had finally accomplished his goal of a unified Terrangus. It had only cost his life. "As empress, I request an immediate ceasefire. No more Vanguards. No more war."

Kolsen looked around. He was clearly out of his depth, looking for someone of a superior rank. "I cannot authorize that. David, if you are a god, can you summon Serenna or Bloom? If Arrogance has truly fallen, we can stop the bloodshed. I don't want this anymore. None of us do."

"I can," said David with a grin, "but I won't. Serenna needs her rest and Bloom is focused on Vaynex. I have spoken the words. Is there a rank above god?"

Kolsen hesitated, then his eyes lit up like he had a brilliant idea. "How about this? You said Francis fell in battle. Can we take the body to Alanammus? That should be enough to satisfy my superiors."

How dare this man? And he called himself a captain? Mary gripped her shield. The thought of bashing it against his skull and separating his jaw from the rest of his face seemed so tempting—

David erupted into an even brighter light. Kolsen and soldiers on both sides stumbled back. They were terrified and, to be honest, Mary didn't appreciate it. The whole point of this battle was to free mortals from the tyranny of gods.

"Stop it," she said to David. "Allow me to broker this alliance. After everything, if I cannot succeed without divine help, I don't deserve it. Trust me. One more time, I must ask you to trust me."

"I do," David said, losing his white glow. "I always did." He stepped back into the castle, and she swore there was a tear in his eye.

Forgive me, my beloved. "Captain, if it will solidify our alliance, I shall escort you to the fallen emperor. But I demand, not as Empress, but as a loving wife and mother, please reconsider your request. Whatever you have lost in this battle, Captain, I daresay I have lost tenfold."

"I just want this to end," Kolsen whispered. "I suppose you have no reason to bluff. When those Vanguards portaled through... Father forgive me, but I nearly surrendered immediately. I thought the entire realm would be enslaved by Arrogance. Swear to me, Empress. Swear to me that he's dead."

"On Calvin's honor, you have my word that Arrogance and his reign of tyranny has fallen. Now comes the hard part. Finding out what to do next."

Kolsen smiled. It was a genuinely happy gesture, like the weight of an entire kingdom had been lifted off his shoulders. "Indeed. Fortunately for me, I'm not important enough for such decisions. Be well, Empress. You have my condolences with the cleanup."

"My son is alive and well. Save your condolences for those who need it." Mary saluted Kolsen then walked forward. "People of Terrangus!" she yelled, brushing back her cape, the way she had seen Sardonyx do as warlord. "The nightmare of serving a tyrant has ended. I will not stand before you and claim to have the answers. What I will claim is that we shall find them together."

Mary brushed the hair from her eyes and slammed her shield into the ground, the way she had seen Serenna do as Guardian leader. "Terrangus shall persevere! Her children shall persevere! Every one of you...every one of *us* has known a kingdom of pain and loss. I don't know if the worst of it is over. Regardless, it's time to start healing. We live in a kingdom built upon scars. You have yours, and the gods know I have my own. Terrangus is not a paradise. It will never be a paradise. It is a cruel home, but one we endure together."

Mary told them the truth, the way Francis had done any time he said that he loved her.

CHAPTER 55

VAYNEX IS YOURS, CHILD

loom materialized within the portal. Without even looking, she knew it was Vaynex. There was a scent here. A feeling that could only be found within the citadel. Bloom sighed and forced herself off the floor. A pile of dead humans was stacked in the corner, near the entrance to the old diplomacy room. If Tempest was still around, he would've had a lot to complain about.

"Warlord? Sardonyx? You return at last!" a zephum yelled. Bloom had seen this warrior before but couldn't recall who it was. She had stopped putting effort into names after losing so many allies. "Something happened to the Vanguards. All their power vanished at once. I wanted to take some for questioning but it ended up being a massacre. Did you…is the Arrogant One defeated? That would be glorious!"

"Glorious indeed," Sardonyx said, staring at the empty spot behind the throne where the God of Strength had used to stand. "Warlord Bloom," he said, which made her a bit nervous. "Speak truthfully: have I earned it?"

"I have no idea what you're talking about, but sure. Whatever it is, Boss, you earned it."

Tradition gave a weak grin. With Bloom's adrenaline fading, it was easier to focus on all the burn marks and scars that occupied his swollen snout. "If only my son could see me now. I hope…I hope

Tempest would've been proud. I have made many tactical errors as Warlord. And many, many grave mistakes as a father."

She stopped herself from placing a hand on his shoulder. Too much time around humans. "There is no such thing as a perfect zephum. If it's any consolation, I am honored to be a Child of Tradition. You taught me the meaning of honor by living it day after day. Listen, I know I was never your first choice. I probably wasn't in your first one hundred choices. Still, you never gave up on me, and not a moment goes by when I don't appreciate it. I will lead the kingdom of Vaynex with honor and glory."

To her surprise, Sardonyx slowly approached and hugged her. It was a *glorious* embrace, though he made no attempt to avoid her numerous scars and bruises. "I am honored to call you my warlord. Vaynex is yours, child. Lead her well." Sardonyx stood straight and limped towards the empty spot behind the throne. Once there, he slammed his bloody sword into the ground in front of him and placed both hands on the hilt. "I shall return, better and stronger than ever. Be well, Warlord. And remember! Strength without honor—is chaos!"

Bloom nodded as Tradition became a statue. Hopefully, it wouldn't be for too long. Strength himself had disappeared for weeks at a time and, to be honest, Bloom could really use the help. Who was even alive anymore to help rule? She turned to the warrior next to her. "What's your name, kid?"

"Um, Warlord? We have met more than once—"

"Name, not backstory. I got a lot to do right now so don't waste my time. Follow me."

"Oalum, son of Ollex," he said, following Bloom as they exited the citadel.

Damn, it was chilly outside. There were a ton of dead bodies, human and zephum alike, and all Bloom could do was laugh. By Tradition's name, it must have been hilarious as the Vanguards regained consciousness only to get butchered. Good work by the soldiers who didn't hesitate and killed them all. Some people are born strong. Others are born lucky.

"What are your orders, Warlord?"

Where to start? One thing was certain: those Terrangus uniforms were a mockery. "Get those fucking humans off my sand. We bury our own, not them."

"Consider it done." It was a relief when Oalum smiled. The kid had clearly seen some terrible things in the past year. To be fair, most zephum had.

Some other nameless zephum approached Bloom. Hmm, this woman was scrawny with no blood on her armor. How she had managed to avoid battle during an occupation was anyone's guess. "Thank Strength you have returned, Warlord. We need to discuss rationing food and water while we rebuild. It's fortunate this occupation came during colder times—"

"Thank Tradition."

"Um, what?"

"Tradition is the god of Vaynex. When we give thanks, we give thanks to him."

"Sure. Of course. Back to rationing. So, I have a theory—"

"Kid, what's your job?"

"Well, I was a diplomat, which didn't pay very well after Tempest fell."

Bloom grinned. "Congratulations. I hereby deem you the master of...commerce. How does that sound?"

The girl kneeled. "It would be an honor, Warlord. I have many theories on—"

"I don't care, it's all approved. Just get to work."

Whoever it was bowed and rushed off, harassing a much larger zephum. Damn, there was a lot of work to be done. All those songs of honor and glory had never included the grunt work that follows a massive battle or economic downturn.

No wonder Sardonyx had taken a nap.

CHAPTER 56

A BEAUTIFUL FUTURE

erenna could barely keep her eyes open as she materialized in the portal. The pain was overwhelming, but the oddest feeling was how it stopped right below her chest. It was like… nothing was there. Crystal magic *did* have the potential to destroy the user. It would be a cruel fate, but she appeared to be alive in her lover's arms, and Arrogance had somehow been slain. Whatever the price, for such a result it could never be too high.

"My room? How…did we arrive here?" she asked Zeen. Maybe it was a dream. She couldn't help but wonder if the true Serenna had died within the gardens of Serenity. "How…did we win?" None of it made sense. David and Nyfe had both died, and there was no possible scenario in which Zeen, Bloom, and Robert had defeated a god. A dream would be acceptable. Even if it was temporary, there were worse ways to leave the realm than to see her home one final time.

"David ascended and became a god after he died." Zeen took a moment to smile. "The God of Hope. My love, it was a beautiful thing. The only downside is that I lost my sword. But who knows? Maybe I won't need it anymore."

Since Death had used a Harbinger in Xavian, that gave them at least a year. Unless… "Did Fear agree to withhold future Harbingers? That would be a relief."

Zeen placed Serenna on her bed. He tucked her under the

covers and nudged a pillow under her head. "I swear it was the strangest thing. Even after everything, Arrogance and Fear died holding each other's hands. Their relationship was more bizarre than anything from the Rinso Saga. I'm glad we're not like that."

"We shouldn't judge," Serenna said, then coughed. At least no blood followed this time. "I doubt most lovers nearly kill each other as often as we do."

Zeen's smile faded as his eyes grew watery. He took her by the hand and trembled. "There are no words that properly describe my regret. I nearly killed you. I nearly killed everyone."

"But you didn't. We made it, Zeen. No more regrets, no more apologies." She patted the other side of the bed. "I don't want to hear any more about the past. Rest with me. Let's regain our energy and consider how lucky we are to be here. There is a beautiful future awaiting us."

He squeezed her hand then climbed into their bed from the other side. They were both a bloody, wounded mess but that would have to wait. Bless him for not trying to cuddle. In reality, he was probably just as tired as she was. "Are your legs broken? You collapsed immediately when I tried to help you earlier."

"I don't know. I don't care. Marry me, Zeen."

Zeen gasped and shot up onto his knees. Maybe he was less tired than she thought. "Truly? Like really? *Yes!*" he yelled and surged forward, then stopped right before her face, probably remembering how injured she was. That did not stop him from planting tiny little kisses all over her—

The door opened. Sophia stared at them in disbelief, holding Calvin in her arms. "By the gods, you couldn't even say hello first? Had to rush right into bed? In case you haven't noticed, I am watching over the son of an emperor who, last I checked, we are at war with. Sardonyx told me nothing. I need answers. I need answers now."

Zeen rushed over, which sent Sophia staggering back. He glanced at the ebony blade on his shoulder pad and frowned. "Oh...of course. Um, there's a lot to explain. Arrogance is dead.

Someone else too but, uh, I don't want to say it in front of certain company. And Serenna and I are getting married!"

"Congratulations! Here is your wedding gift." Sophia placed Calvin in Zeen's arms. It was kind of adorable how nervous Zeen looked as he held the boy. Sophia approached Serenna. Her loud gasp wasn't very encouraging.

"Is it that bad?" asked Serenna, struggling to keep her eyes open. It was a blessing Sophia had found them. Having Zeen call for help in his Terrangus uniform would have ended poorly. "I've never died before but I imagine it feels something like this."

"Rest your eyes, Senator. I will get a healing mage at once—"

"Wait," Serenna said, grabbing her hand. "Find some clothes for Zeen. I don't want anyone to harm him."

"The Rogue and the Crystal Guardian," Sophia said, shaking her head. She sighed as Zeen struggled to get Calvin to stop crying. "He's an interesting one. I suppose I'll have to get used to calling him Zeen Morgan."

Zeen Morgan. The thought of it made Serenna's eyes water. "I wish Father was here. He always wanted to be a grandfather. We won, Sophia. We actually won. It's still...very, *very* difficult to fathom. When is the next election?"

"To be honest, I am unsure. We haven't had one since...the *other* wedding."

"Then I am resigning, effective immediately. I finally have enough power...to relinquish my power."

For whatever reason, Sophia did not appear pleased. "Get your rest, Serenna. We'll discuss all these things in time. I'll be back with fresh clothes for you both and a healing mage. You don't have to rush anymore. Relax, and let happiness linger. You sacrificed a great deal for this moment."

Zeen approached after Sophia left. "Wave to Serenna!" he said, though Calvin did not oblige. The boy cried in his arms, probably missing his parents. Hopefully, he was too young to understand the loss of his father, though perhaps that was a cruel thought. It's always easy to delay pain, but time only makes the trauma more powerful.

Calvin's crying face made her feel so empty. His face was the perfect combination of Mary and Francis, which obviously wasn't surprising, but still startling to see up close. The image of the fallen Francis leaning against the throne made her hold back tears. "Hand him to me."

"Are you sure?" Zeen asked. He then did so after Serenna nodded.

"Shh," she whispered, leaning the child against her shoulder. "It's okay, little Calvin. You are among friends. You are among family. Mylor will protect you as her own."

The boy stopped crying. She handed him back to Zeen and lay back in her bed. "Watch over him, my love. I just need a moment. Just need…a few moments." Serenna managed to wiggle her toes before she closed her eyes. Finally, after so many years of loss and pain, was everything going to be okay? By Valor's grace, she actually felt hopeful. She actually dared to let happiness creep through. For the first time in a very long time…

She wanted to see tomorrow.

CHAPTER 57

YOU HAVE MY BLESSING

t had been nine months since the fall of Arrogance.

David still thought about their victory every day, but mostly for Noelami. No one really missed the goddess except David, which was understandable, but still a tragedy. Oh, if only she could see him now. Maya had risked everything for a drunken, broken mortal. Her ridiculous gamble had somehow created the God of Hope.

No time for such thoughts, for today was a celebration! Serenna and Zeen sat at their own table within the Mylor grand halls, giggling and holding each other while they waited for the wedding ceremony. Yes, it was cute, but David couldn't help but reminisce about Melissa. Their wedding had never come to pass. Still, in the end, David had become the mountain she always knew he was. *Nothing* in the realm could ever take that away from him.

The wedding had originally been planned for later in the year, but a sudden change of plans moved it to mid-spring. The official reasoning was that an earlier wedding would mitigate the risk of a Harbinger of Death. Most people accepted that idea, but David suspected there was a very different reason.

Mary and Bloom shared a table. Out of all the oddities in the realm, the fact the two of them were allies was one of the most beautiful. Like most of the people here, the two of them pounded wine and laughed about old tales, each exaggerating their feats of strength to levels of absurdity.

David's enhanced senses made the scent of wine all the more tempting. Still, he refused to partake in his favorite vice. He didn't know if gods were susceptible to addiction, and he didn't care to find out.

"David Williams!" Sardonyx said, slapping him on the back. They had a bizarre, unspoken agreement to still use mortal names. "Ah, look at it. The joy! The celebration! The inebriation! Isn't it glorious?"

"I can find no better word to describe it. Days like this make everything worthwhile. Not to bring the mood down but have you heard anything about Death? I can usually sense where you are but...I haven't felt Death since becoming a god. The day of his return will come. And the realm must be ready." David watched Serenna rise from her seat and limp over to the food table. It would be a lie to say she moved well, but the fact that she moved at all was a relief. Her Guardian days were over, which probably meant the same for Zeen.

Sardonyx grinned. "You worry too much, human. Give the mortals an opportunity to surprise you. The realm is in good hands... Ah, it would appear someone desires a moment of your time alone. I shall take my leave."

Who is he referring to? David thought, until he noticed Serenna limping over. Her pure white dress was large, fluffy and glamorous, but the added weight probably didn't help her legs. David approached to make her walk less of a trek.

"Thank you for joining us, my friend," she said with a soft smile. "It is an incredible honor to have two gods attend my wedding."

"I wouldn't miss today for anything in the realm."

"I know, but it must be difficult—"

"Stop. The only tears that fall today will be tears of joy."

"Still, I—"

David took her by the hand. He still wasn't sure how his powers worked, but he allowed some of his essence to flow through. Hopefully, it would alleviate some of her pain. "You have a look on your face. Is there something you wish to ask me?"

"Indeed, but not here. I know just the place."

They walked hand in hand out of the halls and into the gardens, leaning over the balcony and gazing out to the far-off mountains. It was unusually cloudy, covering most of the mountains in a pale hazy gray.

"The lilies are finally coming into season. Valor always favored them. I'm not sure if you ever saw her home but she modeled it on the Mylor of her time." After a moment of silence, Serenna finally said, "David, I think… I may…"

"You are. I probably knew before you did. I couldn't understand why I could sense two of you until I realized the obvious."

Serenna blushed. "Ah, of course."

"Why the secrecy? Is Zeen unaware?"

"He knows. I just um, well…"

David snickered. "It's been a while since I made you nervous. Stop thinking of me as a god. Make your request. After everything, you should know I would never deny you."

"If it's a girl, Zeen wants to, well, we both want to…name her Melissa. Only with your blessing."

"It's a girl," David said immediately, to avoid an awkward pause. It was an honorable request. One that should've filled him with joy but was instead a dagger through his divine heart. A new Melissa would mean his was gone forever. She was already gone, of course, but a replacement? Melissa didn't need a replacement. She would exist forever in David's memories, and no one would ever change that.

"Forgive me. I know it was a terrible thing to ask. I wish I could solely blame Zeen, but the desire was also my own. Please forget this conversation ever happened."

David closed his eyes and took a deep breath. "You have my blessing." He forced the words out before he could regret them. In all honesty, he had no right to deny them. Melissa was more than David's lover. She had been a Guardian who guided the team like a mother. Melissa had created her own legacy. It was hers, and hers alone. "I must know. What were you going to name the child if it was a boy?"

"Charles. If we end up with two boys, the second will be Landon. If we have another girl, Everleigh."

"Let's see how you feel after the first one before you make a list of future Morgans. I'm relieved you didn't choose my name. The last thing the realm needs is a tiny David running around looking like Zeen."

Serenna sighed. "He wanted a Rinso."

"Of course he did. My only advice would be to stop after two boys. Otherwise, we may very well see a Rinso Morgan running around these gardens. Serenna, it's time to head back."

"I know but David...we should do this more often. I don't care if you're a god. You were my friend first."

David smiled and said nothing. Her request warmed his heart, but once her daughter was born, Serenna wouldn't have the time to talk to anyone, let alone David. And that was okay.

A mentor's greatest achievement is to be forgotten.

"Take my hand," he said. "I know a quicker route."

Serenna cocked her head, then obliged. She gasped as the two of them flashed back into the wedding halls.

"Your father," Sardonyx said while he held Calvin, "was a glorious man! A mighty wizard who struck terror into the hearts of humans, zephum, and gods alike! Heed my words, little emperor: on one stormy night in Terrangus, we battled side-by-side, and I watched as he burned soldiers into dishonorable specks of dust. It was glorious!" Apparently, Sardonyx didn't share David's fear of alcohol.

"That's enough," David said, taking Calvin before Mary did something rash. He took the boy to an empty corner of the room, the spot where David always felt most comfortable. "You are too young for this sort of thing, though eventually, I wager every person in this room will be entangled in your life in some way or another. Do you trust me?"

Calvin had a wide smile, which made it more surprising when he said, "No!"

"You are indeed your father's son."

322

Mary approached. She walked a straight line, but David could sense the alcohol distorting her senses. Hopefully, she wouldn't ask to hold the boy. "David, um, would you mind overseeing the ceremony? Sardonyx was supposed to but he's too drunk. I don't want him to misspeak and cause another war."

David let Calvin down and sighed. He was never a public speaker. Mary of all people should know that. "Is there anyone else? What about you?"

"David, you're the God of Hope. Act like it."

"Yes, *Empress*," he said with a formal bow. To be honest, Mary was kind of annoying. The longer time went on, the longer he realized Francis had been the perfect soulmate for her. She had never remarried, or even attempted another relationship. The empress wore a scar, one that was all too familiar. Mary approached the musicians, who stopped their current song and started a new one. "A Bevy of Doves" was the title, if David recalled correctly.

Almost on cue, Zeen rose at the first notes of the ballad. He took Bloom by the arm and shuffled nervously to the altar at the end of the hall. Zeen moved too quickly, though he probably had no idea he was doing it.

David took Serenna by the arm. "Serenna Morgan, please allow me the honor to escort you to the altar." Such a task was normally reserved for the father, but…

Serenna nodded and slowly approached the altar. Fortunately, the musicians were skilled enough to loop certain sections to fill in the lost time. "The honor is all mine. Thank you for everything, David. I always imagined my journey would end in tears. It still doesn't feel real."

"Believe me, old friend, it's real. Sometimes I think Noelami had it all wrong. Reality is eternal. It may indeed fail us at times but, ultimately, it is eternal."

"Do I deserve this? I cannot help but grieve for all of those we lost to get here."

"Happiness is somehow the greatest gratitude and the sharpest revenge. Love your family. Give them every part of you."

She opened her mouth to speak but ran out of time as she

reached the altar. To be honest, David wasn't sure how this worked. A senator would usually oversee the ceremony, but Serenna still hadn't given up the title.

Fine, David would do it. All he had to do was say some inspirational words, then ask them both if they wanted to marry the other. David had seen demons, gods, all sorts of magic and wonders, but he had never seen someone say no at their own wedding. He cleared his throat, then got pushed aside—

Sardonyx stood at the head of the altar. He roared then yelled, "I shall not miss the opportunity to wed my favorite humans! *You,* Serenna Morgan, Guardian of Mylor…do you take this glorious man to be your life-mate?"

"Uh… Yes. Yes, I do."

"Glorious! And *you,* Zeen Parson, Guardian of Terrangus, Rogue Guardian, Human Warlord, do you accept this sorceress as your life-mate?"

"I do."

"Then under the watchful eye of Hope and Tradition, I hereby declare you officially joined forever as life-mates. May you frolic with honor, and reproduce in mass quantity to secure your lineage. I can already sense your first daughter training within the womb. Her wrath! Her power! Your child shall be glorious!"

Serenna froze as the crowd gasped. "Sardonyx! You gave me your word!"

"Children of Strength and Valor. When the day comes, I shall await you in the Great Plains in the Sky. Life-mates are joined in life, joined in death, and destined to flow through eternity as one. I shall be your guide, and I shall watch over your family long after your departure." Sardonyx paused, then took a deep breath. After a moment of silence, he yelled, "Speak the words. Speak them now."

"Strength without honor—is chaos!" Zeen yelled.

"Strength without honor—is chaos!" Serenna yelled right after.

"You may now kiss your life-mate."

And so they did…

Gloriously.

EPILOGUE

CHEESE

 elissa watched Mom close the door and step outside, while Daddy sat on his favorite chair and picked up a book. The time was now. She waited a few extra seconds to make sure Mom wouldn't return, then crept up next to Daddy. With her eyes wide and her feet timidly pressed together, she eased her hand to Daddy's and said, "Where did Mom go?"

"Just a quick trip to the store, Honey. Needed some things before dinner. I offered to go but she enjoys the outside air. Honestly, I think she prefers to stay active because her leg never fully healed. Your mother used to run very fast!"

Yep. Sure she did. And apparently, Daddy used to be an awesome warrior. Either old people are liars, or something weird happens after the age of thirty. Fortunately, Melissa had twenty-four more years before that happened. She took a deep breath. It was time.

"Daddy…may I have some cheese?"

He looked at her cautiously, which was expected. Daddy never surrendered on the first try. It would be a battle of wits. "Honey, you know there's no cheese until after supper."

Melissa looked down, trying to get her eyes to water. "But… Mom isn't here. It could be our little secret."

"Secrets and lies are the same thing. We taught you better than that." Daddy laughed, which was a good sign, then he kissed her on the forehead, which was *not* a good sign. Throughout the years, the forehead kiss meant "go do something else while I sit here and get fat." No. It would not work. Not today.

"But… I thought you loved me? Don't you love me, Daddy?"

Daddy sighed, ensuring his defeat. That technique had always worked against him, though Mom was a more worthy opponent. Still, given enough time, no matter who opposed her, Melissa *would* get her cheese.

"It hurts Daddy when you say that. Of course I love you. But you must understand, it is nearly supper time, and I cannot give you cheese."

What? How was he resisting? A change of strategy would have to do. "I hate you!" she yelled and rushed into the kitchen. There, she sulked in the corner and counted down to the next part of her plan.

Five.

Four.

Three.

Two.

One…

"Melissa, please," Daddy said, right on cue. He walked over and picked her up, giving her a large kiss on the cheek. "Do you believe in oaths?"

She didn't, but if oaths meant cheese, she would believe in anything. "Yes, I learned about them in school. They cannot be broken!"

"Good. Here is my proposal: I will give you some cheese, but you can never say you hate me or your mother ever again. Am I clear?"

"Yes, Daddy," she said with sad eyes, hiding the joy underneath. Whoever had first thought of oaths must have been an incredible liar. The ability to get anything Melissa wanted with words was a magic more powerful than her crystal abilities.

"And remember, don't tell your mother. I have my own oaths, and let's just say, I'll get in a lot more trouble than you will." He took his knife and cut little slices of cheese.

Melissa could hardly contain her joy. Maybe one day, Daddy would stop falling for her tricks but, for now, all was right in the realm. Her father was wonderful. What he lacked in brains, he more than made up for with cheese—

Mom entered the room. Everything became quiet, but not in a good way. The angry quiet where someone was about to get in a lot of trouble. Time to act fast.

"I didn't want the cheese! Daddy did it! He broke his oaths!"

"What? You little *brat!*"

"Stop," Mom said, and everyone did. Serenna was scary like that, especially since her belly grew rounder. She had never hit Melissa, but if she did, it would probably hurt. "Zeen, stop letting your daughter walk all over you. If you can't handle her now, what will you do when she's seventeen?"

Part of Melissa was sad to see Daddy get yelled at, but the other part was more upset she never got cheese.

"And *you,*" Mom said, pointing at her. "David is here. Should I tell him what a bad girl you have been?"

"No! I'm sorry!" And she was. Kind of. Not really.

Enough of that. David was here!

Melissa rushed out the door and, sure enough, David stood outside, giving her a gentle smile. He almost never used his cool glow power, but there was probably a good reason for that. "Grandpa David!" she said, hugging his leg.

In a realm of angry, crazy grownups, David was super cool and relaxed. The only strange thing was he never used Melissa's name. He had tried it once, but it looked like it hurt him. What could possibly hurt a god? "Hello, little one. You grow more and more every time I see you."

"I do! And I'm stronger! I can hold *three* crystals at once now! Emily, in my class, she can only hold two. Yeah, they're bigger but more is better. Right? You know I'm right."

David stared at her house. He snickered then said, "Have you been causing trouble?"

"Me? No. Never."

"Lying to a god... Shame on you, little one. What would Uncle Sardonyx say? Listen, don't torment my friend. He loves you with his entire heart."

"I just wanted some cheese."

"One day, when your hair fades from platinum to gray, you will wish to trade all the cheese in the realm to see them one last time." David took a deep breath and looked down. He was kind of weird like that, but it was usually temporary. "You said your crystal powers are increasing. Care to show me?"

Her parents came outside before she could answer. Too bad, she really wanted to show David how awesome her powers were now.

David hugged her father. "Ah, Zeen. You look...happy."

"Are you calling me fat?"

Their conversation was boring, so she stopped listening. David had stopped by less and less over the past year, so her opportunity to prove her Guardian powers was fading. Melissa grabbed her staff off the ground, groaned, and crafted one large crystal spike to float in front of her. She would have made two, but her evil parents hadn't given her any cheese.

"Stop it," Mom said, but Melissa didn't listen. Why her mom was so against crystal magic never made sense to Melissa.

Melissa pointed the spike at a large tree and yelled, launching it forward with her full energy. The force of it made her nose start bleeding. Hopefully, that would stop with some more practice.

David grabbed the spike mid-flight, which was *stupid*. Why would he do that? He held it up close and studied it from every angle. "Remarkable. One can only imagine what powers you'll attain in a few more years."

Great. It was about to get weird. Anytime David mentioned anything about powers or Guardians, Mom always got angry.

"I warned you last time. Don't go there. My daughter will never endure the horrors of Guardian life."

David sighed. "Someone has to. We lost two more in the last battle. Say what you will about Fear, but her tactics were valid."

"Valid? Truly? Listen, David, just because you miss Noelami doesn't make her any less of a monster. Stop trying to guilt me for letting go. I earned this. We all did."

"Your guilt doesn't stem from me, old friend. Nevertheless, I did not come here to cause distress. We can revisit the matter later. She wouldn't be prepared for at least ten years anyway. Maybe her brother will be a swordsman?"

Hold on. What brother?

Daddy walked over and picked up Melissa. He never got involved when Mom and David argued. Maybe he was smarter than she thought. "Ignore them, Honey. They both love you very much. They just...disagree on a few things."

"But I want to be a Guardian! You and Mommy were Guardians, and I should be one too! Why is that so bad?"

Daddy smiled at her. "You are a precious little angel, and I love you with all my heart."

"You didn't answer my question!"

"I did, but it really doesn't matter. You could never become a Guardian, anyway."

Melissa gasped. "What? But why? Am I not strong enough? I will train! I will make spikes and shields that will defeat anyone stupid enough to face me!"

"Because you are an oath-breaker. You are a deceptive little cheese-stealing oath-breaker."

She smacked Daddy in the arm as hard as she could which, unfortunately, only made him smile wider. Her daddy was a stupid man. A stupid, *stupid* man.

The End

MEET THE AUTHOR

Timothy Wolff lives in Long Island, New York, and holds a master's degree in economics and a career in finance. Such a life has taught him the price of everything but the value of nothing. He enjoys pizza bagels, scotch, karaoke, oxford commas, and spending the day with family and friends. The obvious culmination of the past thirty-six years was to write a 400+ page fantasy novel where a drunk teams up with a swordsman, two mages, and lizard-people to oppose god. Why do we write these in the third person?

Strength without honor—is chaos!

He can be reached at:

@TimWolffAuthor on Twitter, X, or whatever the hell the site is called by the time this book is published.

Timwolffauthor on Instagram/Threads

timwolffauthor@gmail.com

Willow Wraith Press is a collective of nerds who write the types of books we want to read. If you have enjoyed this book, please check out the other Willow Wraiths.

Dewey Conway & Bill Adams:

The Tenacious Tale of Tanna the Tendersword

Bill Adams:

The Godsblood Tragedy

Andrew D. Meredith:

Deathless Beast
Bone Shroud
Gloves of Eons

Thrice
Four Scored

Quaint Creatures: Magical & Mundane

Michael Roberti:

The Traitors We Are
A Grave for Us All
The Revenge of Thousands

Timothy Wolff:

Platinum Tinted Darkness
Tears of the Maelstrom
Age of Arrogance

The Whisper that Replaced God

THANKS, ACKNOWLEDGEMENTS, ETC.

Well, it's finished. After a very strange 2-3 years, my trilogy is complete and out into the world. There were many nights where I sat at my computer around 1:30 a.m., trying to figure if a comma was necessary, or if a glorious was better off being GLORIOUS! or *glorious!* In the end, was it worth it? Absolutely yes.

First and foremost, to anyone who sat through the entire trilogy, thank you for being a part of this story. The love and support from readers, reviewers, and the community in general has been nothing short of wonderful. Special thanks to my immediate family of Larry, Joan, and Danny, who have shown nothing but love throughout the entire process, despite not being fantasy fans in the slightest. All the love to the rest of my family, but especially to my cousin, Kelsey.

If anyone actually reads things, you'll know I'm always hesitant to shout out members of the indie community in fear of missing someone. Still, for the last book, I feel compelled to try. An enormous thanks to my beta readers: Amber Lilyquist and J. Flowers-Olnowich, who dredged through the horrors of my earlier drafts for all 3 books. To the Silverstone team: Kavin, Mike, Matt, Dewey, and Bill—who quite honestly has become one my closer friends over the past year. To Jackie, my novella bestie who writes about trees. Ayla, who has supported and shouted out my book since day one. Huge thanks to all my reviewer friends, with special thanks to Jamedi, Eddie, and Matt (Beard of Darkness) for all the support. Special thanks to the friends I've made participating in the indie prompts. I WILL miss people here, and I apologize in advance.

Adam, Faust, Kat, Jason, Dianne, Miriam, Coe, A.J, IndieBook Spotlight, Keren, Steve, Casie, Joel, Cat, Ayrton, Marissa, Nicole, Tim, K.R.R, Jana, Victoria.

Special thanks to my friend and editor, Jon Oliver, whose name I spelt correctly this time. It's been a pleasure to work and learn from an industry professional for the entire series and beyond. I'm still amazed after all the times I rewrite and reread each manuscript to receive hundreds of corrections on the edited MS. And to Alejandro Colucci, who made beautiful covers for each book. I love Age of Arrogance in particular. In hindsight, I'm not sure how helpful "whimsical, yet sinister" was as a description, but Arrogance ended up looking perfect.

It's possible I'll come back to this world, either as a Boulom prequel or a ten-years-later type of thing. Can't say for certain. For now, my novella, *The Whisper that Replaced God*, is coming out later this year, and I'm working on a new series which, hopefully, will have book 1 out sometime next year.